STAR OF ASHOR

T. Niven

To the friends and family who stood by me when I needed it most,

To those who taught me how to care enough,

To those who believed in me when I didn't believe in myself,

It's because of you that I was able to write this book.

Thank you.

Did you know?

The Star of Ashor world was in development for over a decade before this book was written. As a result, there is a lot of background and world building that doesn't fit right inside. Thankfully, you don't have to wonder about those details because the official Star of Ashor website has you covered.

You will find a whole host of Short Form content and narrative there. If you have ever wondered about culture or daily life in the Star of Ashor world, or perhaps, the work and deeds of an un-explored character then look no further. The Star of Ashor world is much more than a single book, and is a large scale world building masterpiece. As a result, exploring the official website will bring you unprecedented insight into some of the details that helped shape the world in which the novel takes place. If you are a Star of Ashor fan, an avid world builder, or someone who just loves fiction, you will find something to enjoy.

In addition to the Short Form content library, you will find the author's blog on the official website. Take a spin and read about a variety of writing and creative topics, including world building, character development and even specialized techniques for handling various topics or creating interesting conflict for a narrative. The Star of Ashor blog is made for anyone who has even a passing interest in creating narrative content, with an eye toward helping writers and creators, be they of novels, video games, comics or anything in between, to craft exciting, compelling and most importantly, interesting narratives for those with whom they want to share them.

Use the official blog to learn, and the official site to get in contact with the author, then, stay a while and expand your Star of Ashor knowledge! You'll be surprised how much time flies! Visit any of these domains and you will be awash in Star of Ashor goodness:

http://www.starofashor.com
http://www.starofashor.net
https://www.starofashorbook.com

"Targeting?" The quick, urgent query from the ship's captain sounded, "Do they have us?"

"Unknown sir..."

"Shut down that damn transmitter!" another voice, the ships executive officer sounded, following with, "Clear the tank!"

The holographic imager folded away immediately and Tony stepped forward to Kirashira. He tugged her arm to move her aside as she stepped back, confused, "What's going on?"

"Your patrol ship isn't responding and it is coming in aggressively," Tony replied.

"What!?" Kirashira seemed more than just surprised, she was offended, annoyed even, "What kind of accusation is that?"

Tony almost rolled his eyes. She couldn't even understand the conversation now taking place around the holographic map in the holo-tank.

The image had shifted from nothing to the NovaCore destroyer at the tank's center. Spheres representing various perimeters and distances from the ship glowed faintly as a detailed three dimensional model of the incoming Hil'Raigh patrol ship closed. It was of course, small in size as the distances were large. Even so, the speed of approach, the vector, it was something Tony knew spelled trouble. As he thought it, a curse erupted from the Captain as he examined the situation.

"Deflectors Full. Engage full burn evasive pattern Teros Negal. Charge Points!" He barked. The bridge replied immediately.

The order resounded several times. Once was enough of course, for Tony to know he and his partner were going to be leaving the bridge with their charge rather soon but there was always the chance that she was able to talk to someone. Thankfully, one of the bridge officers had already been thinking the same, approaching the trio and motioning for them to follow.

"Come on Princess," Tony requested grimly, "We might be able to stop this from becoming a fight..."

Prologue

The ship on the display was a reminder of the price of an unceasing war. It was an older generation ship, a destroyer from the end of the war with the alien Hil'Raigh. It was harder to identify with most of the deflector projection systems blown off. An engine nacelle was missing and there were more than a few new holes in its armor plating, ones that were not in the blueprints. The vessel had been towed to berth in a shipyard and this one was likely to be put into service once again. With an intact core, and a strong keel, the older destroyer still had some years of service left. Looking at the face of the second in command during the briefing earlier that day however, had made Admiral Thorsh question the longevity of the crew, at least at present. They would need some rest.

It was the latest, and perhaps most brutal of confrontations on the border in some time. Such a skirmish had not been seen since the days immediately following the armistice. At the time, the Hil'Raigh had hailed it as a good way to stop the fighting, and for their part they had largely stepped away, at least, with the official military operations. Thorsh scoffed.

It was all privateers now if anything, privateers and opportunistic pirates. Even if the would be fighters on the border were doing things the Hil'Raigh Federation's government found to be illegal, the official government had painfully little incentive to chase them down as long as they were preying on the neighbors instead.

A harder stance, tougher escorts and full convoy protection had been the norm for Thorsh's NovaCore homeland on the border for years. Despite that however, it appeared that the privateers felt bold enough to challenge even those measures these days.

Was this to be a trend? Surely the privateers would lose steam, but there was always some glory seeking, former captain among the aliens; some hired hand willing to put in with a clandestine raider fleet for the promise of riches. For the NovaCore, such a situation meant it's navy had been up in an endless game of cat and mouse, preventing its full fleet readiness in the case that the Federation as a whole, decided to resume hostilities on open terms.

The winds of political change had been blowing in the NovaCore's neighbor for years. In the post war era, there was little appetite among the aliens for violence, but that memory was already fading and the saber rattling had begun again. Years ago it had been whispers in intelligence briefings. These days it was a duke or a nobleman openly calling for a 'fitting conclusion' to the war. It was only a matter of time before those nobles or dukes were kings instead.

The NovaCore had by grit, determination and resolve, managed to fend off the advance of what still billed as the strongest naval powerhouse in the galaxy. The alien's bravado and ignorance of their new opponents had given Thorsh's people the edge they'd needed. The Novian's superior FTL technology had given them a deployment advantage too.

The war had been shocking to both sides, but the aliens were not stupid. They, like the NovaCore had been spending their time studying, improving, and adapting. They'd rebuilt ships and navies and though Thorsh was loathe to admit it, their industrial capacity on a grand scale was larger than his own nation could match. Only by virtue of the fact that his own people were so much more collective and focused on their own defense, had they managed to keep pace in naval production.

If the Federation's economy however, switched to a serious war footing, even the hardiest of Novians would have to pause for breath against what they were capable of producing.

This was of course, fully independent of a continuous security threat posed by privateer vessels. The Hil'Raigh did not even have to officially support or reward the privateers, just do nothing about their actions. That was enough. It kept their enemies busy while they churned out new ships with no torpedo damage to the superstructure. Fresh crews would fare badly against experienced NovaCore, but when ships were lost in full, their crews tended to take mass casualties. The experience advantage would wain with serious protracted fighting.

Thorsh sighed, shaking his head. His was not a position he would wish on anyone but it was the job he had asked his fellow citizens to elect him to. He was a member of the Admiralty, tasked with their protection and defense above any other goal. He was a military commander yes, but more than that, a standard bearer for the NovaCore itself.

For years, his posting had granted him the chance to get a snippet of conversation here or there with a Federation dignitary or leader. They were ineffectual conversations, hollow overtures by the aliens, at least for the most part, but the urgency of the situation had never been more clear to the man than it was today. He was as close to a diplomat as anyone had ever been with the Hil'Raigh in the last decade. He spoke their language with fluency, he knew their culture and customs, largely because he liked to study his adversaries. He'd even bothered keeping up on politics, at least as much as he could. Nevertheless, it was something more than many of his comrades could say for themselves.

There were no true allies across the border, no voices for peace, not now, and there had not been for years. As Thorsh turned away from the wall screen and sat in his chair, slumping noisily into it, he let out a long sigh. The picture on the desk before him, a smiling visage, one lost to time and fate, greeted him in response to his uncertainty.

"What would you do about this Keiy?" he said exhaustedly, looking to the image. She had looked so happy in that image, that was why he'd kept that particular one instead of the most recent. It had seen him through the war back then, and it was burned into his memory. In the woman's arms was his niece, a small round faced child so young at the time that she could scarcely sit up without assistance. He often took a moment here or there to talk to his sister, or at least, her image. He often wished that she was there to speak with him in person but she was not.

What would she do anyway? What could she offer? She could have asked the very same people for inroads, made the overtures and met with the same response, that was just how the Hil'Raigh were. Some of the alien Federation's member states wanted war, somehow, someway, to salve their bruised egos and that was that. But did all of them? Thorsh had tried to find out who among their governments would listen but had met with nothing.

He stared at the image of his sister in thought, and then, he felt new gears churning in his mind. He always asked his sister for advice, despite being her older sibling. He was technically the leader, and yet, he tended not to act without considering the opinions of the others in his family, even back when he lived at home. It was not law but it was his way.

What if it had been the law? What if he had to have permission from every sibling to act? True, not all of them held the same level of danger to him in a contest of raw wills, but if someone outside of his family had perhaps, convinced his sister to restrain him, he would have had no choice.

He leaned forward and tapped away at the control console for his workstation, the screen blaring to life. While he knew he'd never reach anyone in the particularly hostile governments, there was one 'little sibling' in the Hil'Raigh Federation that had never been too enthusiastic about the wars in the first place. They had never been a diplomatically involved power with the NovaCore, true, but their voice was enough. The Starlight Compact, as they were called in a literally translated fashion, shared a large border with the NovaCore. While relations had always been ice cold between Thorsh's own people and the Compact, it did have better relations with a mutually friendly power who bordered both. The Compact's king was unconventional, by some accounts a trouble maker, but a trouble maker to some was and always would be, a visionary to others. Thorsh quickly keyed for his assistant's call channel, and the junior officer's voice filled his ear piece a moment later.

"Jael, I want to speak to the Imperial Consulate. I'd like to see if I can get a chance to make a formal introduction with the King of the Starlight Compact."

The affirmative response was immediate and the Admiral glanced to the cherished image on his desk once more, in gratitude.

PART ONE

UNLIKELY RESCUE

1 - Vacation

Summer's hot afternoon air had subsided as Major Tony Karo walked down the seaside boardwalk. At last, he felt like it was comfortable to be outside. It had been a particularly hot summer on the planet of Ashor but that had done nothing to curb the number of street vendors and small commercial stalls that were making every use of their rented spaces on the boardwalk. If the community had been a desert rose, then the cool temperatures of the evening air were like a welcome rain, bringing life out onto the streets as they did each night. The open spaces were filled now, with people of all shapes and sizes, a general cacophony of carefree society dominating the atmosphere once again.

The town of Kolos was a tourist hot spot if there ever was one. As a result, even though he was not a native to Ashor, or the Hil'Raigh Federation in general, it was hard to pick him out of a crowd unless one was careful about it. Karo, like most of the people here, was dressed in a pair of loose fitting shorts, extending past the knee, clad with an equally loose fitting shirt above. He had eschewed any sort of the normal fair, opting instead for a simple shirt with no buttons, no collar and short sleeves. His sandals were a bit small but they had been inexpensive, something he had insisted on when searching for them, though the quality was not all that impressive as a result. Other than his lack of pointed ears and a decidedly non-native hairstyle, his clothing let him blend in as well as he could hope.

Unlike the native species, Tony's eyes were round and blue. His relatively short black hair, styled into a lightly parted but not entirely unkempt affair, was mildly helpful in going unnoticed only because of its color. The taller stature and more muscular build he had however, made him easier to spot amongst the thin Hil'Raigh and shorter Kul'Raigh species regardless. His chin was stronger than the locals and his nose was a bit wider than most of them too. His brows were naturally bushy and his eyes were deeper overall, giving his face a detectable level of foreign blood under any scrutiny.

Blending in was something of an art form and despite the difficulty it could present, there was no shortage of reasons to do so. Living here on a foreign world, stationed as emergency protectors for the NovaCore ambassador, he and his partner had to make at least passable efforts every day to look their part. It was an act that Tony had not chosen, but one that had been 'statistically proven' effective for maintaining cover in situations like this. Even so, as his partner returned carrying what Tony had long ago learned was the Hil'Raigh equivalent of ice cream, he caught himself smiling. Doing his duty, being a good member of NovaCore intelligence, meant that at times he had to make sacrifices. He often found however, that maintaining cover, especially with Truth as his company was something he enjoyed. It was not that he enjoyed every aspect, but Truth's presence ensured that at very least, he could endure it with relative ease.

He eyed the treat and spoke, "Kolos blend?"

It was a mixed feeling for him: pretending to be a couple with his partner and best friend. Though the two had been together since they graduated from the advanced training program, it always felt a bit odd to play at a fake romance for the sake of cover. Despite the fact that he had been challenged to befriend Truth at a young age, the forced beginning had started the most important relationship he had ever known. Truth was as close to a family as he had ever could have hoped to have and even in the tight knit service community of the NovaCore intelligence division, the bond the two shared was one of a kind. Despite how awkward it was at times to pretend, Tony had to admit that the mission itself had made him question the possibilities of such a relationship.

His musing however, was cut short as Truth replied, her warm voice carrying just the right way, as usual, "It is your favorite if I recall."

Tony nodded, reaching and taking the spoon as he scooped some more. The tart flavor mixed with the sweet in a way that did indeed make the Kolos blend flavor the most enjoyable. The fact that he had told Truth and couldn't recall doing so however, made him realize just how much the few days had blended together since they had come to this particular part of town. It was only half a week so far but it felt like so much longer in his mind.

He had to admit to being challenged at times by his role here. His partner never seemed to lack the composure or ability to remain in character but perhaps that was because she looked so much more like some of the natives than he did. For the obvious foreigner, blending in properly as he could was a consistently challenging affair. At times he envied the fact that when Truth disappeared into a crowd without him, no one would take a second look at her.

She had almond shaped, striking green eyes and dark black hair. Those features, coupled with an olive skin tone let her blend well by color alone as a native Kul'Raigh. Her shape however, added considerably to the illusion of being a native. She boasted the same characteristic wide pointed ears as all of the Federation natives did and she had even had some custom earrings made to fill out the look here in Kolos. Her well trimmed brows and rounded cheeks complemented her relatively full lips. Overall, her face and stature let her blend in almost completely if she were alone. A light dusting of the popular cosmetics and a healthy number of bracelets, rings and necklaces worked together with the shorts and tank top she wore, to help her look not only native to the Federation, but local to the beach side community.

The illusion that the pair were indeed some sort of couple had worked well enough to allow them to rent the small apartment space they had been able to find nearby. For local landlords, the prospect of renting such a property to a foreign national alone would have been preposterous. Even with Truth's help, they had been rejected several times before finding a suitable location. As much of a native as she appeared to be, her appearance came with its own set of drawbacks.

Despite the advanced nature of the Federation, the overall warm atmosphere of the Starlight Compact state, and the generally forward thinking societal attitudes in most subjects, the Federation had its own difficulties. Difficulties? Perhaps traditions, Tony was not sure that some of the things the Federation did could be reasonably separated into either category alone. So it was, that even as native as Truth looked, she was scrutinized for being a Kul'Raigh.

Years ago, when Tony had first learned about the Federation in school, he was not alone in his confusion about what the difference between a Kul'Raigh and a Hil'Raigh were. It was all the more confusing as the entire nation in which both peoples lived, was called the Hil'Raigh Federation. Over time however, like anyone who learned about the Federation, the distinction became clear enough to be understood, even if some of the nuance was lost in translation.

While most nations in the galactic sphere hosted only one major population, the Hil'Raigh Federation was different. Of the five major countries that had sprung up in the history of the galaxy to date, only one of them hosted such a unique population.

The NovaCore and Novian Empire were inhabited almost exclusively by Novians, the species of which Tony himself was a part. They had evolved on the same world and shared a common history as a species, despite the genetic variations among them. The split in their national populations had only occurred for political reasons and even now, both populations retained most of the same genetics.

As far as aliens went, there were of course others, the Terran Hegemony for one, but they too, were a mostly homogeneous people. They were a relatively new species to the grander sphere of the galaxy and they too, shared only one major genetic pool.

The Federation however, was populated by what it called "two halves of a whole" in the Hil'Raigh and Kul'Raigh. The two cultures shared a substantial amount of genetics, having apparently come from the same planet at some point in the distant past. The similarities broke down a bit when one looked at each population in detail however, with the Hil'Raigh generally being taller and more slender. By contrast the Kul'Raigh were generally rounder. Common coloration in skin, eye and hair colors varied as well, with green eyes and black hair being the most common genetic set among Kul'Raigh. Hil'Raigh generally had lighter eyes and hair colors instead.

There were other differences too of course, with a myriad number of them arising out of genetic engineering that Tony had no illusions about understanding. Regardless however, the differences were generally enough that one could identify between the groups. The division not only served to visually identify, but for some, served as a litmus test on a range of things beyond simple genetic makeup. Some used the distinction to determine the moral character of an individual using only a glance, while others made even more interesting assumptions based on the same.

It was not entirely uncommon among any culture in the galaxy really, but it was an oddity to be sure, for groups united under one national banner to make such distinctions of each other. It was something at least, that Tony had not seen much of in the NovaCore. He knew that on some level, that was because unlike the people living their lives here, he had grown up with something else. Tony's upbringing had been spent mostly within the confines and direction of state military academies. With most of his free time going into such an environment, he had to admit that he never felt he had much time to categorize his fellow cadets. As a result, dissecting the entirety of the Federation culture based on obviously deep rooted feelings was something he avoided. To the pair of NovaCore, it had been enough to get the place they needed, and with the landlord they had found, they were in no worry, or hurry, to leave.

The Federation, for all its flaws, certainly had its own share of good people, criminals and scum. Tony imagined that it was likely the same anywhere, but had to admit that thus far, his stay here in the Federation had not challenged his sense of security much. Perhaps it was because he knew he looked the part of a foreign citizen. Perhaps it was because he did not look as friendly or oblivious as some of the tourists that passed he and his partner now on the street.

People in Kolos were generally well adjusted to anyone, as long as that person did not demand anything other than a good time. It also helped if the good time that arrival was willing to have, was one that would inject a healthy sum of credits into the local economy. More than once upon arrival Tony had been the attempted target of "tourism pricing" by street vendors and it had prompted him to learn exactly how locals behaved in response to the same. Overall he guessed it made him look or act colder, but the lack of pamphlets or intrusive sales pitches more than made up for any sacrifice in personality. There were things about Kolos though that Tony felt he could learn to miss, given the time at least. Of course, loud crowds weren't one of them.

As a particularly rambunctious group of visitors entered the line for the dessert stand, Truth motioned to her partner and stood. Complying, he readily accepted the offer and the two set off down the boardwalk. There was no shortage of noisy groups here, especially in the evening, and especially in the summer, at least, that's what he had heard. Despite living on planet for a month now, the pair had yet to make many friends, other than those who served them food in exchange for money. It was a relationship Tony guessed was a bit one sided.

Even so, the atmosphere of the town was something he liked. Truth finally spoke as they left the noise machine of tourists behind, "Did you get that watercraft rental taken care of earlier?"

"I looked around but didn't decide on which of the places to rent from yet," Tony replied calmly. Truth was as relaxing company as he ever could have hoped for and he caught himself smile without having to act in character to muster it, "Ideally, I'd like to find a place that lets us take out a boat whenever we want so that complicates things a bit. At least that's what they all said."

Truth nodded. She had explained earlier that it was apparently a standard practice at most water sports clubs to allow use of the water craft during the week since most locals still had to work. Those that didn't were wealthy enough to own their own berths. Tony had suspected after the third boat club had become squeamish about his on demand criteria that they simply did not want to rent to him directly for some reason.

"Exploration is a never ending endeavor, Even when it is cultural." Truth replied, adopting a scholarly tone and drawing a laugh from her partner. The holo-ads for the Royal Deepspace Exploration Society had certainly gone into overdrive lately with the news reporting almost nothing other than the society's press releases as of late. Even the penchant for petty politics that the Federation had such a mastery of could not seem to muster the strength to unseat the current stories from their places in prime time.

It was of course, big news. The Royal Deepspace Exploration Society, or The Explorers Society as it was referred to locally, had apparently announced, through the Royal Press Corps of course, their discovery of what was purported to be one of the first worlds on which Federation feet had stepped in the galaxy. Of course, it had yet to be verified but despite the cautionary tone that followed such warnings, none of the news outlets seemed to care. It had for all intents and purposes, catapulted normal political discussion into an entirely new realm, a potentially transformative one, at least for the Federation.

Tony doubted personally, whether the Hil'Raigh nation was, like it claimed, originally from a far away place outside of the galaxy. It was such a tall claim, and one that could not be backed up by their current technological expertise. The method they relied on for interstellar travel was far from capable of bringing them across galaxies, or they would have done it already, or at least, again.

No, Tony guessed that the lack of historical record surrounding the period was the result of what many civilizations had endured in their pasts, a period of intense civil war or strife. He guessed it was one that had for one reason or another, caused the victors to push everything about those days under the largest rug they could find, subsequently burning the rug and its contents unceremoniously. Doubts or not, it was a rather interesting discovery: artificial construction on a world that was uninhabited and far from civilization as a whole.

The energizing news had done wonders for the historical tours here in Kolos. While the city was modern, there were several old cultural sites in and around its boundaries that most definitely had seen increased traffic as of late. It had fueled local business in turn and even the nightlife had opened up. The beach side open air pubs here in Kolos, a staple really, had become hubs for visitors and with the extra crowding, visiting any of the places had become increasingly taxing. Despite that however, the city was relatively clear of trouble for the most part.

It seemed that this night was an exception to that general rule as Tony and Truth departed the board walk and moved forward down the nearby street. A small group of Hil'Raigh had cornered what appeared to be a single Kul'Raigh, who was all but backed against the side of a building. Though it was not entirely dark out yet, Tony guessed that the group likely had enough of a reputation to make sure no one asked questions about their brazen impropriety. It was one of the few explanations he could come up with as he and Truth approached the street corner.

He still wasn't sure in his mind, what the group would do in response to strangers showing up, but as one of them took a belligerent swing, striking the Kul'Raigh roughly on the cheek, he knew that he and Truth were getting involved. It was Truth who first spoke up, calling to the group. Her voice was emotionless and flat, but underpinned with a sort of confidence that betrayed her feelings toward them, "Quite bold to hit a lone Kul'Raigh in the street."

There was a pause, a hiccup in the assailant's second motion, likely another strike. He dropped his hand away from the Kul'Raigh's face and turned, his green eyes piercing enough even from a couple meters away. There was a level of disbelief in the body language of the trio of Hil'Raigh, a swagger of sorts that showed all that Tony needed to know about who they thought they were. This was after all, their town, at least in their eyes. Finally the apparent ring leader, the one who had taken the swing initially, replied. A sarcastic drawl covered each of his words as he eyed Truth, sizing her up in disbelief, "You'd best keep out of this Kul'Raigh. You and your foreign friend..."

Tony glanced to his partner, eyeing the trio and deciding which of them was likely most threatening. The ring leader of course would be the one to make the mistake of attacking Truth first. She was after all, small enough in stature that she looked the part of a native Kul'Raigh, with features to match. Years ago, careful genetic engineering had yielded Truth's unique characteristics with no intention of replicating the decidedly alien appearance. However, the mix of Kul'Raigh genes had been the catalyst for an advanced immune system and other enhancements not native to the Novian genetic code. All told the work had ensured that any future generations of genetically engineered soldiers would reap the benefits without having to look like a member of the Federation at all.

Even so, the thug had no idea what he was up against. He could never have known about Truth's augmented, artificial muscles and metal plated skeleton. Nor could he have known about her enhanced reflexes and the intense combat training that she had mastered in her lifetime. No, from the outside Truth was unassuming and relatively harmless looking, yet Tony knew it was a guise from experience.

Years of friendship, cooperative training and missions together had netted him a unique insight into Truth's prowess and though she had struggled with her implants and neural interfaces when younger, her teenage years had changed all that. Ever since the academy days, Truth was impossibly capable, so much so that she had few peers who could match her skill in any aspect of her duties.

The irony of the Hil'Raigh confidently striding to Truth therefore, drew a smirk from Tony as he watched, waiting for what would definitely be a quick exchange between the two. Truth stood about to the man's shoulder at best, looking up to him without giving ground as he stepped uncomfortably close.

In what had to be the standard for untrained technique, he moved to swing, his body language and motion giving it away before he ever got his arm moving appreciably. Those small cues were all Truth needed to respond. She stepped out, pivoting on one foot, letting the man's arm fly past. He stumbled a step with it, proving just how much energy he had planned to put into Truth's modest frame.

The extra step however gave Truth all she needed to exploit for an opening and she sprung into action. She leveraged her pivoting step, coiling up to launch a return attack. An instant later, she had struck her unprepared victim.

The stumbling Hil'Raigh's face registered mostly surprise, probably because no pain had set in yet. Truth had closed her hand like a sort of tight claw, her pointer and middle fingers extended past the rest. Then, leveraging her artificial strength, jammed them into the man's armpit with vicious intent. A strong pressure point for Hil'Raigh, the cluster of nerves there made for a terrible place to be struck. A seasoned Hil'Raigh fighter might have endured the blow with only discomfort, or blocked it entirely.

A foolish drunk however, never would have had the sense to prevent exposing himself and his error was laid bare now. Truth retracted her arm almost as quickly as it had struck him, letting the man list forward. It took a moment for Tony to see the Hil'Raigh's eyes finally glaze a bit. It was the realization of the shooting pain in his arm taking over. The sight was short lived, his stricken face hidden from view as he roughly slammed against the ground in the alley.

The sudden exchange was over so quickly however, that it took a moment more before the two remaining, less drunken friends of the man were able to register it. Finally however, the two gave away their surprise. Of course it came in the shape of anger or righteous indignation but it was all the same to the two NovaCore.

Despite their threatening posture, the pair of remaining thugs hesitated, one glancing to Truth and one to Tony. Both seemed more than willing to give up the fight and for a moment Tony almost gave them the option. That was until one of them lunged forward. This man's blow was much less drunken, a bit more finesse to the swing. Rather than take the blow however, Tony snapped his arm into the oncoming forearm, deflecting it to the side. The block had precluded any return strike and so as Tony repositioned, he was immediately faced with another ill fated swing. This time the blow connected only briefly, glancing off Tony's shoulder. There was a hint of pain but nothing compared to what greeted the attacker's stomach.

A curled punch into the man's vulnerable gut sent him reeling immediately. He let out a defeated groan as he fell back. Stumbling to the side, the unfortunate man clutched his unhappy midsection before toppling to the ground. Now, he curled into a ball as he groaned, his eyes fastened shut by pain.

His remaining friend was already in the process of failing to make his blows connect with Truth. As he missed another of his strikes, Tony caught a glimpse of Truth bringing her knee to bear. The man lurched up from the blow as Truth pulled her leg away. Her elbow jabbed in precise place between his shoulder blades. There was a thud as he was sent careening downward, connecting with the paved ground in even more dramatic fashion than his leader. He however, didn't have the luxury of having passed out. He was left groaning helplessly, flat against the ground and unable to desperately clutch his bruised body.

The scene was not all that out of the ordinary really. The pair were trained to deal with far worse than a trio of thugs in the street. The desperate attempts at dominance that this group had made thus far, had done painfully little to cement their position. Instead they had bitten off far more than they could chew and paid the price.

Finally, satisfied that the brazen Hil'Raigh weren't going to be getting up for any more failure prone attacks, the NovaCore turned their attention to the Kul'Raigh who had slumped to a sitting position against the wall of the alley.

As Tony approached he got a better look at her face, which was bruised at least a bit on the left side. Despite that, her eyes, a rich brown color, traced he and his partner without fear. Her skin, aside from the bruise bore the fruit of what was probably a fair bit of sun exposure, a warm olive tone to it, complementing the most common of hair colors among Kul'Raigh: black.

Her hair was pulled into a loose ponytail behind her head and she wore what appeared to be normal wear for the locals here. She was clad in a loose fitting halter top and some shorts, not unlike the clothing Truth had chosen to wear.

Tony could never tell just how old Kul'Raigh were, but she looked about as old as Truth was and her stature he guessed, was about the same as well. She sighed as Truth approached, closing her eye and speaking aloud, if briefly, "Thanks"

Truth nodded and stood nearby, Tony approaching as well. Finally Truth spoke in reply, "Let's go somewhere else and we can see about your bruise."

The Kul'Raigh cracked one eye, obviously having been tired by whatever ordeal she had endured. She scanned Truth carefully and nodded, standing shakily.

"They harass you often?" Tony asked calmly as Truth helped the native to her feet.

"No," She replied, looking over to Tony, "I don't even live here, just visiting."

"Sightseeing?" Truth injected quizzically.

"You could say that," replied the Kul'Raigh, wincing and rubbing her ribs.

"I've never heard of people randomly attacking tourists here. What did they want?" Tony pressed.

She sighed and was silent for a moment, "It's a long story, dunno if it would make sense to you."

Tony shrugged, he was not going to force her to talk, though he was curious at least. Having helped out, he figured she would have been a bit more forthcoming than that. Regardless, she kept walking with the NovaCore until the trio reached the street corner when she spoke once more, "I know a beach side place out here, should be able to get a cold pack or something if we go there."

Truth nodded, motioning for the Kul'Raigh to lead the way and the NovaCore followed. This time, Truth spoke, inquiring candidly of the stranger, "What is your name?"

"A'Shir," She replied.

***

The warm coastal air had done wonders for the Kul'Raigh's energy but she still pressed a cold wet cloth against her cheek every so often. A'Shir, as she was called, apparently knew the owner of the eatery that Tony and his partner had decided was one of their favorites in the short time they had been in Kolos. It was of course an interesting coincidence and perhaps would be useful in the future. When the owner had seen Truth and her Novian counterpart escorting A'Shir into the establishment, he had asked only a few questions before getting them a seaside table and having one of his staff assigned to take care of them. Tony couldn't complain at least, even the non-alcoholic drinks on the menu here tasted good enough to sip at all night.

"Thank you again for your help," A'Shir broke a standing silence that had covered the table since the trio had received their drinks.

"Not a common occurrence I hope," Tony replied. The Kul'Raigh snickered a bit then shrugged as she pulled the rag away from her cheek and sighed.

"No, that's never happened before," she said, "There is a reason some people are on the Guild's no service list I suppose."

"No service list?" Truth inquired. She had spent most of the time drinking and as she spoke Tony noted the half empty cup.

"Yes, I had no intention of meeting them but I guess I need to be more careful about where I go these days," A'Shir replied, "People are on edge because of the King I guess."

"King Ren'Tauru huh?" Tony replied carefully. He knew only a little of the King of the Starlight Compact save that his family claimed a connection to some of the oldest of Hil'Raigh royalty. His family line, Ren'Tauru, was apparently as well connected as any other royal but the current head of the line had a habit of making headlines.

He was a controversial figure, one who had started his reign with marriage to a Kul'Raigh companion over twenty years ago. Since then he had been a fairly passionate voice for whatever cause he felt was important at the time. Tony had not kept up on, nor did he care to know the details of the man's motivations but knew that he was both loved and hated in the Federation.

It was therefore not impossible for Tony to imagine him creating some controversy. What was it now however? He was unsure. Despite his best efforts at keeping up with the politics of the country, Tony had to admit that he had no idea which issue was going to set off the populace of the Federation at large, on any given day. As enlightened as the Hil'Raigh always claimed to be, they had a propensity for the dramatic.

"Yes, his immigration proposals," A'Shir replied, "I'm sure you've seen the news."

"I haven't been watching as closely as you might think, finding an apartment and settling in took most of my time."

"And you?" A'Shir turned to Truth, who simply shrugged.

She laughed in disbelief, "I hadn't thought anyone could... miss... Those details but..."

Truth replied calmly, "I had heard that he was planning to change the border control law and allow more Kul'Raigh into the Compact on a permanent basis."

Truth had a habit of being as unassuming as possible at times but somehow managed to surprise most everyone with her conversation. She had always been that way though and for Tony it was a normal part of life. Thankfully, it was apparently enough for A'Shir who nodded, and interjected with a warmth permeating her voice, "That's right, I'm glad one of you is paying attention to current affairs."

"So many people thought things would change when the King married Queen Shiyara but I guess traditions are hard to bend when they have been going so long hmm?" A'Shir continued.

Tony shrugged, he had always been skeptical about the more colorful parts of the Hil'Raigh histories, chief among them the claims about having come from another galaxy thousands of years ago. He voiced his skepticism plainly, "You really think that this has been going on that long?"

"Of course," A'Shir replied, "We and the Hil'Raigh are quite different, I wouldn't believe someone if they told me we always got along."

There was a certain logic in the reply that Tony had not expected. It was true after all that both races were different, culturally at least a bit, but probably more biologically. Tony was no scientist and always felt he had no hope of telling Hil'Raigh apart but Kul'Raigh were far more alien. He guessed that despite what he had learned of their biology, that generations of genetic engineering had made them much more homogeneous than his own or even the Hil'Raigh species were physically.

The Kul'Raigh were a decidedly homogeneous looking species, something unique to their population and though they were supposed to be biologically compatible with Hil'Raigh, Tony could never really tell much about what made particular Kul'Raigh an eligible mate for anyone, especially since the Kul'Raigh sexes shared most of the easily visible characteristics of their appearance with each other

The species itself was something of an oddity in the galaxy with most other species following what seemed to be a more common division of biology. Novians, Terrans and even The Hil'Raigh seemed to have clear distinctions between their sexes but the Kul'Raigh did not. That fact was one of the few pieces of evidence Tony could say truly lent credibility to just how alien the Federation claimed to be.

"Some people think the King is trying to buy influence among the Kul'Raigh and lure them to the Compact, especially with the discovery by the exploration society happening so recently," A'Shir explained. "If it were any other royal house, or if it had happened at another time in history, I don't think it would have been so controversial."

Tony smirked and sipped his drink. He knew he wouldn't be able to keep himself looking all that surprised at this rate. Despite the fact that covert protection teams for the NovaCore ambassadors to every nation were common place, Tony had to admit that the briefing before this particular mission had been injected with a fair share of urgency about the charged political climate.

Whether it meant anything or not he was not sure but time would tell. It was only a few hours in fact until the next communique from the NovaCore would arrive.

"I wish I could do more to say thank you," A'Shir smiled at the pair and took a sip of her own drink. She was a fairly nice person and it helped to have friends among the local population, even if those individuals didn't realize they were befriending personas more than actual people.

"Actually, we were planning on taking a boat trip sometime, out into the archipelago. Do you know of any places that do boat rental on demand?" Tony injected.

He and Truth had yet to settle on a boat to rent but that was one of the definite prerequisites to communicating. Taking calls from out of orbit was not something just any communications gear could do discreetly. As a result the long range passive antennas had been buried undersea near one of the islands in the bay. It was not the most efficient means of communication but it was secretive enough that it had yet to be found. It also helped that it was only for intelligence briefings and non time critical communication. Anything that needed to reach the operatives quickly could just as easily be routed from the ambassador's office. Of course, doing so gave away any covert protection team and so it was used for emergencies only. Truth was the final fall back for emergencies, with a long range radio implant that, in a pinch, could just barely reach orbit with any sort of reliability. The range of her communication antennas was limited however due to the fact that it was unable to be larger than the body containing it.

Getting a boat to travel to the island chain outside of Kolos would be one of the simplest ways to pick up the latest briefing, and any kit that happened to be deposited there waiting for pickup. Though he hadn't yet bothered finishing his search, Tony figured asking the Kul'Raigh about on demand rentals would be better than continuing blind, if she knew anyone that was.

A'Shir looked thoughtful for a moment, then nodded, "I think I do know someone actually. There's a Hil'Raigh I am on good terms with that runs one of the boat clubs in the bay, maybe he could help."

"Wonderful," Tony replied, adding, "Though I did kind of blow a lot of my money getting that apartment, something cheap and reliable would be the best. It's only for the day and we weren't planning on taking anything out very often."

Truth nodded, adding to the assurance that the would be couple was in fact rather tight on funds. In reality, there were no real limits on spending but any kind of excess not only looked bad on the mission reports but drew suspicion. No long term resident would bother paying exorbitant fees and so, neither did the two NovaCore.

"He runs single rentals as well as memberships, so I think you will find something in your price range, I'll put in a word for you as soon as I'm back in my hotel," The Kul'Raigh chortled. She gave a warm smile and sighed, drawing a small thin plastic card from her pocket and sliding it over the table to Truth with a calming grace, "That's my contact card at the guild in Dau'Kore, if you are ever in town, let me know."

Truth accepted the small item after a moment of examination, taking it in her fingertips with intent before finding the right place for it in the small carrying pouch she had bought the day before.

"Thank you A'Shir, I am afraid we do not have any contact cards to give you in return," She stated, her gaze fixed on the Kul'Raigh.

A'Shir nodded, "Of course I wouldn't have expected it. It would be especially impolite of me to insist upon that sort of thing after I'd already found myself in your graces today."

There was a pause and Tony took the moment to finish his drink. He glanced to Truth who had long since finished her own. A'Shir's was about half full but she had been fiddling with the ice pack for much of the conversation. In the grand scheme of things this particular person was probably not going to ever hear from he and his partner again but Tony had to admit that he was glad to have met her. At very least they would be getting a better deal on a boat rental. Even so, there was a warmth to the way the Kul'Raigh received them that Tony had to guess was something of a talent she must have had. It made the fact that anyone had attacked her all the more confusing to him, but then again, he didn't ever pretend to understand the Hil'Raigh mindset.

"Well I think we should be heading back to the apartment for now, it was nice meeting you A'Shir," Tony finally said. Truth nodded and the pair of NovaCore looked to their acquaintance.

She cocked her head affirmatively and smiled, a small smirk of a smile as she replied, "Thanks again, I hope you enjoy your time in Kolos."

With that, the NovaCore stood from the table. If everyday ended with a fight, Tony guessed he would probably enjoy the place quite a bit.

2 - Boat Trip

The dock master that the Kul'Raigh A'Shir had mentioned was indeed a stroke of luck for Tony and his partner. He had been cordial enough that it was easy to see he had little to hide. His docks were in good order, his watercraft in pristine condition and the whole marina had been rather well kept. While he was only one of the three operators out of that particular facility, he had specialized in smaller scale vessels, ones designed for leisure outings.

As a result, when Tony and his partner had come seeking a two day rental for their planned diving trip, he had been easy to work with. With little haggling, the man had offered a friends discount, low enough that it put any other service to shame and that was that.

That had been two hours ago however, and now the pair were on the open sea, nearing the destination indicated by their navigation system. It was a deep spot in the island chain, but far enough away from land or any prying eyes that the only reasonably close island was a small jungle atoll not more than ten kilometers away.

Tony sat cross legged on the deck as the sun tried in vain to cook him inside his diving suit, tweaking and giving final checks over the equipment he and his partner would soon be donning. Truth stood behind the control console, a pair of over sized sun glasses covering most of her face as she continued to stoically pilot the vessel. She must have been standing there for at least an hour or so now but every time Tony offered to take over, she refused.

It was true that he wanted to drive the boat, but Truth apparently wanted to hog the controls and so, most of the trip had been spent with her at the helm.

"You know I want a chance to drive this thing too right?" Tony joked as he tweaked one of the regulator valves on Truth's diving system. The tester blinked green and he unhooked the small tube from the connection port.

"I am having too much fun to let you interrupt me," Truth replied, taking off some of the throttle. The bobbing of the craft slowed and it sunk a bit more into the water as the engines whined down.

It was a classic vessel to be sure, a single hulled design with underwater hydrofoils for high speed travel. It was a smooth ride even at high speeds and the fuel cells on board would more than cover weeks worth of travel on a single charge. Though Tony was familiar in part with tactical craft, he had never really had the chance to operate a leisure vessel and so as Truth dashed his feeble hope of taking the helm, he adopted a mock tone of disappointment, "So harsh. Your gear is green."

The front deck of the boat was open to the sun, a ring of seats around the inner portion. The control console was in the middle of the vehicle and behind it near the rear, was another couch. A small internal cabin was accessible from the fore-deck but was only really large enough for a bed and a small set of appliances. The craft was no luxury vessel and definitely not equipped for long term travel either. However, the weather report had been accurate and no foulness was expected at all, making today's job all the more simple. At least as simple as it could be really.

Finally, Truth cut the throttle and the boat gave in to the waves, gently bobbing to a stop. From where he sat Tony guessed she had also put the boat in automatic station keeping before leaving the controls and coming to the fore-deck with her partner.

As was procedure, she attached the tester to Tony's rebreather and began the routine. It took only a couple seconds but she cleared the device a moment later, announcing, "Yours is green."

"Good crosscheck," Tony replied, taking his device. The newest generation of rebreather was a bubble free affair with a small profile. A majority of the system, save the gas bladder was contained in the mouthpiece while the latter portion took the form of a small pack. On the special issue diving suits, that bladder was discreetly fashioned into the lower back of the suit rather than standalone.

Tony reached out as Truth stood, spreading her arms out sideways while he patted down her back. There was a decent give in the suit, the air pocket obvious enough that he declared her suit ready and able. Turning, she repeated the actions for him and the pair readied, grabbing their respective mouthpieces and attaching the tubes for input and output to the two ports on the shoulders of their diving suits.

"Physical map?" Truth asked as she finalized her connection.

"Check," Tony replied, patting the pocket on his torso.

"Digital map and compass?" She asked.

"Check and Check," Tony replied again, looking to his wrist and tapping the small buttons on the wrist computer housed there.

"Bleed tac?"

"Check," Tony patted the small pouch hanging from his belt. The putty like resin contained within was useful for helping to deal cuts that could occur underwater.

"Lamp?"

"Check," Tony tapped the small headband like device slung around his forehead and behind his skull. The lamp provided a range of illuminations in the spectrums that his ocular implants would easily detect. Though his eyes were not as capable as Truth's fully synthetic ones, neither of the pair would be stuck relying on standard lighting underwater, an asset for them both.

Tony gave a final visual check of his partner now, her hair tied back tightly, her wide ears prominent from behind. She looked as ready as he himself felt he was and so, without further waiting, he moved to the rear of the vessel, stepping out of the small safety gate there to lower the ships ladder into the ocean. Truth followed and in moments she was waiting for him to descend into the warm seawater.

Ladder down, Tony descended the quarter or so meter into the sea, feeling his suit contact the water. Though he would have preferred a wet suit for the time being, the suit's breather also featured a filtering and hydration system that kept he or anyone else using the suits hydrated enough despite them being all weather dry suits. He lamented not being able to take a last drink and settled for the fact that the air he breathed was going to be infused with enough water vapor to take the edge off of the coming exertions.

Finally, the Novian sunk into the water, releasing his hold on the metallic ladder. He felt his body supported effortlessly now as he slid out of the way for Truth to do the same. She slid unceremoniously into the water and in moments she turned around. Both of the pair had joked about how silly the other looked wearing the systems but Tony was the first to get his goggles down this time, completing the look. Truth followed, sealing the mask against her face before she turned like a natural born sea creature, in a small roll and slipped underwater without a sound. Tony followed, slipping into the water with a bit more noise than his partner had made.

The ocean water felt good, at least, what he could feel of it's temperature through his suit. As he was encompassed by it, a clear view of the ocean floor several meters below was granted by the light from above. Because of the archipelago, the seafloor between islands was relatively close to the surface of the water in this area, a key reason it had been chosen for the long range antenna array.

The array currently only tasked with talking to satellites or ships in orbit from its position on the seabed but existed for the sole purpose of ensuring plausible deniability to the ambassadorship. The diplomats did not know it existed, nor would they ever be told, just as they were never told anything about the officially titled "relief security forces."

On the one hand it added a layer of complication to the real relationship with the Starlight Compact, but it suited the desires of the NovaCore admiralty to have a quick response force available for their ambassadors here on Ashor. Because of the rough history between the Hil'Raigh Federation and the NovaCore, there was no official embassy here on Ashor. In fact, the Starlight Compact had been the only nation out of the three major powers within the Federation, to even grant for a diplomatic presence. The relations had been icy enough that the NovaCore had made sure to officially title the mission with the use of the Compact's Hil'Raigh language name, Ashi'Teya. Thus, the Ashi'Teya Diplomatic Mission had been born. As a matter of course, months later, the first rotation of quick response team had been made. It was unfortunate that the lack of an embassy and general distrust of the NovaCore by their alien neighbor precluded an official security presence. Even so, something was better than nothing, and at very least, it was good cultural immersion practice for the teams who would be rotated through here over the coming months. Thus far, the Federation itself and the Compact's own government had made no indication that they had noticed, or at very least, cared about the team's presence.

It made sense, given that the Federation had never really had to interact with any major political powers outside of itself for so long. Who among them therefore would have expected the NovaCore to bury an antenna on the ocean floor?

The answer was at very least a small number, Tony mused as he followed Truth. There were always suspicious people in governments and militaries, that was just how things tended to work. He stopped his musing and looked to Truth. She had found the ground and was now sweeping carefully along, looking for one of the long tendril like cables that made up part of the antenna array. She carried a small metal detector in her hand, running it close to the sandy ground, quietly and carefully moving along.

The search was complicated by a liberal helping of kelp like plants, though thankfully, marine life other than the plants themselves appeared to be fairly sparse. There were a minor number of fish and other aquatics, most of which were on the move away from the intruders into their home. Finally, Truth looked to have found something, her course changing abruptly.

Tony traced what he thought was her intended destination and gave a renewed effort forward. Next to a collection of uninteresting rock, a non descript metallic cylinder rested, half buried in the sandy ocean bottom. The device was about twenty centimeters in diameter, big enough to be obvious from this distance but small enough not to be noticed easily from afar.

The pair approached the device, with Tony slipping an access recorder from its small pouch at his waist and affixing it to the outside of the container. Rather than a keypad or plug, the system simply used a wireless proximity transmitter, pre-configured to download the latest intelligence briefing stored inside.

The entire process was encrypted and if anyone ever did find the antenna, it would look more like a piece of forgotten ocean monitoring equipment than a radio antenna. Even so, the system regularly wiped the received content to be sure, filling the memory with realistic looking readings on the surrounding ocean until a new message triggered hidden programming.

The download process was quick enough, finishing in several seconds. The light on the small recorder turned green as it indicated the same. Tony pulled back his recorder, sliding it against the computer system in the forearm of his suit. As he did, the keypad lit up and he keyed through some options. Moments later a textual representation of the briefing was filling the display. He skipped through the reading and a small map came up next. Indicated prominently on the map was the location of a kit drop. One of the uninhabited archipelago islands apparently now hosted whatever was inside the container from his comrades.

If the islands were larger, or more hospitable, it would have been possible that some well off business mogul or celebrity maintained a presence on one of them. Given the regularity of storms and the utter lack of sturdy building foundation that most of the islands had however, that didn't seem to be the case.

While undersea living was apparently all the rage in some areas of the planet Ashor, this archipelago was for the time being, too far away to be considered a good real estate investment even if one were to build an underwater house. That had all been in the pre-mission briefing, or at least, that's what Tony remembered of it. At times it seemed like the mission had started only yesterday, but when he thought about it more carefully, he could always identify something that had happened between now and then that reminded him otherwise.

The island that had been indicated on the map was one of the smaller ones, maybe worthy of a night of camping at best, and near enough that it would take only ten or so minutes to get there. Tony gave his partner a thumbs up and headed for the surface with the newly acquired data. She followed at a few meters distance, and when Tony finally broke the surface near the boat, she was almost immediately at his side.

Treading over to the ladder, the Novian grabbed hold and hefted himself out of the water. His weight returned as each centimeter of his frame was lifted from the warm seawater until finally he felt himself at his normal weight on the rear deck of the vessel.

Truth followed, climbing the ladder as Tony moved past the small safety gate near the ladder's head and removed his goggles. Next came his breather device which he unplugged carefully from his suit. A glance at his forearm told him everything had disconnected properly and in a moment he had moved to set the un-needed equipment in the duffel bag on the foredeck of the ship.

Looking over his shoulder, he noticed Truth firing up the boat's engine and stood, moving to her side as he showed her the map.

With such a good memory, Truth would have been able to navigate off the image alone, but it helped that she was able to use a variety of extra information from implanted sensors. Her neural interface fed the information she needed to her mind and in moments she was throttling up the craft.

Now it was time for actually listening to the brief, and figuring out what was in the kit drop. Tony had not guessed there would be a drop and so, his curiosity was piqued. A mission like this was relatively straight forward and nothing about it would have pointed to requiring any kind of heavy gear. Tension always seemed to be high in the Federation, so the presence of extra gear meant that someone in the NovaCore command structure was nervous.

Not wanting to wait any longer, Tony keyed his computer to read the message that had been contained within. The nasal computerized voice sounded in his ears, and certainly Truths as well, transmitted to their communication implants.

Tony nodded through the boiler plate and finally started paying attention as the meat of the brief began. The cryptically simplistic wording of the brief served only to further illustrate some sort of gravity to the message. "Believe an incidental event is possible within Ashor ruling body that may put ambassadorial staff at risk. Primary mission in such case is to provide escort of staff to ambassadorial vessel embarkation by any means required. See scenario Alex Riding Ether, Kit for escort hardening mission. Further investigation pending. Notification of host government pending."

The sound of the vessel's engine and the surf of the foils in the water was an oddly quiet backdrop for the message. The brief was clear. NovaCore analysts apparently thought something big was possible, something that could put the ambassadorship in danger. Things had certainly not been routine lately, but this revelation cast the entirety of the mission in a new light. What exactly did they think was going to happen? It was a question that Tony was beaten to asking by his partner, her voice breaking the silence.

"Well? What do you think they are expecting?" She asked calmly.

"Alex Riding Ether," Tony replied sarcastically, "Ambassadorial Rescue and Extraction, I think they are expecting the apocalypse down here, but you know intel, they will say that about anything."

"I have never heard of anyone being called for code Alex Riding Ether before Tony," Truth replied, "I would question whether this is normal over reaction or something more concrete."

Tony felt the same to be sure, but was hoping that his partner would be the lighthearted one. It was a vain hope this time. He mused aloud as they moved forward across the sea, "Escort Hardening huh? How are you on those procedures?"

"I am as expected, completely proficient in those task. How about you?" She replied glancing to him.

He had them in his head too, line after line of simple, repeatable procedure. Instead he began the unofficial steps aloud, "Make up a plan. Execute insertion as if we had no plan at all. Secure escort target via luck. Verify planned exit strategy wont work. Execute new exit strategy, making it up as you go. Did I miss a step?"

Truth smirked, "I wonder if command would be happy that you remember the joke version better than the real one."

"If it helps you remember the rules for real, no harm," Tony shrugged. He and Truth would most certainly be spending most of the next week shut into their apartment. It would be hours of planning, working and most importantly, programming everything into the nifty portable holo-projector that they had on the table.

"Do not forget a step or I will quote it at you, line number and all," Truth snickered, glancing around over the ocean as she navigated.

"It's easy to memorize plans and regs when you have the entirety of them stored in your robot brain, give us normals a break," Tony replied with mock offense. In reality he was always grateful that Truth had that ability, the ability to recall most anything she needed. It was her blessing and her curse and because it was such a curse for her at times, Tony always tried to highlight how grateful he really was for it. Truth's neural interface had given her many challenges over the years but Tony felt that accepting both the good and bad was his best way to be appreciative. Truth knew that she could count on him to be there when it was troublesome, and that he was always willing to let that unique ability aid them both when it could. It was part of their bond now, and it had been long enough that it no longer needed to be said aloud.

Truth shrugged, a small playful smile, innocent to a degree, covering her lips for a moment as she graciously took the joke and replied in as deep and grating a tone as she could muster, "Don't test me flesh bag, I can fold you in half."

Tony snickered. The quote had become one of her favorites, originally from a movie they had seen years ago. Truth liked quoting the evil robot in the movie simply because it was one of the worst, most hapless villains to ever be put to hologram. The budget of the production was decidedly on the low side, and as a result the robot's dialog was the highlight of the entire experience.

"Wisdom for the ages from Orios, " Tony replied, adding another quote from the same film, "A damned fine robot, and an even finer soldier."

The truth was that most militaries had long since automated whatever they could but nothing automatic could ever blend in seamlessly. Meaning that no matter what the future held, Tony guessed that people filling the role he and his partner currently occupied, would last quite a while.

Despite the best attempts from across the galaxy, continued setbacks, or even laws against artificial intelligence development, had barred the creation of sentient artificial life forms. Truth was about as close as it came, artificial in the sense of having been cloned, but using natural biological processes in many ways despite her implants and artificial organs.

It was even easier to regulate such efforts in the Hil'Raigh world however, because their culture had long stigmatized the development of real artificial life. The philosophical argument made by their race was simple: when a people created artificial life, the temptation to denigrate it below themselves would be too great to resist.

As a result, the society as a whole had focused more on other technologies, ones that they viewed as more natural. Cloning and genetic engineering were not something Tony thought of as natural, but apparently the Hil'Raigh did. Even so, an already strained dynamic with the Kul'Raigh painted a clear enough picture on why the Federation had avoided creating synthetic people, regardless of the ethics.

It was not a sentiment shared by all but despite the advances of technology over the decades, artificial life had always struggled to find a broad footing and was rarely constructed to fully imitate people. In cultures without the Kul'Raigh, who dominated the service sectors of the Federation economy, such creations were a bit more commonly attempted but by no means ubiquitous.

Tony guessed that it was a sort of natural balancing act. So much of peoples lives were already surrounded by technologies of all kinds that perhaps they yearned for living breathing company. He was never sure though. Especially with Truth already blurring that line.

To the outside observer she was a normal looking Kul'Raigh, despite her Novian eye color and some facial features that were not normally in the gene pool of the species. On the inside however, she was far different. It was a topic they sometimes talked about, Truth's gut being full of machines, but it never seemed to bother her these days. Perhaps in times past, but not now.

The official reasoning that had always been given for Truth's bevy of artificial parts was simple. It had been a matter of survival. As far as Tony had learned, Kul'Raigh genes did not mix well with Novians. They had to be spliced together artificially to make things work. It had raised the question of course of why it was done in the first place.

Truth had been told that it was because of several factors. Despite the shorter than Novian size of most Kul'Raigh they were regarded as the most resilient species of humanoids in the galaxy. Their immune system was strong, their bodies dealt with stress well and for the most part, their metabolism was relatively hard to slow down, keeping them rather energetic. Despite all of this they did not age quickly and had a resilient genome that was resistant to disease and the copy errors that would otherwise result in genetic disorders.

Those characteristics, combined with an already refined strain of genetic material from the NovaCore's admittedly less advanced genetic tinkering, had proven to be a combination of great interest among the NovaCore research teams.

As a result, research was started on finding a way to combine the genetic material of the two normally incompatible species. Experts in the subject had worked together to produce, through a cloning program, a variety of different combinations. It had all gone well enough that they were given the go ahead to clone embryos, then later people, or at least, create artificial children, Tony and his partner had been created as the end result of the program so he couldn't quite complain about it even if he had no particular love for the engineering involved.

Tony liked to think that he probably shared the test tube next to Truths and that fate had re-united them later in life but the reality was he had no idea about the project, other than that Truth had apparently had some pretty severe complications toward the end of her gestation. For one reason or another, the staff had decided to give her a chance and there she had been.

At first she was billed to be a bit sickly, but survivable, probably not soldier material at least. Later though, the aggressive nature of the Kul'Raigh genome had reared its head and resulted in some genetic problems that had never existed before Truth. It was all hear say of course, Tony was not a scientist and though Truth was as sharp as anyone Tony could imagine, she too had only ever been trained in her role. The difference though was that she had a near perfect memory of the conversations she'd managed with those who claimed to be in the know. When she had shared them it had been quite a detailed affair but neither of them could fill in all the gaps despite their best efforts.

The two clones knew precious little about the program from which they had come, not even as much as the star system it had happened in. Tony had a relatively easy time of life growing up, not getting sick and being healthy for almost every day he'd been alive. Truth had been the one that needed replacement organs, things to do the job of natural faculties that just weren't working properly. Artificial as they were, most of them were a mix of synthetic biologies, allowing them to grow, to a point at least. Truths growth had been stunted once she had reached optimal maturity for the Kul'Raigh genome. Her stature was locked, even a couple centimeters below someone like A'Shir who they'd met only yesterday.

That of course was only the tip of the iceberg when it came to Truth's origins and while Tony enjoyed musing about it, the approaching coastline of a small atoll made him perk up enough to sit straight and take a good look over it.

Sea grasses covered some of the small landmass, a few trees here and there too. It was a small piece of land in the chain of larger islands that stretched out across that part of the hemisphere, but this particular pile of sand was all the more valuable than its neighbors, at least until the kit pod dropped somewhere on it, hopefully unburied, was removed.

Truth cut the throttle as the bottom of the ocean ramped into view even from the surface. She turned the vessel around carefully before cutting the engine in what had to be barely a meter of water and setting the anchor with the push of a button.

"The pod has a beacon on it," She announced as she secured the steering wheel. The back of the boat to shore now, Truth moved to the rear deck, kicked the small ladder down and hopped into the calm ocean water. Tony followed, his feet sinking into the thick sand underwater just a bit before he stopped. Truth waded to the shore, looking rather comical, a wide legged almost helpless stance. Tony felt like he fared a bit better, but the smirk he got from his partner as he shook blobs of caked sand from his feet told him he had not done any better.

Thanks to the small radio transmitter in the pod, Truth quickly honed in, making a beeline straight for the metallic cylinder, which had been lovingly concealed under a bed of sea grass. Tony made a mental note as Truth pulled away the covering, that he should thank the drop team for their care in the matter.

Truth knelt next to the box amidst the weedy grass and sand, her fingers tracing a thin line that made up one of the edges of the container's lid. She found the catch on the device, a small metallic bulb, and thumbed it easily. The case popped open part way as the tension of the lock was released and Truth easily lifted the hinged lid out of the way, letting it hang in place under its own support as she exposed the contents to the air.

Inside the kit pod was everything Tony had expected given the sparse yet foreboding briefing information. Covert combat uniforms, one for them both filled the bottom of the box. On top of each were ablative combat vests, and finally on top of that, a pair of high powered rifles, a sidearm for both of them and some boxes of ammunition and powercells.

It had only been a week or so since Tony had layed eyes on his railgun back in orbit on the ship that had ferried them here, but seeing it in the kit pod, neatly arrayed with the rest of his gear made him glad he had taken the time to properly clean the weapon before he'd left. Truth's weapons were equally pristine and both of the pair had been issued what had to be the newest of uniforms and vests, since neither of the sets of pants in the pod showed any signs of wear in the knees.

"Well, I guess its good they gave us most of our own stuff. I do have to say I will miss the way those old pants fit" Tony said, hunkering down next to his partner.

"At least the boots did not change with this iteration, these are the old ones," Truth said pulling the top of her combat boots out from under the uniforms for Tony to see.

She then rifled through the uniform pieces, looked over the weapons and inventoried the ammo and powercells in short order, nodding and sitting back on her rump in the sand, hands behind her back and legs out forward as she stretched away from the pod, "All there I guess."

Tony nodded and crossed his legs, tugging at the sea grass as they sat, tossing the piles of it onto his partner's leg. The ocean was so calm at the moment that there were no waves crashing onto the island, not loudly at least, and the wind really had little to say either, occasionally rustling through the grass and fronds of the taller vegetation. Otherwise however, it left the two NovaCore alone together in the middle of nowhere.

"Well, as far as I can recall we have the boat for another eighteen hours, why don't we see if we can roast some Toks while we are here hmm?" Tony finally said, standing and brushing some sand off of the bottom of his suit. "Plus I want to change into some shorts, this thing is hot."

"You stuck Toks in the rations?" Truth giggled, her voice said enough, she couldn't believe the announcement.

"Sure, you love Toks," Tony replied casually, Truth standing to follow him back to the boat.

"Yes but you hate them," She educated.

"Oh yeah. Well I guess it was dumb of me to stick them in the food bag," He shrugged as he stepped into the water, "Suppose that means you'll have to eat em all."

With that he sauntered into the water toward the boat, no more than fifteen meters from where the pod was resting on the island. It was a rather small place to camp but with the weather promising to behave, Tony was sure that he could enjoy at least a Tok or two for his partner's sake. Besides, napping on an island in the middle of a paradise like this would probably not be something he'd have the chance to do if things went like intel suggested. No, for now, relaxing a bit while the weather really was calm, would be the best way to wait for the coming storm.

3 - Unlikely Associate

There was noticeable tension in the air, it had of course been building for the greater part of the year. The public part of it at least. For Vaerlin and some of the other nobles, those who had been privy to the initial proposals, that sense of dread had been building far longer. A change for certain, but for the better? No, no it was a disaster in waiting. The balance of power among existing nobility would shift, political alliances to the Nobles of other states would collapse and have to be rebuilt. It was a drastic change, but it was all so well packaged.

Vaerlin knew that he had no prayer of opposing the reforms alone, especially since he was already being put on review. Even from the beginning he had always been in the middle ground, not in the King's good graces but not one of those slated to lose a council seat in the next quarter either. He had carefully towed that line for years even despite his disagreements with the Monarch. Now though, the reforms would change it all.

It was not just about the Kul'Raigh, but the way council seats were awarded, the way nobles retained their properties and holdings, a centralization of power so absurd that Vaerlin had never believed it would gain any support at all. Yet, here, listening to the blithering idiot of a Noble from Kylos, he was hearing it, actual support, from a noble, of the centralization reform.

As quickly as the man's speech had started, it ended, amid silence. It was the final argument presented for the session and it was sure to be among the last chances anyone got to take the Advisory Council floor in such presentation. To the chagrin of Vaerlin, the supportive camp had more voices than anyone had expected and it left the oppose camp undermanned for the political wrangling. How could anyone in good conscience support centralization, especially when the next in line was not even a Hil'Raigh? It was a question Vaerlin asked himself several times over the course of today's session.

The amphitheater remained in silence until the King took the podium at the center. He looked around the room, and though from this distance Vaerlin couldn't see his eyes, he knew what the man was doing. He was scanning the faces he could see, gauging them, sizing up their mood. It was a talent the King had, reading people, and it was because of that talent that Vaerlin had chosen a seat far from the Monarch during today's proceedings. The sound of King Ren'Tauru's voice sounded at last, amplified by the speakers in the room.

"We've heard many arguments and though there have been some compelling ideas put forth, I think it is in our best interest as a nation, to move forward with the slated reforms to policy in the next quarter. I understand that this is an issue which draws out the passions in all of us but I must confess, that I feel our passions alone cannot dictate this policy."

He paused. There were some murmurs before he continued, "The needs of all of our citizens should weigh most on our minds as we consider what is in their best interest. For that is why all of us are in these Council Chambers. I suggest that the reforms move forward thus far, with minimal changes, and for now, I feel we should adjourn this council."

There were open murmurs, some discontented ones, at least from where Vaerlin was seated he could hear them. However, none of the opposing camp dared stand and shout or risk anything that would put them on the fast track to losing a council seat. The reforms would necessarily reduce the number of council seats that the King gave out to his nobles in the coming quarter, and as a result, no one wanted to put themselves in the cross-hair. There would be political wrangling for certain, Nobles trying to discreetly push others into that dangerous position. Vaerlin knew of a couple people he could try to assure himself priority over at very least. The King's primary Adviser was really the last hope that any of these changes could be averted but unfortunately he had not been openly opposed to the reform during deliberation. It was entirely possible he had sided with the King already.

Therefore, as Vaerlin moved out of the amphitheater, he headed for the man, hoping to catch him before anyone else managed to soak up his time. It was a desperate move really, because something about the King's candor earlier had made Vaerlin worry that no one at all could change the Monarch's mind now.

Vaerlin felt he would probably retain most of his influence, his holding, but he distrusted the King's daughter and the way she would undoubtedly ruin him when she finally took the throne. She was already frustrating enough and having to deal with her as the queen someday certainly made Vaerlin cringe. He hated the idea that the halfbreed Kul'Raigh would be in charge of a truly Hil'Raigh nation. He mulled it over in his mind as he rehearsed what he'd open with when he finally reached the object of his hurry.

The Adviser had stopped, the stone corridors of the council hall echoing with conversations, some heated, a few debates, but mostly quiet talking. The council was out of session for now but that did not mean there would be no further business discussed here today. It meant that Vaerlin's time was essentially limited, he would not have long to make his case, at very least for delaying the reform.

He cleared his throat loudly as he approached the King's right hand man, a tall Hil'Raigh, thin, a bit gaunt in the face but quite a loyal leader nonetheless. He turned at the sound, facing Vaerlin wordlessly until the nobleman spoke.

"Adviser Tolem," He began

"Duke Vaerlin," replied the adviser, even as he continued to walk, "What can I do for you?"

"Ah of course, I wanted to talk to you, briefly at least," Vaerlin said.

"Well you have my attention," replied Tolem. He looked a bit tired, perhaps from the deliberation.

"It's about my council seat," Vaerlin began, "I just can't accept being put on review like this, not with these reforms pending, not with all that's going on. A mid season change like this is highly irregular."

The adviser sighed loudly, motioning for the Duke to follow, "I understand your concern but I don't make the final determinations on that list...."

"But you do have input, input on whose names get considered at all...." Vaerlin replied. He was trying to avoid being outright accusatory but the frustration he felt within was making that difficult.

"And why should that change how the King reacts?"

"Why under the stars am I on this list?" Vaerlin practically exploded with frustration.

"I don't know, I didn't suggest your name...."

"I can help the King secure support for the reforms if he takes me off the list..." Vaerlin replied, trying to speak as smoothly as he could bear. Being on report was a devastation, a danger. If he lost his seat on the Federation Council he would be indebted permanently to those he had already chosen to make deals with. No, he could not let this happen without a fight.

"As I recall, Vaerlin, you oppose the reforms..." The adviser stopped walking, facing the Duke directly. His eyes were scrutinizing, almost as if he was making an accusation of his own.

"I'm a reasonable man Tolem, and I have good influence in the Federation Council as well."

"If I didn't know better I would feel you were suggesting your place is outside of the King's jurisdiction Vaerlin..." Tolem quipped. He looked downright annoyed now, he was definitely calculating something, his eyes, his body language, they all pointed to it.

"I have been in the council for decades, I know who pulls strings and I know how the Council works Tolem. No matter what the King claims, he has always been an outsider. His Queen isn't a representative for the Compact and so far his daughter shows almost no political promise either," Vaerlin replied, he felt bold admitting what he felt aloud, but it was true. The King had never made many political allies and the fact that he was a leader had been enough to get some of his ideas onto the floor of the council. It was only because of noble support that he had really had any success in anything outside of the local governing of the Compact itself.

"Are you saying you don't need to be loyal to your Monarch, Duke Vaerlin?" Tolem raised a brow now, he was accusing Vaerlin of treason. It was nothing of the sort, Vaerlin had no need to be treasonous, not with this. This was simple fact, a reality which could not, would not, be ignored.

"I am merely stating fact Tolem," Vaerlin countered, "Without noble support the King of this nation is as good as imprisoned when it comes to Federation politics, none of the other nation's Nobility trust him with how centrist he is. He fancies himself a people's man but ignores the very people who help him make things happen. His daughter is more of the same, cut from the same vine. Not to mention she's a Kul'Raigh halfbreed…."

"I find that lack of respect for your King rather disturbing Vaerlin, especially after King Ren'Tauru's family has been so good to your own. How long has Vaerlin been the line of Dukes now? Two, three generations?"

"And through all of it, there has been a reasonable exchange, Tolem. A reasonable return to those who help get things done. With the Kul'Raigh changes, the reforms, who can say what Ren'Tauru will do next…."

"And now a surname alone describes your King. Vaerlin, you must not be so naive as to think you should not be on review at this point." Tolem scoffed openly, "Listen to yourself speak and consider just how much it mimics what the silver tongues said decades ago in the Sho'Alar state…."

"And now the Sho'Alar dynasty is in the hands of the regent…" Vaerlin replied, "A weak ruler breeds a discontent that cannot be quelled by simple loyalty to whatever misguided cause he undertakes…"

"You may not believe you are worthy of disdain Vaerlin, but I find the King's decision to place you on review, quite shrewd," Tolem replied. His brows were furrowed, a deep scowl in his face as he replied and turned away, "You are certainly a boisterous, if impaired member of the Nobility, Vaerlin."

The Adviser moved away without another word. He was sure of course, to repeat the conversation to the King. There was no going back now, the King was most certainly going to take away Vaerlin's Council seat. Perhaps he could get a foreign noble to intervene and help. A foreign nation could always protest the removal of some other nation's council member if they thought it was in the Federation's best interest to maintain someone's spot. He had heard rumors, shufflings really among some of the other nobility, most of them well entrenched, that they were tired of the King. Perhaps he could count even on local Nobility for help. He did not directly oversee or control any of the other Councilors but was certainly on the list of people who shared their common interest. In their minds he had to be a viable political ally. Even so, moving against his own king with the help of a foreign dignitary would be seen as the move of a desperate obstructionist. Worse still, even if possible, it would likely never come to be regardless. His potential ally would taint their own political reputation in the process, not only in their own nation but internationally. There had to be something, some reason for which Vaerlin could reasonably receive the foreign help, but how was it to occur?

As Vaerlin mused, he heard someone clear their throat from behind and turned to face the noise. He was given to see a thin faced Hil'Raigh with long ears and a narrow nose. The eyes on the man's face were the shape of small almonds and his thin lips barely pink compared to his skin. Overall he looked like an old stereotype for a librarian, save the fact that his hair was black and tied back into a ponytail rather than flowing free. He wore robes not unlike what most councilors wore here in the Compact and had a confidence about him that made Vaerlin question whether he had met the man before.

"Excuse me?" Vaerlin called to the man. The pair were in the mouth of one of the side corridors, with Tolem having lead Vaerlin along. Now, Vaerlin was alone save for the stranger nearby.

"You are Vaerlin?" The man asked, leaving off his own name. In most situations that was a sign of rudeness, but the body language, the circumstance, they made it something else. Vaerlin cocked his head and eyed the stranger as he approached.

The man spoke again, "I overheard just a bit of your exchange, it seems like you are having a rough time with the reforms..."

Vaerlin scoffed, of course he was unhappy with them but he was not about to incriminate himself further, not when he was already doomed thanks to Tolem. Instead, Vaerlin quipped sarcastically, sounding rather condescending, "What do you know of them?"

"I know your voice is not the only one to express what you did, I hear it often," the man replied with a friendly, if deceiving smile. Vaerlin stood straight as he saw the expression. Whoever the stranger was he was not a Councilor or someone Vaerlin knew.

"Who are you?" Vaerlin finally replied, his voice full of gravity. He wanted to know who exactly had such a boldness about them. It was uncommon for anyone to even voice an opinion like Vaerlin himself had, but to support it even after having overheard it was ludicrous.

"A representative," The man replied calmly. He began to pace, his hand gestures betraying a definite confidence and understanding of whatever message he had prepared. He was rehearsed and ready, Vaerlin was not. Being off guard like this made the Duke uncomfortable on a level he had not felt for years. For so long he had been able to be on the upper hand and now, someone else had him in a difficult position. Instead of pushing into that opening however, the man continued, "I represent a majority of voices in this affair."

"Majority of voices?" Vaerlin felt a chill down his spine. It was of course, something simple to hear, yet it carried a foreboding secrecy to it. A majority of voices, voices sympathetic to his own. It was almost too good to be true, perhaps a trap. Vaerlin shook his head and sighed, trying to regain his outward confidence, hoping the man had not noticed his vulnerability.

"I have no interest in jokes or traps friend, move along."

"And leave a friend in need?" The man smiled and eyed Vaerlin carefully, he seemed to pierce the Duke's defenses but his face did little to reveal what he thought he might be seeing. Instead, he simply paced some more, "You are thinking ahead Vaerlin, why would anyone want to trap you for that?"

There was an appeal to what Vaerlin heard, something he realized he was displaying openly when the man smirked. However appealing it was he could not risk open conversation with this man, not here, not about this. He had no idea whom it was and how he could trust them. No, he was going to send this man away or call security. At very least he could win back some of the points he had lost with the King by doing so. As he was about to raise his voice however, he noticed a change in the visitor. The man's demeanor became one of momentary surprise. That had certainly got his attention.

"Of course this place isn't ideal for such a discussion," The man quipped quickly. He approached Vaerlin and lowered his voice, "The majority would rather you lead this nation into the future, they trust your policy more than the King at this point, Vaerlin. If you want to hear what they have to say, you can simply ask them yourself."

With that the man handed Vaerlin a small contact card and smiled, "To a brighter future."

They separated and Vaerlin eyed the man as he vanished into a crowd of people from a lesser, regional council while they filed into the Council Chambers. Eventually the man's form was lost amid the sea of faces and Vaerlin was stunned to find that he could not make him out at all once the tide had passed. There were guards at the door who would have noticed a stranger sneaking into council however and so his first reaction was to wave over a security guard. He gestured visibly to one of the posted guards who smartly approached. It was a Kul'Raigh, shorter than Vaerlin himself but wearing a vest and uniform.

"I just met someone who I don't think should be in the chambers," Vaerlin began.

The guard nodded, "Of course Duke, where did they go?"

Where had the man gone? That was a good question, one Vaerlin could not answer right away. Would revealing the conversation however, implicate Vaerlin himself? He mulled it over and then finally told the guard, "I.. I confess I lost him, though I had little interaction with him."

"I see," the guard sounded dismayed, "What was his description?"

"Black hair, brown, no... hazel eyes, with ears that had sharp points, He wore his hair in a ponytail and looked a bit thin for his robe..." Vaerlin stated, confident in his vivid mental image of the man.

The guard nodded, then glanced around the room, her head tracking at a slow pace. The Kul'Raigh cleared her throat and then finally replied, "There are... several councilors that match such a description Duke... perhaps you misjudged one of them?"

"No I..." Vaerlin paused, "Perhaps... but please be vigilant..."

"Of course Duke," She replied, "We strive to do our best at all times."

"Right," Vaerlin gave her a flat response, looking around the room himself. He had certainly been had. He should have called out to the stranger. Now all that remained was the contact card. The Noble's mind waffled now as to whether he should hand the contact card over or not.

If the man legitimately represented a group like he had claimed, they would never let the King's security forces find them, so turning over the card would simply make Vaerlin look bad. On the other hand it could have been a trap. It was not unheard of for monarchs to set up such honey-pots to catch disloyal nobles. King Ren'Tauru however, had never done so, and as such, Vaerlin doubted it.

No, from the man's confidence to his words, he seemed to exude the idea of representing what he had claimed. The card he had given was smooth, completely featureless metal, not like normal contact cards which usually carried a logo or writing. Whomever the man was, he had also claimed to have Vaerlin's interest, and not just that, but the interests of the majority of supportive Nobles on his side.

With that kind of support, perhaps Vaerlin could force the issue, get rid of Tolem of course, and push the King toward something more workable. If he could prevent his own Federation Council seat from being taken, he could definitely help any Nobles who were on his side that lost theirs in the reforms. It was only a win for Vaerlin, if he could get to contact with the stranger.

"Thank you guard," Vaerlin finally said, "That will be all for now."

She nodded, saluting, and turning on her heel before heading back to her post near the council chamber entrance. Vaerlin sighed, this was not like the Federation Chamber, a place where he may never have set foot again, it was a simple place, a place where small minded Monarchs and foolish Advisers made claims and deals that were in nobody's best interest.

It was decided, Vaerlin would have to give this stranger a chance, and at very least if it turned bad, he could probably report the whole conversation to the Security Council. Such an occurrence could definitely ensure he retained his seat, even under current circumstances. The Duke shook out the anxiety that had been building in his aging frame for the past several minutes. He calmed himself as he finally took his wrist communicator to his mouth and spoke aloud, "Be'Ran, prepare my chamber. I have a bit of research to do."

4 - Prepaid Price

The smells of the lower city were certainly something Vaerlin had never intended to understand. Now that he had been here for some time however, he found himself oddly familiarized with the scents entering his nose. It was a sooty smell, like exhaust. At least, that's what Vaerlin guessed.

He had never really owned any machinery that actually output exhaust gasses, save perhaps the hover cars and limos that carried him about the world of his daily life. Regardless though, he had smelled fire, ash, and if this smelled of anything it was reminiscent of those odors rather than nature alone.

The air itself felt musty, closed in and like it was hanging here, crushed under a blanket of freshness above in the upper city blocks, but such was the price of a metropolis. There had to be something under it all, propping it up, keeping things running. People needed factories or industry close to the commerce and since space was at a premium, things just went vertical instead.

Like most Federation capital cities, Dau'Kore, the Compact's own, was a metropolis not only in raw land area but in height. The average height of structures in the city had long exceeded fifty or sixty floors, with the center of the city so pin pricked with skyscrapers that the skyline there was more a solid line of buildings before an abrupt cutoff into the air.

Vaerlin looked up, scoffing. From the underside all of the interconnected platforms, walkways, paths and means of normal navigation in use by the citizens of the city, gave little in the way of beauty. It was on the underside that all of the piping, climate control, logistics and water ways were hidden. On the underside of the platforms between skyscrapers were the structural supports, those oh so needed yet inelegant pieces of engineering. Here, function was all that could be seen and everything reflected it.

The lowest levels of the city operated in a relatively dark environment, given just how clustered the space between buildings above had become over the century. As a result, most of the light here was fake, harsh, artificial. Everything had a greenish tint to it, even Vaerlin's own skin and the muck of grime. The messy, undefinable liquids that dotted the ground here resided in various places around the patchwork of walkways and physical roads. They were already ruining the bottom hem of Vaerlin's robe.

It was a good analog for politics. The shiny public exterior was what people saw, but the down under, grimy muck on the bottom side that made it all possible was something people preferred not to know about. It was a sort of irony, but it did little to distract Vaerlin in the long term. He was rather nervous about the trip and since he had never even been to the lower city, let alone this part of it, he was sure he would get lost or be attacked.

Crime was not common in Hil'Raigh society, but then again, most sensible people also avoided the underside of the city as well. Who would be assaulted on the broad, well-patrolled paths above? There was a stark contrast though, to how the underside worked. Despite having never been here, Vaerlin was aware of the fact that this part of the city followed the same sort of distinction as the overall world did. It had its own underbelly, something worse than itself upon which it rested. Some called it crime, some called it corruption, even further still, opportunity.

Vaerlin preferred filth. He hated the underside and even with reasonable assurances that his wrist computer was in fact still leading him on a good navigation route, he had become increasingly uncomfortable with the idea that he was to meet the new stranger alone.

The man that had approached him earlier was dignified and presentable. It came then as even more a surprise for the Duke when he had fully scanned the man's contact card, that the proposed meeting location was in the underside of the city. If the offer, or rather, Vaerlin's desperation, had not been so strong he would have considered not even coming, but a single check up call from one of his contacts in foreign nobility had worried him enough that he was now willing to do even this.

Thankfully it had not rained for days, making the grimy ground relatively dry and avoiding large staining on the hem of the robe. Even so, Vaerlin had tied some of his clothing up into his belt to prevent it dragging as much as he could.

There were few times in his life when the noble ever remembered doing so, but when the prospect of his Federation Council seat being taken reared its head, he buckled down mentally and trudged onward.

The prospect was not all that unheard of, Vaerlin had seen it happen before. However, like most long term members of his nation's Council delegation, he anticipated a sort of tenure after all this time. Maybe it had made him complacent.

The Compact like all member nations in the Hil'Raigh Federation, had its own delegation, a limited number of members that split its total voting power. Unlike its neighbors however, the compact had long had a tradition of having a smaller delegation, concentrating the power among fewer voters.

While the ruler of the nation carried the highest amount of voting capital in the Council delegation, people like Vaerlin, because of the fact that they were nobility in the Compact rather than its neighbors, faired far better in influence than their peers. Over the years that balance shifted, but largely remained stable and it was a good, working system, one steeped in tradition and effectiveness.

Kings and rulers were kept in check on the international level by Federation decree, which their own delegation members voted on while, in turn, nobles and other appointees were largely at the mercy of the leader's whim at home. The monarch decided on whether they kept their appointed place. Removals and additions to the delegation were limited to a percentage each year, making sure each delegation slowly grew or shrunk, never suddenly becoming too lopsided and ensuring more stability.

For the past decade, King Ren'Tauru had kept the delegation at the same size, filling a few seats, replacing a few here and there when it was required. Now however, he was cutting seats, as many seats as he could under Federation law without some sort of emergency authority.

Vaerlin had never seen it coming until days before the last Ruler's council meeting at the palace. He had assumed it was a potential, non-finalized list of names slated for review but when he had realized how short that list really was, he knew it was little more than a formality. While he was supposedly under review, there was little doubt in the Duke's mind that his council seat was simply being taken away and the worst part of it would be that there would be no replacement. At least if the seat had remained, Vaerlin could have used the new delegate as a middle man, got some things done through him. The King's plan however, utterly compromised that hope.

That internal struggle, the desire to remain in council but at the same time, push beyond the King's direct influence had made Vaerlin open his mouth to Adviser Tolem. It was all but assured now, Vaerlin would lose his place because he had spoken. Though it was likely before, it was all but promised now. No one spoke so ill of their king and retained his place in the delegation. Any ruler worth their position knew that much.

What King Ren'Tauru and his Adviser had not anticipated though, was the apparently wide spread opposition to these kinds of reductions. Those delegation changes combined with local reform were apparently rubbing the influencers the wrong way. That was at least, what Vaerlin had to surmise, given that one of these shadowy figures had approached him rather brazenly.

That was a sign of boldness, or rather, political desperation, if framed properly. Vaerlin knew that no one would take a risk, say the things that the man had said, allude to what he had, without a vested interest in a resolution that favored them.

He had talked of a majority of voices, the need for a face to lead those opposed to unchecked centralization of power and it had all made sense.

Still, had it made enough sense for Vaerlin to believe what could have been an elaborate and potentially lethal hoax? Here he was, a duke, alone, in the underside of Dau'Kore, listening to the echoes of machinery through the forest of skyscraper bases, hearing above, the pounding racket of life on the top of it all. Every so often, the sound of the monorail system running above caught his ear, rushing past and going quiet again. How would anyone want to be down here for any length of time? How could anyone want to actually spend time down here, let alone have a meeting?

There was only one real hope, one silver lining to the locale, and that was that few people would venture after the Duke. As far as anyone knew, including his own staff, he was on a private appointment in the city and could not be disturbed. Even that little bit of misdirection had cost him a favor with one of the locals who served as part of the unspoken bridge between the upper and lower worlds. Vaerlin just hoped it was worth the time now.

Thus far Vaerlin had not seen a single person, or vehicle even. Normally that would have been welcome, but with such an unfamiliar place surrounding him, the Nobleman felt only an increasing sense of dread.

No matter how seductive the stranger's message had been, this was probably a mistake, he decided. It was not easy to find non-private access to the underside, especially considering so much of the underside was technically privatized property. Even if Vaerlin did want to leave early, and he was increasingly considering it, he would have to find a way up.

Going back the way he came was always an option, but if he were being pursued, that would be exactly the chance someone would need to lay a strong ambush for him. The Noble adjusted the rings on his index fingers carefully, just in case. While it was not a guarantee, each of them was equipped with a toxin filled needle that could be deployed simply by slapping the appropriate place of the ring against someone's skin. The poison would incapacitate the target and was laced with chemicals that made it impossible to treat outside of a hospital. Anyone who had it in their system was willfully admitting to assaulting a noble when they checked in to save their lives. Even then however, the chance that assailants simply held him at gunpoint was equally high and so, as he walked, Vaerlin adjusted the projector belt he had under his robe. The small device would protect him from most of the heat from a shot or two, but it would still be painful if he were to be shot regardless and so, on his hip he carried his own small pistol.

Like all current standard weapons, Vaerlin's was a pulsed plasma weapon, a device which used an extreme amount of energy to ionize pockets of atmospheric gas and contain them in a small magnetic field before propelling them forward. The pockets would rupture on impact with any surface, releasing their superheated contents and dealing significant damage, largely via heat transfer. Vaerlin's own weapon carried an enhanced gas mechanism, mixing more easily utilized firing material into the mix and making the whole process more dangerous. He was grateful for that, though it added some bulk and made his weapon classified as a military grade piece of hardware instead of something one could officially own for sporting purposes. Any noble in his position owned something similar, even though most of them refused to admit it. They all practiced in secret but that was not too difficult when one was influential enough.

What Vaerlin had never done however, was fire the weapon at a living target. Simulation and testing were all fine, but Vaerlin had never actually had to defend himself with a pistol, let alone the poison rings. Part of him worried that he would never be willing to pull the trigger, but that part was always overshadowed by the fact that the Duke was very fond of his own life. When it came down to it, he always knew he would if he had to, it was only a matter of motivation.

Still, despite all the confidence and assurance in himself that he could muster, the Nobleman's quiet anxiety was no less intense. He wondered as he walked whether he had seen someone ahead or whether he was just paranoid from being alone so long. A shadow or a face? Probably neither, but that did not stop his mind from racing at a speed that he found entirely uncomfortable.

How long had it even been since he had first cracked the door to the underside? The duke paused, checking his watch. It had only been ten minutes, but it was a windy confusing ten minutes to be sure. The navigation software was having only the barest of luck giving him the sort of direction he now sought.

He reached down to the device and keyed the controls once more, eying a small holographic projection of the surrounding area for a moment, before he finally settled on his destination. He was at least, close now, with maybe a minute or two at most, even at his relaxed pace. With any luck the stranger's meeting place would be temporary and the two could talk like civilized nobles, in the confines of an actual building rather than between the shelter that the shells of other people's structures formed around them.

There was another shadow ahead, and this time, rather than vanishing as Vaerlin approached, it took form. A Hil'Raigh man stepped out from against one of the buildings. Vaerlin felt his hand slipping into his robe pocket, caressing the hilt of his small pistol. He had no idea who the person was or why they were there but one thing was certain, if they attacked him he was going to defend himself. Of course the man would try to get close quickly, and so Vaerlin paused, circling wide rather than walking past.

The two locked eyes, the stranger puffing from a long vaporizer as the nobleman passed him. The person had to be a thug, he had a leathery face, skin that had obviously spent its share of time in the dirt. His features were harsh and his nose was just a bit crooked, meaning the man had broken it at least once but never bothered to pay for a good doctor. His hair was short cropped, a crew cut and he wore a faded gray jacket with little decoration, except on one of the shoulders.

A wave of realization passed through Vaerlin's mind as he saw that the stranger was likely a former Akal'Maru military member. The armistice that ended the war with the NovaCore was still holding even today, decades after it had been declared but that meant little for the Akal'Maru who had been in the thick of things. Many of them had left their home nation after finishing their military careers, many of them doing so out of frustration at what they labeled weakness in their home government.

Vaerlin had been younger then, but he had been watching the headlines daily. The Akal'Maru were poised for amazing gains near the start of the conflict but by the end, their forces had been run ragged. The official story was that the leadership wanted peace after all and that they had finally made a breakthrough with the NovaCore but Vaerlin had met enough of the nobility from Akal'Maru's war era to know otherwise.

Terrible decision making and a tendency for micromanagement by Akal'Maru's rulers had hampered their military response and capability. They had assumed it was a sure thing, going against the arguably inferior military of the NovaCore. Technology was on the side of the Hil'Raigh and the Federation at large had committed to the war effort.

A combination of overconfidence and some confusing capabilities from a species so young, had been the seed of destruction among the Akal'Maru fleets. The NovaCore had a tendency to appear out of almost anywhere and even now, hushed conspiracy abounded over just how they managed it. Some claimed it was collusion with people in the Federation, others claimed they had found out how to make a faster subspace travel. Some even claimed that it was because the NovaCore could travel faster than light without hyperspace, something that experts the galaxy over agreed had to be untrue.

Vaerlin had no idea what it was in practice but the headlines were clear; losses were heavy and disproportionate, some vessels were boarded and scuttled, some destroyed outright and others had to surrender when brought to their knees alone.

Everyone involved, from top to bottom, had been living down the shame for years, except of course the King of Akal'Maru and his closest leadership, who styled themselves as heroes of peace for ending the conflict. Vaerlin knew better, and politically, it had looked more like giving up, retreat in the face of a foe who should not have been a challenge at all.

It had left many without a cause, and the man that Vaerlin had met was most certainly a result of that time period. There was a moment where Vaerlin found himself feeling a bit of compassion, but he knew that regardless of who this person was, he could not be trusted. He was after all, hanging around the underbelly of the city and though Vaerlin himself was also, he somehow found himself on the moral high ground anyway.

There was an uncomfortable tension as the stranger moved, idly striding toward the fence gate Vaerlin had been moving to. Vaerlin tensed, and only as he did, realized that there were more than two people here. Off to the right was another, and the left. At least two or three more in total. Shooting any of them was going to end poorly if any of them were also armed. Vaerlin glanced around, none of them had spoken but they had certainly been closing the distance toward him.

The motion was clear and Vaerlin cursed himself for falling victim to this of all things. He wished at least that whichever rival had orchestrated all of this would have simply done the job himself rather than have some hired hands do it. Of course, Vaerlin had to admit that if he had been trying to remove a rival in this fashion, he would have hired too.

"It seems you are at a disadvantage here Duke," the man with the vaporizer finally spoke, shaking the vaporizer out as some drops of the oil that had been in it splattered about. He had a voice that was hard to read, one that told of his time in Akal'Maru's service.

"Who sent you?" Vaerlin replied condescendingly.

"Who do you think?" the man replied. He took a couple steps forward, slowing as Vaerlin's hand found the grip of his pistol.

"No need to try and shoot me Vaerlin. My friends and I aren't here to make a mess, we're here on behalf of a mutual friend."

Vaerlin tensed, but eased his grip on the firearm in his pocket, eventually withdrawing his hand and taking as calm a posture as he could muster, now counting five strangers in total.

"If a friend sent you why did he send five of you?"

"In case you brought friends, against the instructions on the card..." The man smirked, stepping forward, reaching out his hand in gesture, "One last instruction for you though, could you hand me your pistol? Oh and take off those rings of yours too..."

Vaerlin glanced over his shoulder, the others were Hil'Raigh men as well, some of them wearing coats like the apparent ringleader. All of them had visible weapon holsters and none of them looked at all relaxed. The Duke took a breath, nervousness overtaking a part of him that he tried to keep hidden from view as he removed his rings and set them on the ground.

When he reached into his pocket for the pistol he expected a reaction from the leader, a flinch, an extra instruction, but nothing came, and so the Duke slipped his fingers around the grip and drew the weapon out. A glance around him told Vaerlin that the others were more than ready to pounce if he decided to try and use his pistol.

Vaerlin's mind played out a scenario as he handed the weapon over, what he could have done, ways things could have played out. None of them ended with him living though and as he handled the barrel and extended his arm to the stranger, he felt a sense of dread fill him when the man's fingers curled around the grip.

"Not a bad design, military issue even," The man quipped, "I hope King Ren'Tauru doesn't find out about this little gem, he might be insulted."

The weapon was slipped into the stranger's coat with no fanfare and in a moment, a gesture from him had his cronies moving to Vaerlin's sides. One of the pair pocketed the two rings and the Duke guessed he'd never see them again even if he did get out of this alive at all.

"What now?" Vaerlin asked, genuinely curious.

"Now," The man explained, "We go to the meeting, you are very punctual Duke Vaerlin."

A bit of relief filled Vaerlin's mind as his hope that things would be alright after all took hold. The man he had met in the council hall was enigmatic enough and it followed then, that whomever he represented would be equally careful about who they met with. It did make sense after all, they had revealed what some in Ren'Tauru's court would have thought to be sedition. After that, none of them would want to be public about it. Vaerlin had to admit that despite how uncomfortable he was currently, he likely would have tried to set up a buffer too. If he were as the initial contact had claimed, 'a representative for a majority of voices' who did not agree with the King, discretion would have been his course of action as well.

"Loty you owe me thirty credits. He came and he did it on time." The ringleader quipped as he motioned for Vaerlin to follow. The group, like a small ring, prevented Vaerlin from going anywhere but where the leader was going and he headed straight to one of the buildings nearby.

"You bet on whether or not I'd come?" Vaerlin was mildly amused, he had heavily considered not coming at all and wondered now what the conversation would have been like had he not.

"Call it a friendly game for those who have nothing better to do," The man smirked.

"You still have not introduced yourself..." Vaerlin quipped, hoping he could impose upon the man's social senses for some sort of introduction.

"Tamur," he gave Vaerlin only a glance as he said it, his eyes were scanning even in the short look, trying to size up the Duke constantly.

"From Akal'Maru yes?" Vaerlin asked.

The man glanced at him again and, instead of speaking raised a brow. He turned away and picked up his pace, leading a brisk walk now as the group approached a large cargo door. When they reached the wall, the ring of thugs led Vaerlin off to the side as Tamur keyed on the control pad. In moments the door began sliding upward in its track, each segment bending into the gloom above as it was sucked into a neat roll. Immediately visible inside was a vehicle, a limousine not unlike the one's Vaerlin himself used most of the time. It was black with no identifying marks and an engine arrangement that said it was the newest model. It probably had a good speed to it as well.

Tamur moved to the door of the vehicle, motioning to Vaerlin as the group parted to allow him passage. He gave one or two of them a look, brushing off his robe and trying to look all the more dignified as he headed to the vehicle. When the surly Hil'Raigh cracked the door and pulled it aside, Vaerlin could finally make out some of the interior. The space looked plush enough and at this rate Vaerlin was finally sure he found the right place. He ducked into the interior carefully, and as he did, noticed a familiar face on his left side near the drivers compartment.

The passenger area was arranged in a square ring of sorts, all seats facing the middle of the floor. Vaerlin quickly took one opposite his riding companion.

"Good of you to come Vaerlin," The man said, it was the same regal looking contact from before, his dress and appearance enough to remind Vaerlin just how much more comfortable he was with other people from his social class. The door closed from the outside and with that the vehicle began to move.

It was a good place for a private meeting at least, Vaerlin decided. A glance out the window gave the Duke a parting look at the group of toughs that had picked him up.

"Of course," Vaerlin replied finally, he was nervous now, perhaps more than before. He was face to face with someone who was at least familiar with how noble politics could happen.

"I hope Tamur and his goons did not give you too much trouble?"

"Not at all, though, they took my gun, and rings..."

The man snickered, ignoring the comment with his reply, "I am glad to see that you understand the value of a coherent society your eminence."

"Of course, that's why I'm here," Vaerlin replied, he leaned back into the plush chair, noting how comfortable it felt.

"I had a good feeling about you Vaerlin," The man smiled, "You understand how things happen in the real world, not just the world of ideals like King Ren'Tauru."

Vaerlin nodded, eying the man who seemed quite content to let the Duke ask a question or two. He said nothing for a long while until finally, Vaerlin himself broke the silence, "So what is it you want to do about all of this then?"

"Oh yes, you remember our talk? You are a born leader and we want you to be the face of the new Compact going forward." He replied. His voice was filled with a deep calm, one that exuded his confidence.

"Like Sho'Alar?" Vaerlin inquired. He knew what had happened there. The real king of the Sho'Alar state had been killed, as had his son and nephew. A regent had been put in place and now, as Vaerlin sat across from this stranger he wondered just how involved the man might have been in all of that.

"Good connection Vaerlin," he replied with a smile, "Yes, like Sho'Alar. It's easier though."

"Easier?"

"Yes, when the heir is a Kul'Raigh there is not much you need to worry about with ending a royal line. That was done for us. Now we just need history to catch up with biology."

Vaerlin shuddered a bit, this man was indeed candid, veiled, but candid. He was cold, that much was sure. The way he spoke about simply having the King and his daughter killed was something of a potent combination. It did little for Vaerlin's nerves however.

"And the consort?" Vaerlin asked, he was genuinely curious.

"Probably sell," The man shrugged, "She can't rule without her husband or daughter's express blessing to do so and I see no reason to waste a perfectly good Companion of her renown."

"And you want me to take the throne?"

"Yes," came the reply, "It is better that you do it than someone who thinks they can run the world with hope and dreams Vaerlin."

The duke felt hurt by the comment, at least a bit. Had he no hope? No it was not that, it was simple, he, Duke Arash Vaerlin was a realist. He wanted to hope, but hope did not make deals, hope did not get things done. Hope was an idea, action was what Vaerlin had always relied upon, even if it was behind the scenes. He took a breath, feeling empowered by that realization.

"We decided," The man continued, "To ask you to accept the position now, rather than… foist it upon you later…"

Vaerlin nodded, "And what is one of the goals of my new Compact?"

"So receptive," The man smiled deeply, gratified as he nodded, "You just need to hold things together while the transition happens, make sure that you append a few to the Council Delegation, expand the noble base a bit, not too much, but a bit."

"I see, and when I am done holding things together?" Vaerlin jabbed. He knew better than to trust.

"Ah," The man snickered, leaning back and spreading his arm on the back of the cushion to his side, "At that point you live a long happy life as the Compact's ruler."

"That sounds like a wonderful plan, but how can I trust your end of things?" Vaerlin pressed.

"No reason to put you in and then get rid of you Duke," The man explained, "It would be simpler to put the right person in the first time and avoid a nasty repeat of upcoming tragedies."

"I get to decide what happens to the queen…" Vaerlin added. He was going to push for negotiation and make himself an obvious player in this game. He had to find ways to ensure he showed that he was not along for the ride. If he did not start strong he was doomed and even then there were no guarantees.

He had this group on his side for now and the less he asked about the details of how they worked, the more likely he was not to put his life in danger. Even so, as he eyed the contemplative Hil'Raigh before him, he knew he had his work cut out for him. He had to find out anything he could, discreetly and quietly. He would have his people find names, organizations, affiliates, anything, and store it away secretly in case he ever needed it.

"Deal," the man shrugged, "You can keep her if you want. I don't care too much."

There was a silence between the two now, and though Vaerlin was guarded still, he felt as though he had gained some standing.

A flying vehicle was not the most calming of places to negotiate, with the cityscape of Dau'Kore whipping past as the vehicle made the aimless rounds required to give the occupants time to speak. Vaerlin finally stole a glance out the window, noting that they had climbed quite a bit higher than the underbelly, where almost no flying vehicles were. They had entered some of the more active traffic corridors, lazily moving along in the slower section of traffic as the driver traced a random pattern of whim through the sky.

Vaerlin's contact brought him back from his musing with a continuation of the conversation, "You will be having Tamur's assistance in this, he's the go to. You will interface with him and that will reach the rest of us."

"You sure he is trustworthy?"

"He's proven," The man winked, "His people are capable and efficient."

"When?"

"The Princess' birthday party is coming up and it is probably the best time given how busy people will be. If you can ensure some of Tamur's people get into the pool of security staff for the event they will be able to take care of the details themselves," The man finished with a casual smile. He was rather nonchalant about the whole situation, something that made Vaerlin wonder just how much safety there really was in this deal.

"That wont be too hard," Vaerlin replied, "I will have a few assigned into my own security detail. Unfortunately, I may end up detained on the way to the party...."

"Tamur's people may hit some targets of opportunity among the existing nobility Vaerlin, I think you should know that since you have a few allies among them."

"Why?"

"A number of reasons, but good ones nonetheless. I must say I can't tell you any of the details."

"Of course not," Vaerlin sighed, the idea of all of this weighed on him now but it was too late to back out.

"A wider net is less easily traced Vaerlin, the trap has to be large to deflect scrutiny."

"How does one explain something like this?"

"The NovaCore of course. The war never ended and we are aware that they have been keeping security details on Ashor since their ambassador was allowed back. That information is set for public dissemination soon after the dust settles."

"Security details? The King suspected it but never confirmed...."

"We don't know where they are, just, that there is very likely something on world already. It's not hard to find Novians, especially because details like these are usually pairs."

"Spotting a pair of Novians together... seems like that kind of direction to the public will generate a lot of false reports..." Vaerlin trailed off and shook his head. The plan had obviously existed longer than he had been an active part of it.

"It will be next to impossible to determine anything concrete, but just in case, our people are going to be using some acquired NovaCore weapons for the job."

Vaerlin was silent now, impressed by what had already been laid out. There was little room for error in a plan such as this but then again, it was already taking many things into account, or at least it seemed to be. There might have been some hope for success after all.

"Alright, well I guess I will need some of the names for Tamur's people," Vaerlin said, his contemplation ending.

The man across the limo reached into a small bag on the seat next to himself and withdrew a large data slate, handing it to Vaerlin. The clear crystalline display blinked to life as Vaerlin touched the edges and in moments he was looking at a sort of comprehensive list, mostly about Tamur's people.

The details on the screen looked like they would be clear enough with some actual reading, but for now Vaerlin opted to skim over some of the wealth of information. In moments he had scanned over several profiles, mostly looking at the pictures to see who of the listed individuals was in Tamur's little group down in the underbelly. After finding several of their faces Vaerlin set the slate aside and eyed his contact for a moment.

"Those are the contractor identities, already clean and ready for jobs. It should help streamline things," The man smiled and turned to look over his shoulder at the driver. A tap on the driver's compartment of the vehicle was all that followed but the course of the drive changed quickly.

"I'll have our driver put you down at one of the monorail stations nearby, it's in An'Jea district so it should look as normal as one would expect of the Duke's visit to Dau'Kore city."

"Alright."

"I won't be contacting you directly for the next while, you'll be contacting through Tamur and any other assets we assign to the job."

Vaerlin nodded as the vehicle found its path. Out of the side windows Vaerlin noted one of the landing pads near a larger one of the central An'Jea monorail stations as the intended destination. The driver slowed and moved into an orderly queue with the other vehicles as they each took turns coming to the pad momentarily to offload passengers. There was a collection of taxi vehicles at the current head of the line but at the pace things were going Vaerlin guessed it would not be long. The city of Dau'Kore, its tall spiky skyline, millions of people and its many districts were completely oblivious to what was going to occur rather soon here at the City's heart. An'Jea, the richest of the districts would probably never be the same, given that the Kul'Raigh Guild Hall was at the center of the area.

Vaerlin sighed as his ride came to an end, the vehicle setting down. Slipping the given slate into his robe pocket he took another look at the broker of the deal that would forever change his life, the lives of the entire population of the Compact, even the Federation. For dealing in such business, Vaerlin was surprised at just how casually the man let Vaerlin key the door and slip out onto the platform. It was a confidence that made Vaerlin realize he had made the right decision. He already planned to make sure he got as much information on his allies as he could and the smug satisfaction his contact exuded right till the end solidified his resolve to protect himself. He would avoid the same fate King Ren'Tauru and his daughter were to receive.

5 - Princess Kirashira

So many names, so many different faces. Kirashira set down the slate she had been viewing and sighed loudly. A moment more and she had collapsed onto her back, spreading her arms and legs in a long stretch as she yawned up at the roof. The guest list, or at least potential guest list for her celebration was longer than she had ever imagined and full of names she didn't recognize.

It was ironic really that she was being asked to plan her birthday, or at least be involved in it when she had so little control of who actually was going to come to the party. So far the list was full of dignitaries, nobles, people who worked for her father, foreign governments, even diplomats. Of course that was standard fare for a royal birthday but it was always something she disliked about her life in the royal family.

At the very least, her mother had pulled some strings and had the Kul'Raigh Companion Guild Hall lined up as a venue, a place much more equipped for hosting the number of guests that would be traveling from far and wide just to see Kirashira celebrate her twentieth year of life. It was adulthood, officially, and it meant a bigger role in the kingdom's affairs as well. In a way, once the party had finished, it would be as if she had crossed a bridge she could never return to, a one way trip to responsibility.

Even so, the task of digging through names and faces just to pretend to send some kind of personalized invitation to them was as far from a desired responsibility as she could imagine. It was more fun to select the kinds of table coverings or the music. Even looking over the catering menus was more exciting than trying to sound genuine when dictating yet another half hearted letter of invitation.

"Shan'Li I really think you need to insist that this invitation business just be done in bulk, I can't even remember meeting most of these people," the Princess finally said aloud, calling to her bodyguard and friend.

The familiar pitch of the Kul'Raigh replied from across the room, near the book shelves. She had probably borrowed another of Kirashira's collection of print books again. Print books were antiques these days, especially the collection that the Princess owned, amassed over years as gifts. The entire collection habit had started with the young Monarch displaying an interest in a copy of her father's historical compendiums years before. Now it was a sort of well known fact among the people of the Starlight Compact that their Princess liked print books.

It was not that she read them all the time either. She liked filling her shelves with them, opening them and turning the pages. The different textures and the calm reflection and imagination that were unique to those volumes made them interesting enough to warrant her attention. Shan'Li of course, being a good bodyguard and maid, took an interest in them as well, now even more of an avid book reader than her mistress.

"Your mother already forbade me from bothering her about that on your behalf," said the bodyguard teasingly, "You knew that though."

Kirashira sighed. She had guessed, but knowing and guessing were different beasts. Who knew that Queen Ren'Tauru could be so cruel. That sentiment came out aloud, "I don't even know most of these people, they met me when I was three, or five, people who came by and said 'Hello Kirashira' once in my life..."

Shan'Li giggled heartily as she slipped one of the juicier encyclopedias from its place. She liked those ones in particular, reading them in order. It was odd of course since the topics were always arranged by alphabetical order and most of the time that meant things had almost nothing to do with previous entries. Even so however, Shan'Li seemed not to mind, always picking out those books in particular when she was able to relax in Kirashira's room.

Years ago, that would not have been as easy. Ever since the Princess had been old enough to be delegated those kinds of choices around the palace however, she had made sure that Shan'Li, one of her only true friends, had time to spend here.

"You may not know them but wouldn't it help your father to pretend?" Shan'Li replied, it was definitely a rehearsed line, or at least one given to her directly by the Queen.

"Did my mom make you say that?" Kirashira jabbed, sliding her feet over the edge of the bed as she slid toward it.

"Probably," Shan'Li laughed, "I can never remember when it seems like something she'd say herself."

"You sound like a little echo of the Queen sometimes Shan'Li," Kirashira retorted in jest.

"As her highness says," Shan'Li replied, making a valid escape from the topic. Shan'Li was nothing if not quick to wit in etiquette. That was partly why she had always been in the good graces of the royal family. She had, from a young age, been a servant here in the palace. Over time her tact and composure had given her the clout one would need to get personal duties from the royal family and now, she was practically a sister.

Socially, of course, she was never to be an equal, always a Kul'Raigh servant at most. A royal servant was still far more than most would ever be however, despite their parentage. At times Kirashira wondered what she would have felt being in Shan'Li's place, a plain Kul'Raigh without royal blood. She wondered if it would bother her to be in a place like the palace, but instead of being in charge, being beholden to the whims of the family living there.

The Princess had long ago concluded that she was glad not to be anyone other than the child of the King, granted a unique place and privilege, especially as far as Kul'Raigh went. It was not as if she shared any common parentage with Shan'Li though, with her servant being entirely of common birth. At very least, Kirashira's father was the current head of the Ren'Tauru Royal Line, one extending back thousands of years. He carried on the tradition of the oldest dynasty and was the only child of it. When he had opted to marry a Kul'Raigh instead of another noble then, it had created quite the stir, at least, that was the story.

That was over two decades ago now, but even today there was still political friction floating around over that singular choice. It was a choice that had given Kirashira life, her unique 'half' genetic set and features, a mix of some of the best traits of both, fine tuned with genetic honing and tweaks to ensure the absolute best offspring possible came to be.

Being a half Kul'Raigh monarch was something that at times had been puzzling but in recent years, Kirashira had decided to avoid the issue entirely, mostly by eschewing some of the cultural norms that followed Kul'Raigh her age. Instead she opted for the life of a royal Hil'Raigh, immersing in the more accepted culture.

Her mother had been more than supportive, despite the fact that at times, at least in Kirashira's estimation, it was not easy to teach her own child to live the culture of a different people than her own. Due to that instruction however, Kirashira, without any overt or dedicated effort toward the goal of being so, felt decidedly more Hil'Raigh than Kul'Raigh even though she was genetically more of the latter.

Even though she was technically a Hil'Raigh monarch, Kirashira still had a soft spot in her heart for Shan'Li's caring service. The Kul'Raigh had always been loyal and compassionate to her mistress, even when Kirashira had to admit that her own moods had left much to be desired. Maybe it was simply duty, maybe it was just a job. The Monarch wanted at very least, to believe that there was something more to it, a sort of mutual friendship and understanding that transcended the societal barrier that put the two on unequal social footing forevermore.

Kirashira finally slipped over the side of her bed and stood, stretching again as she straightened her hair a bit. Her servant sat quietly now, reading the encyclopedia.

"Are you up to Jras yet?" Kirashira called, looking over to the shelf a meter or so away.

Her maid shrugged, "No"

The room was well lit, overlooking the palace gardens outside. It was a place that Kirashira increasingly found herself as of late, especially with the birthday planning taking its stresses to the farthest reaches of her mind. Outside, the dusk of another ending day waned and the trees and ponds seemed to coax a bit of relaxation back into the room. That coupled with Shan'Li's calm demeanor made things decidedly relaxing, a bit lazy feeling even.

Kirashira examined her friend carefully, the light skinned Kul'Raigh's brown hair and long pointed ears being some of the few defining features visible from this angle, her face aimed into the book's pages. Both of the two shared about the same height, their bodies weighing almost the same amount as well. While Shan'Li was attractive however, her figure did pale a bit in comparison to Kirashira's own.

A combination of genetic tweaks and a rigorous selection process was the real champion of appearance and figure in the modern world but Shan'Li's natural beauty had always been something of an enjoyable addition to most situations. Even better still, the maid did very little to take away from her mistress' own efforts at being attractive.

That sort of effort was not uncommon among servants for royalty, but the fact that it did not seem to bother Shan'Li much at all made things far more comfortable. It was probably going to be a permanent part of the Ren'Tauru line moving forward really, the beauty that had been brought to the family by Kirashira's mother. Because of that, servants and supporters who could truly take pride in their supportive role would be all the more valuable.

"Have you picked out a dress yet Kirashira?" asked Shan'Li at last, flipping the page of her book. She asked the question without moving her eyes from the page, sitting on the reading couch lazily with the encyclopedia in her lap.

"I thought about it, the two we looked at before were nice," Kirashira replied, recalling both garments. One was more traditional, decorated and trimmed in a decidedly noble fashion. The other was a bit more adventurous, lending itself better to a well figured individual with a unique "Companion" flair in some of the styling. One of the two was something Kirashira would have expected at a dignitary function and the other was something she herself felt lent itself to a celebration.

"The second one is nice for a party, but I will probably get both tailored anyway just in case," Kirashira finally replied, still not completely sure which one she really wanted at all.

"I think you would look fine in either, but you'd steal more eyes in the second one. Maybe that would be good if its your own party." Shan'Li mused. She was right of course. As the Hil'Raigh aesthetic went, Kirashira was definitely on the better end of it, a pinnacle within that ranking structure really.

"I think you are right, I'll go with that," Kirashira said, "Don't forget mother wanted you and Fa'Sha to get measured for your outfits too. By tomorrow..."

"I took care of that thanks to your previous reminder Princess, but I appreciate your concern as always," Shan'Li smiled up from the book. She had a nice warm smile. It was friendly and as much as Kirashira felt confident in her own appearance, she had to admit that Shan'Li's winning smile was one of the most relaxing things about her.

"And Fa'Sha?"

Shan'Li paused her reading, looked thoughtful and nodded, "I'll make sure she does so as soon as possible, I don't think she finished that task yet."

"Good, thank you." The Princess felt satisfied. At very least Shan'Li was imperfect enough that taking the time to remind her of something had made a difference. Though Kirashira herself was not the most organized, she had been trying to be better about that sort of thing. Shan'Li was so good at remembering most of the time that the Princess had grown to rely too much on the servant and had made an effort lately to burden herself a bit more with keeping schedule.

She imagined that her father had gone through some similar phase as the prince before he took the throne but it was entirely speculation. As far as Kirashira knew, her father had always had the same mannerisms and capabilities, being a well formed monarch as long as she could remember.

The Queen, Kirashira's mother, always made the effort to keep any of her husband's past weaknesses and their discussion out of her daughter's mind and as a result it was hard for the young royal to recall any specific time when her father had not executed his duties with the candor of a king.

She sighed. Part of her wondered if she would measure up to that sort of responsibility, a sort of dread, despite the fact that her father was still relatively young and quite healthy. He had many years left, many years to train and teach his daughter on the various duties and responsibilities she would inevitably take on when becoming the queen someday. Such was her responsibility as the only child.

It was possible that at some point she could have been gifted a younger sibling but the oldest child, Kirashira, was always going to be the heir to the throne anyway. She could not escape her eventual duty.

Perhaps she mused, that was why the party planning had been so stressful. Everyone of course had some idea of what they thought should go into the guest list or the food, even the events. What no one had an idea on, or at least no one had offered to do in any meaningful way, was convince Kirashira that becoming an adult in her society was something she wanted to do.

Ahead lay challenges she had never faced, an unknown world that expanded far beyond the palace walls. Here inside, she was safe, she was free to do as she pleased. Out there, there were cameras, watching eyes, judges and juries, all waiting to cast their own assumptions into the forum. Could she measure up? Would they be so generous to her now as they had been up to this age in her life? What about being half Kul'Raigh?

The questions bumped around in her head aimlessly and she stood. She was lost in thought as she gazed out the window to the garden for a moment, "I need a walk Shan'Li"

With that the Princess reached to the handle of the sliding door pane that separated her room from the palace gardens and pulled it to the side. The door slid open quietly and as Kirashira glanced over her shoulder, she noted the obedience with which her servant had set down the book and come to her side.

It was a tradition for the children of royalty to be accompanied by their guards at nearly all times when outside the safety of palace walls but at very least, with Shan'Li it didn't feel forced most of the time. She was a good conversation partner and given the closeness the pair shared, it made the tradition easier for Kirashira to deal with.

The Princess' uncovered feet connected with the warm sun bathed tile on the patio outside her room and she wiggled her toes in delight as she felt the breeze on her skin. It was definitely a summer evening here on Ashor and the gardens were a wonderful place to spend a portion of it.

Like most regal estates, the Ren'Tauru Palace featured a large central garden around which much of the actual architecture was placed. Especially important however, was the fact that Kirashira had been given sole jurisdiction of an entire wing of the palace a couple years ago. It was essentially her own home within the palace, though she shared meal times and services with her parents in the rest.

Because of the large garden though, the fact that the palace wing was connected did nothing to dissuade in Kirashira's mind, the feeling that she really had her own independent space to occupy. She had a head of staff that managed most of the affairs for cleaning and other services of course, but there was still a sense of pride she got every time she looked across the courtyard rather than next door, to see if her parents were out and about.

Unsurprisingly, her father was not on the patio for the royal suite, nor was Kirashira's mother. Her father was most certainly still in council meetings, dealing with nobles who were up in arms over the reform regulation. She had no idea where her mother might have been though, save for doing some behind the scenes party planning.

Kirashira smirked, it was probably the case that her mother was doing something secret, a surprise for the upcoming celebration. Regardless, the Princess hoped it would be exciting while at the same time avoiding an embarrassing situation. It was her birthday party after all and even her mother would respect that, despite a penchant for silliness.

Kirashira disliked her mother's playful nature at times but it was something she found herself admiring. It made her so much more than a mom, but an entertainer, a friend. It was probably intentional, given her mother's experience in life, but even so Kirashira never felt that her mother forced that warmth with anyone, even the most humble of servants.

That was one area where the King and her mother differed almost certainly. While they both treated their servants with respect, Kirashira's mother took special care to uplift and encourage all of them, sometimes so much that it made Kirashira herself feel awkward by proxy. While it was nice, friendly and admirable in its own way, it certainly was an unusual trait for someone in her mother's position.

Some people disliked that, the Princess was sure. Some probably talked about it in hushed whispers or behind closed doors and while it was not something she liked admitting, the young royal had to agree, that she saw at least partly, why it happened.

A Queen with those kinds of eccentric traits was rare enough, but combined with being a Kul'Raigh and one of the most famous former companions ever to see the light of day, Kirashira's mother was hard pressed to win over her detractors, though if it bothered her she never showed it.

Because she herself was not of royal blood, Queen Shiyara was forbidden from directly ruling the kingdom at all, just as with any of the major Hil'Raigh states. The fact that her past had shaped her personality and skill set so heavily however, was something that had always been a talking point when people criticized the King.

His choice in brides, they would claim, was unsuitable for a king. Kirashira did not agree, her mother was her mother regardless, but at times, she wished that just for a bit, that Queen Shiyara would restrain herself and fit a royal mold more completely. Her daughter was managing just fine, why not the queen?

Kirashira moved ahead, taking in the trees and plants, the garden paths paved with smooth hewn stone. The warmth and texture of the path, as she stepped off of her patio, reminded her of how nice it was to remove her tall shoes and walk without them for a while.

Normally, due to her relatively short stature, the Princess opted for shoes that granted her a measure of extra height. They unfortunately had the side-effect of tiring her ankles a bit. Days like today, where she had no real need to leave her own wing of the palace, made living without them a sort of treat to fall back on. Because she lacked the height afforded her by her choice in footwear however, her servant was a bit taller than her now, despite their similar statures. Shan'Li was ever so slightly taller in any event and because she had actual shoes on her feet, she stood a good few centimeters taller as the pair walked on Kirashira's favorite route through the garden.

It was a path her father had taught her, one he walked himself, and so, when Kirashira had started taking a fancy to the gardens, she had decided to try the fabled route. It was a great way to relax, the variety of foliage and decoration taking a sponge to the stresses of life, soaking them away. There were Yalek trees and their long drooping fronds, a number of bushes no one remembered the name of, a pond, even some Klipa and their colorful shells that lived around it.

Kirashira led the walk in silence, reaching out to examine a leaf here or there, even stopping to kneel before some of her favorite smelling flowers for a scent. The time in the garden tonight felt especially meaningful already.

As she neared the pond, taking in the particularly colorful Klipa laying on the large rock next to it, she finally noticed that her father had come out to the garden from his room's patio.

He took the small set of stairs down to ground level quickly and moved in his careful deliberate way, toward Kirashira and her servant. His robe spoke enough about where he'd been, definitely in council, with the royal trim one would expect him to wear there.

"Hi dad," Kirashira chortled with a smile.

"Kirashira," he said with a nod. This was the point where, instead of talking to Kirashira directly, her mother would have greeted Shan'Li as well. It was out of the ordinary for a royal to do that, but the Princess never failed to notice when it did not happen these days.

"How was council?" Kirashira asked, glancing to one of the critters as it slid into the pond with a thunk.

"It was long, tiring," the King replied. He did look a bit tired and he was holding his hands inside his robe sleeves too, something he always did when he was conserving his energy. His narrow eyes betrayed the beginnings of exhaustion taking hold of the man. Unlike her own, or her mother's, the Kings face always had a shrewd look to it. It was one that made him into a negotiator automatically, at least in the eyes of those who met him.

His eye brows, like all of the upper class Hil'Raigh world, were thin, well kept and trim and his cheeks, while healthy, were not as round as his half Kul'Raigh daughter. That was one characteristic of the Princess' genes she had certainly been given from her mother alone. In truth, Kirashira looked far more like her mother than she did her father in most other ways too.

While his ears were angled back just a bit, Kirashira's own were wider, more pronounced and far more Kul'Raigh. His nose was relatively small and thin, more like Kirashira's own than his lips, which were thin and less pronounced. His jaw and facial structure showed one of noble lineage, a thinner, more angular face as compared to the rounder visage looking back up to him. He looked down and regarded his daughter calmly, his taller stature one of the last reminders Kirashira had of the stark differences in their genes. Genetic engineering had certainty made them look quite different.

Kirashira's eyes returned to his robe sleeves for a moment. The rim of his robe's sleeve cuffs met in the middle as they always did when he was tired. It completely masked his arms and because he wore a long robe, his limbs were all but invisible. At last, he spoke, "How is birthday planning?"

The Princess frowned and looked away, finding a particularly interesting plant to look at across the pond as she replied, "Long, tiring."

Her father made a noise, one of understanding, "I hear you have decided to skip the ceremony?"

Kirashira's stomach knotted, not this conversation again. It was awkward enough with her mother, but the Queen had understood it well enough. Why didn't she explain it to the King instead of making Kirashira do it herself? She was after all, far more convincing and articulate.

"I guess I felt like it was inappropriate," Kirashira shrugged and turned back to her father, who eyed her critically.

The way he looked, examined, made him seem like he was capable of looking through someone and this was no exception.

"Inappropriate?" He scoffed visibly, "How under the stars is it inappropriate?"

Kirashira rolled her eyes, it was the same conversation again. She did not want to have the coming of age ceremony, a Kul'Raigh traditional piece, play a role in her party. She had already explained it all.

"I told mom already, she said it was fine," Kirashira replied, appealing to the wisdom of her mother in agreeing already.

"Regardless of how….tolerant your mother was of your choice, I will not be," The King stated authoritatively, "You'll have the ceremony, for your mother's sake."

"I'm not a Kul'Raigh dad, I'm half and I am a Hil'Raigh royal." Kirashira retorted. She did not want the ceremony being the headline of her party; she knew exactly how it would play out. The tabloid pictures were already coming to mind.

If it were any other ritual, it would have been fine, but the coming of age ceremony was a Kul'Raigh antique of a tradition, not needed, not required, especially not for a Hil'Raigh royal.

"Maybe you forgot that most of the blood in your veins is your mothers and not mine," The King replied cuttingly, "Or have you so little respect for your mother?"

"It's not disrespect dad, I just don't want to pretend I'm something I never was."

"And here I thought you were my obedient daughter, I suppose I was wrong about that too." He stated. In terms of etiquette it was as devastating a blow to Kirashira's resistance as she could imagine. There was no proper way to retort, not to the king, not to her father, especially not when it was the same person. Even so, she pressed onward, part of her mind warning her off but failing to stop the words.

"I'm not a child anymore, that's what this whole stupid party is for, me being an adult. If you think I am so adult why don't you let me make my own choice?"

The King's ire was clear, but the fact that he was stunned was surprising. Kirashira had never actually pressed beyond that automatic barrier. She had never tried to defy, not like this. Her father's icy tone, his command and authority were always enough before.

"You must be right," he began, "Because my child would never turn her back on her father's guidance so flippantly, let alone disrespect her mother in such a blatant and disgusting way."

Kirashira wanted to reply, the fighting part of her egging her to find something but her common sense, or was it guilt, led her to stay silent. Her father had managed to pierce her armor, not with punishment but with his outright and undamped disappointment.

Now, the Princess, instead of a desire to avoid the conversation, felt sick. Was she really so selfish? Would she turn her back on an event that was certain to have been something her own mother had looked forward to for years?

The King stared at her without a word, his face stern. He was not going to move until Kirashira replied and she knew in her mind, that she was going nowhere until she mustered the strength to conquer her ego and open her mouth. Was it going to be justification again? A plea? No, it was shame.

"I'm sorry father," She mumbled softly, hanging her head. Yes, it was shame. This was the feeling Kirashira hated more than any in the world, her father's disappointment. It always cut so cleanly and effectively, but it was so very rare.

The rarity perhaps was what made it so potent, yet here it was and worse yet, Shan'Li had seen it all, Shan'Li the Kul'Raigh.

"You are free to organize your party as you see fit, Princess Kirashira. I see I have nothing more to say to you for now," her father finished, giving a small bow to Shan'Li.

This was the prison, at least for a few hours, that Kirashira would endure. She was not allowed to cross the barrier that her father had erected in the final moment. She was to wait, to stew and to feel bad, at least for a bit of time, before she was allowed to approach him about the issue. That was how her father dealt with flippant disobedience and she hated it. She wanted it resolved, she was even willing to have the stupid ceremony now. Instead, she would have no more pleasure in her garden walk, no more pleasure sitting in her room. A miserable night to cap off the day.

She furrowed her brow and huffed, glancing to her servant. Shan'Li's ever supportive face gave her a tiny smile, one that said enough. It meant the world and in that moment Kirashira felt a bit of her shame and guilt melt away. The smile said it all, things would be okay, at least eventually.

The Kul'Raigh nodded now, putting an arm around her Princess as the two headed back to the room from which they had come. She stayed silent, respecting the gravity of the King's words to his daughter by letting them hang in the air. They remained as a monument in Kirashira's mind, the last sound the Princess had heard aloud. It was a subtle reminder to the young monarch, that her servant knew full well the rules, the etiquette and the responsibilities they both had, despite how different they both were.

There was a long silence as the now anxious Princess meandered, trying to make the most of the time she had given to her walk. Despite that though, things did not feel the same, not at all. She had trouble finding any beauty despite being surrounded by it. Finally, after a fruitless minute or so of walking, Kirashira spoke once more, "I guess I never thought father would make such an issue out of that ceremony."

Shan'Li shrugged, "Respectfully, I would be honored to have Queen Shiyara give me my adulthood gift in the ceremony."

Kirashira nodded. Shan'Li had no family because she was a first generation member of the house staff. That meant she had been chosen at a young age from a pool of eligible, mostly parent-less children in the Compact. One of the ways that the loyalty of guards like Shan'Li had always been assured was to ensure that those who were allowed to have the closest of contact with the royal family were not influenced by outside relationships. It was essentially a blanket ban on what most people would have considered normal social experience. Instead, most of that was taken care of by interacting with other staff members and the royal family themselves. It was not forbidden for the staff to spend time together and become friends or develop relationships but it was generally frowned upon for someone in Shan'Li's position to pursue a relationship while she was still expected to devote energy to her duty.

"Maybe I can ask her to do that for you someday..." Kirashira said after a moment, feeling quite guilty at the words of her servant. Shan'Li would have happily accepted such a ceremony from Kirashira's mother because she had none to get a gift from. By contrast, Kirashira was so worried about culture clash that she was opting to avoid the ceremony entirely. It made her feel selfish.

"I think you should give your mother the chance..." Shan'Li finally suggested, it was a bold statement and Kirashira almost reprimanded her guard right then. Instead though, she contemplated the words, her mother, their relationship and the culture. Her mother was very much Kul'Raigh, despite how many concessions she made to be Hil'Raigh enough for the position she held. She had the mannerisms of a companion and a culture that clashed with the idea of being the queen, at least in the eyes of many. Though it had been a while since Kirashira had reflected on the duality of it all, the dichotomy was still quite fresh to her mind. Over and over she had to ask herself just what was her mother saving face and what was genuine. Was she as hurt by the request as the King had made it sound?

Possibly, if she were she wouldn't have told him though. If anything it was his assumption because Kirashira's mother rarely, if ever, voiced such a concern to her husband. She kept quiet about the cultural things, mostly for his benefit. Instead, such challenges scraped away at her grace and candor for a while until whatever problem she was experiencing was resolved. Her father must have picked up on that instead.

That had to be it. The Princess had seen it before. When her father observed that his wife was offended or sad, he chased down the problem like a hunting animal. It was something that Kirashira had to admire, even if it turned out frustrating at times. At very least, she always knew where her father stood when it came to cooperating with mother. His strictness toward honoring and respecting the queen was partly motivated, Kirashira guessed, by the lack of respect many in the Hil'Raigh nobility gave to her, at least in private. Publicly, no one dared say much, but privately in gossip, people said what they wanted. It was inevitable that some of it reached the King's ears and it always annoyed him more than anything else did.

"I guess I forgot how protective he is of mother," Kirashira admitted.

"He always has been," Shan'Li replied, "But we take for granted what we see everyday, perhaps that is why you forgot."

The Princess smirked and shook her head, "You excuse me too much Shan'Li, I don't think you would have forgotten such a simple thing."

"I forget many things," She replied, ever modest, "I just don't publicly mention that I did because it makes me sound much more authoritative than I would otherwise be. Sometimes only the fool opens their mouth."

Kirashira sighed, the old saying was as true now as it had ever been, "I suppose that describes me tonight...."

There was a long pause, the pair stopping near the drooping fronds of one of Kirashira's favorite trees. It was flowering, as it always did around her birthday. She sighed as she examined the myriad blossoms. It was a tree her mother had planted years ago and had always been a place of refuge, either from the sun, the rain, even tutors.

"Or maybe it describes the whole idea of asking mother not to do the ceremony at all...." said the Royal as she reached out and cupped a few of the blossoms in her hand. They were small red blossoms with creamy white centers, Kirashira's favorite colors.

"I understand why you were afraid to look too Kul'Raigh Kirashira, your mother does as well." Shan'Li added in consolation, "Don't let guilt change your mind on this. If you want to do the ceremony, your mother would want you to do it for the right reasons, not because you felt bad."

Kirashira shuddered, exhaling. The words chilled her, not because they were scary, but because they rang so truly in her ears. Shan'Li was right, about both points. Not only did her mother understand, but she would never have forced Kirashira to do anything. In fact, she was probably chastising the King right now in private, for having jumped into the middle of the situation. If anyone in the entire Compact understood just how difficult being a royal and a Kul'Raigh was, it was Queen Shiyara.

The guilt and shame, the feeling of wrong doing eased in that moment, as Kirashira remembered her mother's warm expression, her calm, her love. It made her pause in earnest. Her mind was made up in the instant. She was not going to avoid the ceremony, she was not going to do it because she was guilty. She wanted it now, to show solidarity with the person who had given her so much. That was what it was supposed to be, what it was always for. What better reason could she have than that?

"I found the right reason Shan'Li," she said with a broad smile, her eyes wet, "Thank you."

6 - Birthday Celebration

That was a running theme tonight. Kirashira felt invigorated at seeing some of her peers in the Federation but a bit nervous despite. Impressions were key with royalty and the noble houses. Even people under her father's rule were going to be scrutinizing her heavily. Rather, they were probably the most intently scrutinous of their potential monarch.

Kirashira couldn't blame them. She was now an adult officially under the law, meaning she was allowed, even encouraged, to take on running parts of the Kingdom under the guidance of the current head of state. Her father would undoubtedly have a new selection of staff assigned, and in a few months, Kirashira would be officiating some of the internal affairs of the Starlight Compact.

Her age alone meant that she was entitled to some of the voting power of her father in the Federation Councils, becoming the most powerful Non-monarch voice in the Compact's delegation overnight. It was because of the changes, the new power and the responsibility she was heading to that she felt increased apprehension about making a bad impression. She needed the nobility and power brokers to be her political allies now, so when she finally did take the throne in several decades, she would have an established base of support in the nobility.

Hostile nobles could cause trouble, something her father had been lamenting now for weeks in his own dealings. She wanted to avoid the same troubles he was now going through and it meant making herself look effective and capable. It was for that reason, instead of choosing a date or a friend to cling to tonight, she found herself having small conversations with various nobles or delegates. She wanted her parents to know that she was ready, her father in particular.

Kirashira had changed her mind on the Kul'Raigh coming of age ceremony, which she now intended to have her mother perform. Despite that however, she was still worried that letting her father down before meant he would not be at ease even if the ceremony went through. He claimed that it was just the realities of ruling that made him so tired today but she couldn't be sure.

To make it up to him, she now found herself conversing with new faces and their wives or husbands, all of them Hil'Raigh. The nobility was actually quite a bit more varied than she had anticipated. Where Kirashira herself had assumed so much about the lifestyles and interests of each of them before today, she was taken aback by just how interesting some of them really were. Despite the reputation of the nobility as would be royals, it seemed to the young Princess that there were some at least, worthy of the trust they had been given.

It varied of course, based on who one was speaking about, but in general it made sense that some held title. Others were a bit confusing, some seeming out of touch or simply unqualified. While her father was not one to outright strip titles from his subordinates he had certainly shifted the Federation Delegation membership recently.

There was an awkwardness in conversing with the few who were slated to lose their Federation Council seat in the coming months but none of them were allowed to say much negatively about it. It was after all, etiquette. One would not insult a member of the royal family even if they were in disagreement over the politics of the time.

Even so, Kirashira found Duke Vaerlin to be quite aloof and cold this evening. No matter really, his holdings were fairly stagnant at this point due to his failures to manage. He had not made sure to improve what he had and he'd instead spent too much time forging bonds with foreign nobility.

The Duke did not seem to recognize that even now, and Kirashira understood why the man was losing his seat at this point. Another was losing her seat because of mismanaging resources granted by the King himself and some of the others had lost challenges to their seats since they were only minor nobility and thus open for the challenges each season. Of those leaving the delegation, only one was doing so happily, to retire and spend time with his family.

Overall, Kirashira felt confident that she had done as well as she could. Whether that was good enough for the myriad judges in attendance tonight however, was not something she could guess at. She knew that some of them would never be satisfied and some others would be full of praise no matter how poorly she conducted herself. She had long ago learned that with the nobility, the most middle of the road reaction was the most realistic representation of her overall level of acceptance.

From the middle of the room Kirashira had a good view of the surroundings. The function hall was well decorated, well lit, and clad in the finest. It was hard to believe when standing in such a massive room, with such high ceilings, that the party was taking place in the city's largest building. The Kul'Raigh Companion Guild Hall was not only the largest, but one of the oldest fixtures of Dau'Kore, making its unique place in the skyline an iconic part of tourism and memorabilia. It was a place that was always bustling and busy. As a result it fit the party well if a bit more than was needed.

The Guild Hall towered above its neighbors as a proud spire. It was impressive on the outside of course, a structure that contained everything from housing to commercial markets and business halls. It was in one of the upper floors, near one of the private external landing pads, that Kirashira's party was taking place tonight. The Princess found herself wishing that perhaps she could have left a bit less to her mother's imagination and more perhaps, to her own planning instead.

Her mother, a former companion and still the Guild's un-equaled darling, was definitely used to such events and it showed. The setup was enough to make even Kirashira blush. No party she had yet attended had been given such attention to detail as this and tonight there was no expense spared. The upholstery on the chairs and couches near the edges of the room matched perfectly with the perfect table coverings. The dinner utensils were of the finest silvers, materials fit for true royalty. The floor was polished and the marbled finish of the tile made it shine with the perfect attention to detail that even the most stringent of architects would have approved of. Every detail, down to the coordinated, matching sets of jewelry given by the Companion Guild to the lucky companions who were in attendance tonight, showed the opulence that had gone into the planning. Kirashira had not dared say anything since arriving, mostly overwhelmed by it all. At very least she knew that no one could question her mother's ability to operate among the nobles and their varied tastes, not after a party like this. Especially not after the expensive food trays and the exotic offerings atop them.

This was most assuredly the best the Companion Guild had to offer, and knowing her mother's relationship with them, Kirashira was certain that the price of such a gathering had been considerably discounted for the Queen they loved. Indeed, the services on offer, not just the venue but all of them, showed an obvious intention on the part of the Companion Guild. Was it trying to curry favor with the now adult Princess and her father? Was it trying to prove a point to the Hil'Raigh nobility? Kirashira was not sure what the motive was, but she did appreciate it even if it was a bit too flattering at times.

The venue consisted of not only a large ballroom style hall and its dance floor, but included a selection of private suites for guests in the floor above as well. Tonight, those rooms had been promised to guests from afar, nobles whose holdings were near the borders or had significant stake in the current political climate. Most of the people in attendance were guests of her father's political influence and not Kirashira's choosing, but such was life in the King's family. The momentary offering of such an expensive accommodation was a not so subtle way for the King to send messages of trust and support to a number of the nobility he was relying on.

The only access to the private suites was a rather artistic looking set of stairs across the room, in the corner of the ballroom. The room was connected to a single corridor, one that allowed access from the foyer that served as a sort of gate for the entire venue. From that corridor, another, lesser decorated space, served as an area for even more guests to congregate. Like all venues rented privately in the Guild Hall, access was easy to control since it relied on the common foyer area.

The smaller secondary hall served to funnel the less connected, less important guests away from the most upper of echelons in attendance. The space of the suites, the ballroom and the secondary hall together, were something of a marvel in a building so tall. Both halls were two stories high inside, both with large flat windows extending to the outside world and here in the main hall, Kirashira had a good view of the city below if she got close to those nearly invisible barriers.

Situated in the corner of the building, this largest space made for a unique and breathtaking view of a city so often monolithic and boring from within. From here, the glittering lights, the thousands of whisking dots out to the horizon seemed to serve only as reminders of the power Kirashira was now approaching. It was a realization that had humbled her tonight, one that made her nervous. She had been past trays of the most expensive of appetizers and dutiful Kul'Raigh attendants, serving both refreshment and the pleasure of wonderful company. She had been showered with praise for almost nothing but reaching the age of adulthood, something anyone so well protected would be able to do. There were people she would never see again, all clamoring for her attention, to meet her and her father. She was truly a member of royalty and yet, she almost felt as if she would trade it.

She had caught herself wondering what it was like to be someone else. She tried to put herself into the glamorous and expensive heeled shoes of some of the Companion's she had seen here tonight, wondering if that was what her mother looked like in a fancy gown back then. Was it easier?

Nervousness was the biggest feeling, perhaps apprehension. Regardless, Kirashira knew that she had to maintain her composure as best she could. She had been greeting, smiling, hugging and dealing with all manner of stranger and acquaintance alike. The party had started with such a procession of guests she thought it would be over before she ever got to do anything on her own.

Like most royal birthday parties Kirashira's own began with greeting guests. She and her parents would stand at a predefined place for the first hour of the party and the guests were each expected to come introduce themselves and receive thanks for coming. Mercifully, Kirashira's mother had some of the staff deal with handing out the small thank you bracelets that were being passed to them. It had been painless, if a bit tiring.

The train of guests however had finally trailed off some minutes ago and Kirashira had been able to say hello and walk about on her own. The process was less exciting than she had hoped, her nervousness impeding her ability to carry on much meaningful conversation. In something of a mixed blessing, the party plan now came to her rescue instead, whisking her away from the last of dry conversation she hoped she would have to have tonight.

Now, it was finally time to have her mother give her the first birthday present she would receive as a real Kul'Raigh adult. There was still the nervousness of course, but seeing all the work that her mother's influence had brought to pass tonight made her respect the Queen in a way she never realized she could.

It was not just her relation to the Guild but her ability to discern that had made things so special. The Queen knew Kirashira so well, all of the things her daughter had wanted tonight were accounted for: the food, the dance, the music, even the order of events was as close to Kirashira's personal taste as it could be while still falling in line with the norm. That was why Kirashira was glad to finally hear her father's voice pipe up over the loudspeaker.

He cleared his throat as his daughter approached, the crowd quieting quickly as he spoke, "I am glad you all came and, as you know we are proud to have you here with us to celebrate our wonderful daughter's adulthood."

Kirashira blushed hotly as she was showered with congratulatory applause and as the approval subsided, her father continued, "It's Hil'Raigh tradition on the twentieth birthday for a father to share one of the things he loves most about his child with those who come to celebrate, and I suppose that means the privilege falls on me tonight."

The King paused, glancing to Kirashira with a warmth that she had learned to love. His gaze was one of adoration and care and as he smiled, the nervousness she had felt earlier in the evening melted away in an instant. There was joy in his eyes and his voice as he continued, looking over the crowd and giving his wife a tight squeeze at his side.

"I love how contemplative and careful my wonderful Kirashira is. Even if she is impetuous or frustrated, she always thinks about her actions and tries to improve. She inspires me to be a better king and father with the joy she shares with those around her." The King proclaimed boldly, finishing with a genuine smile to Shan'Li who nodded in agreement. She stood at the edge of the cleared area where the royal family stood with some of the happiest looking house staff Kirashira had ever seen.

Inside, the Princess felt a flood of emotion as she took in the faces, her eyes watering profusely, coming to full tears as she looked over her closest friend. None of the staff had to smile, they didn't have to care, it was a job. But here they were, happy, sharing a joy with her family.

In that moment, the young monarch felt closer, more equal to the people around her than ever. Her father's words were not entirely praise, but guidance.

Mercifully, he began his conclusion as Kirashira wiped her eyes, "Thank you all for sharing a joy that only grows with each year. The life of the only child I could ever ask for."

With that the king finished and turned, embracing Kirashira so tightly she almost gasped. There was a need in the embrace, a closeness that let her melt. She was safe, happy, and most importantly, she knew she was loved.

Kirashira returned the embrace enthusiastically, amid some clapping at the conclusion of the traditional display. Finally though, the King released his daughter, giving her another large smile. She nodded to him and readied herself, prepared to speak from where she stood. She cleared her throat and lifted the wristband she wore, the piece of technology that rarely left her body.

"Thank you for coming to share this day with our family. I hope that I can live up to all of the good things my dad claims I do." She began, adjusting the position of her improvised microphone even as her voice was rebroadcast over the speakers in the room. There was some laughter and she breathed a sigh of relief, encouraged to push forward.

"I wanted to share with you all tonight, something that is a special part of my family culture, something brought to us by my mother. In Kul'Raigh tradition a mother gives their child a gift on their adult birthday, the first present they receive as an adult," Kirashira began, recounting information that most probably knew, but feeling a duty to explain it once more, "It's a gift that reminds a child of the gift of life, and it's a chance for a parent to re-affirm their commitment to be a gift in their child's life. I can think of no greater gift than having my mother guide me through everything and because of that, I'd like our family to be able to share this with you all."

The room was fully silent now. Kirashira glanced around and noted that the guests were still looking quite respectful, more than she had anticipated. Her mother stepped to the edge of the clearing in the center of the group and retrieved a large cloth-wrapped gift, a flat object almost a meter in both directions. She carefully carried her soon to be gift and then set it gently at her own feet, resting it against her robe as she smiled, waiting. Unlike her father, and unlike her, Kirashira's mother seemed to see no need to broadcast her voice. She simply spoke aloud, and to her credit, her words carried well despite having little help.

"Kirashira, you are the greatest gift I've ever been given, so I'd like to give you one of the things that is important to me," The Queen stated carefully. Her gray eyes were full of care and warmth, she looked perfect in her robes, custom tailored white with red trim, the royal colors. No one looked any more like royalty than Kirashira's mother did in that moment. It was not just appearance but candor, demeanor. She was truly remarkable and Kirashira glowed inside, knowing she had decided to go through with the ceremony after all.

After a moment of silence, the Queen lifted the cloth from the object she had acquired, revealing an intricate metal disk. The circular object was only a centimeter or so thick but inlaid with glistening red gem stones. The silvery metal revealed its flawless construction and craftsmanship. There was no question of what it was in Kirashira's mind.

It was one of the crowns her mother had acquired over the years. They were expensive accessories that few could afford, and a crown so large was out of the reach of almost any buyer. Queen Shiyara had been given one of the most unique and valuable crowns years ago when working at the Guild and now it sat at her feet, ready to be passed on. Such an accessory was one worn by the affluent or, at very least, the attention seeking. Paired with a proper control device, the disk would form a sort of halo behind the wearer's head, framing them with its impressive presentation.

This particular crown was a symbol of one of the most elegant, beautiful people to live in the Federation now, well known and iconic. Now the reason that the Queen had worn one of her lesser accessories to the party was clear. Kirashira had wondered where the vaunted piece of jewelry had gone to and her mother had been coy about the whole affair. She had not worn it because she wanted to give it to Kirashira, as if she were giving a part of her beauty away.

"We'll get you a hairpiece made soon," Kirashira's mother whispered playfully, giving a smile as her daughter reached out and took the priceless gift in her fingers. It was a magnificent object, one that would definitely remind the Princess of her mother for the remainder of her days. Kirashira caressed the smooth metal gently, seeing her own distorted reflection in its surface, knowing that this was a gift that meant more than any other object her mother could really offer. This object was a representation, not only of love, but of willingness, of sacrifice. Her mother had given away a life of luxury and fame, one where she was free and under far less scrutiny. She had chosen to burden herself with the challenge of taking a child of her own into the world, and now, she was saying with more than words, but silent devotion, that she would do it again, that she always would. Kirashira's eyes moistened as she recalled the tales she'd heard about her mother, about the things she had overcome to be her mom. She felt pride inside for the one who was her eternal ally. There was nothing in that moment she could have wanted more. The ceremony was the right choice, and now, she understood why, with pure, untainted love flooding her heart. A glance back to her father showed that he too was brought to a rare display of emotion. Pride, liquid pride, was pooling in his eyes.

"Thank you mother," Kirashira replied happily, reaching out to embrace her mother. There was some clapping and a few cheers, no pain at all. Kirashira was glad, she had made the right choice and it was never more clear to her than when she felt the loving squeeze of her mothers arms.

Like her father's earlier embrace, there was a pride conveyed in that hug, a sense from parent to child that their bond had only just begun. Kirashira felt wonderful, happy and cared for all at the same time. She felt important, but humbled. Needed but supportive. A feeling like this would be hard to forget, no matter what.

As her embrace ended, she turned to look at her father once more, a broad smile on his face. He stood out against the backdrop behind him, the chorus of city lights and a cacophony of reflection from inside the Guild Hall itself against the outside windows. Though, something was wrong with the way the light was showing, as if it was moving?

Confusion crossed the Princess' face as it seemed the world slowed. The light, the time, something was going...

There was a crash, a loud, ear shattering thunder filled the air. It was powerful and dire, a feeling that sent Kirashira from her feet, tumbling backward amid a blast of warmth. The heat was as if the maw of hell itself had yawned open outside the Guild Hall window, outside the party and spit forth its brimstone against the glass. It was reinforced, protected window glass, resistant and strong, something Kirashira remembered from the tour she had taken hours before. Now however, it splintered and broke away in the face of the malevolent onslaught against it.

Shards of jagged glass nipped her robe, her skin. There was an instant chaos and screams of terror from a chorus of voices sounded around her. The world was swimming in her vision, a blurred mess of reality from which she tried to escape by rubbing her eyes. There was so little coherence to what she saw until finally enough of the focus returned.

The restoration of some vision was enough to extend the torment of a damned soul to the Princess' heart. A desperate feeling of denial filled her mind as she finally laid eyes on what had formerly been her smiling father. There was fire, a lot of it, spewing forth from metallic hunks. There were bits of what had to be a vehicle of some kind. It had come unceremoniously through the windows on the outside but whatever it had been carrying, perhaps an explosive, had devastated much of the room. A good two meters from where he had been standing, lay Kirashira's father, the Starlight Compact's Monarch, face down and unmoving.

Amid the desperation of helpless guests, amid the cries of anguish from the injured, the Princess felt nothing at all, a sort of numbness that only the most pained of souls could comprehend. She scrambled, beside herself, toward her fallen father. Her feet slipped, her shoes coming out from under her and bringing her down hard as she attempted to gain her footing.

Shots of pain arced into her knees as she hit the thick floor. She was undeterred, a morbid curiosity mixing with the darkest of fears. They beset her confused heart as she crawled across the floor.

Her dress was ripped, she realized, torn in several places. Contrary to how she felt, the fact that there were cuts on her arms seemed to juxtapose oddly with the lack of feeling her extremities otherwise provided. She could feel the ground, the coolness of it, compared to the heat of the fire in the air and yet, the gash she had suffered seemed all but inconsequential.

To her right there were knocked down, hurt or injured people. Some being nursed by others, some struggling to regain a sense of direction but the cries of the hurt or the devastated played out like a choir of tormented victims around her.

Her father lay limp. The powerful, strong protector that had given her life now inert ahead. The Princess, shaking now, reached his side. She nudged him with timid helplessness. She could barely understand the words coming from her own mouth. The voice speaking them, her own voice, sounded so completely foreign. There were words certainly, but the feeling within that voice was not hers. She felt like a passenger in her own body, even as she spoke. It was the feeling of one so utterly lost that she scarcely associated the movement of her own mouth with the uttering of a single transcendent word: father.

She repeated it with the reverence and need of the most helpless child as she tried, tried to roll him over. Even as she did, she was struck with a sickening fear. What would she see if she succeeded in rolling him over? Would she be able to endure his face? She had to know, she had to see. Her curiosity won out and despite the failing control of her limbs, shuddering in a helpless panic, the Princess managed to roll him over at last.

Now it was her turn to add to the cries of the mournful around her. Her heart ached, burned, melted and died all in a moment. Every feeling she had ever felt paled so utterly to this. Every moment she had lived now seemed a dream and every hope that had lingered in her heart bowed to the pain she felt. There was nothing in all of her life that would have prepared her to look upon her father's bloodied face in that moment. His eyes, his gentle loving eyes, unmoving and lifeless. They were staring into the void which had taken him, almost as if they had watched him go.

Even as part of her told her it was too late, that she had no power over the forces who had robbed her, she clutched his face in her hands and begged. She begged desperately, for her sake, for her mother's sake. It did not matter why or how, it only mattered that he not leave.

She wanted him to stay.

She wanted her father to protect her like he always had.

She wanted what she knew she could not have and yet the smallest shred of her refused to believe that this was how her father would leave her. Not here, not like this.

Her eyes flooded with liquid despair, clouding her vision as her cries became increasingly frantic. Her helpless, shaken voice, giving way to the bitter depths of hell she felt welling inside. She pushed, she shook, she begged, she whispered and clutched her fingers into his. His hands were still warm. His face was the same gentle face that had hugged her so many times today, the one that had smiled and shown her love for so long and yet, there was no breath. There was no life here. It had been driven from its shell. It had been forced to flee, forced to leave her behind, alone.

The separation, the void already forming between her and the man she so loved loomed in ominous majesty over her heart. How could a world like this be just? How could a world which took away someone so important ever be right? Her ancestors, the stars above, they had all promised her more than this. Why had they betrayed her?

She was not ready, she had so much to say to him, so much to share with him. She had so many things she wanted to learn from him but most of all, she just wanted to keep loving him. How was that too much to ask? She just wanted to give back the love he shared, bring happiness to him like he had to her and now, he was gone, stolen.

The Princess leaned close, taking in his face. Timid and broken, she whispered her love with the devotion only a child could muster for a parent and yet, it felt so unfair to know that he could not hear her. His heart could never know just how much he meant, not now. The only time she had ever managed to say it so plainly, so openly and with such purity was the one time his ears were closed forever. The words came until at last the inescapable truth was laid bare. He was gone, and not even her pure love, her desperate need for his guidance and love, could call him back from where he had gone.

Kirashira yielded to her pain once more, the pain of one who had been robbed of everything and yet, even that was not enough. Nothing was enough. No word, no sound, no desperation could express her anguish and so she simply reached across the once powerful chest of her father, holding him desperately as she wept the most bitter of tears.

Her father was gone, he was gone and she wept. Her tears fell freely. All the careful preparation for her appearance tonight melting into the anguish that poured against her father's robe. They were soft, they were comfortable, just like she remembered.

Her mind raced, part of it trying to decide what had happened and yet, somehow the logical, analytical part had put something together. Something had crashed into the building, violently; a vehicle. Even as she analyzed, though, her mind was ripped from the solitude it had created.

There was a crack, loud as lightning from another part of the room. Was it starting again? Another crash? The Princess was struck with a sinking feeling, one of dread as she laid her pain bare. Another crack, this time with an anguished cry.

Even amid her sobbing, she felt a new kind of despair, the hair on her neck standing on end. The curiosity, the helpless need to explore, to see, to understand, overtook her so powerfully that she managed to look past her knot of hair and forward to the other half of the great hall.

There was so much smoke in the room now it was hard to see very far, at least if one was standing, but from where she rested it was clear. There were so few people standing on their own that the few who were, their legs at least, were immediately obvious. Glinting metal, dark and sinister, met gloved hands and suited bodies. The kind of body armor Shan'Li trained with when she was re-certifying, the kind of armor a soldier would wear.

Their demeanor, the casualness with which they were exploring the devastation nearby, it was enough to make clear their intent. A lightning crack from one of the invaders, one pointing the long metallic weapon he appeared to be carrying, ended the anguish of some un-named noble in his way, one who had been groaning.

Kirashira recoiled, sinking against her father with an overpowering nausea filling her stomach. She was so shocked she couldn't even manage the scream she had tried to vocalize, her body refusing to even make the noise.

Her father's body was lifeless at her side, her mother was nowhere to be found, nothing she knew or understood applied now, save one overriding need, to survive. The sickness, the pain and fear, it all fell away into the tingling desperation that crept over every millimeter of her skin, overpowered every loving care and urge she was capable of. Her hands released their clutch on the bunched up robes of her father, her white knuckles uncurling as the primal instinct sent her scrabbling, as quietly and carefully as she could, toward one of the few exits she could see in the room; the now damaged staircase.

She glanced over to the trio of invaders as she scurried along, they were checking the Hil'Raigh women and the Kul'Raigh specifically, as they approached. She turned her back as another blood curdling shot rang out from behind. Passing a chunk of mangled vehicle debris, one that still burned with fuel, the Princess skirted the damaged doorway and managed to carefully move herself into position on the precarious staircase. The metal creaked beneath her feet, a long groaning sound accompanying her movement until she reached an un-damaged section above. She heard the footsteps of the strangers below, in the other room, someone yelling about the King, someone who was uninjured, healthy and strong, yelling to his friends.

As soon as she was able, she curled into the darkness of the hallway she had entered. The thin, almost light-less hallway offering no cover from prying eyes save that of darkness alone. The corridor was lined with doors, portals to various suites, ones that would have housed the guests for the night, but now, now Kirashira was not sure what they were to house. Perhaps they would keep vigil for the dead? Perhaps one of them would become her final resting place.

She crawled and stumbled down the dark corridor, the lack of lighting as suspicious as anything else that had happened. Even now, her tears still wetting her cheeks, her hands slick with the salty reminder of her loss, she moved down the hall until finally she realized, she was at the corridor's end. There were noises behind, enough to renew her fear and she ducked helplessly into one of the doorways lining the hallway. She rested against the door frame, curling her knees to her chest, holding tightly, quivering and shaking.

There were footsteps now, a set of heavy boots coming up the very stairs she had come up to escape. The ascent was apparently remaining cooperative enough for the stranger to gain purchase, at least temporarily.

A loud crash sounded, the sound of metal, damaged architecture. Even so however, a curse from whomever had made the ascent sounded at the top, rather than the bottom of the staircase. Kirashira quivered and curled tightly, willing herself to vanish into nothingness as she heard an exchange, one she couldn't fully hear both sides of. The stairs had collapsed, but it was too late.

Her heart raced, her body shuddering, her legs readying to run. Where? She didn't know, but her mind screamed now to run and hide. Fear won, she stayed, curled, hidden, trying to be a shadow in the dark. The nameless pursuer who had made the climb now meandered for a moment, finally deciding to go down the hall the same way Kirashira had run.

As the heavy, booted footfalls neared the edge of the doorway she had chosen for her departure from mortality, Kirashira whimpered aloud and there was a pause, a long pause before a set of sounds she couldn't identify. First a rustle of clothing, then, then a disgusting, grotesque gurgling. A thud followed as something, some form, fell lifeless only arms length away in the hall.

There was a long silence, then finally, a voice unfamiliar, sounded in the darkness. It was a whisper, one with an accent not common to nobility, nor servant. It was not a Hil'Raigh, and definitely not a Federation dignitary.

"Princess," The voice sounded pained, labored. In the darkness, Kirashira chanced a nervous glance toward its source. In the minimal light, the near blackness of the corridor, she made out a face.

"Please..." She began to whimper.

"I'm not going to hurt you."

The speaker had a rough, deep voice. Whoever it was must have been a foreigner and in moments, he had grabbed a small light from the fallen invader's body. It was enough to reveal him. It was a diplomat, a NovaCore man. Kirashira recognized the face as the ambassador who had introduced himself earlier. He was a man with short cut black hair, probably in his forties and with a build mostly hidden inside of a decidedly NovaCore uniform. His hands were bloodied, as was his face. The abdomen of his tunic was damp, probably with the same liquid, and he seemed to labor for even a bit of breath. His face was a mask of controlled agony already. Nevertheless, he spoke, "Let's get to a window"

Kirashira's mind and heart told her he, like the others, was a danger, not to be trusted. She had no idea who the invaders were, only that they were out for blood, her blood. Even so, the injuries the man had suffered made her question just how dangerous he could be. She scooted, wordlessly, against the door of the room she was resting against, her back to it flatly, as she examined the man and his weakened frame.

The invader, one of the three who she had seen earlier, was an obvious dead man, a grotesque cut across his throat, pooling his crimson life on the once pristine carpet. The Princess heaved helplessly at the sight, thankfully avoiding a second taste of her dessert.

"Oh Stars....." she gulped, "What's going on?"

"No idea Princess. Help me to a window and we can get you out of here safely," The man scooted himself, it was finally apparent that one of his legs was not only hurt, but unusable. How he had managed to cut the stranger's throat was a mystery, a disgusting one which Kirashira's mind refused to consider further.

"A window?" Kirashira asked, confused. She had no idea what to make of the man or the situation.

"A window, for my beacon." The man replied laboriously. He held up a cylinder in one of his hands.

Kirashira shuddered, replying quietly, "A window, I think I can help..."

The man nodded and for the first time Kirashira took a good look in his eyes, the eyes of a dead man who had not yet died. His expression said it all, the blood on his face, his clothing. He had probably been hit by something, perhaps the explosion, the glass. There were scars from days past, contorted with the concerned folds that had manifest in his pained visage. His eyes were distant even despite his apparent clarity. Rather than being ripped away in an instant, this man would make his way slowly to the afterlife. Kirashira gulped and tried to force herself to look away from him, force herself to hide the mutual understanding they both most have had.

"Just help me move, that's all you need to do," He directed, reaching out with his arm, the arm on the side of his body that seemed most injured, the side with the leg that it appeared he couldn't move much.

His hands were sticky but it didn't matter. Kirashira was to help him find a window, that was all he wanted. She gently took his hand in hers, and he huffed at the gentleness with which she directed his hand in her own, a whimper of self pity from someone who was obviously trying his best to be strong and in control of himself. At this level, in this place, he was laid bare however, his vulnerability shown to the timid, the Princess of the Compact.

"Thank you," He said quietly. He was heavy enough that he had to help Kirashira get him off the ground but once he was up he stood taller than she would have. There was possibly a window down the hall and around the corner, opposite the dead end the pair now occupied. She had no idea what to say, no words of comfort, no questions, nothing she could ask that would ease his obvious suffering. She simply moved when she had to, supporting him forward as the two moved away from the dead attacker's body.

The two labored back down the hall, moving in unspoken understanding of their need to minimize the noise made, especially as they passed the former stairwell. The hallway showed promise however, light cascading in from around the bend ahead. Reaching it at last, the demure Princess helped her rescuer around the corner. The man spoke up as they neared the glistening of the window glass ahead, "Damn thing came through the window and got my leg pretty good, glass got the rest."

Kirashira shuddered, she had no desire to know, to see, to visualize what had happened to the poor man's broken body and yet he continued laboriously "Never thought diplomacy was going to be the way I left the world to be honest..."

They reached the window and Kirashira's mind was still blank. The man eased himself to the ground as they approached the pane and with a sudden burst of concentrated care, managed to make a meticulous effort of placing the cylinder he held against the glass, sticking the end on the pane. It adhered silently and the Ambassador sighed, "Thank god, the windows have the right metal in 'em."

"This is a radio device? Like... an emergency call?" Kirashira asked finally, watching the device as several lights on the apparent transmitter blinked to life.

A soft hum emanated from the machinery, a high pitched chirp resonating through the window every couple seconds.

The Ambassador nodded and sighed, scooting himself backward to a wall which he leaned against, breathing heavily, but with a wince on his face at times, "I hope its enough..."

His simple word choice underscored the fact that he was probably not the longest serving ambassador to ever speak the Hil'Raigh language.

"How long have you been the ambassador to my country?" Kirashira asked carefully, gently.

The man smiled and laid back against the wall, slumping now, "Not long really, a couple months. They rotated the previous ambassador a while ago..."

"I'm sorry," Kirashira replied, knowing it sounded hollow.

"Don't be," He said, a chuckle resonating through him, one that revealed fluid in his lungs, "I died doing my job, can't say I'd complain about that really."

Kirashira was silent, watching the man, wishing she could help, wishing she knew what to say, how to comfort someone in need. She wished she could have done the same for her father, a fresh pain rolling in. The sincerity of the man's words however, rocked her from renewed self pity, at least for now.

"You're gonna make it Princess, I promise. Just don't go too far away from this window..."

The Princess nodded, slipping into a nearby door frame, one that offered far more shadow than the pale light leaking through the window provided to the corridor.

It was an odd feeling, knowing that only one floor down there was a fire, armed killers and a bunch of dead party guests. Kirashira was sure that she was still entirely in some kind of shock, some kind of mental block responsible for her continued coherence.

As she sat, waiting, listening perhaps for the sounds of people making their way up the stairs, she heard some banging metal and some yelling but not much else. It went on for minutes, minutes of hearing the attackers below fiddle with the damaged staircase.

While she waited, listening, her ears caught the sound of a gentle, soft melody, one that was imperfect and improvised. Only after a moment more did Kirashira realize the Ambassador was quietly humming a song to himself. She eyed the Novian carefully, realizing he, like her, must have felt so alone now.

Her desire to hide, to be concealed, fought now with a sense of gratitude for at very least the small amount of time this dignitary had granted her. She was sure that whatever his device was, it was not going to do much, how could it? If the local authorities were not already here, then what chance did his machine have of summoning them?

She didn't want to point those things out, feeling a tinge of hopelessness. Even so, she crawled out of the shadow and sat next to the Ambassador as he hummed his tune. After a moment she worked up the courage to reach out with her hand. She wrapped it in his and gave him a squeeze.

The man sighed deeply, and with his eyes closed, kept humming. His desire to be strong, to present his best, as Kirashira had heard most NovaCore tried to do, meant that he never looked at her. She never saw his eyes again, but knew from the small tear that eased its way out of them, that there was soon to be only one alive here. His song continued for a minute more, growing softer still, less enthusiastic, until finally, the next note never came.

⁊ - The Guild Hall

The checklist was complete, or at least everything on it was accounted for. Even still, it was not something Truth was looking forward to. Rather, she was at best, ambivalent, not knowing quite what to expect from the fact that the Ambassador's emergency signal had been activated in the heart of the city.

The signal was emanating from the Kul'Raigh Companion Guild Hall in the center of town currently, from one of the upper floors. Since the structure was so large, that broadcast had managed to reach both Truth and her partner even down on the maze of catwalks and pedestrian routes high above ground level here in Dau'Kore's bustling heart.

The pair had been on their way to deposit some of the gear from the kit they had recovered the previous day, at a secure location in the city when the signal had come in. It had therefore been possible to equip themselves while in the city rather than returning home first. It was a stroke of good luck amongst the terrible reality that there was an emergency mission on the table now.

Unfortunately however, the pair were not going to be able to acquire easy public transportation to the middle of the city, where the Guild Hall was located. No matter how well they could conceal their gear, it was all but assured that the location was on lock-down already. It meant that they had opted instead, to don the equipment rather than store it.

Their dress, NovaCore light contact gear, though not entirely obvious to the untrained eye, was definitely out of place to most. Law enforcers in the city would pick up on the pair rather quickly as a result and with a definite emergency on their hands, there was no point in risking such a complication. The rifles they shouldered, were wrapped in simple cloth wrap cases, ones commonly used by the NovaCore on such missions. They gave the impression of a simple instrument or piece of sporting equipment to most while allowing the owners rapid access to their weapon without having to go through the trouble of opening many clasps or zippers. Regardless, there was not a soul who would be able to identify exactly what they carried now as they raced along on borrowed transport.

Truth still remembered the face of the man whose vehicle they had procured. Though his expression was much different after he had noticed they were driving away on it. He had stopped to buy a snack at one of the shops on his route and had come out to find the pair of NovaCore making off with what must have been a prized possession of his.

It was after all, quite well kept, and expensive looking as Truth could guess. A quick query from her co-processor on the city's business networks told her that the mag-lev hover-bike retailed for an average year and a half salary for a normal resident of the city, something that was apparent in its trim and paint. Still, it was getting a work out now, one it might never have received otherwise.

Weaving traffic was one thing on a mag-lev bike but doing so without a good knowledge of city streets and flying for better or worse on the moment to moment lookups of her neural interface was challenging even for Truth.

The stolen vehicle was fast enough that it demanded most of her attention to control. That fact was complicated by her need to pay attention to both the police radio channels she was monitoring and the navigation data. Overall, it was an experience she did not envy.

Law enforcement had been notified only a few minutes before Truth had picked up the ambassador's signal and as a result, were still, according to their radio chatter, creating perimeters and moving in to secure the Guild Hall as a whole.

Of course, they were likely not to cooperate with the idea of Truth and her partner moving in themselves to rescue their ambassador and as such, beating them to the building as it were, was of the utmost importance.

Vehicles whipped by on the roads, most of them so slow Truth could barely get a good reading on what the types of each of them were as she passed. She realized as she watched a wave of police vehicles make a fully airborne trek overhead, lights blaring, that perhaps a flying vehicle would have been the better thing to steal in this case.

Tony clung to her from behind, letting Truth's expert reflexes take the helm of what was normally one of the most dangerous vehicle classes the pair had ever operated.

"Looks like we are going to have our hands full getting past them," Tony chortled over the small radio in Truth's ear. She nodded and glanced at the line of several cruisers as they moved past down the a corridor between buildings and made a sharp turn out of sight soon after.

The air way the police were taking was far more direct to the hall but the highway on which she and her partner were stuck, was configured in such a way as to make a direct drive to the same location rather hard. Truth set her interface to work on a solution as the pair raced onward.

"Shoulda stolen a flying car," Tony finally said, echoing Truth's earlier thought. She almost sighed, it seemed so obvious now but who was to say it would have worked? Flying vehicles were almost always bio-metrically authenticated in the

Federation, making their theft quite hard. In addition, dedicated pilots took the helm of each, something an average person would lack the training and experience to accomplish.

Those two factors together made finding a stray vehicle rather difficult, most of the publicly usable ones being taxi service vehicles or commercially owned equipment. While stealing a flying vehicle would have been quicker, there was no guarantee that it would have been possible at all.

"I was thinking the same but I do not know how effectual that plan would have been," Truth replied calmly, dodging a large cargo vehicle that decided to change it's heading unexpectedly.

A loud horn followed the Novians as they raced by, whining into a quick nothing due to their speed.

"I'm telling you I learned some good jacking techniques from Roshe last time we had training conference, shoulda let me try," Tony added.

Truth had heard the story yes. Tony had claimed to have learned some new ways to exploit the security on some models of vehicles from one operative Roshe, another of the NovaCore intelligence operatives that had come out of the academy around the same time as Truth and her partner had. He was older, a bit of an older brother to Tony, more of a distant acquaintance to Truth.

"Roshe's jacking techniques require software if I recall," Truth quipped.

"I have it on the wrist machine," Tony said, a verbal shrug as it were, accompanying his words as he hung on tightly.

Truth's interface came back, finally, with an idea. She would veer off the highway soon and drop down to one of the monorail tracks. The plan drew a smirk from her face but it was what she had hoped for. The monorail track system had lines that, if properly negotiated, ran through the middle of the tall Companion Guild Hall, making it possible not only to reach the structure, but reach a potentially unsecured place in the building. The monorails were one of the first things to be diverted away from their intended destination in an emergency. As such none of the police would expect someone to arrive via the tracks.

"You know I just realized the guy whose bike we stole is gonna have to tell one hell of a story to get off the hook today..." Tony mused as Truth edged ever closer toward the side of the road, closing on her sudden turn.

"We are jumping," She announced, and with sudden force, flipped the rear of the vehicle wide, sending it into a weightless slide, sideways down the highway. The lack of friction thanks to the magnetic levitation carried the bike at more or less the same speed as it had been moving forward, though Truth had leaned heavily to retain balance.

Sliding now, her mind painted the picture, super imposing digital maps in three dimensions onto as yet unseen geometry, giving her the perfect picture for pre-planning as she looked ahead.

Even as she and her partner passed to the gap between buildings down which the monorail line ran, Truth had already punched the throttle again and cut down the slide of the bike.

Like most Hil'Raigh bikes, the magnetic force could be adjusted for assist in navigating and thanks to some practice and quick optimizations with her neural interface, most of the control techniques were already coming in cleanly.

The rear slid further as the mag pads hitched themselves to the road bed and in moments the bike had changed directions from a sideways slide to a mix of forward and sliding.

It was a well planned maneuver, one that let the bike sail lazily down the six or so meter drop to the monorail track, which, in Hil'Raigh fashion, was equipped for mag-lev vehicles as well.

The track had been shut down earlier, the trains that normally ran on it now out of the question. With no potential traffic to contend with, Truth twisted the accelerator of the bike heavily, the thrusters whining and the whir of the engine core picking up volume as it continued accelerating.

Now, even with her capable senses, artificially enhanced, her vision managed painfully little detail recognition on the buildings they passed. Windows, mostly, because they were traveling down the monorail corridor but some pedestrian walkways both above and below, made brief appearances in her view.

In all, the entire monorail corridor was no more than twenty meters wide, and the excessive speed the stolen machine was capable of became quickly apparent in the confined space. The wind whipped past, Truth's ears filtering out the noise as best they could, but even then, the sound was quite loud. At these speeds, the air itself felt thick and unmoving, and for a moment, the ripping currents of air convinced her skin that indeed, she had begun to swim rather than ride.

As she raced forth, a small flick of the wrist here, a gentle lean there, she guided the bike froward, all the while urged on by the projected map ahead. The Guild Hall was no more than a kilometer or so away at that point, its outline clearly visible behind a line of skyscrapers hedging in the monorail track. Eventually, the obstruction would pass, opening into the large empty space that surrounded the Guild Hall and accommodated the monorail tracks and landing pads for shuttles and ships.

The Hall was the closest thing to a spaceport allowed in the middle of such a busy city. Reaching it once one was within the rather large perimeter around the building, was made easier thanks to the large exclusion zone, one filled with gardens and open space rather than easily manned choke points.

That was not to say that the open space was a positive with no caveats however. Open air meant that the local police forces would easily pick up the approaching bike, riding at unsafe speed toward a blockaded building that was under lock-down. Furthermore, it was being driven by a pair of questionably dressed individuals with obvious intent to reach the interior.

The saving grace of it all was of course, that because it was late in the evening, seeing a vehicle so small, especially one operating without its headlights, was going to be hard. The police force surely was not expecting the kind of insertion Truth and her partner had planned, but there was no room for error. The rail stations at the Guild Hall would be guarded well and even though the vehicle they had acquired would be hard to see from the gardens and promenades that surrounded the place, it was still likely to be spotted before it made the entire journey.

The time for speculation ended abruptly as the NovaCore finally emerged from the shielding forest of skyscrapers on either side of the rail line. The claustrophobic corridor opened into a grandiose use of space the likes of which was surprising even after seeing a map of it all.

There was a sense of scale here and several smaller satellite buildings ringed the open space around the Guild Hall. The hall itself stood atop a central building in the middle but featured a set of four large structural legs. They were likely to spread the weight of a top section that was decidedly larger in its diameter than the supporting main structure was. The design was intensely Kul'Raigh, shrugging off many of the standard architectural conventions of the Hil'Raigh city and moving for a spire like, flat sided structure. Underneath the large overhang were a selection of gardens, walks and of course, the rail station.

The open spaces beneath, spidered away with artificial paths and routes toward the smaller buildings. Each was equally distinct in it's own way and created a maze of pathways that Truth had no interest in attempting to analyze. Though her implants had retrieved and processed the map data, her artificial eyes now gave her as much data as they had neglected. Despite the dark, Truth could make out most everything clearly, and immediately began scanning likely landing locations for police transports and squads. In the night sky above, a billow of fiery smoke spouted from one of the flat sides of the guild hall. Making the section look more like a malfunctioning candle than a skyscraper.

The fire was not extremely large, rather small in comparison to the structure in its entirety, however, the implications were clear.

Whatever had occurred had certainly breached the outer skin of the building in some significant fashion and was likely related to the fire. Details were scarce though, traveling at such speed and trying to navigate the bike effectively. Truth turned away in an instant, back to her driving, noting that the rail station was only a hundred or so meters away now.

On platforms in the distance, a couple stories above the level of the station itself, a steady stream of shuttles, mostly civilian, appeared to be landing and taking off in haste. It meant only one thing really, that the Guild Hall was still being evacuated and that meant rail station security would be minimal. With the trains shut down and the civilian population generally kept out of the area, there would be little need to guard the monorail platforms at all. Because of the chaos in the distance and perhaps some useful concealment, the Novians had yet to be detected.

The foliage and gardens that surrounded the monorail line on either side were remarkably capable at keeping the pair from view, far more effective than the map would have indicated. It was only when Truth could make out a collection of four patrol officers walking the platforms at the station ahead that she realized they would surely be detected. Rather than give them an easy time of it however, she fired up the engines and as the tracks widened out to allow access to the several boarding platforms found in the station, she followed them wide and aimed for one of the platforms itself.

Much could be said of magnetic levitation in vehicles, even more however could be said for the Hil'Raigh propensity to design all of their buildings with curvature all over. The interior of the rapidly approaching station fit the bill for generic Hil'Raigh architecture quite well, decidedly different in its design than the building it was servicing. Truth guessed it was some sort of city planning decision but the importance of who had decided on the particular arrangement of the platforms was less important than their reality.

Barreling through the platform and sliding hard into one of the access tunnels at speed was definitely unsafe, something no one would have expected or trained for. That particular combination of factors however, made it the best possible course of action and it was only moments away from being tested as Truth heard the first yell of consternation from one of the police.

Two were in the way ahead but their survival instincts took over and they lept out of harms way as Truth had expected. The others were far enough away that they had not been in direct danger and so, instead, they had time to yell as the bike passed.

"Go!" Truth urged her partner as she took the vehicle into a tight slide, one that imbalanced it enough to cause the levitators to fail. She made out with vivid detail, the surprise on one of the peace officer's faces as her vehicle turned, giving them a fraction of face to face time.

The slide caught ground enough to rapidly slow the vehicle and Truth punched the downward thrust hard at the same time. While still rather unsafe for dismount, she knew her partner was going to take his chances. The vehicle lurched and skittered, even further out of control now as he lept from the rear seat, square into one of the guards.

Truth dismounted then, only fractions of a second after her partner had, choosing her own target like a hungry cat. She too connected, barreling into the officer with her rifle and assessed as she did, another police officer behind this one. Her target went down and as he connected with the ground she let her rifle slide out of her hands. The hefty, durable weapon slid noisily over the tile of the platform and Truth herself coiled into a roll over her target.

In moments, she uncoiled, reached out to her weapon and took the muzzle in one hand while her other took the grip backwards. Across her body now, she had optimal leverage, pulling the hand on the muzzle back and thrusting aggressively with the grip as she twisted the weapon upward into the stomach of her second victim.

The blow was far less brutal than the response of the officer might have indicated. A pained expression settling over the woman's face as she still struggled to process what exactly had happened to her partner. She lurched backward, staggering and breathless. Her own Hil'Raigh weapon fell from her grip and Truth scurried toward her with practiced intensity. Rather than plunge a knife into the target's neck however, the Novian opted to move from her crouch to standing as she kicked the rifle away from its owner with gusto.

The weapon clattered noisily off of the platform and onto the rail track below, unbroken but far out of its owners reach.

Truth turned to assess her partner's situation. Tony had incapacitated his initial target and the guard had sustained an apparent injury in falling. The last and final member of the patrol team however, was standing enough to give Tony's rifle butt a good place to hit his stomach. The Hil'Raigh officer curled helplessly around the abusive blow and winced, clutching his midsection.

Calculated violence was the name of the game, well calculated violence being the optimal balance between effect and avoiding permanent injury to bystanders. Truth had to admit though that she might have overdone the blow to her second target and so, as she motioned for her partner to make his way over, she knelt and checked the woman's ribs. Amid some groans, and with some help from various imaging modes she was reasonably assured that her target would fully recover within a day or two, though she would definitely bear the bruises of the assault for a while.

Now, with relative security assured, the pair of Novians turned their attention to the access tunnel leading toward the central spire of the Guild Hall.

According to the maps Truth had found on the Guild Hall, the structure's central spire ran the height almost entirely, providing express elevators and some local elevator access in various intervals along the length of the structure.

Securing the entirety of such a structure would be nigh impossible in a situation such as the one experienced tonight. Even so, it was a sure bet that the levels connected to the outside world would be heavily patrolled. That meant the rail station and the promenade floors were likely crawling with security. Additionally, the incapacitated police would call their friends soon, reporting the assault and complicating matters.

The final difficulty however, would be gaining access to one of the express elevators without the help of the attendants who normally operated them. While ascending stairs manually was not impossible, it was fatiguing even for the two Novians. As Truth considered options, her partner spoke up.

"Sounds like there is a bigger issue than just the cops."

Truth eyed him carefully, waiting for his explanation as he continued, "There are hostile actors in the building still and they are calling for help upstairs, sounds real bad from the radio."

Truth nodded and turned, leading the way toward the tunnel to the inside of the building. The shops competing for real estate around the train platforms lined both sides until finally, a set of doors indicated the building proper. There were food stalls, clothing stores, places selling shoes, underwear, about anything one could want or expect. Most of them looked to be specialty shops and some of the others were part of well known chains. All of them were eerily empty now. If Truth could have given the Hil'Raigh credit for at least one thing tonight, it was evacuating the Guild Hall's extraneous places relatively quickly. The two new arrivals speed, was of course, limited when it came to the Guild Hall proper, a building heavily populated at all hours of every day. Reaching the intended location inside therefore, was going to carry its own set of challenges. Being discreet was most probably the best course of action within.

Such a plan would require blending in with the evacuating people inside. With the local officers placing such a high priority on civilian safety, it would be far easier to sneak amongst them near the elevators.

An idea popped into Truths head the instant her mind realized it and she quickly queried her partner, "Where is the evac stage area? Have they discussed it?"

"Not on this channel, I can poke around..." Tony replied, reaching to his ear awkwardly and poking at the ear piece. Most Hil'Raigh radio's on the market were of similar design, they did not fit inside the Novian ear all that well but Truth had neglected one of her own. Eventually, as they made their way through the double doors, Tony piped up again, "What level are we on?"

"Fifty five," Truth replied, "From ground level"

"Sixty is a flight platform, they are still evacuating people so I'd imagine they are using that as a staging area at least...."

Truth nodded and as soon as she saw the sign for a staircase, she made it a priority. The pair would stick out certainly but they had yet to be identified and with enough luck they could make their way into one of the express lifts and coerce its operator into helping them get up the tower.

It was a risky plan but without the elevators there was little chance of reaching the upper floors quickly. With any luck, Truth and her partner would be able to take advantage of all the confusion to make their way to where they needed to be.

"We might have to revise our exit plan," Tony said as Truth led the way up one of the staircases, several levels remained until they would have to choose.

"I was thinking the same, we will need a vehicle to extract the ambassador safely," Truth replied, her interface set to work looking for places that extraction might be possible in the Guild Hall. Remarkably, there was a parking garage for hover cars just a few levels further up.

"There is a garage on level seventy five, I have no idea how many vehicles may be inside however," Truth announced.

"Better than nothing, I don't think we have time to bring ourselves back down though with the cops already asking for help up there." Tony mused, "Maybe I should get us a car while you sneak upstairs, probably easier for you to blend in."

The idea was as sound as anything Truth herself could come up with. It was not out of the ordinary for operatives in this kind of position to perform concurrently in different capacities. Both were trained to work alone or with their partner and both were confident enough in each other to make the call. A nod from Truth set the new addition to the plan in motion and with a burst of speed, Tony continued up the staircase while Truth exited on the floor hosting the evacuation.

Tony vanished up the stairs rather quickly and Truth hastily adjusted the covering cloth of her weapon as she strapped it over one shoulder once more. The cloth case was about as inconspicuous as one could hope for with a railgun strapped to their back, but it was enough to delay identification of the weapon long enough for a discerning operative to exploit most situations. Here however, Truth's Kul'Raigh features would hopefully prove invaluable.

The side corridors were littered with some offices, probably commercial, reminding the Novian just how much variety of business really was conducted in the Guild Hall, despite it's obvious associations. It was really the upper levels that managed the Companion Guild as a whole and its affairs, at least if the floor maps were any indication.

Save the fact that the halls had the markings of some hasty departures, the building was otherwise pristine here, with no real law enforcement to be found in this remote section of the floor, at least for a moment.

Truth briskly picked up her pace, heading to the central area, hoping to catch a glimpse of an advantageous situation. The sounds of general ruckus, some panic, some attempted calm, told her that she was indeed approaching the right place. She only hoped her partner was having luck on his own.

The garage would certainly be under lock and key from the police at this point, no flight traffic would be allowed this close to the hall and surely no one was going to be leaving law enforcement custody without being vetted first.

In reality, it was a nightmare of sorts. The local police could never have known who was potentially a bad actor here tonight, and so, they had painfully little to go on, able to check evacuees for weapons at most. That was how a situation like this often played out at least.

Despite the negative situation, Truth and her partner had both received training for such scenarios, not just response but exploitation. The saying went that one should never waste a good tragedy and Truth was certain this one qualified, being a poster child for the saying as a whole.

As she approached what her interface had determined was the central corridor, she hunkered low and crept forward to the edge of the wall ahead until she was able to take a quick glance around the corner.

The scene was one of mildly controlled chaos, with groups of patrons from the building flowing hurriedly out the doors amid an overwhelmed contingent of peace officers. Recoiling behind the wall again, Truth unwrapped the cloth gun cover from around her shoulder strap and slid the strap from her body quickly. Kneeling over the rifle she carefully wrapped her weapon and cinched the ends and middle.

She hefted the weapon once more, now covered in a nondescript black cloth on her back, one that was unlikely to slip loose as she moved. Though one with training would be able to identify what it was with a careful examination, even from a distance, the temporary cover would provide all the delay Truth needed to get to one of the elevators. Of course, one would have to admit that her clothing did not look all that convincing either. It was sure to be a giveaway for anyone who got a good enough look, making it all the more important that Truth avoid being examined as long as possible.

Given the sheer number of people, She was increasingly certain that she would be able to acquire use of one of the express elevators to the upper floors.

Truth skirted the corner again, looking perturbed and upset, nervous. They were emotions she conjured to her face at will, making a good mask of her features as she made her way toward the evacuating crowds.

The inside of the Guild Hall's central area was a large open space punctuated in the center by a collection of elevator shafts. Several stories tall, several floors from above had an open view of the floor on which Truth now walked. Tables, plants, chairs and a general attention to interior aesthetic showed that while the space was currently shuffling people out of the Hall en-mass, it was designed to be a sort of traffic hub in any case. Several moments passed before Truth was finally able to decide on which of the shafts so many meters away were likely to be the express lifts.

The one she chose had just released a crowd of hurried people and was likely to sit at ground level for a few moments while another of the elevators moved instead. Truth guessed at least, that the response teams who had secured this area would have disabled the use of most of the elevators and kept a limited number online at once. She hoped as well, that it meant they would be staggering or alternating the use of each of them because it would give her the time she needed.

Though she came from an awkward place across the concourse, no one seemed to question the arrival of a non descript Kul'Raigh carrying some personal item on her back as she approached the crowd. Any of the details of what she wore or carried were given to distance and distraction for the time being. There were a few attentive eyes on her from some of the police as she approached one of them but a burst of noise amid the group of evacuees took their attention for a critical moment.

Truth felt her heart rate increasing now as she closed to within meters of some of the security teams and by the time she was a meter or so away from the elevator shafts themselves, she could hear the pounding of her heart in her ears. She had devised a plan but it was off the cuff and quick.

She chose a guard near to the door of one of the shafts, the one she had guessed on earlier and got his attention with a timid hello. The man turned, glancing at her dismissively then back at the exiting crowd as he spoke, "What? Move on out and you can get the rest of your stuff later."

Truth, added as much helplessness as she could to her voice. She wanted to be ignored, persistent enough to get an answer but innocent enough not to be interesting, "Did this elevator just come from upstairs?"

She glanced past the man now, into the open door of the lift, there was no one inside at the moment. Around the guards neck was a small lanyard to the front of which a card holder was affixed. The markings on the card were non visual but a quick look with wireless sensing equipment revealed the card as one that would have control over the elevator system.

"Of course it did but there's a fire upstairs you can't go back up.... Look I'm busy please just move along," the man replied, giving Truth an annoyed look. A quick look toward the exiting wave of people told Truth that she had an opening and at the same time, the posted officer finally seemed to notice something odd about Truth's personal belongings.

His skepticism showed in his eyes and as he reached for his own weapon, Truth lunged into him and grabbed his hand snatching it mid motion. Twisting around behind him, she took his forearm and bent it across his back, lifting it away from his spine with ease. The immediate submission of the pained individual was a welcome response and Truth was able to tug the man backward into the lift. There was a moment when the stunned victim must have been contemplating what to do next but as he began to yell out Truth wrenched his arm hard, turning his yell into more of a pained groan.

The man collapsed to his knees and shuddered in pain as he twisted awkwardly to try and relieve the pressure on his shoulder joint but to no avail.

Reaching around his neck, Truth ripped the lanyard from him with a vicious tug, one that likely left a mark on the man's skin as the thin plastic cord separated with a snap.

By now, several people had turned, some evacuees and some other security as well. The sea of people being herded out of the way however, afforded Truth enough time to shove her victim forward and kick him roughly. The kick sent him splaying out of the elevator and even as he hit the ground Truth had moved to tap the lift door closed. A quick scan of the access card later and she was given a floor selection.

There was a bang on the door as Truth's fingertips keyed the estimated floor number she had calculated earlier, definitely near the top, and in a moment she had confirmed the selection.

No doubt the selection process had been long enough that at least someone had noticed what had happened but by now it was too late. The lift would make most of the trip before anyone could effectively communicate the issue and as long as it was within a reasonable margin, Truth would be where she wanted to be rather soon.

It was as the lift hummed to life and Truth felt her stomach lurch toward the floor that she decided to see if she could have her neural interface look up some detailed blueprints of the place. While publicly available maps were useful to an extent, they lacked most of the data for the upper floors. Truth guessed it was because the upper floors contained so much that was meant to remain private, like various halls and large hosting spaces for events and banquets. The Guild Hall was after all, listed as one of the best places to book something like that, or so it claimed on the wireless data network.

Rather than be content to guess, Truth set to work in her mind, mulling over every detail she could muster about the beacon and its possible location from what she had observed earlier.

She knew it was up high, high enough in fact that it had been visible in other parts of the city, or at least, it's transmission had been. Second, the beacon had probably been affixed to some heavily reinforced glass up near the top of the Hall because of the way it's transmission had been attenuated by the time Truth's own antennas had received the signal.

The final piece of course was the worst bit of information, the reality that the origin point had appeared painfully close to the columns of fire and smoke sputtering from the top of the Guild Hall earlier. There was certainly trouble afoot but what had transpired, the details at least, were still a complete mystery.

It was no coincidence that the same Guild Hall hosting what the news had reported as Princess Kirashira Ren'Tauru's twentieth birthday party celebration, had also been the sight of an emergency call from the NovaCore ambassador. Clearly the two were related but Truth hated to think about the implications that a relation between the two would have. Only time, precious little of it in fact, would be able to provide answers but somehow Truth knew that she would find only more questions up above.

8 - Party Crasher

Truth pulled the final piece of her kit from the small satchel and set the empty bag aside. As with any rescue operation, procedure was to bring a towline rifle, wing harness and an emergency care kit in the now empty bag. All of the parts of that kit, save the medical pouch and the broken down towline rifle had been removed from their holder and Truth carefully double checked all of the straps on her harness. The idea of using the wing harness at this point was rather outlandish but protocol was protocol.

Normally such gear was used in the case that entry into a particularly problematic place was required. The glider harness coupled with the towline rifle provided a good way to get around, at least as long as the towline rifle had cables.

Normal kits like this carried only a few, three at the most. The cabling was wrapped into spools and hosted a piercing anchor at the head. All of the gear was tailored to work with the cityscape of Dau'Kore, the capitol city here on Ashor, but unfortunately, the Guild Hall was not a place one could simply glide to from the surrounding buildings.

Both Truth and Tony had tossed the idea around but it was quickly discarded due to the sheer height of the structure. A stolen motorcycle later and Truth was putting on the kit anyway.

With any luck her partner would be able to acquire a vehicle and bring it to the VIP landing pad that the building schematics Truth had found during her elevator ride, had finally revealed upstairs. It had taken some sleuthing and probing, it was likely frowned upon by the Guild. Regardless, Truth had already planned a route as it wasn't far from where she gauged the Ambassador's beacon to be located.

The express elevator had been moving nonstop for minutes now, making Truth wonder just how prepared the locals really were for responding to the attack. If they had been properly staffed she assumed the elevator itself would have stopped already. She eyed the smooth metallic frame of the near hollow box and waited, watching the floor number rapidly ticking upward on the wall display.

The lift shuddered with a sudden violent intensity. Screeching metal and the whine of what had to be the emergency brakes overwhelmed the small box, and like an echo chamber, the lift only amplified the already horrendous noise. Even as the lift ground to a halt, the control panel blinked and a calm computerized voice began playing.

In eloquent Hil'Raigh, the lift described an obstruction in the shaft above and carefully instructed the passengers to wait for assistance.

Having braced against the handrail on one side of the lift, Truth regained her footing, taking note of what sounded like creaking metal outside. The lift itself was now useless and as Truth mashed the open door button, nothing happened. Thankfully however, lifts such as this always came with an emergency exit built into the roof.

Truth scanned the area around the roof mounted light in the center of the lift, locating the coveted emergency exit hatch in the corner above the control console. A small red button on the console, previously un-illuminated, had finally come to life and Truth tapped it after examining the glyph on it's face.

The exit above retracted amid the sounds of a whirring electric motor and gears, before disappearing from view. Truth reached up to the artistically crafted nooks in the wall beneath the newly opened exit. The button had opened the door and even a ladder to ascend.

The Novian took careful grip of the handhold, lifting herself as her toes hooked into a ledge below. She had to admit that the space was rather limited and that combat boot toes did not fit quite that well inside the surfaces. Her foot slipped and she felt a tug on her fingertips and arms as she scurried to get footing once more. Having regained her pose on the ladder, she followed with a careful ascent and despite the lift's single story height, the climb continued for what felt longer than it had actually taken to make the trip. At last, Truth reached the top and poked her head out of the hole above.

The air was acrid here, the smell of metals and electronic heat forming a scent that immediately assaulted Truth's nose, making her eyes water. She could make out, amid the odors, some steel and other particulate, probably from the lift's cables and brake system.

Above, far above, there was more light than Truth would have expected in an elevator shaft, and amid the darkness, it proved rather capable of illuminating the roof of the lift itself.

With calculated care, Truth rested her arms on the threshold and began pulling herself free of the confines of the lift. At last, she got her torso up, then, rolling to the side, pulled her legs free as well. At last she noted the cabling for the elevator, the brakes on the cable clamped tightly. A glance over the edge of the lift, in the gap between the wall and the box from which she had escaped showed not only were the brakes on the cable engaged, but a separate set had all but dug into the walls of the elevator shaft. The scene explained why the ride had been so violent when the lift had gone from its high speed travel to an abrupt, jolting stop.

Above however, the light's source became increasingly clear. Flickering and an uneven naturalness cascaded through the illumination and one final scent added itself to the mix. There was smoke above, the kind of heavy smoke that could only mean there was a fire.

Truth remembered seeing fire on the outside of the building before entering the train station minutes ago but if the fire was this far inside, the situation was far more dire than she had anticipated.

The fire was a floor or two above her current position, and glancing at the walls of the elevator shaft confirmed just the same. An emergency access ladder lined the wall near the exit doors and moved up the shaft toward the obstructed surface.

With a fire above and the lift rapidly on course to fill with smoke now that it was no longer in motion, Truth quickly moved to the ladder and grabbed hold. Unlike the careful crafting of the lift interior, the industrial ladder proved easy to grasp and far more accommodating to her gear. Slinging her rifle on her back and the kit bag containing her medical kit and towline rifle above her rump, she began her ascent.

Her intuition told her that the fire was on or near the level where the Ambassador would be. He would have been nearby whatever event caused the fire when it happened and as a result Truth would want to get as close as she could to the fire without climbing through it.

The shaft was not all that tight a fit but even so, with a fire above and a stalled lift below, it was nonetheless claustrophobic. Truth's enhanced frame was able to withstand high temperature, the debilitating odors and even the nervousness that came from hanging onto the emergency ladder here in the elevator shaft. No matter her capabilities however, the idea that at any moment, some hefty hunk of metal or equipment would collapse through the inferno above and take part of her body with it was inescapable. She hurried, working quickly and keeping herself going with deep breaths of the acrid air.

Even despite her artificial lungs, and the extra filtering afforded her, Truth's neural interface began a series of reminders to her about leaving the environment as quickly as possible.

Hearing so plainly from the implants in her brain was odd. It was as if she was hearing the sound of warning through her own ears and yet, it was entirely internal, generated by the computer coprocessors and transmitted directly into her nervous system without interruption. It was intrusive and at times, annoying, but served to remind her that even she had limits, something she often forgot about. She willed the environmental warnings to silence at last.

A small internal conversation followed, the computer talking to her mind in its own unique way, a bit of back and forth until finally, Truth agreed to accept it's tactical analysis data. The information now streaming into her consciousness was always available to her but rarely was it so detailed or robustly calculated. In moments the normal world had overlayed infrared, sound, structural and all other sensory data Truth's implants and sensors could provide. Visual color and hue were all there of course and yet, even more so, extra information beyond simple sight was being mixed in.

The transition from trickle to deluge was always jarring and it quickly tired Truth's mind if she did not exert herself carefully. Mental fatigue was a real possibility when operating with such a bevy of information at her disposal. However, there was a marked difference in her abilities in such a state. While she could unconsciously call on that extra information from her sensors, the near constant stream of data now, changed the way her thought process worked.

Even climbing the ladder was a different experience. Rather than simply climbing, her mind was instead, conscious of the pressures exerted by her toes and fingers, the strength of her muscle grip, the level of fatigue that each of those artificial muscles was experiencing and the rate at which they would tire.

Reaching the highest level she dared visit with the fires above, Truth carefully reached toward a previously identified wall switch. Her hand grabbed the small bar and she pulled the switch down. It resisted but gave in after concerted effort and finally there was a loud airy pop from the door nearby.

The two halves of the once sealed door cracked open and Truth carefully reached out to the closest one. A series of grips on the inner face of the door allowed her, with one arm, to make slow progress in opening the doorway. The other half, linked by the door mechanism, followed the progress of its partner and in moments she had opened enough of a gap to pass through herself.

Truth slid from the ladder to the lip of the door, a few stories above the disabled lift now. She took one final look down at the elevator as her feet found their place with careful precision. Gripping the door handles, she shimmied a few steps until she got her feet to open ground in a corridor. There was little light in the hallway, save the reflected light from the shaft.

The scene cast a small window of light on the floor outside the elevator door but beyond that the gloom had taken hold. Whatever had happened above had likely disabled power for a couple floors at least.

Truth moved into the darkness without worry, her implants and interfaces working in perfect harmony. Where normal light failed, infrared and thermal readings gave her vision back. The integration of the data was so seamless and automatic that she had to remind herself it was occurring at all.

Here on this level, the beacon signal of the Ambassador was strong enough that Truth's internal radio gave an audible ring to each of the pulses it was emitting. From where she was now it was two floors up at most, far closer than before, assuming of course, there was a way to ascend.

A glance at the elevator door, from the outside of the shaft this time revealed the floor number and in moments Truth had called up a route to the nearest staircase, only a few meters away. The path would take her to the main event hall and above that the Ambassador's beacon was blazing away. Triple checking the plan as she went, Truth set out, un-shouldering her rifle and carrying it low as she moved.

The acrid scent of her former prison leaked into the hallway with less intensity as she left it behind. A meter or so now removed from the elevator shaft, Truth dialed her partner's radio frequency. After several moments, still no response had come, leaving Truth alone in earnest, at least for now.

The architecture in the halls was one of smooth form, with rounded edges on the doors and the walls themselves. Unlike most normally constructed buildings, the Guild Hall featured regularly interspersed decorative archways throughout the corridors, each of them coming to a rounded point at the top. It reminded Truth of the NovaCore starships on which she usually made her home, with heavy durable bulkheads separating compartments.

This building however, did away with all of the tactical niceties of a warship and instead of easy access to maintenance and a lack of interior decoration, the Kul'Raigh had opted to cover the bare metal with a smooth layer of well applied paint. The color was impossible to fully understand in the dark, bombarded by a bevy of information about its infrared and light reflecting properties.

The facsimile stone floor was exposed only on the sides of what Truth guessed was the longest run of carpet she had ever seen in the hallway. She followed the carpet in near silence until, according to the map, there would be a foyer and from there, a variety of rooms sprung off.

Entering the foyer, Truth scoped out the largest of openings across the way, one with a wide set of stairs leading to the banquet hall on the floor above. To the right was a route that led to what was probably a private landing pad and on the left was a set of nondescript rooms with no information on the map itself.

The foyer here, like the central foyer so many stories below, was decorated with plants, a sweeping architecture and trimmed in what had to be gold. The entire room was reminiscent if not entirely more extravagant than the main area downstairs. There were fountains, small jets of water still running while the main lighting, a chandelier overhead appeared entirely dead. Instead a small selection of runner lights along the bases of the walls of the cavernous foyer provided minimal lighting.

Truth traced over the stairs ahead through her rifle optics, skimming the top edges of their railings, then following it clockwise as she herself moved in that same direction around the room along the wall. Eventually she had broken line of sight with the open stair top and finished scanning the opposite side of the room, pausing in her crouched stance to take a knee.

The air here in the foyer, at least according to a array of sensors Truth could never hope to name, included a measure of smoke and some other gases. Some was probably a result of the fire but everything she could see about the temperature in the foyer indicated that the blaze from the elevator shaft was having little effect.

With apparently more than one fire alive and well here at the upper levels, Truth questioned just how much planning had occurred before whatever had taken place. Any reasonable accommodation would have been expected to provide an automatic fire suppression system and, as Truth glanced over the roof, she found what had to be the detectors and sprayers for one. Each of them sat idle and lifeless, seemingly unaware that their job was being neglected.

Satisfied as she could be that there were as of yet, no assailants waiting in the shadows across the room, Truth skirted the wall until she came to the staircase to the next floor. Sticking to one side, she crouched low and moved up the staircase at an angle, biasing herself toward the side she was on. Once she reached the top she would sweep from one side to the other to clear.

As her line of sight crested the final step, she instantly snapped her weapon to a form on the ground but the reaction stopped short of a trigger pull. Truth eyed the corpse carefully, and, seeing that the top of the staircase was clear, checked the hallway behind the top of the stairs.

The space was more of a portal, only about a meter in depth before it opened into a much larger room on the other side. Truth felt a chill run down her spine as each meter she observed told a more terrible story.

There was more than a single casualty here, a series of corpses in various states of apparent flight. All of their efforts had been met with weapon fire, halting their progress with finality. The once pristine carpet, already crimson, hosted dark pools and there was enough smoke wafting around in the room beyond the connecting hall, that a nearby fire was all but certain. The incident Truth was responding to, she realized now, was nothing short of a massacre.

After yet another body picked out of the haze, Truth called her partner in reflex. The radio chortled, popped once and yet, nothing came back. Taking a breath, Truth paused her forward motion and steadied her mind. Entering this unknown alone, despite all of her training and confidence, was something that gave her pause. Her instincts, her natural will to survive urged her to turn back. Steeling herself against the weakness, Truth tightened her lips and moved forward, her implants churning away now in a frenzy. Each body was analyzed even if it lay inert, life signs were confirmed non existent before any single one of the casualties was allowed out of her view. Despite that, even before they were confirmed dead or otherwise, each was numbered, a path was built in her mind, the gun motion from target to target was set and the reflex of each trigger pull was anticipated. A single magazine would do the job if she aimed properly.

Again, she moved, steadily, classifying and watching every detail she could muster. Her rifle led the way now like an extra limb, scouring, ready and willing. It's owner was much the same. Her objective was painfully close, dozens of meters to her left and somewhere above.

It was at that moment that Truth heard something scraping against metal in the next room. The banquet hall here was covered in smoke, blood and death, but the next room, listed as a ballroom on the map hosted some sounds.

Truth picked up her pace, careful still but more concerned about the life in the other room. She rounded the corner of one of the arched portals in the banquet hall and was greeted by debris and fire. A quick inspection of the room ahead revealed a mess of smoke, torn metal and flaming wreckage. This was most certainly what she had seen from the outside before arriving here.

Skirting into the room, following and hugging the wall as close she could, Truth was forced to break away from it as she was confronted with a raging bonfire. She moved slowly, her footfalls careful and quiet, as she managed to inch past the obstruction.

The room was a mass of carnage, some the result of wounded people while the rest was the apparent result of what looked to be a destroyed shuttle of some kind. The fuselage of the vehicle was broken, battered, destroyed beyond usability, but the hunks of it that had strewn themselves around the room contrasted with it's blunted nose. Whatever it had done was more than a simple crash.

Damage around the room looked to be from an explosion of some kind and the hunks of metallic death that had showered the room had done a number to those who had met their ends here. Overturned tables, lifeless Kul'Raigh attendants, dead guests, all of them lay quiet. There were bodies, some of them looking all the more regal than others, but all of them having shared in a common fate. Amid overturned trays of food, fuel soaked hunks of shuttle smoldered and burned even still while the pyre of the main body continued bathing the room in a hellish heat. Truth examined the map she had acquired, trying to fix the beacon with a possible route toward it.

The map detailed a selection of suites above, a privately accessed area only available to guests of this function hall. It was interesting construction, uniquely unconventional but unsurprising given the oddities of extravagance Truth had found thus far.

A scream from above sounded and in a second Truth had burst into action. She charged forward to where the stairs on the map should have been, her feet gripping even against the bottom of the vertical surface that served as a wall there. With a practiced lunge, she managed to reach her fingertips upward, noting at last that a large piece of the shuttle had demolished the support structure for the stairs that she had clamored over to reach this point. The lip, having been wrenched violently free of the connecting staircase, was jagged enough that it hurt her hands despite the gloves. Urging her muscles onward Truth pulled herself upward with the ease that only her training and implants could provide. As she crossed the threshold she noted what had to be blood from someone's cut on the edge as she passed. Whoever had made their ascent last had certainly not had an easy time of it.

A whimper of pain sounded, along with an angry curse, someone yelling about trying to escape, someone yelling about their dead comrade. The sound was loud enough that it was easy to locate. Truth hung left immediately, submerged in the darkness of this extra private floor. It only took fractions of a second to identify an armored Hil'Raigh silhouetted against the light streaming into the window at the end of the small hallway. He was armed, carrying a rifle, the ambassador's beacon was less than a meter from his position.

Truth dropped to her knee, taking aim. The main artery above the man's heart, leading to his neck and head was acquired, a virtual overlay of vital areas placed over the figure in real time as Truth clicked the trigger.

A pop sounded loudly in the hall as Truth's weapon lurched against her shoulder, spitting forth the power of it's deadly projectile. In an instant, death struck the unsuspecting figure squarely at the point of aim. Truth had already pushed off the ground surging forward. Adrenaline continued to fill her body as the window behind the target fractured and exploded outward. A shower of plastic, the man's blood and fragments of his body armor preceded him as he was carried helplessly out of the make shift exit.

Truth's footfalls fell as noisily as they could while she charged, hoping to round the corner. Readying her rifle, she prepared to bash a potential target with it before they could ready.

In the second it took her to reach the corner, Truth heard shuffling and a scramble.

She rounded the corner and immediately felt her nerves go white hot with pain. She lurched and stumbled, almost falling out of the now wind swept precipice her rifle had created out of the window. Her implants wailed, her body cried out and she felt herself struggling to maintain any kind of order.

It had to have been a Hil'Raigh sidearm. The plasma weapons would certainly have done that kind of damage so close. She had to avoid passing out. Her mind fixated, desperate on the training techniques she had been taught to avoid losing conscious when struck by such weapons.

A curse followed the shot as a heavy boot took to Truth's ribs. She grunted angrily and, mustered every bit of strength she could. She dragged her rifle with one arm to aim at the assailant's other foot. Yelling aloud, a guttural cry of defiance, Truth hammered the trigger and her rifle bolted its response into the assailant's body.

He cried out as Truth watched him go down, likely without a foot now. With a desperate motion she summoned what she could to swing her rifle wildly against his torso. He stumbled and in a moment Truth had struggled toward the inside of the hallway.

Her left shoulder arced with throbbing, unbearable pain and she felt herself tearing up despite her will to do otherwise. The shock had not yet set in and until it had, she would never be able to deal with the damage.

A quick assessment told her all she needed to know. The ambassador lay dead against the nearby wall, bloodied and silent. Nearby, a quivering Kul'Raigh in fanciful robes lay crying.

Unable to effectively hold her rifle now, Truth huffed and, pressing her burnt flesh against the wall began to use her legs to push the incapacitated assailant toward the broken window. The agonizing pain of the severe burn on her shoulder made her mind desperate and she cried out helplessly in pain. She pushed with all her might until at last, the Hil'Raigh tipped out of the window and disappeared from view.

The hallway was immediately quieter without him present but the exertion sent spiderwebs of light across Truth's vision and she nearly collapsed then and there, her shoulder protesting in a way it never had. She cried out desperately, rolling to her stomach, fumbling for the small pouch on her belt. She grit her teeth, taking out the trauma syringe contained within, then rolled to the side, plunging it into her thigh helplessly.

The lance of pain in her leg was far from competitive with the urge to simply give up consciousness and Truth huffed in agony on her side for moments until finally, the welcome bliss of the nerve dampener took effect. Her entire body tingled now, much of it going numb. But for her implants she would never have been able to feel anything at all.

She rolled to her hands and knees, huffing loudly as she crawled over to the ambassador. He was certainly deceased, probably for minutes. He still held a bloodied knife in his hand. The utensil matched the cutlery from the floor below, barely sharp enough to be considered a weapon. The fact that it was thus tainted with some unknown victim's blood then, meant that the ambassador had been involved in some kind of struggle already. His expression was one of serenity however, suggesting he had not been killed by the pair Truth had dispatched.

Truth fumbled into her medical kit again, drawing out another trauma syringe as she neared the Kul'Raigh. The helpless figure recoiled but a wince of pain crossed her face and she was unable to scramble more than an arms length before she came to the ground hard, clutching her body.

"I'm not going to hurt you!" yelled Truth angrily. It had taken an impossible amount of effort for her mind to get her mouth to open with all of the dampener in her system. She felt it now, the impossible to control adrenaline still pumping. An internal battle raged as her mind all but attacked her implants and interface over the continued deployment of the sometimes life saving chemical.

Her body quivered as she reached out and grabbed the Kul'Raigh by the hand and repeated, this time with less effort. "I won't hurt you..."

The flighty figure paused, her cheeks streaked with the traces of tears that had been running through her heavy makeup. She had a gentle face, perfect proportion, almost artificial. She wore her hair in a fanciful way and had a number of cosmetics on her pale skin. Her black hair framed her face and Truth could have sworn she had seen her before.

It was in that moment that she realized just who she was staring at. She was taken aback, surprised and appalled all at once as she blurted aloud, "Princess Kirashira..."

The Princess sobbed helplessly as Truth spoke her name and the Novian quickly realized she had no idea what to do. Her plan had been to reach and rescue the Ambassador but he was dead. Now however, Kirashira Ren'Tauru, Princess of the Starlight Compact lay before her, bruised and devastated.

"What happened?" Truth finally asked. She gripped the trauma syringe and eyed the royal, who, rather than responding, buried her face in her knees and sobbed.

Truth eyed her for a moment. Assessing the situation, she turned around and moved back to her gun. She carefully put it on, stringing it over her good shoulder as she did so and then, with marginal confidence and bad balance, moved into a low crouch as she pulled the Ambassador's emergency beacon, still pinging on the radio, from the window. The pristine surface remained untainted by its neighbors destruction, the wind whipped hole providing a strong contrast to the intact pane. Truth shoved the beacon into her pouch and took a breath. Her shoulder was still throbbing.

As she approached the Princess again, she heard now, the sound of people clamoring at the staircase behind and down the hall.

"Tony!" She finally called over her radio once again.

This time, despite prior silence, the radio replied, "On my way, got a limo."

"Hurry, we have casualties," She replied.

"Casualties? How many?"

"One survivor," Truth replied, eying the Princess, who was still huddled into a helpless ball.

"Copy. Ambassador?"

"Negative, Royalty,"

"Say again? Royalty?"

"Affirmative," Truth replied. The noise of conversation echoed from the ruined stairs, and the topic was clear enough, in moments Truth would have additional company. "Tony I have an idea..."

Truth eyed the Princess and, scooting toward her, jammed the syringe in the Kul'Raigh's arm. The Monarch's eyes went wide with surprise as she uncoiled from her timid, balled-up form. Her expression went glassy in short order and in mere moments her small frame was overcome with the dose.

"I am going to use the wing suit..."

"Wait what? What about the casualty?" Tony's voice came back, surprised, incredulous.

"With the casualty.." Truth replied. Being boxed in up here was not an option. If there was one group of people on their way up the staircase already, there would be more soon enough. Even if Truth could hold off a few of them, it was likely that she would be overrun eventually.

"You...." Tony stuttered, "Okay, I'll try and ... snatch you out of the air... I guess..."

The lack of confidence in his voice betrayed his surprise, however, like he always did, he agreed to the unconventional plan.

Truth asked her interface calmly for a status report of the suit and fed it a guess as to her and the Princess' combined weight. The system replied negatively, because of course, it had never been designed for more than one passenger. The gliding wings would not provide the kind of lift two people needed to make a safe landing speed.

"You will have to meet me in a dive..." Truth announced shakily.

"Of course I will," Tony replied, a mix of sarcasm and worry in his voice now.

Truth reached out, kneeling before and scooping up the Princess. She carried the unconscious royal by her waist and stood before loosening her rifle strap. She slipped it around over Kirashira's head and under one of her arms before pulling it tight again, giving a small measure more of assurance to the plan. With that she carefully carried the sleeping monarch toward the broken window.

Even as she did so, she heard a yell from down the hall, an order to stop and in that moment she leaned over the edge, Kirashira's extra weight carrying them both out of the window. As Truth felt herself leaving solid ground, she wondered exactly what the two Hil'Raigh had thought on seeing her exit in that way. Shaking the thought from her mind, she focused on holding the Princess tightly enough not to have an unfortunate accident.

The royal's rather small size made it easy to grip her tightly, her weight clocking in about half of Truth's own, something the Novian could easily measure now that they were both in free fall.

Truth, now meters away from the window, willed her wings to open and the suit complied instantly, a loud pop sounding as the magnets energized and the now polarized sheet of wing material deployed between them. The deployment quickly rolled Truth to a position above her cargo.

"I have a radio beacon on, follow it," Tony called over the radio. Truth located it moments later, panning her head to find the vehicle her partner had taken. As if the situation could not get worse, Tony's stolen transport was already causing a ruckus from the police vehicles down below on the Guild Hall grounds. There would only be one chance to intercept it, one chance to live.

Truth raced downward now, her wings sending wordless machine signals of protest to her mind via her interface. They told her she would probably crash at this rate and of course, they were right. Her projected trajectory highlighted eerily, showcasing the fact that she and Princess Kirashira would become a single pancake only twenty or so meters from the edge of the Guild Hall grounds, right in the garden. There was a level of irony to it Truth decided, crashing into the dirt of a serene garden at high speed, but until she missed her partner's vehicle, she decided against further speculation on an impact.

The sight of Tony's stolen car entered the view now however, nearing the trajectory carefully. Truth called out to him again, "I'm relaying the impact location to your HUD."

"Aye," Tony quipped and his vehicle assumed an intercepting path. "You aren't making this easy."

Meter after meter shaved away, quickly and helplessly. Truth fell, with her cargo gripped tightly in her care as she neared the rear of her partner's vehicle.

The limousine broke into a dive as Truth neared and even from this far away it's straining engines were audible over the wind.

The air whipped past as Truth came closer and closer to an untimely end. Within meters now of her partner's vehicle she finally spoke once more, "Thanks for trying."

With that Truth clenched her teeth and tugged heavily to the side, asking her gear for all the assistance it could muster. The maneuver brought her over her wings again, Kirashira plastered to her chest. She curled her torso, trying to make the suit give one last bit of climb. The wings protested loudly and as she rolled. She heard the metal rods disengage as the stresses became too much. After a barrage of malfunction warnings, she willed them closed and, for a second or so more, was in complete free fall once again.

She reflected on the mission thus far, and realized there was room for improvement, probably room for a new partner at this point really. After all, this maneuver would most certainly result in her crash into the ground with precious cargo.

The crash came, but it was not with the dirt of the garden. Truth felt herself connect with the limo suddenly, the extra weight of Kirashira crushing her beneath as the roof itself gave way to her frame. Another half meter followed and Truth felt herself hit hard ground. Almost instantly, her stomach was churned, Kirashira shoving down heavily on her as the vehicle loudly buckled and strained out of it's dive. She felt her body in flames now, all over, but especially her shoulder. She felt crushed against the floor, crushed under Princess Kirashira, feeling like she was being squeezed between two large rocks. Even so, her shoulder dominated the chorus of pain that invaded her body, throbbing with an intensity so virulent that she could scarcely keep her eyes open. She looked up at the stars, hurting everywhere, and finally realized, that perhaps laying here for a while was the best course of action after all.

9 - Joyride

Tony's stolen ride did little to assuage his concerns. The engines had already started sputtering, not meant for such high speed descent. Even so, he aimed the vehicle nose down and watched as the path Truth's systems were relaying to him vanished. The trajectory disappeared from view as a loud thunk sounded from the roof of the vehicle. The feeble sunroof above the passenger compartment punched in behind him like a weak serving plate, upon which were Truth and the apparently royal guest that had come along for the ride with her. The two careened into the open space behind the drivers seat with a deep thud against the once pristine carpet of the limousine. Tony immediately began pulling away from the rapidly approaching ground as he called back to his partner.

There was a mumble but nothing approaching words, until finally, a familiar tone sounded in his ear. Truth's neural interface relayed to him, in an oddly calm fashion, that Truth was currently in no good condition to speak. She would likely require his assistance but she was certainly alive.

With that small assurance in hand, he turned his attention to banking hard and moving toward the nearest gap between skyscrapers. The towering needle-like structures dwarfed his comparatively tiny vehicle and in seconds he had decided on one particular exit from the Guild Hall grounds.

A remote monitor on his dashboard quickly lit up and indicated that the vehicle had been shut down by local law enforcement, or at least, that's what the vehicle thought should have happened. Tony glanced down at the override kit he had plugged into the vehicle's auxiliary port, the same kind the Hil'Raigh authorities equipped on their own vehicles. He looked back to the air ahead and blew out of his lips in a self gratified fashion, even smirking.

Stealing that box had taken longer than it had to get the limo. Thankfully however, someone had left their own patrol vehicle parked in the landing area, ripe for re-appropriation. Tony, benevolent as he was, had opted to steal only the override kit instead of the whole vehicle and its contents. He mused that it had at least saved the assigned driver some of the extra paperwork they would have otherwise had to fill out.

Though he had managed to avoid having his vehicle perform a forced landing once, he was not so sure that a second attempt, with more convincing tools like guns, would not be employed against him and so, he angled into a crevice between buildings.

The traffic lanes were far above and crowded, especially because of the closure of airspace. The ground lanes below were packed as well. Tony illegally strode the line between both, occupying the air normally reserved for ambulances, something his vehicle continued to remind him about with an annoying chirping noise, something he now wanted to disable.

Of course, not even an override kit would allow one to disable such simple safety features since even the police vehicles had to be aware of their airspace. It was something of which Tony was reminded as he fumbled ineffectively through a control menu or two. Finally, he gave up and ignored the sound as best he could.

As he drove, Tony's radio beeped in a distinct pattern. A familiar voice sounded over the link, grizzled and trustworthy. Unfortunately it was a recorded message to which he could not reply.

"Ground Team this is Knight Slayer, we have received the Ambassador's signal, please provide pickup location. Extraction team is underway and will break atmosphere in fifteen minutes."

The message repeated once, then went dead. What Tony would not have given for Truth to be handling that already. Of course, he had no idea what had happened. It was uncharacteristic for her to pass out from exertion and so, he had to assume she had been hurt somehow. He doubted that her current state was the result of crashing through the roof, probably something that had transpired in the Guild Hall. Unable to move to help, he continued piloting, every so often speaking her name and of course, getting the same scripted reply from her interface. At very least, the automated response was not imploring him to seek medical as soon as possible. It gave him some small modicum of assurance that he could make a discreet exit from the center of the city before he was intercepted in force.

It was eerie at times that his partner's mind, even when unconscious, had a way to communicate with the outside world. Well, it was as close to her mind as anything could be, but it wasn't really. At the end of the day it was a computer regardless, one powered by her body but not a natural part of it.

With Truth currently unable to participate in any sort of planning effort, Tony was left to his own devices and his mind considered an array of ideas on exactly where he and Truth were to extract. Of course there was also someone whom Truth claimed was a royal in the rear compartment to consider. Despite his partner's normally accurate assertions, Tony found it hard to believe.

He looked over his shoulder once more trying to get an idea of who she had rescued. The individual was hidden from view for the most part, still collapsed against Truth and as such Tony could not get a look at their face.

Long black hair and a bit of an overdone hairstyle, combined with clothes that appeared at least, extravagant enough to be those of royalty were the only discerning features of the person. Chain earrings like most in the Federation wore hung from golden bands, wrapped around the top and bottom edges of their ears and the tips were capped in gold as well.

Whoever it was at least, was certainly someone of some affluence but if it were a royal it would have had to have been the Starlight Compact's Princess or the Queen. With the stature and build visible it was most certainly a Kul'Raigh rather than a Hil'Raigh frame.

Tony returned his attention from glances and examinations in the rear view mirror to the sky ahead, directing his vehicle as carefully as he was able. He was for all intents and purposes, qualified to pilot this kind of vehicle but he doubted that the Hil'Raigh authorities would have agreed with him on that point. A marginally unsafe lurch around the corner saw to what would have been the revocation of his license if he actually had one.

The first order of business was to decide exactly where the landing zone would be in addition to relaying it to the incoming extraction shuttle. Truth normally would have handled the latter with a bit of extra oomph to her internal radios but Tony lacked such specialized radio implants and as a result, was left wondering whether he should wait for his partner to come to, or whether he wanted to find an appropriate radio beacon somewhere in the city. A large business or other network might have what he was looking for, but the average person did not have radios designed for communication with ships in orbit.

Given that he was unable to proceed with his second objective, Tony opted to aim for a landing zone, one on the border of the city, or at least, outside of the forest of skyscrapers that was the inner section. Like many Hil'Raigh cities, Dau'Kore was layed out in a circular pattern with the inner most of concentric rings being the most densely populated.

Even though the town he and Truth had lived in up to this point, Kolos, was many kilometers from the Guild Hall, it too was considered part of Dau'Kore's metropolitan area. On the outskirts, opposite of Kolos, was the primary spaceport, one of the busiest in the galaxy. That section of the city would be a non option due to the density of people and the accompanying presence of law enforcement. Needing the beacon and knowing that Truth was still unconscious, Tony made a series of moves that took him on a path out of the central rings of the city and toward the seaside town he had come to know.

As he made the course corrections, he heard someone stir in the rear compartment. Taking a glance in the mirror, he was delighted to see Truth moving, albeit little.

"Truth!" he called, "We need a radio..."

She was silent for a moment, undoing her rifle strap which she had apparently wrapped around her cargo's body.

"Right..." She replied groggily. Finally she slipped out from under the guest, leaving the Kul'Raigh laying sideways.

"What happened?" Tony asked as Truth wobbled in a low crouch toward the front seats. At first it looked as if the flight itself were the cause, but as she tipped against the seat next to him before attempting to sit in it, he realized the expression of marked discomfort on her face.

"I was shot," Truth replied, too matter of factly for Tony to immediately absorb the words.

"Shot?" Tony asked, "By a PPR?"

"Yes..." She replied. She collapsed exhaustedly into the seat next to him but leaned forward, her breath heavy. Tony glanced over and got a good look at her shoulder. Her left upper back and the shoulder itself were burned, her skin charred enough that Tony grimaced as he looked at it. She was calm and quiet, even when wounded but the subtle way her fingers curled was one of the many signs Tony had learned over the years to recognize an internal struggle.

"Meds?" Tony asked quickly, reaching with one hand to the pouch at his waist.

Truth shook her head taking a breath, "I used the dampener on myself already, I can't take a second dose yet. It does not work very well when you crash on the wound..."

"Burn spray then.." Tony replied, drawing the appropriate tube from his belt pouch and holding it. With his eyes off the flight for a moment, Tony took the cap off of the spray and squished the small button on top of the silver tube. It responded by putting a cloud of clear spray on Truth's shoulder area. The spray, on contacting her skin began to foam until there was thick layer of it over her burn. Truth huffed, clenching her hands tightly as the froth formed.

"That never feels comfortable," Truth said as Tony finished. A wound such as the one she had suffered was going to take time to recover even after they were extracted. Hil'Raigh weaponry, unlike NovaCore firearms, used magnetically pocketed plasma made mostly from a careful mix of atmospheric gases, or in some cases like vacuum, gas canisters.

Firing the hot bursts of energy meant that they required no physical ammunition except in rare and specialized circumstances. The Hil'Raigh weapons were also quite capable of incapacitating their targets even if they did not outright kill them, through severe burns and painful injury.

Tony himself had never been hit at such close range with one of them, having been skimmed a time or two at ranges that made the impact far less damaging. It also helped that NovaCore military uniforms were treated these days to withstand and distribute the shock and heat of impact.

Unfortunately for Truth however, the close range shot she had taken had easily burned away the limited protection she had been afforded by her quiet kit suit. Unlike normal combat gear, the quiet kits had to skimp on bulk to be easily stowed, and that meant minimal protection.

At this point, Tony guessed Truth would be in recovery for at least a week, which, by modern standards was still quite a short recovery period. In her own standards however, that was quite a bit of time. No matter how many nano-robots were there to assist in treating injury, the process took enough time that someone as active as his partner always felt the sting of being out of action. Truth had quite a number of the things floating around amidst the other ingredients in her veins but as hard working and capable as they were, even the small machines had a considerable amount of cleanup to do under the surface. Tony had to agree that it was for the best that she not be in recovery too long anyway as she usually refused most painkillers. He couldn't blame her for that, not after what she had dealt with before. The past was for another time however, they had a mission to finish first.

"I'm thinking Kolos for an LZ, there are some open spaces on the edge of the town that could make for a relatively discreet landing," Tony said finally, watching the navigation console in the middle of the vehicle's control area.

Truth nodded, "I will send out Kolos as the rough location with the exact position to be determined then. The drop shuttle is close enough for my radio at this point."

Truth closed her eyes for a moment, looking a bit relaxed and after several seconds, she opened them once more.

"Done," She said, "Tentative LZ in Kolos."

"Thanks," Tony replied, adding, "Let's hope we can get out of here with no more gunshot wounds..."

"I hope so," Truth mused, stretching her shoulder and wincing visibly.

"So the Ambassador was dead huh?" Tony asked finally, he had been wanting to but had waited until the more immediate objective was dealt with. Now that they had selected a rough landing zone, the whole town, he felt more comfortable diverting his attention.

"He appeared to have died before I arrived, however the Princess was being held in some fashion by a pair of Hil'Raigh," Truth explained, "I neutralized them both."

Tony nodded, glancing over his shoulder at the passed out royal. That really was the Princess then. He still couldn't believe it.

There was something about royalty, even unconscious ones apparently, that bugged him. Was it the way they lived in such luxury? Was it undue influence? Was it simply that he viewed them as self-centered and self-important? Probably all of those things.

The royal, Princess Kirashira, was entirely helpless now however, something he was forced to admit to himself. He doubted she could threaten anyone very effectively and she certainly did not look old enough to be a head of state. No, she was probably only grown up in half of the ways that mattered. Her face, what he could see of it, was that of someone who had lived a pampered life. She wore clothing with puffy red fur as trim and white expensive cloths in several layers made up the bulk of the robe. Tony had no idea what exactly passed for an expensive form of fabric in the Federation, but managed to catch the glint of subtle embroidered designs, even in the barest looking parts of the robe. Gold made up any clasp or button on the outfit, though it was the workmanship that really counted in this day and age. He did not have the time now to fully classify the clothing but overall it gave him a distinct impression on who he was looking at. She had probably never worked once, and like all good royals, would wake up with a furious case of NovaCore hate that was rivaled only by Akal'Maru Kings.

He shook his head, "You sure we weren't better off leaving her there?"

Even as he spoke, he knew the answer. Of course it was better for his partner to have performed a rescue on the one survivor she had found. He knew that, but even so, his distrust of most things Hil'Raigh finished the sentence for him, despite his moral reservations.

"I assumed she would have been killed," Truth replied, "Given that one of the assailants was carrying what appeared to be a facsimile or genuine NovaCore rifle, coupled with the way many of the guests appeared to have been killed, it seemed prudent to rescue Kirashira."

"NovaCore weapon huh?"

"Yes, a rifle, not unlike yours or mine, an older generation model perhaps." Truth stated darkly.

"So not only is this bad but someone is framing the NovaCore for it? Great," Tony sighed loudly.

"It appears that may be a possibility, though the armament of the two I dispatched may have been mixed... At very least two Hil'Raigh corpses in body armor with weapons will turn up on the Guild Hall grounds soon."

"On the grounds?" Tony was puzzled.

"Both of them were neutralized in cooperation with the window of the hallway I was in..." Truth explained matter of factly.

"That's a rather diplomatic way of putting it," Tony chuckled, "Two Hil'Raigh pancakes in the garden and you word it in such a sanitized way."

Truth shrugged, "It is entirely possible that my neural interfaces and combat sense are still affecting my judgment and word choice..."

Tony nodded, it was not unheard of. Sometimes when Truth was in direct communication with her mind's computerized parts for a while, she seemed slightly more... robotic. It didn't bother Tony at all, but he wondered if she recognized it when it happened. She had certainly become better at avoiding that particular social pitfall in recent years however.

"So what do you think we'll do with the Princess?" Tony inquired genuinely.

Truth looked thoughtfully at her partner, tilting her head, then back at the Princess. She spoke after a moment more, "I do not know yet. I did not think that far ahead."

"Hopefully someone in the Federation will be thankful then," Tony replied, a grim tone taking hold of his voice. With no peace treaty ever signed and with facsimile NovaCore weapons on some of the assailants, the officer doubted that anyone in the Federation would willingly say thanks.

The fact that Truth had already seen evidence that undeniably showed he and his people were going to be framed in some part for it all, made him both frustrated and nervous.

While he himself was not afraid of fighting, he had to admit that many of the early victories the NovaCore had scored in the war with the Federation years ago, were the result of arrogance that had been abandoned in the modern Federation tactic. Not so much that they admitted this to their own people, more so that, to avoid a fiasco like the last time, their military leadership would certainly rely less on confidence and bravado, preferring proven, realistic strategy.

A renewed conflict with the Federation as a whole would most certainly spell a continuation of a long war and undo anything that having an ambassador in the Starlight Compact had established, "Maybe she can help us out in exchange for saving her life..."

The Novian seriously hoped that at very least, even if Kirashira Ren'Tauru ticked all the worst boxes of royalty, that she would have the sense to stop her Federation from witch hunting the people who had saved her life today.

"Let's check LZ 1 to dump this thing," Tony said as he began going over a mental list of all of the pre-screened landing sights he and Truth had observed while living in Kolos. The first of these was a public park not far from the apartment they had rented.

Tony angled the vehicle toward where he remembered the park to be. His memory was true enough, but from the air, Kolos was not as easily recognizable as it was from the ground. The paths he had become used to were not the same here and he searched for a landmark to align himself fully.

After some examination and deceleration, Tony was finally able to catch one of the higher buildings near the apartment complex. Their building was not more than three stories tall and most of Kolos was rather short compared to anything over in Dau'Kore. The closest exception to that rule was a five story apartment building with a set of shops on the first floor. It's unique construction made it stick out even from here, one of the few classically styled brick buildings in town.

The park came into view shortly after the building gave Tony bearings and Truth eagerly leaned toward the window of the vehicle as she looked downward to the semi lit park. At this hour, that particular park was mostly empty, save the few people who would walk through it. It was open though and offered enough unobstructed space that it was a respectable landing zone.

Truth turned to Tony for a moment and shrugged, wincing as she did and leaning forward with a pained expression. She could apparently see no reason why it wouldn't be acceptable. The best landing zone for ditching the limousine.

"What do you think for..." Tony was cut off by a lance of white hot energy streaking past his window. The beam was a bit too hastily fired, something for which he was grateful as he checked his rear view.

"Company!" He said in controlled alarm, "No sirens and shooting first, pretty good bet they aren't official."

Truth sprung into action, or rather, as much action as Tony could have expected. She moved quickly, but there was little she was going to be able to do to counter fire at this point and so he called to her, "Don't bother, I'm setting us down in the park."

Tony dove, the vehicle lurching and its safety alarm chortling in protest. He found a good looking open patch of grass next to one of the paths, a few meters more from that were some trees that could provide good cover from any potential attacks by air, or at least, airborne rifle fire.

Another shot rang out, this one connecting with the limo's hull. Tony felt the controls shudder as the emergency light on the control console blinked to life. One of the engines had been shot.

The descent increased in speed and Tony angled up just enough to shut one set of alarms up. The maneuver lasted long enough for another to begin chiming, this time about being too close to the ground. Normally that was not a problem, but going so fast near the ground was not entirely safe.

Wrestling to regain control, Tony felt one side fighting, the controls increasingly less responsive until the main drive began to sputter. The vehicles engines were all starting to give out and the rear of the vehicle began to limp lower and lower.

It was only a few meters now, and any hope of landing close to where he had planned vanished as the brakes on the limo pretended not to exist.

"Hold on!" He called back to Truth, who was already in motion, dutifully strapping the Princess to one of the couches with a safety belt before buckling herself as well.

Meter after meter vanished until finally, Tony was sure the rear of the vehicle would hit ground. In that instant, he nosed forward and leveled out. There was a rough slam, warning sirens coming on about a myriad number of now non-functional systems, added themselves to the chorus already sounding.

There was an immediate smell, smoldering electronics, rubber, some mixes he couldn't identify. The vehicle slid loudly, roughly, like a boat trying to drive through the grass, tearing up the immaculate landscaping as the gentle sloping ground of the park picked up and set down the fuselage roughly, time and again. A patch of gravel here, a flowerbed, some shrubs, most of it coming over the front of the vehicle as it skidded to a halt. The once proud transport faced almost entirely backward to the path it had come in on. Through the front window, Tony was able to see the ruin that had heralded his arrival here in the park. There was no way anyone who lived adjacent to the space had missed that.

Cursing, Tony unhooked himself from the driver's seat and moved into the rear compartment. He reached down and unbuckled the unconscious Kul'Raigh royal before moving to his kit bag and rifle.

Tony debated fiddling with his medkit and shooting a syringe of something to wake the Princess, into her leg, but Truth was already measuring out a dose of her own.

"What were her wounds anyway?" Tony asked as he drew his rifle. The sound of engines moved overhead once, twice, three times, the last one sounding as if it were circling back.

"I did not fully examine her, she has some minor burns, bruising and several contusions at very least. I do not know about broken bones..."

"Lets hope her legs work," Tony replied, hefting his gear and practically kicking the passenger compartment door off of its hinges as he opened it and shoved it aside. A pop sounded and a boiling pool of melted dirt appeared next to Tony's foot as he stepped out of the ruined vehicle.

The heat had been enough that he'd felt it through his pants anyway. Whoever these people were they were in no hurry to take prisoners and Tony guessed he knew why. Like most royals, Kirashira certainly had a tracking implant somewhere in her body, in case of hostage situations. Most of those were relatively short range but in public, royals had a garment or something else that would act as an antenna. He should have thought of that earlier.

Slapping his rifle on the side, he felt the chamber lock into place and made a feint toward exiting the vehicle again. Another shot came, this one the same as the first, but sizzling at the vehicle's hull above and punching a hole. Molten metal rained down centimeters behind Tony, peppering the passenger couch. The sharpshooter was using a high powered long range rifle. A Hil'Raigh rifle like that had a cool down period long enough for a return shot.

Even as his brain consciously processed the information, he had leaned out of the door, his rifle to his shoulder and sight picture finding near instantly, the offending vehicle. Clicking the trigger, Tony felt his rifle lurch, then pop, more violently than the Hil'Raigh weapon had when firing at him. The angle was clear enough and Tony guessed that the engine noise meant the craft was hovering instead of moving.

A bright line traced the rails of his rifle, connecting to the target in an instant. Metal fragments and a shower of anything not tied down to the hood of the vehicle came spraying away and it dipped wildly from its hovering position.

The shot sent the Hil'Raigh sharpshooter's own continued fire wide and Tony took advantage of that fact to trigger a second round. This one burst through one of the obvious engine nacelles on the hostile vehicle. Returning in kind, the favor the shooter had given him initially, Tony clicked off a third and fourth round. The nacelle was already disintegrating from the first shot, the wildly lurching vehicle finding itself riddled with two more holes. The two followups sprayed violent fragments throughout the front compartment of the vehicle and Tony ducked back inside as he saw a gout of flame erupt from the damaged engine.

"If you want to shoot at me you make it count," He muttered to himself as he looked over to his partner. Truth had coaxed the Princess back to relative consciousness and she had the look of a scared animal. She seemed at a loss before her eyes finally seemed to focus.

A loud crash sounded meters away, the unfortunate, probably pilot less vehicle Tony had taken down, making its own landing pad amid the once pristine park.

The moment the Princess regained any semblance of real thought however was clear; she immediately struggled and tried to run.

The Kul'Raigh squirmed and rolled off of the couch with a small thud, betraying how little she probably weighed. She scurried a bit before Tony finally called to her.

"Stop right there," He ordered sternly.

The frightened, shuddering Kul'Raigh clutched her apparently bruised midsection through her fanciful robe, her eyes darting frantically over Tony and then back to Truth.

"What are you doing to me..." she whimpered.

The engines of two more vehicles got more prominent and in seconds Tony guessed there would be landed company.

"You want to live don't you?" He retorted, poking his head out the door. It was clear for now, there was no movement at the other vehicle's crash sight. "Get rid of your homing antenna, now!"

"Princess, please, we are trying to help you..." Truth began from inside the vehicle, "I promise, we will not hurt you."

"Let me go..." The royal tried to scurry past Tony and out of the vehicle, she was a quick one. Already in the doorway, blocking her was simple enough, but Tony knew he would be annoyed if that continued.

"You wanna go get shot go right ahead you imbecile..." Tony said impatiently, "But there's no way in hell I'm letting that happen until you make saving you worth while..."

The Princess froze as Tony stared her down. She had probably never been threatened like that before. Was it a threat? Not really, not to Tony, but her sudden attention told Tony that whatever he had said had struck a chord.

"Princess," Truth was still calmly trying to reason. "Your homing antenna, please take it off and leave it here..."

"Maybe you should've let her stay unconscious, a sack of potatoes would be easier to carry than a finicky royal..." Tony said to Truth as he stepped out of the vehicle.

Truth began coaxing the Princess inside the vehicle as Tony exited. He swore he was not going to let that damn royal get his partner into anymore trouble than she already had. Being shot at had the immediate effect of making him value prudence and action, something the Princess was certainly inhibiting right now.

Finally though, the royal emerged from the vehicle, sans a single bracelet that probably contained her homing antenna. With that device gone, it would be slightly easier to run.

After she exited, Truth followed, laboriously carrying her rifle. It was clear the way she held the weapon that she was going to have to fire it with her non dominant hand. Thankfully her implants and the like made ambidexterity in combat easier than it was for Tony himself.

"Come on," Tony said to his newly acquired charge. She eyed him, then began to follow. Tony led the way forward toward the nearest bank of buildings. The closest landing zone other than the current one was some minutes away and with no way to verify what kind of weapons the enemy possessed, bringing the drop shuttle here was not an option.

"What do you think of finding a new LZ for the shuttle? If the hostiles have these here already, who knows if they have something heavier on the way."

"Open spaces? The marina might work..." Truth replied.

The idea was sound enough. The boat club where he and Truth had rented their boat days ago was open to the air, with plenty of space. It was of course, a bit of a soft landing since most of the space was simply the oceanic surface. There were only a few adequately sized places on land and the docks themselves were too small to support the weight of a drop ship, unless of course it was hovering.

"Call up the shuttle, the marina docks. Tell them to get to the long L shaped dock on the south end..." Tony finally instructed, recalling the layout of the place, "It's gonna be a hover landing, use the rear ramp."

"Affirmative," Truth replied. She looked like she was concentrating but now instead of closing her eyes she moved with Tony and the Princess.

Tony glanced over his shoulder at the would be monarch trailing behind and though she was following she looked flighty nonetheless. A few good shots at the trio from their pursuers would probably determine whether she was immediately killed or decided to play it safe with her rescuers. He hoped at least for his partner's sake, that she would do the latter, given that Truth had already been injured on the Princess' behalf.

Of course, not being shot at would have been preferable to any of what was going on right now, but there were no complaint departments in a firefight. Based on the pursuit force having three vehicles and only one of them going for fancy trick shots from the air, Tony guessed that the remainder would likely split up. The vehicles would remain airborne eyes, with a gunner at most, while a non determinant number of boots were put on the ground.

If Tony were in their position he would have one group land and be a pressure element on the rear of his pursuit target. That group would also check on the wreck of their allied vehicle and render aid. That meant it's forward motion would be retarded, possibly halted until the second element, a flanking element, moved in to cut off the assumed path of travel for the pursuit target.

Tony played out the scenario in his mind and turned, remaining in the park and finding a small rise in the ground. It was enough of a vantage point that he found a target in the leg of one of the freshly arrived mercenaries. The man had slung his rifle on his shoulder to begin digging into his comrade's wrecked vehicle. As Tony had predicted, even the mercs started with helping their comrades.

Thankfully, the rough parking job Tony had been forced to employ had put them amidst enough foliage that he got a quick shot at the man he had spotted before any of his comrades could react.

The shot was glancing, Tony having aimed to wound. The grazing strike was enough to incapacitate the target but require aid to be given. Even a grazing wound by a rifle like the one Tony was using was enough to ensure that medical attention would have to be present. It would tie up at least one more pursuer and there was still the matter of potential crash survivors. The wound all but assured that the current crop of adversaries was not going to be giving chase anytime soon.

A single return shot met the embankment as Tony dropped behind it reflexively. Truth and Kirashira had already hunkered down, out of view.

"Tied up most of the pursuit element, let's move," Tony said quietly, making deliberate use of the Hil'Raigh language to make it easier for the guest to understand.

Truth gestured forward and Tony began on his way, having now chosen a new path out of the park. He couldn't currently hear any airborne vehicle engines and that meant that they were either far away or high enough to be unheard. Either of those options was likely to result in continued conflict but Tony decided he preferred the latter. At very least if the vehicles were up high they were avoidable.

Skirting the edge of the park, a place accessible only by foot from a ring of apartments and a nearby plaza, was not an ideal movement situation. Local residents were to be already roused from their night time routine by the sounds of crashing vehicles and it was only a matter of time before some well meaning fool inserted themselves into the thick of things.

"Why are you bringing me with you?" The Princess finally inquired, it was a timid inquiry but given the situation, an unexpected one. The trio moved in silence for a moment more as the question hung in the air before Tony finally paused at the edge of a building. He poked around the edge, examined the intended path forward and moved on. Truth followed on the rear and the Princess stumbled along between them.

"Well, if your police were any good they'd already be on top of us," Tony replied, "You heard any sirens yet? How about badges or a 'Lay down your weapons and surrender'?"

There was silence in reply and so, Tony continued, "The people chasing us, or, probably you, don't seem to be too worried about the police. That means, you should be more worried about them than us."

The way forward was clear enough, Tony sticking to the sides of the more narrow alleys of the town as he led onward. It would be several minutes of tense careful movement, sticking to shadows where possible and hoping he could lead the trio to the marina before the drop shuttle actually made its final approach.

The approaching NovaCore ship would wait unless waived off, and that was the biggest reason for his renewed pace down the alley. That would make them vulnerable to attack as long as they were loitering.

The smaller paths here in Kolos were lined with one or two story buildings, most of them in traditional construction. Wood paneling and slanted roofs were all the rage here and that made each one of the many exteriors they passed blend together in memory.

If one was not paying attention, the maze like side streets of Kolos' densely packed construction would have made it seem like one big circle. The layouts of entry ways, the punctuations of small landscaping bushes and sometimes a high privacy fence of brick and metal, broke an otherwise uniform set of buildings into discrete sections.

Kolos, like any Federation town of size was lacking in open space. Yards were almost non existent and so ruining the park as the Novian had earlier meant that at least some group of people were soon to have a disruption in their life.

Most plant life in Kolos probably occupied planter boxes, especially alleys like this and it made each entry way a sort of contest for owners to see how much personality they could cram into the limited space. Apartment building, residence or randomly placed family owned store, none of them shied away from the competition of appearance.

During the day it all seemed inconsequential, but now at night, under pressure, each nook and cranny, every variation had to be examined and assessed. Thanks to the tightness of the alleys an ambush would be easy even from the ground, and that didn't include looking at the edges of rooftops. Thankfully, he had Truth who, despite her injury was undeterred from keeping herself alert.

The pair had always been good at noticing potential problems or spotting danger when together and Tony hoped that training and practice would pay off once more. They always did, but when he was in the thick of it, he rarely believed that those were enough to win the day. He was right in a sense, after all, practice alone without wit and experience kept someone weaker than those who possessed the latter. Combining all three was the only way to be assured of success.

Another turn, Truth quietly notifying him, wordlessly via radio, of which ways to go for the best route to the marina. It was a simple process but each corner was checked and rechecked before he led the way out of cover and to the next place. He hated continuous movement like this at times, especially when out numbered. Sometimes he felt the need to stop in a shadow and look. At those times, he did, taking in his surroundings carefully before moving.

The alleys were dark enough that aside from the occasional porch light most of them were adequately concealing but one could never be too sure. From shadow to shadow, sliding along walls the trio moved on. The Princess was already looking far more winded than Tony had expected from a royal. Perhaps it was due to her injuries.

Either way, when he heard the familiar whine of vehicle engines move overhead not twice, but once, he froze in the shadows. The pursuers were probably still sweeping by air before dropping any more people off. The single set of engines gave him confidence that his delaying action earlier had been fruitful and based on the size of the vehicles that had been pursuing earlier, he guessed that three or four were the most that the remaining vehicle would be dropping off if it indeed found a place to put them.

If Tony were in their position, he would have kept his people on board until he was certain that putting them down was going to net him a gain against his target. Since the vehicle had as yet, not appeared to locate the trio, he assumed that they were doing the same.

Unfortunately, no matter how many meters more of cover he had, once they reached the larger roads they would have to cross to exit the current city block, whatever cover they had would be stripped away. That brief exposure would be enough for an astute crew of whoever was giving chase, to identify their targets. Though he had been able to dispatch their sharpshooter with relative ease, he guessed that a squad at once was going to test he and his partner both. Without injury and unhindered by someone requiring escort, there was definitely no possibility of a fair fight with a squad, the enemy wouldn't stand a chance. As long as a VIP was in the mix however, the chances of things going horribly wrong were high enough that Tony hoped to avoid more shooting.

There was still the matter of Kirashira's tracking implant however. Even without it's antenna there was a good chance it was potent enough to attract attention from an astute observer if they got close enough. As a result, every time Tony heard the vehicle making a pass, he wanted to break into a run.

The tension, pass after pass, over inconsequential or already explored space by the vehicle above, came to a head finally as the trio met a ground road. Though mag-lev vehicles were uncommon at this hour, being run into by one was still a possibility as was being seen crossing the pathway.

"I'll go first, when I reach the other side, send her after me," Tony stated carefully, examining the sky both ways down the road.

It was as clear as he could have hoped and in moments he was in a speedy run across the expanse. He felt exposed, vulnerable, silly even, for breaking cover like that, but it was the only way to cross the space. He ended up in a relatively shadowy position and called to Truth via radio.

The royal waiting with Truth finally hunkered down. She scurried forward more timidly than Tony had hoped. Her progress was slow and worthy of being spotted. Thankfully it appeared that the vehicle had not come by this road as the obvious monarch took enough time in her crossing that Tony could have run across and returned before she herself had made the trip one way.

Finally, Truth followed, she began at a speed that made Tony a bit jealous. Even injured, she could still outrun him. As she neared the near side of the road however, Tony spotted the one thing he hoped not to see. The vehicle of their pursuers, one of them at least, was skirting the same road, and only a hundred or so meters down wind at present. The engines were barely audible here but an abrupt course change, followed by rapid descent into parts in the next city block told Tony enough.

Truth must have noticed the vehicle too, gaining more speed but it was already too late. It was now a race against the pace of their pursuers.

"We're running, you are keeping up." Tony informed the Princess as he began moving now at a jog. The corner checks were faster the movement less patient and overall Tony felt his hair standing on end. There was a clear tension now, a renewed enemy, one with eyes in the sky. The tightness that came with a surge of adrenaline found his muscles, his chest constrained and his grip on his weapon becoming more and more like a vice. Every corner was taken at a quick pace, one practiced and tactical. With his rifle scope leading the way, Tony was ready to fell any target foolish enough to find itself there.

The motion of the trio was now more dire, filled with purpose. It would be only moments before the pursuing foot soldiers caught up, at least if the Novians and their VIP were too slow. A good pace would keep the enemy guessing.

For now, Tony avoided a direct path to the marina, hoping that he could not only close distance but throw the enemy off of their intended destination long enough to break across. They were only blocks away now, one or two. The narrow streets of Kolos were going to slow the pursuit. True, that also made his own forward progress slower but he hoped that it was having equal affect on both he and those pursuing.

Of course, the enemy had an advantage, something airborne. The rush of the engines from the very same vehicle sounded again, only a few streets away now. It sounded as if it was rising into the air, meaning it had dropped some measure of its crew off.

"How long until the drop shuttle gets here?" Tony asked. He hoped that perhaps the arrival of the NovaCore drop ship would either put the vehicle into retreat or, if need be, provide the power to shoot it down without remaining exposed. After the trick Tony had pulled before, this pilot was probably not going to give him an easy time, floating perfectly still for an overconfident sharpshooter.

"Not long, they are on final," Truth replied, sounding a bit ragged. Tony looked over his shoulder to his partner and her fatigue was clear enough. She was fading fast, trying her best to keep it together long enough to extract. A mix of gratitude and apprehension filled Tony as he turned his attention once more, to crossing a street, one closer to the marina now.

His gratitude was for his partner's will, her strength and the power she had to keep going. Apprehension came because he wondered, even if he did not want to admit it, how long she would be able to last. Most people didn't walk after being shot with a PPR and a throbbing rigorous heartbeat would make the burned area flare up painfully.

Sweat dripped from his own brow, Truth had her share, more than usual and the Princess, well, the Princess was holding her own, despite Tony's initial judgment of her fitness. Of course, she was not wearing a combat harness or a quiet kit, nor was she carrying any firearms. She could at least keep up with the slowest combat withdrawal Tony had ever conducted, but he'd expected less and so, couldn't complain too much.

One corner, then another, a house and a doorway, a check here, a sight picture there. The checks kept coming, the corners kept arriving and Tony kept poking, then moving past them until finally, across the street he saw the fence of the marina dock. The office of the establishment was a three story affair, hosting a bistro on the first floor. The location of the marina next to one of Kolos' boardwalks did wonders for the place, or at least that's what Tony had been told by the owner days ago.

The facility was closed at this hour but as Tony rushed up to the wall, he hoped that the anytime pass he had been given for being a friend of A'Shir really worked like it had been claimed. Even as he reached the wall, meters ahead of his party, he heard the engines of the pursuing vehicle flare from above and behind. It was not stopping, just keeping eyes on target. He beckoned to his partner and the Princess as he shuffled through the pocket of his pants. He was grateful that he had shoved his wallet into this pair when he and Truth had changed.

Finally, his hands found the shape of the marina gate key and he slapped the plastic card against the reader with rough intent. A moment passed, a long moment given the circumstance, before the light blessedly turned green and the gate popped open at one end, sliding along the rollers in the roadway. An automated message proceeded to let Tony know he was required to put in a call to the dock house attendant before he'd be allowed to actually remove a boat from the wharf but he had already run inside.

One by one his party moved past the gate inside and finally, he moved for the control mechanism on the inside, if he could close the gate then it would effectively lock the enemy out.

A blaze of PPR fire lit up the ground ahead. A spray of white hot bursts melting neat holes in a chaotic pattern and setting the concrete surface of the roadway into disarray. The heat and the smell were enough to clearly indicate that it was indeed fire, but it took a second for Tony to realize that the vehicle pursuing them from the air had at least one gun toting person inside. If Truth were uninjured, she probably could have hit the vessel with her rifle enough to force it off but with her injury...

Another burst found Tony nearly out of cover and he dove for a set of boxes near the path normally reserved for arriving vehicles. The shipping containers were small affairs, neatly stacked. Each was a cubic meter or so in size and they made a passable pile of defensive cover, though not ideal. Some more plasma singed through and Tony quickly began searching for a more permanent place to hide. Unlike the previous shooter, this one kept fire up at random, with a large magazine in their weapon and an apparently good thermal manager. Given the volume of fire, this was a squad automatic or some other variant, dangerous, especially without cover.

A glance told him that Truth had managed to get Kirashira into cover meters away, amid a rack of out of service watercraft and as Tony heard a lull in the fire, Truth bent around the cover and took a loosely aimed shot at the vehicle as it slowed for another pass. The shot grazed the hull, a loud metal din sounding, but didn't appear to do any critical damage because the spray came without interruption in response.

A few seconds more however, a swiss cheese of cover now forcing Tony to his stomach before finally, the craft pulled away, probably to let the gunner reload. The small gap in fire meant that Tony would have to move and probably, that the enemy foot soldiers were reaching the gate already. Getting to the pier here would be hard, there was no cover.

A volley of semi automatic fire began grazing Truth's position and Tony took the chance to fire some hasty shots as he broke from his own. There were a trio of bodies entering the complex, moving and spreading to their positions with practiced efficiency. One moved, the others covered in good form and tactic. Whoever it was had certainly received some good training, at very least from a PMC or state military. Their motion made Tony lean toward the former rather than the latter but he was never completely sure when it came to the Hil'Raigh.

A battle of suppressive fire was not something he and Truth would win at this rate. The enemy had an air asset and more guns in play, likely more ammunition as well. The firing rate of the railguns was good enough to keep heads down, or blow them off even behind some cover, but the shots had to be placed well and these shooters kept moving. At very least they knew they were fighting NovaCore.

Even as one of them went for an ill fated flanking maneuver, Truth evened the score with a loud crack from her rifle. She was a meter or so away, with the royal nearby. The boats had covered her well enough but the ruined boxes Tony had already abandoned had not protected the Hil'Raigh who had scrambled to them to push forward.

A disturbing thunk sounded for a fraction of a second and no one emerged from behind the boxes afterward, evening the body count. That was of course until the renewed whine of the airborne gun came back into play.

A withering hail of fire resumed, probably a high capacity energy cell this time, the firing rate was as dizzying as before, at least fifteen shots a second now. The fire, though not ruinous to the boat hulls shielding Tony and his partner alone, began to eat away at the metal, molten hunks of it streaming down the expensive water craft's sides as they were pierced by deadly plasma. It didn't take long for a shot here or there to tear through but there was little either Tony or Truth could do. Tony was now being focused by the incoming fire from the remaining ground team and Truth's shot from before had certainly made the gunner angry, he focused her position with intent.

Tony tensed, if the vehicle was not driven off it would mow down Truth and the Princess in a few more seconds, exposing to fire at it would be suicide. He made the choice and double checked his rifle, mentally steeling himself before he rushed around the corner. Back to cover, he took some deep breaths, probably the last full lungs of air he would have.

He hesitated, instead of running out in a single instant he paused. He wondered even as he stood against the cover why he was not moving. He glanced over to Truth and nothing had changed. He stared for what seemed like an eternity until finally he realized why his body had stopped him in the first place.

The rescue tone was playing on his radio. A repeating pattern broadcast to NovaCore radios when an evacuation ship was on station. It was an anthem really, a song that had never once failed to rally or uplift those it was meant to inspire. No one gave up when they heard that song, no one. But the song, the tone, it didn't come alone.

A high whine filled the air and in seconds the sounds of devastating fire from the enemy craft were overwhelmed by the sounds of it's hull being ripped to pieces mercilessly. Rapid explosions, so many they were innumerable, sounding like an infinite chain, one so tightly packed that it almost blended into one single monotone cacophony.

There was a loud crash as what had to be the enemy ship's remains came to an end somewhere in the marina. There was a pop and the acrid smell of fire followed soon after. Whoever was chasing them had not counted on this.

Tony looked out to where the saving sound had come from and, growing ever larger, the undeniable shape of a NovaCore drop shuttle greeted him. It was practically sliding sideways through the air as it barreled toward the pier. The ship descended rapidly, its rear ramp open and down already. Inside a single figure manning a defensive weapon began a new bead.

The fire started again, a hyperactive whine, the sound made by the streams of fire coming from the gun. Tony loved the sound, it was the sound of salvation, one deliberately engineered for psychological impact both on behalf of the NovaCore and against anyone unfortunate enough to be caught in the wake. The suppressive bursts halted any return fire that the two remaining foot soldiers had to give and now they had presumably hunkered down, praying for life.

The tide had turned now, and as Tony looked to Truth she was already in motion, wasting no time. She coaxed, then finally shoved and pulled Kirashira along, the royal so shell shocked at the sudden firefight that she had no faculty left for movement. Truth moved to the edge of the dock, where the shuttle was settling.

The rear ramp had come to rest barely on the edge of the dock and Truth dragged the bewildered looking Princess up inside the ship, even as Tony broke cover and began a quick jog toward it. The radio chatter from the flight crew came in clear, all Novian.

The meters vanished rapidly as Tony finally felt his feet hit metal. Even as he passed the door gunner he felt the shuttle lurch heavily and lean forward as the engines kicked on. The rear ramp began retracting quickly afterward.

"I owe you a drink," Tony called to the gunner. He then looked to Truth who sat beside the medical alcove further inside the main compartment even as the flight surgeon began to look her over. Kirashira was plopped in front of a medic of her own and despite her look of shock and denial, seemed relatively unharmed. As missions went, Tony decided, that was far from the worst one he had been on.

Even so, the NovaCore Ambassador had been killed and, based on what they had encountered here in Kolos, the body count of the night was far higher than just the Ambassador. The Princess had been alone, what about the rest of the royalty, what about the rest of the nobles that had been there tonight? Whoever had accomplished the attack, had, at least in part, succeeded in undermining every peace that the Starlight Compact had known until today and Tony guessed that they were only getting started.

10 - Welcome Home

The shuttle rattled one final time as it came to rest. The rear ramp cracked a moment later and began lowering slowly, opening the inside of the ship to the much larger space outside. The air here was metallic, almost to the point where Tony could taste it compared to the planet below. At very least he had to admit the environment on board a starship was far different from that on Ashor.

The ramp finally settled down, completely open. Tony stood and headed to exit, following Truth. Her shoulder looked no better than it had a while ago but the flight surgeon had a larger supply of anti-infection compound for her burn at least. Her discolored flesh was clearly visible through the artificial layer of skin that now covered the area. Her unremarkable sport bra was all the covering that remained on her upper body at this point and Tony hefted her rifle alongside his own. The rest of her quiet kit and damaged glider suit had been put into one of the duffel bags he began to lug after her. Their footfalls rang hollow on the ramp of the drop shuttle as finally, Tony was once again on solid ground. Solid enough at least.

The docking bay was a large structure, many stories tall. It was a long rectangular room on both ends, but constricted near the middle where the docking control tower was set into the wall. On the outer side of the room a series of armored door locks kept the atmosphere inside away from the vacuum of space, at least when the plasma fields were offline. Through the gap between the halves of the bay, was a mirrored setup, the same as this one.

The tower was in the middle of the bay wall, with a series of windows overlooking the mechanical clamps and hanging gantries that serviced this destroyer's complement of smaller support vessels and the limited strike craft it carried. On the deck floor, were the heavier or more often used ships, in this case, drop shuttles, all assigned to their own landing pads.

Even as Tony and the flight crew stepped away, the support crew for the shuttle had already begun their post flight inspection and were in the process of checking the outer hull for damage. They had heard there was a firefight and of course, had to make sure there were no potential hazards lying in wait as a result.

The shuttle bore a heavy fuselage with a set of delta wings at the top edge that ran most of the length. Double tail fins extended from the rear most portion, over the access ramp and a set of boxy variable position engines made their homes within the wings themselves. They were currently stowed inside for space flight and landing in the mothership. Tony had always admired these shuttles, maybe because they were the ships usually bailing people like him out of trouble when the time came.

"Come on out," Truth called to the figure poised on the edge of the ramp. Princess Kirashira stood, confused, coaxed a bit by the flight surgeon from behind and finally, by Truth's voice. It was likely because Truth was the only person speaking Hil'Raigh to her but Tony was not completely sure.

"We're going to see a doctor, okay?" Truth added as Kirashira closed the distance. She stayed close to Truth, closer than she was to anyone else at least. Her eyes glanced around the bay quickly and she seemed willing to exit the shuttle. Tony doubted it was because she felt more comfortable outside. Having lived a life of authority and power, it was probably quite jarring for the royal to find herself on board a NovaCore ship, especially one she did not know existed until she'd set foot on it.

That at least, was understandable. She was in a completely foreign place. She had asked where she was being transported and Truth had taken it upon herself to explain that the drop shuttle was taking the entire group to a safe place. She did however neglect to mention it was starship. It was entirely possible therefore, that the royal thought she was on a space station. She could not have missed the view from the drop shuttle's admittedly small windows, the blackness of space was too distinct, but then again, she could have never bothered looking out the side that would have shown her the planet below.

How far of an orbit, Tony didn't know, but based on how long the ascent had taken, he guessed it was something bordering on geosynchronous. The planet Ashor was now quite a ways down and any chance that the Princess' pursuers would find her had vanished the moment that the NovaCore drop shuttle had broken atmosphere.

Like all NovaCore starships, this one was probably operating as quietly as possible in orbit, nearly undetectable to those on the ground and hard enough to find even if one had the right tools to look for it. Tony didn't understand all of the technologies completely but had read about some of the engineering challenges associated with trying to hide a ship like this in space. Regardless, he was clear on one fact, the ship was safer than any place he had been for weeks.

"I'll meet you two in the infirmary in a few minutes I guess," Tony said to his partner, noticing a uniformed officer approaching.

The officer wore the standard black and red uniform of a NovaCore command officer. Gold trim and buttons completed the look of the long tailed jacket and its wide cuffs while a dark crimson sash hung from the man's right shoulder. His pants had a smooth crease with a long red stripe up the side. A red belt with a golden buckle split the ensemble in half and a billed officer's cover indicated the man was more than just Naval command, but part of the Admiralty, a selection of Admirals that made up the NovaCore ruling body.

Tony dropped his two duffel bags and saluted immediately, Truth bowing instead as he acknowledged her, "Get to the infirmary Truth, you look like hell."

"Sir," She nodded and moved on, bringing the royal with her.

The man turned his attention to Tony next, approaching and calling to him, "Major."

He returned Tony's salute.

"You heard about the Ambassador I'm guessing?" Tony replied.

The man nodded grimly, pulling off his black hat and tucking it under his arm.

He had short crew cut hair, mostly gray, and a face that told a story. It was not a scarred face, not a rough face, but one that had lived. The man had always had that look, as long as Tony could remember. He had never been one to look like he'd aged in all the years that the Major had known him. His eyes were a brown color and the lines in his forehead and around his mouth gave clues to the stresses, and perhaps joys, that had made up his years.

"I heard, but I have some bad news for you both. King Ren'Tauru was confirmed dead about a half hour ago by authorities on Ashor. It just came over the net and I expect Federation news to be carrying it within the hour..."

Tony paused. He had guessed it was possible, given the state that Truth had found the Princess in but a confirmation of the ruler's death was confirmation of a host of problems on the horizon.

"His wife is assumed dead and the Princess is assumed missing..." The officer sighed, running his hand through his hair.

"No good news for you today huh Admiral?" Tony asked.

The man scoffed, "I don't know whether to be glad or... worried, that we now have a Hil'Raigh royal on-board. Worse yet she is the only child that King Ren'Tauru had and that makes her the sole heir to his throne, legally at least."

"Not a good position to be in for either of us I guess," Tony shrugged.

"I already sent a dispatch to the Admiralty, this is going to require their input."

The NovaCore's primary executive body, the Admiralty, was a set of the best leaders the NovaCore had to offer. Each of them had long, distinguished service records and all were well respected. Even so, Tony doubted that the select group would have an easy time with the new Federation problem.

At very least, having Admiral Thorsh here meant that the mission was in good hands. Tony had a deep respect for the man, probably because he had been given unique access to him over the years. It was not common for someone in Tony's position to know one of the Admiralty on a first name basis but the rare exception had followed their relationship since they had met long ago.

Thorsh had been one of the first NovaCore officers that Tony had met, aside from doctors and support staff at least. It had left its mark and thanks to his continued involvement in Tony's program through the years, the two had grown to know each other better than would have been expected by most NovaCore citizens.

Thorsh was a staunch supporter of his people, his nation, and took his responsibility very seriously, like all of the Admiralty. For Tony at least, admiring the primary executive body was easy when it was made up of people like Thorsh and built on a strong tradition of loyalty toward the NovaCore. Imperfect as they were, each were selected for the positions they held by serious considerations from their peers, a process that took months.

Each appointment was made for a five year period and the nine admirals serving were appointed in such a way as to stagger the replacements or re-appointments, keeping the council fresh and dynamic while also retaining the valuable experience that each member had accumulated over time.

Now, Admiral Thorsh was poised for what would likely be one of his most politically charged command's in history, dealing with the Starlight Compact as it was brought low by the loss of its leadership. Ironically, one of the other members of the Federation, the Sho'Alar State, had lost its own king not more than a decade before and with him his two sons. The whole situation was billed as a horrible accident, some kind of ship crash, but now, Tony was not so sure about it. A regent had ruled the place for as long as Tony had been out of the academy and now that possibility seemed entirely too plausible with the Compact.

"I need to run by the armory sir," Tony announced calmly, "With your permission of course."

"I'll walk with you then. We've got plenty to discuss in the coming days." The man replied gravely.

"I was just thinking how this seemed too similar to Sho'Alar years ago..." Tony mused, glancing to the Admiral as he led the way.

The man sighed and nodded, "I thought the same, it seems a bit odd but I don't want to draw any hard links just yet...."

"Of course. What do you think we are going to end up doing with the Princess?" Tony asked.

"She will have to stay here for a while if she's going to be safe…." Thorsh said, he looked a bit concerned as he spoke, and for good reason. He continued, "I doubt she's going to want to stay either..."

"I think you are right, once she gets out of… whatever daze she's in..."

The two moved now through one of the main access-ways to the docking bay, a wide hallway, of three meters, flanked on one side by the armory and the other by a locker room for pilots and flight crews. Tony turned toward the armory door, giving a glance to the watch posted outside as he ran his wrist over the reader near it. The small panel beeped and the door receded sideways into the wall.

The inside of the armory was empty save the large preparation tables near the door and a selection of weapon lockers lining the far wall. On a ship like this the compliment of marines was large enough that about half of the armory was already spoken for. Tony and Truth had their own set of lockers on the wall closest the prep tables. In one corner of the room rested the sighting and tuning equipment for rifles and other firearms while the opposite corner hosted the enhancement printer. The rest of the space was taken up by general quarters equipment, the kind of tools a desperate crew mounting a last ditch effort would use when it came time to put it all on the line. Though this was not the only armory on the ship, it was the only one for marines and guest personnel.

Tony stepped inside and headed right, the Admiral following after he gave the door guard a greeting. It was a small gesture, another quirk that made Tony like the Admiral; the fact that he took the time when he didn't have to.

As a member of the intelligence division, Tony was not required to engage most of the naval crew at all except if he was addressing them directly. It was a general assumption that the intelligence operatives who were stationed on ships would usually be too busy to uphold all of the standard protocols. The same went for the Admiralty, at least generally speaking. Thorsh apparently liked to find ways to add his own touch to the job, even if it was a little unorthodox at times.

Tony headed to Truth's locker and keyed the memorized combination for it as he set her duffel bag down. Each locker used a combination of a predetermined code and an authorization scan to ensure that legitimate access was enforced. Both Tony and his partner had made sure their lockers were keyed to work on either one of their transceivers and both had memorized each other's combinations.

"How long do you think we can keep her up here before things go too far down hill?" Tony asked, glancing to the Admiral as he pulled a wing suit from the duffel he carried. He spread out the damaged harness on the table next to the locker and dug into the bag afterward. An unused ammo box went to the table for later storage but finally Truth's sidearm came. Tony checked the magazine well, then clicked the trigger once in the safety can on the table before slipping it into it's holder in Truth's locker.

"I'm not sure, but I am guessing they will have a Federation Council meeting over it. I would guess that if we kept her much longer past that point we would be risking worse problems than simply returning her to the Hil'Raigh."

"They won't like it either way..." Tony replied with a scoff, "They are Hil'Raigh after all."

The Admiral chuckled half halfheartedly and rolled his eyes, "Don't I know it. If we could convince her that this was for her own benefit, it would certainly go a long way toward making this easier for both of us..."

"Why don't we just return her quickly?" Tony asked, "If it's going to be such a problem I mean.."

"If we put her back now she's as good as dead," Thorsh replied, "And even though she's not a member of the NovaCore, I think even your cynicism wouldn't tolerate sending her to certain death so haphazardly."

Tony nodded, the Admiral had a point. Truth's rifle magazine came next, on the table, then the butt of her rifle was opened. Tony stripped the power cells from inside and set the case of them on the table too. She had fired the weapon several times, according to her report. He glanced inside the magazine, confirming the rounds were missing and then double checking the power cells, found the same number of discharge indicators. Satisfied, he placed the rifle carefully into Truth's locker before replying to the Admiral's assertion, "Right about that, even a Hil'Raigh Royal deserves better than what happened to her...."

Tony trailed off, her parents were apparently gone, all in one night even. Even if she had a number of friends, none of them would be able to replace her family, not really. It was a hard thing to see, Tony had to admit; watching someone lose their family. He had never had his own parents to lose, but he had seen those of his people who had. He never knew quite how to help, what to say, always feeling lost because it was a loss he could not understand completely. He did know however, that he did not like seeing his people go through it and he decided, that even if Princess Ren'Tauru was not one of his own, she could at least have that sympathy given.

"I think we need to give her a reason to feel safe here Tony," The Admiral stated plainly, "And I think you and Truth are the ones that can do the most toward that end."

Tony snickered, "You mean befriend a royal? I think you have me pegged for someone else sir."

"I'm asking you to give it a try at least," Thorsh responded, "No one on this ship fully understands what she is going to go through and I don't think anyone else has the time to try and learn..."

"Right," Tony shrugged, He would try, it was only fair, but he could make no promises. He had a habit of rubbing people the wrong way when he thought they were entitled and selfish. Hopefully the Princess would turn out to be more than a stereotypical royal. If not, then helping her feel welcome would be rather challenging, "I'll give it a shot, but I think Truth is the better candidate for this..."

"Really?" Thorsh smirked, "And here I thought you were the one who could befriend anyone if you wanted to."

"You know that was different, I was just a kid..."

"And now Truth is your best friend.... I'm not saying I don't think you can do this Major, but perhaps I finally found you a challenge you can't handle," The Admiral chuckled heartily and Tony rolled his eyes. The man certainly knew how to prod him to work harder.

"Maybe I'll prove your assumption right this time, just to be contrary..." Tony said halfheartedly.

"I bet you'll try.." the older man shrugged off the comment and sighed, "I'll be heading back to the intel board down near command deck if you need me, but otherwise, I would like to have you and Truth submit your debriefing reports by afternoon tomorrow..."

"What's the duty hour anyway?" Tony asked, he had no idea what time it was on-board.

"Fifteen thirty eight," The admiral replied glancing at a small wrist computer he momentarily uncovered from his sleeve.

With the standard twenty eight hour naval day, that left plenty of time for eating, sleeping and writing the report, with a good few hours of relaxation thrown in.

"Thank you sir," Tony replied, "Let us know when we have a plan of action on this and we'll be ready."

"I'd say it'll be a day or two at least, so stay sharp," The admiral replied with a nod, moving toward the now closed armory door.

The officer left and Tony now remained alone in the armory. Truth's gear was steadily un-filling her kit bag, finding its place on the table and being stowed. The common items like unspent ammunition and magazines were set aside for being placed in the ammo locker until Tony reached his own bag. His gear came next, then, finally after the weapons and kit were placed in their locker, he removed his combat vest and hung it inside. Removing it was a load off and he stretched gratefully as he finally closed both containers.

Tony didn't feel like re-inventorying the ammunition and so, approaching the armory door, he keyed the small intercom button next to it and spoke, "Ammo check in,"

The door opened a moment later and the guard, formerly outside, entered and moved to the table. Tony gave the watch a nod, then relayed just how many rounds he should expect to find in the magazines. Finally, he opened the door and headed into the hall.

While no watch was present outside no one would be able to access the armory without a high level clearance. Given the peacefulness of the current situation in space however, Tony doubted anyone would need to get inside in a hurry. Now unburdened, he set off to visit his partner.

The design of the destroyer class vessels featured a cluster of important services around the docking bay, aimed at facilitating the deployment or recall of dispatch teams if they were needed.

The infirmary was located not far from the docking bay and armory area, allowing the rapid treatment of injured personnel returning from excursions while smaller aid stations saw to non critical needs on other areas of the ship.

For a vessel of its size, the design was as efficient as Tony could expect but was eclipsed at times by the newest versions of the hulls in service in seemingly minuscule, yet effectual ways. The newer designs had iterated on the current one and squeezed just a bit more efficiency into the layout of corridors or the flow of duty traffic at shift change. All of these small things added up to the point where most of the command officers in the Navy recognized the improvements on the newest iterations. Even so, all NovaCore ships, regardless of class, were designed first and foremost to perform their roles as capably as possible. For NovaCore destroyers, this meant interdicting enemy traffic and in many cases dispatching boarding teams. The less common roles included things like surveillance or reconnaissance duties when long term on station presence was required.

The specialization of ships therefore was apparent in design at fundamental levels, from the layout of corridors and crew traffic to the way the power systems worked and how their redundancies were layed out. Each ship aimed to fill its design requirements in the NovaCore Navy, while retaining as much versatility as possible in doing so.

For its arguably small size, the NovaCore Navy was ranked as the second most powerful in the galaxy at present, a designation that had been won with blood and sweat. It was bought with lives years ago in conflict with the Hil'Raigh Federation and its most powerful member state, Akal'Maru.

Lessons were learned then about design in ships which transformed the way NovaCore space operations worked on a fundamental level. While most ships to that point had been designed with knowledge gained from surface naval warfare in the hundreds years prior, ships since that time were heavily skewed toward dealing with common Hil'Raigh battle tactics in their defense and construction.

It made floating in orbit around the capitol of one of the Federation member states less stressful than it could have been, to know that the ship he was on had been built from scratch since the war, designed to evade, destroy and defeat Hil'Raigh opposition. A normally tenuous position here had become one of secret strength.

The infirmary door loomed ahead, the flat metallic paneling of the floor offering quiet if uneventful transport to the sliding metal plate that made the door of the medical bay. Along the walls of the main corridor here were support structures that jutted a good ten centimeters or more into the hall, reminding anyone who observed them that the hulls and workings of all NovaCore ships were reinforced from the inner most portions to the outside. The bright illumination here in the main corridor however, contrasted with some of the side corridors and less traveled routes throughout the ship itself.

Tony entered the bay fluidly, stepping inside as the sliding door found its closed position once more behind him. The general din of noise outside in the corridor was instantly quelled and the room itself was quiet and peaceful. The bay was divided into two main portions with a smaller third one in the back. One of them was a recovery area into which Tony had stepped and where the on duty medical officer took care of any of their busywork or data entry. The room itself was large, several meters deep and several wide, though deeper than it was long. Along the right hand wall a line of medical beds sat empty, waiting for their unlucky occupants. The left wall featured a few as did the far wall. The middle of the room was largely empty save for some displays or other instruments that were mounted on nimble arms hanging from the roof. They ranged in purpose, size and apparent weight and Tony had no idea what most of them were. Closest to the door, at his left was the Medical Officers post. It was a square shaped desk of sorts in the middle of which rested a comfortable looking chair. Behind the chair along the wall was a row of cabinets and the desk itself featured an array of data slates, most of them off, some piled neatly and others strewn in a more haphazard fashion.

Deeper in the recovery area, Truth sat over the side of one of the beds while the on duty medical officer stood nearby, talking to her about something Tony had missed before he walked in. Kirashira was on the same bed, sitting a good twenty or so centimeters from Truth, quietly observing the exchange.

Truth's back was to the door and the doctor herself was standing behind, spraying over Truth's injured skin with one of her medical tools. She finished a pass over Truth's shoulder and pulled the reading glasses she had on the tip of her nose down.

It was a doctor Tony had met before, the same one who had given both he and Truth their pre-departure medical checks, Korin Rohue.

Dr. Rohue, a Captain in the Medical Corps was certainly a standout. Her rounded figure and jet black hair set her apart from her peers by appearance but her understanding of nano-medicine put her on the radar for both Tony and Truth.

She was one of the most qualified doctors in the NovaCore when it came to nanotechnologies and nano-surgeries, two of the medical technologies which Truth's array of implants and interfaces integrated rather heavily. Not only was Rohue a doctor, but a genetic specialist that had worked in clone research briefly before joining the Medical Corps as an Officer.

Truth was definitely in good hands. If anyone knew how to calibrate or coerce a set of Truth's blood borne nanites to work quickly and efficiently it was this doctor. She had the expertise that made her all but a shoe in for the most compatible of doctors Truth could wish for. By extension it made her quite qualified for helping Kirashira as well, given Truth's unique physiology.

The brief glance Rohue made to Tony was concluded almost as quickly and she went back to her work. Tony guessed she was spraying some sort of protein compound that would help Truth's nanites rebuild her skin more quickly, especially because of the glossy translucent look that Truth's shoulder now had. Rather than burned flesh, a gel like, artificial looking, cloudy skin, had covered the area and as Tony approached, the grayish red meatiness of Truth's artificial muscles became visible beneath it.

Seeing that was something that reminded Tony just how much different he and Truth were at times. While both were clones, both from the same batch, Truth's life had taken quite a different turn when it came to survival.

Finally, as Tony neared the bed, Rohue spoke aloud to him, "Welcome to the infirmary Major, what can I do for you?"

She didn't stop spraying or lose concentration while she did it, she just talked over her shoulder as she worked. Tony shrugged and replied, "Just checking on my partner, and the Princess I guess."

Dr. Rohue nodded, "Right."

She finished the round of spray and glanced to the Hil'Raigh royal next to Truth, who had turned her attention to Tony in quiet examination. Her eyes were tired looking, her face one of tension and unease but one so full of those feelings that it looked like it would never let her sleep. When Dr. Rohue spoke in the

Novian tongue, one that the Princess had no understanding of, she almost flinched as well.

Rather than give the Princess half a conversation, Tony kept his words to Novian for now as well, "Well you know us clones, we stick together."

"I can see that, are you hurt too?" The doctor replied, turning and setting her sprayer down on a tray nearby. Truth sighed and slid off the bed, turning to look at her partner.

Tony glanced over, gave her a hello smile and then turned his attention to the doctor, "No I don't think I'm hurt, but I promise I'll come in for a look tomorrow morning anyway."

The doctor smirked, "Alright, just this once...on behalf of our guest."

"How's she been?" Tony asked, opening the conversation to his partner with a glance.

Truth glanced to Kirashira, who had realized she was a topic. Tony's partner politely spoke in the royal's language instead. The mix was awkward no matter how it was divided, Dr. Rohue knew nothing of the language, most people on this ship didn't. Tony and his partner were among the few who did, and possibly Admiral Thorsh due to his potential diplomacy roles. Other than those few, Tony could not remember anyone else who understood the tongue well enough to talk to the Princess in it. Truth's words came with a bit of visible relief on the Royal's face, "How do you feel?"

Princess Kirashira looked to Truth, then Tony and Rohue before she replied, looking to Truth, "I feel… tired I think…. I'm not sure..."

Her voice was something of a tragedy, one that betrayed a feeling deeper than fear or loneliness. Tony wondered as he listened to the way her words rolled away from her mouth, just what she had seen today. He somehow knew that it had to be worse than he had first assumed.

The Admiral was certain that her father and mother were gone, dead, and in that moment Tony's mind came up with at least one reason she might have sounded so defeated.

"We will find a comfortable place for you to rest, a safe place." Truth replied reassuringly. She was quite the diplomat when she wanted to be.

The Princess nodded and hung her head afterward, "I'd like to go home."

There was a long silence. Dr. Rohue, unable to understand the words, understood the context clearly enough. She gave a long sigh then in a near whisper, spoke once more to Tony.

"Truth says she was found with the Ambassador, who was already dead..."

"Yeah," Tony replied, "No idea what she saw but....she's gotta be in shock still..."

The doctor cleared her throat and turned away, "Let me know if she needs anything, I gave her a nanite injection. Truth's calibration worked well enough but I had to dumb them down a bit. Her bruising wont heal as quickly as Truth's will."

"Other injuries?"

"She had a fractured rib, didn't break thankfully. I don't know how she suffered it but...The fact that she was able to run with you tonight was a small miracle really."

"Anything else?"

"Nothing I can treat with medicine..." The doctor gave the monarch a mournful look before turning back to Tony, "Damn shame really, she's such an elegant young thing it all feels criminal..."

"Assassination attempts usually don't give you a good feeling regardless," Tony replied flatly. It was a fact of the situation, not much could be done to make assassinating the royalty any more criminal than it already was.

"We will try to make sure it's safe to go home before we send you okay?" Truth finally said, getting Kirashira's attention carefully. The monarch eyed Truth, her hollow expression looking like it could give in to sleep soon. She nodded and slid off the bed's edge as Truth turned to Tony.

"I am thinking..." she began but Tony already had an idea of what she was going to say.

"Yeah, use our quarters, she can have my bunk. I'll ask the duty officer if there's a free billet nearby..." Tony said, glancing to the royal. There was evidence of some crying having taken place, her eyes were still a bit bloodshot. He must have missed that during the trip to orbit on the shuttle.

Truth then turned to the doctor, "If that is all doctor?"

"For now yes, come in tomorrow morning so I can check on both of your progress...."

Truth nodded and headed for the door, slowly, making sure Kirashira was following. She keyed the portal open after they reached it and exited, leaving Tony inside the room with the doctor.

"Truth's nanites are very effective..." Dr. Rohue began after the door closed, "If I'd done nothing she would have recovered pretty quickly anyway..."

"One advantage I guess..." Tony replied, it was an advantage at least, but at what cost?

"I'm more worried about the Hil'Raigh Princess than I am Truth." she continued, "You are both in this business, she's just… a sheltered…. Almost a child I guess.."

"She's no child," Tony shrugged, she was an adult in both Hil'Raigh and NovaCore societies, by age at least, "But sheltered, definitely."

"So it's true then what Admiral Thorsh was saying, about her parents?"

"No idea, I heard it from him too so I'm guessing its true…"

"This reminds me of Sho'Alar years ago….it just smells bad. It did then too…" the doctor folded her arms, as if in defiance of the memory she had conjured.

"We weren't there to throw a monkey wrench in Sho'Alar. Who knows, we might have made a difference…"

"I hope so, you two did good work, saving her…"

"The ambassador's dead," Tony shrugged, "I wouldn't call that success on a mission, more like less damning failure…"

"Truth seemed to think he was dead before she could have reached him…"

"I trust her judgment on it," Tony replied, "Doesn't mean either of us like it….."

The doctor nodded, "You know, you two are so alike it makes sense you are from the same batch… but at the same time, you are so different…"

"She's, in her own words, a robot alien," Tony smirked, "Not exactly how I'd describe her but it's accurate, if in a crude way…"

"She has an odd sense of humor at times, that much I have learned…" Rohue replied, she moved past Tony and slipped behind the desk which was her post for the next few hours at least, "When are you coming in tomorrow?"

The doctor slipped her reading glasses back onto her nose as she eyed a slate. It looked like it contained a schedule diagram.

"O six?" Tony poised the question hoping the time was free.

"O six," Rohue replied with a nod, "See you then, keep your partner and the precious cargo in your heart major."

"Am I some kind of extra medicine?" Tony replied with a skeptical snicker.

The doctor replied with a roll of her eyes and a playful tone of voice "Get out."

PART TWO

UNMASKED BETRAYAL

11 - Mind's Eye

There was a darkness around where Truth sat, the flat floor almost textureless here. Cross legged, wearing her combat pants and a light sports top, she manipulated the large data glass in front of herself with care. One hand held up the device while the other keyed things on the face of it.

Images played back on the screen, this one featuring her own first person view from the mission. In the video, she took aim, fired and the target was thrown out of the Guild Hall window. The image slowed as the projectile passed through him then she stopped it, manipulating the screen with her fingertips as she set the device in her lap. She stood and the image filled the air around her. Here in her own memory, she was able to place herself between where she'd been and the already dead Hil'Raigh she had fired at.

She took a step, glancing over at herself, the representation at least, hunched in careful aim, dealing with the recoil of the shot even as it moved forward. She turned her attention now to the Hil'Raigh, he was being racked sideways by the impact and the body armor he wore was splintering away from him on the far side, a mix of blood and flesh coming with it.

Truth reached out and tapped the air, a control surface appearing there and in a second, the blood and mess were stripped away, the scene reduced and a different data overlay covered everything. She lifted her hand from the console and stepped out into the air outside the Guild Hall window, straight down was a hundred or more stories but here in a memory, she had full control.

After a moment she tapped at the air, getting a new console before she spoke aloud, "The tactical analysis on this was incomplete..."

The air was quiet and then, a whispering voice, finally culminating into her own, replied, "You did not have a complete viewing angle for a post damage analysis."

"Right, well, file the firing data for use in improving gun handling and marksmanship at least..." Truth ordered.

"Done,"

Truth motioned again and keyed on a pad she'd willed into being. At once, she was back to the dimly lit area again, the large data slate on the ground where she had set it down earlier.

She sighed as she sat down and dug into more memories, replaying scenes from the mission as she did. She had already weeded out the unimportant parts, parts where she did not learn much, where nothing was gained. Instead, combat sections popped up one after another.

"Give me some non combat memories please... I've been filing combat memories and training forever..." She asked the air.

The disembodied voice replied colloquially, "Alright, here are some scenes with planning and leisure...."

Truth gratefully accepted the new slew of memories, keying through a few on the slate. She couldn't remember exactly how long she had been cleaning up, cataloging memories and events, but she was sure it was almost time to wake up regardless. Even so, it was not all that bad slipping into the abyss of memory management with her coprocessor when she ended up doing so. The machine had a personality of sorts to interact with when approached in this state of unconsciousness. It made the whole process of dealing with memory management easier to bear when it was done with some sort of company.

It had not always been easy, especially when the machine was new. The first time it had asked to do memory cleaning and management was a jarring affair where, more than request, the machine mostly insisted on the process. Truth had hated the idea for months afterward, of even going to sleep and until the thing had been updated to be less intrusive, she had refused to sleep at all.

Now, the process of helping the computer works its magic was a sort of relaxing ritual. It improved her learning and capabilities while also cataloging the most important points learned over the past few days. She firmly felt that no one who had no interface of their own, could fully understand the practice.

No matter how she described this place, the memory was never very clear when she woke, but when she returned the next time, it felt familiar regardless. Sometimes she interacted with the computer just by talking, sometimes it used an avatar clone of her to interact more directly. Sometimes it was just Truth by herself inside her mind, working quietly for a couple hours.

The newest system had always been willing to defer to her needs and was quite good at predicting what those were these days. It was rarely intrusive, even getting her to be more cooperative in filing things by tossing dry humor it had learned from its host, back at her.

It was not that the device understood the concept of humor for humors sake, just that it elicited a positive response in Truth's brain. It was built to make things more efficient and so those positive responses had become a goal to strive for, at least from the perspective of the computer system. It was a philosophical question at times, the difference between the machine pursuing its goals and Truth pursuing her own. It had asked about that difference before, curious as it tended to be. Truth had yet to come up with an answer she felt was fair. By all accounts even her desire to help her partner was able to be reduced to a goal optimization problem. When said with such a clinical wording though, it made Truth uncomfortable. There had to be some middle ground.

At times, Truth felt like it was a second personality, one living along side her brain, one without emotions or feelings, one that could never really understand the outside world without its perception being colored at least in part by Truth's own.

When she was awake, she couldn't talk to the interface, it was passive, quiet for the most part. Communication then was by feeling, intuition, automatic and unconscious. If she needed something, it just happened automatically, but here, it was a different story. In the solitude of her unconsciousness, there was a chance for a greater depth of communication.

Part of her wondered at times whether it was entirely normal for this sort of thing to happen, but then again few people had the kinds of computer implants Truth had. It was not as if people were in the habit of tying their brains to computers like this in the NovaCore, despite the potential advantages.

In a way, Truth was a pioneer of sorts, an ethical dilemma at worst. She was a cloned organism made with a mostly alien genetic template. In addition she was one of the only people she knew of that had her brain tied so closely with a machine, perhaps the first in which the system had worked properly.

She was not the first to receive this kind of implant, but the first who had retained any quality of life despite having required it. Truth had never met anyone else who had the digital coprocessor augmenting their brain, but she knew that the number of people who'd received them numbered in the single digits. The only one Truth knew anything about was an individual named Malory, who had apparently met with an untimely end years ago. Whether it was related to her implants or not, Truth had never learned.

There was a nagging feeling though at times, that having a computer system tied to her brain like this was as much a curse as it could ever be a blessing. She had learned how over the years, to make sure she was sharing or not sharing her ideas and thoughts with the device when she wanted to ensure a singular state of mind, but even so, knowing about things like Malory's demise years ago made her nervous if she thought too much on the topic.

Instead, she shifted her thoughts to her wound recovery. The micro-surgeons in her bloodstream had been hard at work for hours now, repairing her body and musculature to ensure that she would regain her full capabilities rather soon. From the time of her injury to the time of full recovery, she estimated to be less than two days, while most people in her position would have been lucky to have that kind of capability back in several weeks.

That was one of the advantages to being a product of engineering she had to admit. She had the most highly tailored micro surgery bots and nanites that were known to exist in the galaxy. That fact, combined with a genetically enhanced, robust Kul'Raigh immune system, made for a seemingly indestructible framework on which Truth's life was built.

"How is the injury?" Truth asked.

"Doing well, your shoulder will have retarded functionality for only a few more hours after which you should start to see rapid recovery of your range of motion," replied the computerized copy of her own voice.

"Good," Truth replied, "And how long do I have left to sleep?"

"You may get up anytime you wish Truth, You have rested adequately for the time being." The system replied, "Though I would recommend getting some food soon for optimal metabolic balance."

"Alright, I should check on Princess Kirashira anyway," Truth replied, and with that, she willed herself awake.

There was a moment of warped reality, sounds peeling into her world from nowhere, finally making sense when her mind was listening to her ears. Her eyes came next, and then her eyelids opened. Her coprocessor was a memory now, a fuzzy one, but no longer a personality, just a machine, a feeling in the back of her mind.

She took a deep breath, feeling the air fill her lungs. She was definitely awake. The sounds of the air recycler were some of the only ones that she could hear inside what had still, to be the medical bay.

Truth was laying on her side in an infirmary bed, her wounded shoulder on the top and her good one on the bottom bearing her weight. The patch of soft gauze covering her glossy burned skin brushing barely, against the thin blanket of her bed. She sat up and moved the blanket from her shoulder, slowly working her wounded arm to see how much mobility it really had.

A dull pain replied, but the shoulder moved, if a bit stiffly and in a few more rolling motions, she had her arm in far better working order than anyone else might have expected.

The air of the medical bay was cool, on the edge of comfort, especially given the sport top Truth currently wore. Thankfully it was not a particularly tight garment and it put very little pressure around her upper back.

She scanned the room carefully, noting that according to her internal clock, it was just past the normal wake up time she usually set for herself on board, though that meant that the lights were on a low setting here in the infirmary.

It was the first watch here, as evidenced by the nurse who sat behind the desk near the doorway. She was busy reading a data pad and paid no attention to Truth other than a cursory glance as the rapidly recovering patient slid out of bed, her bare feet coming to rest on the far too cold flooring.

Wiggling her toes, Truth looked over the other beds in the room. Only one of them housed anyone, the one that Truth identified as Kirashira's bed. She was curled up sideways, but as Truth took a step away from her own bed, there was a stir of motion from the Royal's location. In seconds the Monarch was sitting up. She had probably not been asleep but waiting for someone to do something.

"Good morning," Truth said to the royal, taking a few steps closer to her bed.

The Monarch rubbed her eyes then looked at Truth groggily, "Hi."

"Did you manage to get any sleep?" Truth asked, recalling that her coprocessor had mentioned the Princess stirring several times through the night.

"I.. did sleep some..." Kirashira managed, her voice sounding a bit dry.

Truth nodded, moving to the one and only drink dispenser in the recovery area, setting a small glass under the tap and pouring some water. In a moment she had returned to the Princess and offered it.

Kirashira took the cup in both hands, eyeing it only for a moment before drinking it all down in a gulping fashion. After a moment she stated, "You can use your arm again."

"Yes, I can." Truth replied.

"How can you recover so fast..." The Princess asked, she winced even as she did, having shifted her weight and drawn some kind of pain out of her midsection. The evidence was all over her face.

"I have a special set of small robots in my blood for that purpose," Truth explained. "They are not unlike the kind your people use for genetic modification."

"We use them for surgery and medicine too," Kirashira said longingly, "Do your people not use them on us?"

"I do not think we have any that are capable of operating at peak efficiency on your people. Mine only work on me, the rest do not work as well outside of the Novian body..." Truth said, "I think you received some of mine, they should help you recover at least..."

"Are you still sore?"

"No," Truth replied, "Not really."

"I can't imagine. I saw your shoulder before, it looked..." The royal paused.

"It looked gross," Truth finished helpfully.

"Yeah, I mean, it was all burned," Kirashira said.

There was a long pause and then the Princess spoke again, "Why do you look like a Kul'Raigh?"

"A majority of my genes are Kul'Raigh, like you," Truth announced, eying the Princess calmly. The royal shifted, straightening her back a bit and giving a small huff.

"How are you so… tough, then… I saw you carrying a gun even with your shoulder hurt…"

"I have a number of artificial enhancements to assist me in my duties, Among those are things which allow me to ignore pain more effectively than others."

"Enhancements, you mean tweaks?"

Truth raised a brow, tweaks were, in Hil'Raigh culture, simple genetic modifications that were meant to improve the receiver's life in some way, a far cry from digital implants.

"No, not tweaks, just implants."

The Princess eyed Truth carefully, "So you're a robot… thing?"

There was a sort of contempt in the accusation, a subtle discomfort. Despite it's subtlety however, it was apparent.

"Perhaps we should change the topic…" Truth replied defensively.

The Princess simply looked her over then shrugged halfheartedly, "I guess I can't complain, you saved me after all…. I just never imagined I'd ever meet a NovaCore facsimile of one of my people…"

Truth had learned before, that her status as a partially cybernetic clone was something that drew a measure of cultural scorn from the Federation's various populations. There was a heavy dogma in their society surrounding life and what was and was not a valid representation of it. Artificial life, clones and cybernetics, were seen as improper perversion of that all important natural formula. It was for that reason that genetic engineering was so prevalent among them, removing the need or desire for replacing life with technology.

There was no clear reason why things like artificial intelligence were taboo in the Hil'Raigh culture, not that Truth knew of, but the feelings were quite common as far as she'd had seen.

Given the already unfavorable reaction from Kirashira, Truth decided against mentioning that she and Tony were both clones, instead opting to limit her disclosure of just how much artificial power she had. The Princess, steeped in her own culture was likely not to appreciate it much and it would lead to more conflict rather than cooperation. For the benefit of everyone involved, Truth decided that a relatively cooperative royal was the most helpful option.

"I am glad that you are in a safe place now as well," Truth said finally, latching onto the one good part of the Royal's final statement.

"Where is here?" the question came almost instantly, along with a more assertive tone.

"Here, is in orbit around your home, on a ship, where you are safe from the people who were attempting to take your life away."

The Princess listened and, for a moment looked as if she was going to press anyway, into a demand to return home. She appeared to think better of it however and simply nodded.

"What's your name?"

"I am Truth," Truth said with a small smile, "And you are Princess Kirashira Ren'Tauru yes?"

The royal nodded. Preempting the Princess's normal option to introduce herself by name, was one of many subtle power plays that Truth had learned of in Federation culture. The action drew immediate effect, Kirashira's brow raising a moment but her composure quickly erased the evidence of it.

"Yes, that's me," She replied, "In orbit around my home..."

After a long pause, Kirashira finally spoke once more, "How long am I going to be ... protected by your people?"

"I have no idea at the present time, I would hope that you would remain here in safety while the situation is better assessed," Truth replied. She had no intention of letting the one whom she and Tony had just rescued, who the ambassador had apparently died to protect, be returned to the surface and snuffed out in the instant it would take.

The words though, appeared to hit a chord with the young royal. She eyed Truth critically, her lips pursed, ready to speak, but she eventually closed her mouth and finally nodded. Though Truth considered her own motivations selfish, she guessed that maybe it was a less cynical display in the eyes of the Princess.

"Do you know what happened?" Kirashira asked. Her mind was certainly still on the topic of her home, the life she would no longer have, at least, not in the same shape as it was before.

"I would prefer discussing that with you when our people have been able to better assess the overall circumstance..." Truth began, but she was interrupted.

"No," Kirashira replied, "You came to rescue your ambassador, why did you decide to take me...Our people don't even get along."

Truth looked at her eyes, they were filled with the kind of concern that someone had only when they were worried, afraid, "It is unfortunate that our nations have usually found themselves at odds. However, I did, and still consider your life to be of value regardless. That is why we brought you here."

Kirashira huffed, blinking back a bit of moisture in her eyes. She glanced away. There was a flash of emotion on her face, brief, but visible. A lasting warmth settled over her cheeks, a bit of blood flow increasing there and while the outwardly visible signs faded quickly, Truth's bevy of senses gave her a better understanding than normal sight alone granted.

She eyed the royal for a moment more, until the sound of the medical bay door opening caught her attention. A quick glance over told her that one of the ships crew had entered the bay. Judging by the band on his upper arm he looked to be from logistics. He approached quickly, a small packet in his hand. As he stepped into comfortable conversing distance, he handed Truth the packet, "This is for our guest. Galley access and identity for inventory."

Truth nodded and looked at the plastic sleeve. Inside was an identification card. There was a lanyard already hooked to the sleeve, the assumption being that a guest would utilize the card to interact with any ship system they had authorization to use.

On a ship like this, most of the crew had an identification implant, though some of them used identification cards instead. All crew were required to be identifiable at all times to use the ship's automated systems and pass security checkpoints between sections. Kirashira, as a member of the royal family of her nation, already had a tracking device. Until someone determined whether her device was compatible with the NovaCore access system, the identification card was the normal solution.

Giving someone an access card usually meant they had free reign to do what they wanted within reason, but as Kirashira had no knowledge of the ship, the language the crew spoke, or most of the etiquette on board, Truth resolved to be a sort of guide, "I will stay with her for the time being."

"Of course, let us know if you need anything."

"Certainly, thank you crewman," The man gave Truth a nod and turned on his heel before departing, leaving Truth with the identification card. She looked it over and then handed it to Kirashira.

"This card will let you use things on the ship, like the food machines." Truth instructed.

The royal took the plastic slab and held it in her hand for a moment before replying, "I guess I could use something to eat..."

"In that case, we should visit the galley," Truth informed, "I will try to help you find food that is most agreeable for you."

The enthusiasm of the Princess melted a bit at the reply, but she slid off of her bed finally before realizing she was in a recovery robe. The loose fitting garment was far from the splendor of Kirashira's own clothes but it was far better than a surgical gown with an open back. Her actual clothing had probably been taken to laundry where it would be cleaned. Truth had heard nothing of it and guessed that it had been taken at some point in the night.

"Where are my clothes?" Kirashira finally said, looking around first and then at Truth.

"They may be at the laundry. I will requisition you some clothing to use in the interim," Truth stated, calling up a map of the ship. The laundry was not all that far away. If she visited, she would be able to check on the status of the Princess' own clothes as well as request a set of leisure clothes for her guest. She estimated Kirashira's sizes would be similar to her own. Their height was approximately the same and Royal's build was not shaped all that differently, save a bit more voluptuousness.

"I'll come," Kirashira blurted as Truth turned to leave. It sounded like a last minute decision, and Truth could not help but wonder if the prospect of being alone with a non Hil'Raigh speaking nurse was the impetus for the request. Regardless, there was no harm in it and so, Truth nodded her over.

The pair moved to the door and as they approached the Nurses desk, Truth announced their plan. They would be gone only for a while, long enough to visit the laundry and get something to eat. After that they would return. The nurse eyed them for a moment before relating to them that they could always have the food delivered as they were in the infirmary. Given the circumstance, the desire Truth herself had to walk around, and hopefully the supportive curiosity of Kirashira, Truth turned down the option.

The nurse nodded and the exchange finished, Truth led the way once more, moving to the door which slid open in anticipation of her exit. Kirashira followed, her feet in a pair of warm looking socks. The cold metal of the deck plating felt even more unforgiving as Truth's eyes beheld them, reminding her only that she wore nothing on her own feet.

In fact, the corridor was rather drafty. Truth's light weight training pants did little to offer much warmth, usually reserved for athletic work in the ship's facilities. Her top, while passably thick, left her shoulders and much of her back exposed. Her midriff was completely open to the air as well. It was settled in seconds, that the recovery area of the infirmary was quite a bit more comfortable than the corridor was.

For a moment, Truth envied the Princess in her robe, a robe that surely offered a bit more warmth to its wearer than her own clothing did. The thought was momentary however and Truth began leading her guest down the wide corridor slowly.

The pair had left the infirmary between deck shifts according to the schedule Truth had downloaded earlier, making for clear, near empty corridors here near the hangar. The exception of course, was a pair of naval marines who passed by in the opposite direction wheeling along a janitorial caddy and carrying some mops. The pair gave a momentarily confused glance at the out of regulation intruders into their assigned cleaning space, but after a moment appeared to shrug it off.

Really, Truth did not know how many of the crew actually knew about their guest. Had there been an announcement? Not globally at least or she would have heard it. If anything, Truth guessed that most of the crew didn't even have a clue about what had been happening on the surface of the planet beneath them. As far as they were concerned, things were business as usual.

At most, some of the section leaders or division heads had probably heard about the assassination of the King but Truth doubted they would easily recognize Kirashira as the Starlight Compact's Princess. Most people never bothered memorizing what the children of foreign heads of states looked like. An odd look here or there was a small price to pay though, for being alive.

Truth took care to match her pace to Kirashira's own and the two found a reasonable rhythm on their way to the laundry. Inside, Truth wondered just what her guest was thinking, about the ship, or even her life back home. The short, brief displays of emotion that she had let slip thus far were too minuscule to provide the kind of catharsis that the NovaCore agent felt that the Princess would need. It often took time for those who had gone through such traumatic experiences to come to terms with them. Truth guessed that this would be no exception.

What the Princess had lost was, in a way, a foreign concept, that of family. Truth had always had her partner but he was about as close to family as she could imagine anyone being. The idea that parents and children lived together in a sort of close knit unit for mutual benefit made sense and Truth had seen it in action before. She had never lived it in the way others had however. The academy and it's squads were just not the same as a set of parents. A squad in the academy was trainees leading trainees, preparation for military leadership in the field. Indeed, if squad leaders in any stage of such training felt like they were being relied on as a parental figure it often seemed to irritate them. It made them call for maturity or toughening up, rather than the care that a parent was supposed to show.

Was the Hil'Raigh culture so different that those roles had changed? Did being a royal affect a family dynamic? It was quite probable that there were changes brought on by station and culture and so Truth caught herself musing on the potential differences in hers and Kirashira's nations.

NovaCore culture was tight knit, and though families played a role in that back home, the national identity of the citizenry was invested in the idea of a sort of pseudo familial tie to the others. It was a collective identity that each person shared in, something larger than an individual. Ironically it was probably the most familial organization Truth had ever been a part of. Aside from her partner, the nation itself was her safety net.

For someone in the Starlight Compact, there were differences in almost all areas, many of them quite significant. The Hil'Raigh identity was also steeped in its own history but the modern world interacted with that history in a different way than the NovaCore.

The Federation had a much stronger emphasis on the individual's accomplishment in the public sphere. While the NovaCore certainly celebrated the best and brightest, they were held up as examples or teaching tools more than idols of popular culture. Federation culture, like most in the galaxy, was one which considered its own tenets and ideas to be of superior value when compared to others. It was apparent already, from the brief conversation Truth had already had, that the stigmas surrounding certain things in the Federation were all too real.

It was a moment of reflection for Truth however, as the pair walked. Seeing, hearing someone speak with an obvious lack of appreciation for her own situation made her wonder how often she perhaps did the same. She had felt challenged in a way by Kirashira's implication that she was a robot. It was an awkward feeling to have after being on Ashor for a while.

On the planet, Truth was one of many. People didn't think twice about who they saw when she walked by and yet, to Kirashira, Truth was apparently something of an oddity. She had gone from a place where she blended in almost completely, to a place where the only person she resembled, had a differing opinion. There was a parallel in their thoughts apparently, as Kirashira finally spoke.

"I'm sorry I called you a robot, but... It's not really something we do in our culture, enhance people with machines..." Kirashira admitted, "I mean, we do, to a degree, but I guess I never realized that there is a logical progression in how much you have done..."

"I did not choose most of the implants," Truth replied, the tone of the topic was already more encouraging. Kirashira was at very least, a diplomat in her own right, "Most of them supplement functionality that developed incompletely.

"Developed incompletely?" Kirashira glanced over, looking a bit confused.

"I am an artificially gestated organism," Truth explained, surprised that she had described her own origin so scientifically, "The NovaCore possesses less understanding of genetic engineering technologies than your own people and as a result, I experienced complications when I was young."

"You've always had machines then?" Kirashira's world seemed to expand at the idea, whether for good or ill, Truth could not yet decide.

"Essentially," Truth said, "At least as far as I can remember."

The Princess nodded, furrowing her brow a bit, She finally spoke once more,"Some people used to teach that anyone who got engineered, or tweaked, lost their soul."

"That is quite a teaching," Truth smiled a little, "Though I do not know if I agree. Perhaps I already lacked one."

"Over time I guess, when that stuff became safer, more normal, things changed a bit, it was 'Don't play god with machine people' and 'Don't needlessly replace your organs with machine parts'"

"It would appear, from what I have observed, that the second versions of that teaching have stuck." Truth noted.

Kirashira gave a nod, "I guess it was our people's response to everything being in our control. I was always taught that those feelings came from our need to retain nature, not just around us, but in ourselves. With so much engineering and choice, what made someone real anymore. That was the question everyone wanted to answer with those ideas I guess."

"I suppose I have never thought of the world that way," Truth shrugged.

"I guess it's kind of odd for me to worry about it all. My parents engineered me a bunch." Kirashira admitted with a conflicted twist of the lips, "They made sure I had all the best tools for being a leader, being pretty, being smart, being... anything I guess."

She sighed, a long drawn out one. It was a sigh of longing, one that told Truth that, no amount of colloquial conversation would ever fully drown out the need Kirashira had for some kind of stability or resolution to her situation.

The repeated feeling that Kirashira's words, her desire to talk, were more than just a desire to converse but perhaps, the start of a coping mechanism weighed on Truth heavily. She was far from qualified to provide any sort of emotional counseling. Any meaningful resolution to the Royal's problems would not come from her implant aided brain but probably a therapist. She considered, even as they reached the laundry, asking Kirashira if she wanted to talk to one but refrained.

The ship's crew featured a counselor who specialized and trained in many things, among them grief counseling. Then again, the person likely spoke no Hil'Raigh, almost no one on the ship did. Admiral Thorsh did, Tony did, perhaps some of the crew did, but it was unlikely that any of them were trained counselors.

Perhaps Tony would have been a better counselor. He did not have to contend with unwanted logical analysis of Kirashira's problem. He was better at emotions, he always had been, even too good at them sometimes. Maybe Truth could have him help.

As she opened her mouth though and began speaking with the laundry attendant, she glanced to Kirashira. Something about the expectant look the royal gave her put a hold on all of the partially explored plans she had been concocting. It was a feeling she had never felt before, an obligation mixed with something new, something she decided she needed some time to identify. Whatever it was though, it made Truth wonder if perhaps, despite her obvious lack of qualification for such a job, Kirashira would expect her to help.

The idea of that expectation alone was almost unsettling. Truth was used to obligations, used to helping and being asked to do things that were difficult. She never worried about failure really, because anything she did she worked at until she succeeded. In this situation however, she wondered if there was any room for effort rather than talent.

The dilemma floated around her mind for only a moment or two more, the act of submitting an estimate of Kirashira's sizes to get some usable clothes, filling her attention soon after. Whatever the circumstance, Truth resigned herself to the fact that the resolution to Kirashira's problem was going to be something she had not anticipated.

12 - Sympathetic Regent

The council chambers had long closed, the deed had been done and the proposals made. There was some debate, some agreement, some talking and discussion but the name had been put out for consideration. Vaerlin's name.

He had been expecting it to be mentioned and it had, as had been promised, but when it had finally come, it felt odd. It was an affirmation that Vaerlin was indeed, a traitor to the king he had served for years. He was now irrevocably part of the conspiracy, up to his neck in whatever came, his head on the chopping block if the winds of change willed it.

He had hoped in a way, that Kirashira Ren'Tauru would have been found dead, but alas, she was still at large. His prize, the Princess' mother was secure of course, but the royal blooded daughter was yet to be found. As long as she was out there, potentially alive, there was a danger that she could resurface.

What would happen then? What would he, the likely regent, do if Kirashira were to come out of the woodwork to reclaim her throne. He hesitated to plan for it, hoping it simply never would be, but inside, his mind tried even now, to prepare for all options.

The speaker of the council had nominated Vaerlin for regency, he had been seconded by a lesser noble and the proposition had been accepted by vote from the remaining council members, making Vaerlin the current front-runner for taking over the throne. He hoped that it would happen sooner rather than later.

The conspirators had of course, come through yet again, making sure a sympathetic voice was there to ensure the legacy of Vaerlin's house could continue. There would in the near future be more than a duke, but a Lord Regent. There was glory to be found, influence to be gained and wealth to be amassed.

Despite it though, Vaerlin's mind nagged him increasingly. Was he safe from his own allies? Would they turn on him as they had the king? If they did there was painfully little he could do to defend himself. Of course, after what happened to the king, security would likely never be the same, but it really was a first of its kind situation. In all the generations of Hil'Raigh history, very few had ever bothered trying to kill off the ruler in such a fashion, usually it was with things like poison or court intrigue. Blatant attacks were messy, expensive and hard to cover up but the attack on Gou'Ran Ren'Tauru had changed all of that.

The days of the ideal, the peace, they were gone. It would be a cold day in hell before anyone dared hold a big event at the Companion Guild Hall as well. Even that was concerning in its own way.

The Guild were a huge economic power, and Vaerlin knew as well as anyone that they had their loyalists among the Kul'Raigh population. They would definitely be interested in finding out what had cost them so much potential cash flow, or at least, who had been involved. It was sure to be a long running concern, but at least Vaerlin would be able to count on his allies to help turn them off the trail. As much as he worried that they were going to try and dispose of him, he knew enough about the political game to understand that the uncertainty presented by the Guild was not something he or the conspirators wanted.

Still, he wished he knew more about who some of them were. After the council meeting, with the two that had suggested him, Vaerlin had tried to speak to them and assess their involvement. He wanted to know how deeply they were connected to the plot. His hints, his attempts to draw a subtle response, had come away with nothing, leaving Vaerlin to wonder really, if they were involved or not. Perhaps they were just unwitting pawns, after all, he was promised only that they would propose him at the meeting, not that they would know why.

There would be time for research, time for digging into anything he could later, but for now, he had to tread carefully. Once he was installed as the regent, his ability to remain discreet would increase ten fold, even from his well connected allies. He made no mistake, his allies were only allies as long as he, Vaerlin, was of use to them and that much was already clear.

The number of empty seats in the council chamber was a reminder, the empty throne in the chambers was a reminder. Even Shiyara Ren'Tauru's face was a reminder, the one time Vaerlin had seen it since the attack. She had not seen him. She had stared downward, defeated looking as she was loaded into the holding container she occupied somewhere off planet at this point.

If there was one thing he had not realized, it was how much guilt that damn Kul'Raigh would make him feel just by looking forlorn. He had seen the royal consort tired, sad, even angry before, but nothing was preparation for the glassy emptiness her eyes held as she was led away after the attack. It was as if the life had been drained from her body and a helpless husk remained, undying in her place. The beauty was there, likely the skill, the knowledge and anything useful. Yet, even so, something was different. She was certainly less of a trophy without enthusiasm, and if he had to, Vaerlin would probably just keep her locked away for the rest of her life rather than attempt to fix what he knew he could not. No bribery would ever erase that level of despondent helplessness.

The Duke sighed, pacing back and forth in the lobby of the building he had been staying in ever since the annual council of nobles had begun its meetings weeks ago. The marble floors, the metallic paneling and the deliberately placed plant life did little to lighten his mood. The opulence of his station seemed in this moment, a small comfort and yet, he wanted more of it anyway. Somehow, he hoped that surrounding himself long enough, with enough, would hide all that had been paid to get there. The Starlight Compact needed a leader who was unhindered, and it had to look like Vaerlin was. Thankfully his allies already had an idea on how to use the continued scrutiny to their advantage.

All of the data anyone outside of the plot had gathered, everything they could guess, pointed to the NovaCore being involved on the night of the attack. Vaerlin was not told exactly how they had come to that conclusion but that it was almost completely certain regardless. Since breaking the armistice was not something Vaerlin guessed that the aliens would do, he instead was left to assume that they were involved in some other capacity. He guessed though, that they had something to do with the disappearing Princess and part of him was sickened at the idea that they could have taken her out of reach.

Then again, what would they have done with her? He had no idea but his allies had apparently decided to make sure that not only they, but the entire Federation understood just how dirty the alien's hands were in all of this.

The initial attack had been carried out with NovaCore weapons on purpose, but it was hard to pin anything to the crafty aliens when the Federation had such a historically poor relationship with them up until now. Instead, today would mark a second, more public false flag attack. The Federation as a whole would have to conclude, and rightfully so, that the aliens had indeed chosen to reignite the conflict. Vaerlin understood the logic there.

A renewed conflict would bring about a focus on unity and moving forward, the perfect fertile ground for forgetting the dubious circumstances of King Ren'Tauru's untimely demise. Even the Kul'Raigh Companion Guild would be forced to align itself with the Federation at that point, taking some heat off of covering things up.

It would end in war councils surely, the false flag would provide the basis for what the neighboring Akal'Maru state had always yearned to continue. The Federation had not easily convinced its members to give up hostilities years ago, managing only to get them to agree to a pause in the war. Without the agreement sitting in their way, they would likely renew their push for expansion, even into alien occupied territory. The Compact had been a small player in the first war, with no real military to speak of, supporting mostly its allies but Vaerlin's voice was all a new conflict needed.

Once Vaerlin was regent, he had some ideas of what to do to change things. Perhaps a military conflict was precisely what he needed to catapult the Compact's economy to top tier in the Federation. He smirked at the idea, being a leader in a war. He had no intention of doing much fighting, but if he did half as much as King Ren'Tauru's father had done during the war then he would be passable at the job.

Finally, the doors of the foyer in which Vaerlin had been waiting, opened. In stepped a familiar face, Tamur the well meaning thug and yes man of Vaerlin's allies. He passed an array of well armed guards as he did so, approaching Vaerlin with a confidence sprung obviously from ego. He would have made a fine politician.

"Tamur," Vaerlin said with a sigh, "You are barely on time."

"You'd be surprised how busy I've been Duke Vaerlin," The man replied with a shrug. Busy indeed, busy setting up the false flag no doubt. The duke eyed the mercenary carefully, wondering just what was going to be happening soon. He decided though, as he caught a smirk from the man that he would rather not know. The details of the party attack were few but already, the information he had been told about it had made him squeamish enough, he didn't want to deal with more.

He wanted at least, some distance from this latest attempt at framing the Federation's largest adversary for the attack. Thankfully, between Vaerlin, Tamur and the guards in the lobby, the only one who actually had any detail was Tamur. The guards had no idea who Tamur was, they were just local law enforcement. As far as they knew, Tamur was a private contractor, a protector for the Duke during these troubled times. In a way it was true but if they only knew.

Tamur motioned toward the door, "Ready to go?"

Vaerlin nodded and sighed, following the mercenary toward the sliding doors. As he approached them he realized just how paranoid he was getting. The hair on his neck was already standing up, he was ready to dive for the ground at a moment's notice. Knowing the fake attack was coming did nothing to assuage his concerns that he would somehow be injured anyway. Hopefully the lunk of a man leading the way had been smart enough to plan things in a Vaerlin friendly fashion. The worst the Duke wanted was to be thrown to the ground in order to save his life from the NovaCore assailants. Something told the nobleman that his present company would have no qualms about doing just that.

The promenade outside of the hotel was expansive and broad, planters with trees and ornate shrubbery making up the landscaping on the artificial ground up here in the sky between buildings. This particular level featured an array of well monitored landing pads, on which a variety of smaller vehicles sat waiting. Some of them were taxis, some private transport and here in the An'Jea district the number of privately owned vehicles was quite a bit higher than other places in the city.

It was a district of wealth and influence, an affluent place in the richest city the Compact had to offer. It was probably the safest place in the nation overall, with a low crime rate and a good standard of living. The district took on the shape of a cake slice of the city, running from the middle near the Companion Guild Hall to the outer edge of the metropolis that made up the city center. The unique, concentric circle design of Dau'Kore's layout ensuring that the tallest, most expensive architecture was near the middle, while the farther one got from the middle, the more An'Jea resembled much of the surrounding city. There were of course, pockets of wealth in other districts but none of them matched the concentration of influence that this area had.

It was no surprise then, that Vaerlin's allies had chosen this, the safe area of the city to stage a framing attack. Despite increased security as of late, the most influential of people lived and worked here, they would demand safety, a change.

Safety and change required a strong leader, that was simply a fact of life, and without even so much as a regent to ensure increased security, there was painfully little local authorities would be able to do in the long term. They would need the nation's government to help and when they asked, Vaerlin would be there waiting. In truth, the setup would allow for Vaerlin to gain not only support from the other nobles, but from the citizenry. He could garner support by offering security, something that he was sure his contacts in the other major states of the Federation would be happy to support. Despite the underhanded means, Vaerlin had to admit that the framing was the best way he could hope to come into a unified government. The NovaCore would simply have to deal with the realities that the distrust they had sewn so long ago would come back to haunt them earlier than they'd anticipated.

Tamur and Vaerlin had only gone a few meters before they were joined by Vaerlin's support staff. The official agenda was to go to yet another council meeting this evening. Vaerlin examined them as they approached, most of them robed in the garb that indicated they served the nobility, so few of them who he actually knew.

The Duke cared little for getting to know any of his servants, most of them had a job to do and they did not care whether their lord was interested in the goings on of their daily lives. He had never asked of course, just sort of assumed that it was true because in their position, he would have felt the same. Of course, matters were not helped by the fact that a member or two of his group had been lost in the party attack. Vaerlin therefore, wanted to know them even less than before, given how he had no idea whose number was going to be punched before all of this had finished.

He greeted the few who he remembered with a nod, carefully listening to the explanation of one of his aides as the young man relayed the current state of affairs within the Starlight Compact's council. The explanation was good, detailed in fact. As Vaerlin listened, the man's enthusiasm became more than apparent, he was excited by the idea of helping his lord through the transition. He had an optimism in his voice that rang of youth, something that reminded Vaerlin of days past, days he had buried now.

When the loud pop from far away sounded, something in Vaerlin's mind knew that he had made his first mistake of the day; allowing himself to care at all. The face of the aide twisted in agony as he collapsed forward coughing, a spray of blood fanning out of him as he collapsed. Vaerlin felt himself shoved to the ground by a rough hand, Tamur's own. He landed next to the face of his aide and simply stared into the lifeless eyes that looked through him.

This time there was a personal shock to him. Before, the attack on the Guild Hall, things had been detached and far away. The news covered it of course, but the graphic imagery was for the most part, left out. Now, there was a visceral feeling to it all, the price of revolution.

A second pop rang out as Tamur began to yell, give orders to the bodyguards nearby. His attacking shooters were good. Vaerlin heard another shot rip into the ground beside him. He wondered if it had passed through anyone on its way, but his curiosity was stayed by his helplessness in the situation. If there was one thing he wanted, it was a quick end to whatever was going to happen here, a quick end and a finish to this kind of change. Something about it all felt so costly, at least when faced with it in person.

The adrenaline coursing through his veins threatened to make him sick as he crawled forward against a planter box. A shot nicked the edge of it as he curled against it. The metal rim of the container fragmented violently over his prone form and he felt some of the heated metal bits chewing at his robe. He glanced down at his legs, both of which were shielded against the planter box, neither of which looked maimed. He had heard that being shot by NovaCore weapons left little to the mind. Shock set in almost instantly and death took hold soon after. He glanced over at his aide, knowing it had to be true.

The NovaCore weapons were themselves, angry, violent throwers of death and destruction. They hurled fragments of metal at high speeds despite the increased wear and maintenance needs of such old fashioned firearms. The NovaCore had refined them to the point where all of Vaerlin's security and training classes had referred in half joke, to the best defense against them being simply not to be hit. It was a tongue in cheek way of saying that most of the infantry body armor was hard pressed at stopping the larger of the weapons the NovaCore ground forces would field.

The alien's own armor and defense was probably more effective against Hil'Raigh pulse plasma weaponry than most of the Federation wanted to admit but the PPR weapons came with far fewer downsides and more versatility. Was that really worth it? Vaerlin hunkered down as another large chunk of metal ripped out of the planter only centimeters from his shoulder. He felt a pain moments later and reached up, his hand came away bloody and his mind took a moment to register that it was not a bullet but the torn metal frame of the planter box that had done the damage.

There was a chaos here, under attack from an angle Vaerlin could not identify. He layed, hunkered, hoping. Was this really a NovaCore attack? The Duke was no solider and so, as he cowered there, he wondered exactly how anyone's nerves ever handled such a thing as this. He scanned helplessly for Tamur, who he saw meters away behind much harder looking cover. It looked harder at least, until one of the attacker's rounds tore a hole through it, spraying a mess of shards behind. Tamur had been uninjured but from here at least, there was a measured fear on the man's face, one he never would have shown otherwise.

It must have been impossible to fully prepare for something even as planned as this. Then again, maybe his people were not following the script as well as they should have. Tamur returned fire after a moment, Vaerlin glancing up toward where he thought the man was shooting. He lost track scanning for it when the familiar obstruction of his now beloved planter box blocked his vision.

Even despite the foreknowledge of all of this, Vaerlin still eyed the box as if it was going to be a lifelong friend now. The few other civilians who had been walking the promenade had been unaffected, none of their bodies mingling with paving as far as Vaerlin could see. That was good at least, it made things look more focused. It was one thing to frame an attack, it was an entirely different one to do so with needless casualties. Vaerlin almost chuckled to himself. He was shaking with pent up anxiety and yet he had the time in his mind, to logically process whatever this was.

A loud public warning siren finally flared to life, followed by a less than helpful automated message about finding a safe place to hide. Vaerlin almost yelled back at the loud speakers mounted on building sides and hanging from the lamp posts between landing pads. It was easy to ask someone to find a safe place as long as they were not stuck behind a rapidly disintegrating flower box.

Surprisingly, the wound on Vaerlin's shoulder was near the bottom of his current concerns, some primal instinct letting him know that he would survive a wound that small with relative ease. A small wound, Vaerlin glanced at the gash again, it looked far from small and was sure to ruin his robe with a stain. His body told him it was superficial but his mind was not entirely trusting of the idea. Regardless, he knew so little about first aid or what to do about the injury while he layed there that he opted to let himself bleed instead. Another exchange between Tamur and the attackers occurred, this time the opposition giving Vaerlin's would be hero much more opening to return his fire against them.

The rapid bursts sent out white hot beams from the tip of Tamur's gun to a place out of view, a set of three bursts before the hardened man returned to cover. Vaerlin had no idea how fast NovaCore guns could actually fire, he wondered if they were going easy on his man but it did not matter too much.

Finally, the sounds of police sirens filled the air, rising above the cacophony for the first time. Vaerlin nearly cheered as the fire from the attackers slowed and appeared to stop. He saw his opening and looked to Tamur, who glanced at him.

There was a long pause in everything, everything save the sirens moving in on wherever the attack was supposed to have originated from. The stalemate continued and stretched onward, seconds turning to minutes until finally, Tamur poked out from behind his riddled cover, rifle drawn. The mercenary's composure had returned rather fast, probably once he was no longer under live fire.

He raced over to one of the fallen, calling for help from one of the newly arrived civil service paramedics. Vaerlin had not even seen their shuttle land but he knew that no amount of their effort would save some of his aides. He sat finally, slumping against the planter box as he eyed them, breathing heavily. He reached over and covered his wounded shoulder even as the paramedics scurried about. Some they pulled into stretchers, others they examined and left, they never even went near the aide that had been hit first.

Vaerlin shuddered, amid the sea of help, desperate help, not a single person bothered with the first hit. He knew why of course, it was because the young man had been dead for minutes, but to see that sort of calculated logic play out with real people, was something Vaerlin had never imagined. The calculated loss of an individual was something he had to admit he was not all that fond of. First it was the king, many councilors, and now, a bright young aide.

The Duke watched it all with fascination, knowing that somehow, this was never going to end in a way he wanted, a way he was comfortable with. The people he had chosen, the people who had chosen him rather, had no interest in his moral qualms, only their goal. For a fleeting moment, Vaerlin caught himself wishing that Kirashira Ren'Tauru was not only found, but survived and somehow won. Even if it meant his death for treason. The thought faded quickly but it was damning nonetheless, something Vaerlin could not easily discard with rationalizing.

Another few minutes saw the arrival of a second medical transport, this one carrying enough of a surplus in personnel that one of them finally took notice of the duke himself. A Hil'Raigh woman approached, immediately recognizing the trappings of Vaerlin's nobility.

"Duke," The woman approached hurriedly, only now did he notice how much his body was starting to throb. She knelt down with a medical bag next to him, cracking it open and drawing out some treated bandages, "Vaerlin isn't it?"

"Yes," He grunted in reply. She reached out with her gloved fingertips, prying back Vaerlin's damaged robe and reaching for her bandages with the other.

"Do you have any other wounds that you know of?" She began questioning. Vaerlin informed her that he had no other wounds he knew about, "Just that one..."

"Alright," She replied. She was remarkably calm and collected being here in this scene. Was it callousness? No, probably just experience and training. Vaerlin did not know much about medical first responders and as a result had no idea what their training was like. He guessed that they, like law enforcement would have to be trained to remain as calm as they could even in desperate situations. This situation qualified if anything did. In a way Vaerlin was grateful that the person rendering him aid was able to focus so well.

"Do you have a personal physician who should be notified about your receiving care?" She asked as she applied some disinfectant gel to the nobleman's wound.

"I'll speak to my personal physician in person thank you," He replied.

"We'd like to have you transported back to the hospital for a further evaluation," She informed as she placed the bandage at last.

"I don't think I need to go," Vaerlin replied. The woman glanced down at him as she patted the bandage down firmly. It was cool to his throbbing skin, the numbing of the disinfectant cream already kicking in. With any luck the pain would vanish soon.

"I can't force you to go to the hospital with us Duke Vaerlin, but I would strongly encourage it. If you choose not to come, please note that you'll be responsible for seeking any continued care you need with your own physician," The woman replied. She removed her sterile gloves and threw them in a waste collection cylinder in her medical bag before grabbing a slate from her breast pocket, "Would you like to forgo continued care from the hospital Duke Vaerlin?"

"Yes," He replied loud enough that the recording mechanism on the slate would have heard. The medic glanced at the device, keyed a button or two then nodded to him before she looked around. That was when it hit her. Vaerlin noted in her face, the composure was holding but was not perfect. The dead had already been covered while law enforcement were busy barricading the scene. There were of course, news crews already assembling at various positions outside the barricades, their holo-imagers already blinking to life as the reporters from various networks across the Federation tried to stake out some real estate in the area outside. The barricades themselves would unfold high enough that once the area was surrounded, no one could see inside but until then, the gaps in the wall offered the prying curiousness of the networks their fill of carnage. At very least, it would make for a convincing argument.

Vaerlin did wonder though, what the NovaCore response would be, it would only be a matter of days at the latest, potentially hours at the least, before they knew what had happened here. By that time, public outrage in the Federation would be near boiling. The first attack they would be implicated in would be the Guild Hall, but Tamur's men had failed to complete the mission as prescribed. Some of the good framing evidence was now long buried by Vaerlin's associates. This attack however, would more than make up for anything they had lost. News holos would have nothing else showing for at least a week, maybe longer. There would be talk of a war council in the Federation and to participate in a war council, the Compact would need its regent sooner rather than later.

13 - The Briefing

It was to be a nice change of pace not to have to ferry Princess Kirashira around the ship today, at least for a while. Though Truth had not had a particularly un-enjoyable time with the royal, the previous day had been a learning experience. The fact that someone of such position from the Starlight Compact was on the ship was something of a novelty and everything from the conversation and questions to the standard operating procedures themselves made that clear.

In the NovaCore, no one was a royal, even dignitaries, and a military ship like this was never expected to handle one. There were procedures for important visitors and the like but no one who held such a position existed in the NovaCore. Admiral Thorsh was probably the closest thing Truth had known previously. Unlike Kirashira however, he was a member of the NovaCore admiralty, the ruling body of her home. He had his own quarters, an office, a place in the chain of command. He made decisions in that context and understood his responsibilities, and even his limits, when it came to the ship and its crew. It was warranted that he have such accommodation because responsibility had placed such a burden on him.

Princess Kirashira on the other hand, was not a member of the hierarchy on board and as such, proved a disruption to the social order. She had started the previous day rather softly, only a minor gaffe here or there, but her personality, her behavior, they made it hard for her to understand that she was not in fact, in a position of power on the ship. She had not directly tried to order anyone to do anything but Truth had felt, rather uncomfortably, that the Royal viewed her more as a conduit for exacting her own interests from the day rather than a gracious host. What Truth had intended as a positive trust building experience had ended up as more of a tightrope.

The clothing that Truth had requisitioned fit Kirashira in a way that the alien felt was non flattering. Only after a minute or two of complaining, and finally, an assurance that the ship's tailor could take a look at it later, did she agree to spend the rest of the day in it. Of course that was not until she had requested to be informed of the cleaning status of her own clothes. Truth had not had the heart to let her know that there was probably not going to be any chance to wear such an expensive garment on board, not in the intended way. There were no attendants to help with cosmetics or hair, no one to perfect the look of a young monarch, something which Truth was sure would be requested if things ever got that far.

The food had been hard to settle, with the Princess insisting after getting her tray from the galley, that there had to be something else instead. There were several choices of course, but Truth had made sure that her guest had ordered what had to be the most agreeable to Hil'Raigh cuisine. In the end the food had been 'edible,' something that Truth was not interested in relating to the food processors or the galley crew. The other meals of the day were less dramatic at least, possibly due to the earlier disappointment.

Kirashira was certainly quite different from anyone Truth knew or interacted with. Yesterday's adventures had been a constant reminder of that fact. They were from two distinctly different cultures and ways of life, with their own feelings and thoughts on just about everything. The differences in NovaCore and Hil'Raigh culture were stark at times, monolithic even, when viewed from certain perspectives. Tossing a social class into that mix, one which had not existed in NovaCore society for quite a long time, made things even more unpredictable. Truth had to admit that despite the fact that she was not really exhausted, she was glad to have a change of pace anyway.

That change was granted by a briefing, a time to sit down for mission review not just with the Admiral on board, but with the command staff. As the ship and its crew had been assigned to the region for support, those officers were to be included in most of the meetings that surrounded the potential dangers and obligations that would be levied against their vessel. It was a long standing practice in the NovaCore, one that felt more like tradition than it would have in any other setting.

The scenery would go from infirmary to conference room and hopefully soon, the royal guest would be housed somewhere other than the medical recovery wing. She was someone who was used to her own personal space, probably an inordinate and excessive quantity of it.

The corridor was busier at this hour than it had been the previous morning but not by much. The cleaning assignments had changed as evidenced by the new faces carrying their gear past the infirmary door as Truth exited it. The proper bill of health she had received before leaving was almost enough to make her smile.

Her partner was already waiting in the hall, calling to her as she let the metal door slide closed behind her, "Hey babysitter."

Truth smirked, then shrugged. It had certainly felt that way at times, "Good morning."

"Ready for the exciting world of conference rooms?" Tony interjected with sarcastic enthusiasm. Truth shook her head and did not reply. She did not mind conference rooms as much as he did. His patience for such things was admittedly lower than her own.

"I heard the Admiral had some new developments for us," Truth replied. Tony raised a brow and the two started off down the corridor. Their destination, a transport station, was not too far away and they set off at a comfortable pace.

"I wouldn't be surprised if the entire Federation world collapsed in on itself overnight," Tony replied, "Seems about how they deal with problems, they create one and then over-react to it"

Truth smiled, she had to admit he had a flair for describing the Hil'Raigh in a way that made her laugh.

"How was your day off?" Tony asked.

"Less relaxing than a briefing with Captain Donavan," She replied with a smirk.

Tony snickered aloud, "And that guy's briefings kept you on edge the entire time. World ending shit every day."

"A no-eff boarding action was the kind of thing I expect from first years..." Truth replied, quoting the former commanding officer in as close a voice as she could.

"I do hope Admiral Thorsh doesn't spring one of those on us or we are finished..." Tony replied,

"As I recall, the no-eff was cleared when they found the training charges," Truth smirked.

"Yeah, good plant on that," Tony replied. The old training exercise had certainly been the source of jokes for months afterward but the poor Captain had remained at the butt end of most of them even to this day.

"That was an interesting assignment..." Tony said with a distant, memory laden voice.

"I was fairly upset about the no-eff when he made the claim..." Truth replied.

"Probably the last time you got visibly angry," Tony replied with a laugh, "Other than the academy days."

"All my instances are justified," Truth defended, "Even the academy ones."

"Yeah," Tony replied, "I woulda broken a bone or two in your place if you hadn't done it first."

Truth glanced to her partner and gave him a thankful smile, it was a small gesture but his words meant something. Back in the academy she had indeed gotten into trouble for fighting, but not for the same reasons most others their age would have. Instead of fighting over something petty or juvenile, Truth had punched one of her squad mates for his blatant lack of respect for the then squad leader. Later, the romantic interest of the same individual had picked a badly timed fight with Truth and ended up with a broken arm.

Tony, the squad leader at the time had to punish Truth by order, it was only fair, but since she had defended him, opted to request his own punishment from the campus' master instructor. It had been a worse punishment than Truth was ordered to take but he had done it without hesitating. The incident patched up the rifts in the unit, forcing honesty out of deception and, thankfully, Tony had been allowed to compete in the pre-graduation trials despite the reprimand. Truth had worried at the time that his prospects of competing in the prestigious event were shattered because she had become angry with someone. She'd wondered whether she had the discipline to move forward like her dreams had warranted. Tony, however, despite his sometimes fiery nature had been a voice of assurance at the time. He had provided something that only a friend so dear was capable.

Even now, Truth held a special fondness for that month, the healing that had happened, the growth that had come to the entire group. The squad itself was rebuilt stronger, several of its members, even the one she had initially punched, moving on to greater things. In her mind, that was the doing of then squad leader Tony Karo.

"You should let me do the cracking, my bones are mostly unbreakable," She replied with a playfully smug glance.

"Not fit for duty," Tony replied, echoing one of his favorite instructor's phrases of disdain for under performing recruits. The voice was spot on at least, even if the one speaking the words was too short to give the full effect of the utter contempt the phrase usually carried.

The pair arrived at the tram station at last, stepping into the space and taking up a position to wait for the transport that ran the length of the track. On ships that reached a kilometer or more in size, the NovaCore employed the trams to ferry crew to predetermined stations along the length of the ship. The stations ran along the main axis of the vessel, parallel to the main armament.

This ship, the Knight Slayer, was large enough for the purpose built transportation system, with many stations and six tram lines. On other, larger ships, there would be many more lines, shunting and transferring people from one section to another. The station here, near the hangar, was the most central, another stopped near the main crew quarters and the last made its home near the command deck and the supporting command centers for various departments on the vessel. There were lines on either side of the ship, and at various heights in the deck structure, but Truth never rode any lines other than the central one.

She was not one to visit the command deck often and as a result never had much experience there. However, the general rule was the same on all NovaCore ships. The command officers of the ship had their offices, personal quarters and some basic amenities on the command deck. The deck itself was a section of the ship mounted quite closely to the axial main armament, usually straddling it in the smaller ships. The well armored area had its own backup life support and emergency systems and a set of configurable spaces that could function as anything from cargo stowage to a make shift barracks in a pinch.

The area also held the central command center, the ship's bridge. While the central command center functioned as the nerve center of the ship, other departments like gunnery, docking control and navigation had their own sub command centers. Each of the sub command centers was responsible for directing the affairs of its personnel.

While it was called a deck, for all intents and purposes, the command deck was more like a cluster of them, depending on the size of the ship and its crew. Rather than a single layer on the ship, several at once were housed in the armored shell surrounding it. All of them shared the unique characteristic however, of being inaccessible unless one entered the shell via the main access ways.

The command decks of NovaCore ships had become larger and more encompassing over the years and newer models even housed the ship's central computers entirely within them as well. The ethos of their design was simple however, protect the vital operations of the ship as heavily as possible. Indeed, in the war with the Hil'Raigh, that sort of construction had solidified the importance of the command deck style. Ships that would have been knocked out had continued to function despite severe or crippling damage to the hull or armor. Commanders overwhelmingly attributed the hardiness of the NovaCore warships to the way they had been made.

Because of his status, Admiral Thorsh had his own quarters on the command deck, and the main briefing room for command officers was only a few doors down from the central command center. Truth and her partner would take the tram to the station outside the command deck, enter at the access way checkpoint and finally make their way to the meeting area.

The stations, all like this one, were more of a double wide hallway than anything fancy. On the wall close to the tram were a set of large windows and two sets of double sliding doors. When a tram arrived and parked, it would fill the entirety of the view there and be obvious to anyone who looked.

In prompt fashion, the arrival sound played, a sing song tone indicating the impending arrival of a tram. Truth and her partner moved out of the exit lanes painted on the gray metal flooring, a set of lines dictating exactly where waiting passengers should stand to let those disembarking depart quickly.

The tram came into view, the normally dark tunnel of the tram tube lighting up as the flat faced cylindrical object came sliding to a halt in front of the waiting passengers. Accompanied by a loud buzzer, the doors slid open and a small contingent of riders exited, filtering out of the station quickly toward their various destinations. Truth and Tony, along with a smaller number of new riders, moved into the tram afterward and within a minute, the doors had closed once more. A final buzzer sounded and Truth felt her stomach lurch as the tube train accelerated forward.

The insides of the carriages featured a set of benches along the outer walls and a set of poles running down the middle for those unlucky enough not to get a seat. At this hour, and for the most part on this ship, the seats were usually vacant but Truth reached for one of the metal poles and took hold of it. Tony grabbed the same one and the two stood together, whisked down the tunnel.

It did not take long for the tram to announce the next stop, and, with a cheerful automated voice, the carriage gave it's riders a warning that this was indeed the last stop. The tram would be turning back from here. With only a few stops, even that simple logic might have been overkill but Truth never felt the need to critique it openly.

The doors slid open once more, revealing a station almost the same in layout as the previous, save that across the several meter expanse that made up the station proper, was a wide door about three meters in width. Hanging into the opening from above were the thick slabs of metal that made the locking teeth of the pressure door on this access way. The metallic slab was almost a meter thick from the inside to the outside, reminding Truth that the armored walls of the command deck into which it was built, were even thicker.

A pair of guards, one at each side of the access way, kept watch over anyone who wanted to enter. Both of them, like all sentries in this sort of position, were armed. Truth and her partner entered the command deck at last, passing the heavy door overhead.

If Truth and her partner had been anyone else, they would have been stopped, but having intelligence operatives on board was a rarity for most ships and as a result, the sentries were instructed on who they were. The pair passed through the checkpoint without incident, only two sets of eyes following them into the command deck.

There was an immediate urgency one felt inside this area of the vessel, no matter the time of day or the condition of the ship. It was all business, all the time on the command deck and only the best of the crew and officers on board a NovaCore ship were ever assigned here. While the professionalism of a NovaCore naval crew was quite high by default, the best of them formed the interface that the command deck had with the outside world, either by being posted within it, or by working directly with those who were.

The halls were orderly, those who were in them, always at a brisk pace, heading to their duties with purpose. The intent was reflected even in the decoration, a brighter more urgent aesthetic given to the entire section by near white paneling and dark metal trim at the top and bottoms of each of the wall bulkheads. Unlike the uniform plating that decorated most of the other corridors on-board, this was the kind that would require much more regular cleaning to look presentable. Passing several side hallways, the officers mess and a small rec room, Truth and her partner found the largest of the hallways in the command deck, the one leading to the central command. Down at one end was the brain of the ship and, several meters down the hall from it, the designated conference room.

The two honed in on their assigned meeting place quickly, making haste to be out of the way of those who belonged here on duty. The engaged crew, combined with the decor, gave the command deck an aura of cleanliness and efficiency. The conference room door was set into a wall nearby, now visible as Truth and her partner made their way to it. In a moment more the door had parted, sliding open without a sound as Truth tapped the control panel on the doorframe.

The brightly lit corridor was a far cry from the more focused lighting within, a room that was dominated by a large semi elliptical table. A holographic projector sat in the center of the surface. Beyond the table, a small doorway opened into another room, one that Truth guessed was a presentation space, several rows of seats visible through the portal. If one were to discuss something with command staff peers, it would happen here in the conference room. When it was ready to be sent down the chain as orders, section chiefs and senior staff would be briefed en-masse next door

In the conference room already, were assembled a group of the Knight Slayer's command staff, some of its intelligence analysts and of course, at the head of the table, Admiral Thorsh. The officer, noting the arrival of the last attendees, cleared his throat as Truth took a seat. Tony sat next to her, immediately starting to wobble forward and back in his chair.

"Alright let's get started," Thorsh began. The lights darkened a bit more and the holo-projector sprung to life in the center of the table. A soft accent light lit up one of the intelligence analyst's positions and he leaned over the control pad at his seat before speaking.

"First, what we know." The center of the table came to life with holographic projection, a vision of what looked like a public space on Ashor below. It was a set of platforms, suspended between the tall buildings of the capitol city of Dau'Kore. The officer continued as the scene moved in, the image growing larger and larger until the buildings themselves moved out of the projection, now framing it instead. In the center, remained the image of a group of what looked to be Hil'Raigh. They appeared to be under attack from an angle out of the projection, with only one armed individual appearing to move or return fire. The image gave Truth pause as, it appeared several casualties were already sustained in the projected party.

"It appears that a second attack occurred a few hours ago, we managed to get wind of it through some of the taps we had established on some key broadcasters," The intelligence officer stated grimly, "And the general consensus is that it was a second NovaCore attack."

"I wasn't aware we had done any attacking at all..." Tony replied. He had likely been briefed, but only slightly on the weak ties that were being drawn between the NovaCore and the attack on the royal family before. Truth had yet to receive a direct briefing either, now listening with increased interest as the analyst nodded.

"Right, the links initially were pointing to wounds that would be consistent with our style of infantry firearms," He added, "But we also searched for references to the two that Truth dispatched on the upper floors. We found that the general spin there is that they wrestled a NovaCore rifle from the attackers while performing law enforcement duties. Hence the finding of a broken rifle near where they hit the ground.

Truth remembered the exchange, a tinge of pain shot through her shoulder. She remembered kicking the second target out of the window herself. The first had gone out with the initial volley of her railgun fire and apparently his rifle, a NovaCore weapon had inexplicably fallen nearby.

"Whoever is responsible for the initial attack has been able to effectively middleman the actual investigation by law enforcement," Thorsh summarized with a sigh, "As far as I heard, we are assuming that they are linked to the second attack?"

"That's correct Admiral," the analyst replied, "We have no concrete ties yet, but the profiles for the two who fell out of the building are as whitewashed as we would expect from planted operatives. That makes them consistent with Truth's debriefing."

The man gave a small nod to Truth, who felt at least a little vindicated to know that her own people were already making progress not only to corroborate her story, but move forward and plan accordingly.

"Those two alone didn't lead us anywhere but one of the analysts on board recognized the face of this man. After we did a look up on who it was..." The officer continued, the projection slipped inward on the firefight scene, now paused until it was focused on the arguably blurry representation of the apparent bodyguard of whomever was under attack.

Truth had no idea who the man was, but then again she did not have complete access to the NovaCore databases that kept track of such people. The expansive program of identifying and cataloging potential threats to the NovaCore was however, fairly focused. As a result, she knew that for an analyst to recognize someone they had been prominent at some point. The holo-projection switched from a combat scene to a much more crisp, detailed rendition of the individual in question, a Hil'Raigh man with a strong jaw. His ears were as wide as any Hil'Raigh, though his skin showed signs of stubble and weathering. Overall it was the kind of person Truth expected to be a grunt for an actual problem, given the Federation's usual history.

"This man has shown up before as an Akal'Maru military officer, former special naval warfare in fact," The analyst explained, "He was apparently responsible for an attempted boarding action back during the war. Went south and he dropped off record until he appeared after the war again."

"He appears to have taken the time to find new employment, as, the next time he showed up was working as a trainer for Shae'Lun," The man stated. There were some murmurs of understanding around the table. The name Shae'Lun carried some weight in military circles.

The largest private military organization in the galaxy, Shae'Lun had been one of the most effective portions of the overall Hil'Raigh military campaign against the NovaCore. Using the same technology as their peers, they had made for more difficult enemies than the Akal'Maru navy themselves had been. They had used a variety of tactics, adapted more quickly to changing conditions and were, overall seen as a bulwark in the conflict. The culture surrounding the organization had catapulted its reputation since the days of the war and they were now the subject of anything from holo-dramas to documentaries and public praise by the Akal'Maru government.

Of course, for the NovaCore, Shae'Lun was anything but popular, retaining instead, infamy. Their operations in the war had been more effective than their counterparts but the real thorn they presented was in their support for a number of privateer groups. Their involvement after the war with privateers had put them on the map in a semi-permanent way for NovaCore intelligence services. Most viewed them as a front for the Akal'Maru state to continue an unofficial, yet state sponsored war against their neighbors.

"So a raider turned merc shows up as a what... a bodyguard?" Tony quipped, eying the holographic face critically. Truth knew the look, he was sizing up the man from his holo. She regularly did the same and wondered if she adopted a similarly thoughtful expression when she did so.

"Looks like it," The officer replied, "He has not been on Shae'Lun's official payroll for a while though, which is why we think there is more to it than meets the eye. Notice especially, that while there are a few dead already, the one with the rifle, our friend here, is miraculously not dead."

"I do not think we would have missed," Truth finally stated, to which Tony grunted in agreement.

"Does he have a name?"

"An alias at least, Tamur Hal'Aen" came the reply, "The name may be fake. The face match turned up a few more but that is the most commonly used alias at least. Importantly, it's what he appears to be going by now."

"You managed to look it up that quickly?" Thorsh piped up, his voice carried a tone of cautious optimism.

"No, we were tipped, and then looked it up. It checked out." The officer replied. "Actually that brings us to the second part of the briefing..."

"Tipped?" The question came from one of the ship's command officers. The captain, as Truth recalled, one Captain Defrae He was a completely bald middle aged man with wrinkles to show for his years in service. Defrae had never really been introduced to Truth but she had taken the liberty to do some research on him, as she always did when she was stationed to a new ship.

He had apparently served in the war, then moved on to command deep cover missions into Hil'Raigh space as part of the effort to preempt renewed violence. The missions he engaged in of course, were not things Truth could read about, but her clearance afforded her at least the basic idea of his career. Judging by the medals on his breast pocket, some of which were quite rare, he was something of a standout. It made sense after all, that Admiral Thorsh would have him out this far.

"A message passed to us, along with some problematic looking intel..." The intelligence officer brought Truth back to the briefing mentally as he replied to Captain Defrae's question.

There was a pause and then the image in the holographic projection shifted. The light garbled then rearranged to a picture not unfamiliar to Truth. Two individuals were hunkered down behind some cover on what looked to be the edge of a building, both had weapons that looked NovaCore. As the analyst rotated the projection a bit however, Truth began to see the problem.

Perched in admittedly blurry form was an individual who strikingly resembled Tony. The equipment used to capture the scene had obviously struggled for detail meaning it was probably at a distance. The image however, was unsettling to say the least. Truth or what she guessed would have been her, was next to him but somehow less clearly defined.

"Oh, I don't remember this one," Tony said sarcastically to the image.

"This is what our informant labeled as, perpetrator footage." The intelligence officer explained grimly.

"Framing us for the second attack too?"

"Apparently with better detail," Truth added, "At least it is an actual picture this time."

"We believe they may have pieced it together from scanning equipment they had on board those vehicles that pursued you in the Kolos suburbs," The analyst added, "But that's just a guess."

"Who sent us this?" Thorsh interjected seriously.

"A Kul'Raigh, claims to have contact with Tamur, claims she met both the Major and Truth in Kolos"

There was a hush of silence with the Admiral glancing over the table to Tony who looked a bit lost. The man then fixed his attention to Truth, "Well?"

"What was the name of this individual?" Truth finally asked, sounding unfortunately more skeptical than she had planned.

"A'Shir is the name, but other than that..." The officer shrugged.

The name drew back memories, recollection and finally, a face, one that was bruised, "Yes I do recall her now, we detailed our contact in the briefing, sir."

The admiral nodded, "Alright, though I can't say I am glad to know you were remembered so easily by someone you met under cover."

"The brief message she included with the correspondence said that she recalled you both when she saw the attached footage," The analyst stated.

"And how in the galaxy did she see this footage?" Tony's skepticism mirrored the rest of the room's own. There were a few quizzical glances, a frown or two from those whose expressions always seemed a mask of unhappiness.

"She didn't explain that detail," The officer shifted the discussion, motioning to the Admiral, "She mentioned that she would be able to contact our people briefly, but it's soon and its on the surface. A relatively small window. After that she said she's going dark even if we haven't made contact..."

"Trap," Tony exclaimed dismissively, "Last time I help someone on the street..."

Truth had to admit she felt the same, it was all so perfectly timed, it seemed too good to be true. The Federation had proven that it was not above deception, and given the situation, how desperate the real attackers appeared to be to frame the NovaCore for wrongdoing, she was wary of the magical help.

Still, despite that uneasiness, it was a lead and she had a feeling there was a mission in the works.

"What evidence do we have to suggest this is not a trap?" The Admiral finally asked. His implication was clear, he wanted a reason to believe it rather than faith alone. There was a nod from the presenter and he spoke again.

"The name traces out to a registered companion, well connected in the Companion Guild. Normally this wouldn't be much to go on but..." The man stated, he paused and continued, obviously venturing into unverified territory with his theorizing. "...the King's wife was a former companion, loved by the Guild and the Kul'Raigh alike"

"What do we lose if we do nothing with this?" The captain of the ship asked finally. There was a long pause.

"As long as we have Kirashira on board, we risk a number of things," Thorsh began, "Worst of all is that this kind of thing is the impetus the Federation would need to re-enter the war."

"Ren'Tauru leadership was historically against the conflict," The intelligence officer added, "If they are replaced by a more sympathetic individual, it could mean a new war council..."

"Who would replace the King?" Tony asked.

"There are a few names floating around but one noble appears more often than the rest. Duke Arash Vaerlin."

"Never heard of him either..." Tony replied, "But I have a feeling we should have?"

"He's a pretty well connected nobleman, but he didn't see eye to eye with the King on a number of issues. Notably, he was due for removal from the Starlight Compact's delegation to the Hil'Raigh Federation Council. With Ren'Tauru gone, that plan is out the window."

"Awfully convenient," Tony stated, "And he's who the second attack happened on?"

The analyst nodded. Truth ran over what she had seen in her mind. The attack had apparently failed to do the kind of damage it would have been intended to do and the Shae'Lun mercenary was the bodyguard of the man against whom it was performed. The situation seemed pretty clear.

"Interesting confluence of characters," Admiral Thorsh said with a hint of irony. The collection of related names in all of it seemed a bit too much for coincidence.

"What kind of policies does Duke Vaerlin advocate?" Truth inquired.

"Vaerlin has in the past, shown sympathies to the school of thought which paints Gou'Ran Ren'Tauru's daughter, Kirashira, as a potentially illegitimate heir due to the fact that she has a Kul'Raigh mother. Otherwise he's part of the expansionist mindset, one that sees the Starlight Compact opening up its economy to Federation Council control more than it does currently."

"Vaerlin as a Regent would certainly reverse a number of political inroads we made with King Ren'Tauru. It was hard enough getting him to agree to an embassy, I doubt Vaerlin will even consider the idea...," the analyst added.

"Then we go figure out as much as we can before this shit is plastered all over every holo on the planet, sir," Tony stated finally, "I say we meet the Kul'Raigh despite the risk.."

"I agree sir," Truth added. Preemptive action was something both she and her partner preferred, especially to feeling like a caged animal, waiting for the captor to prod them once more.

The admiral sighed, remaining quiet for a moment. He glanced over to the captain of the ship and finally spoke, "How quickly can you modify the orbit for a quick insertion over Dau'Kore city?"

"Right away sir," the man replied quickly.

"Good," Thorsh nodded, "Mission is go. Get underway as soon as you can."

Truth and her partner nodded in the affirmative and the quiet meeting room transformed into a flurry of action. In orderly fashion, officers filed out of their seats and out the door. The captain and his commanding officer headed down the hall toward the central command at a brisk pace. Even as Truth and her partner began in a jog back toward the tram station, she heard the captain giving the order, his voice carrying through the hallway.

14 - Good Karma

The summer rain was a fact of life here on the ground, thankfully keeping most of the sometimes curious citizenry of the Compact hidden under umbrellas or indoors. From Tony's shoulder hung his rifle, in a convenient, non-descript case which served to conceal it from prying eyes. The long box shape hung from one of Tony's shoulders and Truth, next to him, had one hanging from hers as well. Most people they passed on the street were too busy trying to get out of the rain to notice anything about the two as they walked along. It helped however that Tony and his partner were sharing a large umbrella and wore matching long coats. For all anyone knew they were simply a pair of people going to exercise or something else. Of course, the fake ears were annoying to wear and the cosmetics Tony had put on to mask himself were not ideal either. It was a necessary evil to protect from what was sure to be a media blitz with his face all over it however. The rain was a welcome diversion for the day, making sure that people were more concerned with remaining dry than finding a would be criminal.

He was glad no one was looking or wondering, because it made things like this easier. Being no stranger to walking around armed in places he should not have been, Tony could only imagine how much nervousness someone with less experience would have shown. Training and practice however, allowed him all the calm he would have in the case of being armed or not.

Testing the broadness of the invitation that had been extended by their contact, still weighed on his mind. It was unlikely that anyone who knew anything remotely valuable would be unwatched. It was even more unlikely that the meeting place would be insecure enough to allow the pair weapons, especially given the affluent neighborhood they appeared to be wandering around in.

Truth had been leading in a route she had planned that was constructed for as much apparent randomness as possible while still giving them a destination. Though he was good at directions normally, Tony found himself only just now, recognizing the street thanks to some buildings further down the way.

Their apparent destination stuck out pretty obviously, and even before Truth pointed it out, Tony had a good idea that the building with the most ornate looking entry front, was probably their goal. Like all of the buildings here, it was polished, clean, and tall.

For a completely clueless visitor to the city it would have been difficult to tell where the general city itself morphed into this expensive district. Unlike the less expensive suburbs that dotted the mountain to the city's northern side, the An'Jea district as it was called, filled out a large chunk of the city's inner area.

Tony had heard that the average height of all the buildings in Dau'Kore was about one hundred twenty five stories. Unlike any of the Novian Imperial cities he had visited, this one was laced with catwalks and multistory promenades that connected building to building. One could spend their entire life never setting foot on the ground below, if they so chose.

As he glanced over the railing next to him, he guessed the building entry he had spotted was probably at least the tenth or fifteenth floor of the massive building in which it was housed, an ornate park style garden spilling into the open space between buildings out front. The area was one of obvious intent, a space for people to mingle and gather. On any other day, one with good weather, it was probably a sort of social hot spot. In the rain, not even the food carts were open today.

Well dressed companions, sharing umbrellas spoke with random groups of passerby despite the rain however. Tony sighed to himself as he examined from afar, several of the affluent looking Hil'Raigh entertaining themselves with conversation. Something about the way that Hil'Raigh high society carried itself bugged him no matter how much he tried to ignore it. It was either that or the fact that even within ten or fifteen meters, he and his partner drew contemptuous stares from some of them. Thankfully, most of them turned back to their talking as they saw his partner's features.

A smirk crossed the Novian officer's lips as he caught the sneers of several bystanders to his partner. For a companion, and especially in this area, she was definitely under-dressed, and no Kul'Raigh coming here would be anything other than a well established guild member. Tony cleared his throat as the pair drew under an awning and closed up their umbrella. Truth glanced at him with a one of her sly smiles as he took the umbrella and shook it out on the ground. She had definitely noticed the attitude.

Even before Tony or his partner had moved to the sliding doors to enter the building, someone emerged, a cheery practiced voice of greeting in perfect, High-society Hil'Raigh. "Hello Honored Guests."

Tony traced the voice to a well made Kul'Raigh with meticulously done hair and clothing, whatever makeup she wore was designed to be near invisible without scrutiny. Either that or she was wearing enough that he never saw the real skin beneath. He was not entirely sure which was the case. She greeted Tony and his partner, with a warm smile, a stark contrast to the Hil'Raigh outside.

"We are here for an invitation appointment," Truth replied quickly, her hand dipping into the deep pocket of her coat and coming out with a thin plastic slate. The card contained the single use digital invitation that had been sent to them by their supposed contact. Tony waited for a question about his weapon case and eyed the greeter quietly.

With only a glance at him, she smiled and took the card from Truth's outstretched, gloved hand. Tony smiled, she always liked wearing those fingerless gloves of hers.

"Please come, On your behalf, I will put your entry into our system." the Kul'Raigh announced happily.

Truth nodded, "Thank you."

Tony caught a slight surprise on the attendant's face at Truth's reply. He guessed that she was not used to being thanked for doing her job.

"Would you like someone to carry your bags, I am sure they are heavy," she announced as she led the pair through the sliding doors of the building.

"No, we will be keeping our luggage on our persons," Truth replied calmly, "They are personal items."

"Of course, I'm sorry for the assumption" the Kul'Raigh replied with a smile. Tony wondered if her face was capable of anything else. Smile smile smile, he wondered how crazy it would make him go if he had to smile at every thing all day, especially at people who were annoying him or being an average Hil'Raigh. He snickered beside himself, causing the Kul'Raigh to blush brightly. Whatever she was wearing did a terrible job of hiding her embarrassment.

"Don't worry about it, I was just wondering if you ever stop smiling. Don't think I could do it."

The Kul'Raigh did not lose her pace at all, leading the pair through the ornate foyer. Either this was some kind of extremely expensive hotel, an apartment complex, or both. Tony couldn't tell. The few attendants in the foyer were all Kul'Raigh but the rest of those inside were Hil'Raigh. After a moment Tony settled on the idea that this place was probably a combination of both.

The foyer was filled with expensive, lavish chairs, gold trim and red satin. Expensive, ornate looking rugs covered the floor in various places, while lighting was provided for the most part from the windows on the front and rear of the room. The foyer extended to the opposite wall of the building, with what looked to be a bar or something at the far end.

Tall golden lamps with upward facing cone shaped lights also added light to the room, and along the walls, lights aimed to create a sort of downward facing cone against the normally dark interior wall, provided an art gallery feel. Some of the wall lights were helped by small spotlights, which illuminated some kind of art piece or painting. Perfectly kept potted trees were interspersed at calculated points around the room, which Tony finally realized was actually two stories tall. Using so much space on nothing was probably one of the most obvious signs of opulence in a city where space was at such a premium.

Finally, the trio reached a rounded counter, behind which the hostess shuffled noiselessly. Smiling yet again, she presented the card for Truth to see in the flat of her open hand, "One moment please."

With that she expertly tilted her hand down, letting the invitation slide, until twisting her hand and grasping it to slow its descent and push it into the reading machine behind the desk. Details like that surely mattered in keeping the reputation of a place such as this, providing a near royal treatment for a guest. Tony was not sure exactly what the meaning was, but had observed small mannerisms like that at times. He was sure there were a load of them that he had missed and Truth could tell him about if he ever cared to ask.

"Your appointment is scheduled and the invitation is accepted," The attendant chirped happily, drawing the card out with more fluid grace and presenting it once again, with both hands, to Truth. As his partner took the card, the Kul'Raigh bowed slightly and spoke once more, "Please use the card at the elevator over there, it will take you to the correct floor. An attendant will help you should you have any questions."

Truth nodded, thanking the attendant with no return in smile, just her normal calm expression.

Approaching the lift doors, Tony was unsurprised as one of the attendants standing near the elevator hit the up button on their behalf, before they had even reached them. By the time they he and Truth made it to the elevator, the chime had sounded and the attendant motioned to door with a smile as it opened.

Wordlessly the pair stepped through, and of course, there was yet another attendant inside, "Your card ma'am?"

Truth nodded and handed it to her. She slid it into a slot next to the button panel then returned the card in the same dexterous fashion as the hostess had. The doors slid closed afterward and there was a jolt as the lift began on its travel.

As the lift moved, Tony lost track of the floor display, thinking too much about how many more attendants had to be crawling over the place. He hated the idea that everything he wanted to do had to be done by someone else instead so that he wouldn't have to lift a finger to accomplish it.

"Do you do anything but stand in this elevator?" Tony asked frankly.

The attendant smiled, if she was not used to questions like that, it did not show in the slightest. "I have many responsibilities here sir. Thank you for taking an interest."

And I bet there's another one outside the elevator too, because the hostess said there would be, thought Tony as the door chimed and parted. The elevator attendant motioned to the door with a smile and bowed as the Novians exited, "Enjoy your stay!"

Once the door closed behind them, another attendant's voice sounded. Tony nearly rolled his eyes as yet another person took Truth's card and slid it into a small kiosk on the counter she stood behind. He half expected she would lead them by hand to the room but thankfully, she didn't budge. Instead, lights set along the base of the wall illuminated with an inviting pattern. They began pointing the way toward the room indicated on the invitation.

As Truth took the card she began leading the way. As she walked, Tony noted that the lighting seemed to adjust, only pointing them where they needed to go but shutting off in places they had passed.

"Their computer is tracking the locater in the card by the way, might want to remember that," Tony whispered to his partner quietly.

"Of course, thank you for the observation," Truth's voice sounded in Tony's ear only, her lips unmoving as usual when they were communicating discreetly.

After a minute or two of winding through the building, the two found the appointed room and slid the card into the door lock. With a soft click, a light on the lock panel of the door turned color and the directional lighting in the hall turned off in the same instant.

"Wonder how many people are stuck working here," Tony wondered aloud as Truth pressed the button on the door lock a second time. The door popped then slid aside with quiet discretion. The inside of the room was nice, with large windows on the far wall.

"I am sure the pay is quite good, it may not be such a terrible job if one has the ability to endure some of the guests," Truth replied, this time verbally.

The pair entered the small entry. The shape was almost the exact same as some of those rooms he'd seed in the Companion Guild Hall blueprints. Now, the post mission learning he had done had at least borne some kind of fruit. A suite like this at the Guild Hall would have had similar windows. The only difference here was the lack of a balcony.

Tony moved to the window to give a look outside but something strange about the view caught his mind.

"The projection screens in place of windows are quite good, it would be hard to notice without augmented vision," Truth called from behind, putting words to what Tony was trying to identify, "Our current position is actually closer to the middle of the building and I doubt there are windows here."

"What do you do if the place starts on fire then?" Tony chuckled, "Jump out the hologram? Guess it doesn't matter this high up, you'd just turn into a puddle if you did."

Tony rapped on the glass over the holo-screen once, at very least forced to admit that it added a lot to the room.

Before long there was a knock at the door. Tony slid his rifle case from his shoulder and stuck it next to one of the couches. Truth set hers on a counter for the small kitchen area near the door, after which she moved to it and answered.

The conversation was not very loud but the Hil'Raigh was clear enough. The same voice that had left Truth the digital message was greeting her, the same voice that had met them in Kolos. Truth invited her in and as the door closed, Tony glanced up to see the arrival.

She wore an expensive looking robe that seemed to fall open at her shoulders just above her bust line. The ensemble, from her clothing to her hair was a far cry from that which she'd been wearing the first time they met. It reminded Tony of a saying he'd heard many times before, about not rushing to judgments based on appearance alone. A floating, shiny metallic disk of some size hovered lazily behind her head, completing the extravagant look.

"'Hello again" She said as Tony took notice of her, a deep respectful bow accompanied her speech.

"Glad to see you are okay," Tony replied.

"Thank you again for your help in Kolos" A'Shir praised. Her voice had the same calming tone as before, "I would not have been able to enjoy my vacation with an injury."

"You are welcome," Truth replied quickly.

"I'm sorry to bring you to the middle of the city under the circumstances," the Companion began, entering the room further and moving to the center of it. The apartment style room featured a nice living area which Tony had already begun to occupy. He sat on a wide lounge chair across from the couch that A'Shir moved to sit on. Truth closed and locked the door before joining them both.

"So you offered us some interesting information," Tony began, "We'd be interested to know where you got it."

"Ever since the attacks on the Ren'Tauru family, the entire Companion Guild has been mourning in a sense. Lady Shiyara was one of the finest to ever grace our halls," A'Shir began, "But when her body failed to turn up in the investigations, some became hopeful that she was alive."

"Right, no one found her dead," Tony replied.

"After a while, rumors started, that she was not dead but taken," A'Shir explained, "For the Companion Guild, having someone so important to us stolen is too great a wound to bear, and so, some decided to start looking into things that normally receive the benefit of their discretion."

The companion paused, "I must confess I didn't originate the rumor personally. I don't even know who did, but when I heard a rumor that the NovaCore was responsible for the attack, I felt like there was a missing piece to the puzzle."

Tony nodded, but as he watched. A'Shir paused, visibly struggling for composure. He glanced to his partner, who shrugged discretely. Finally, the companion began again, "After the attack on Duke Vaerlin, one of my dearest friends disappeared. She had been seeing new clients lately, security people she said. After she vanished, I got a little package in the mailbox and inside… was the data stick with the footage and some copies of mail messages."

Tony was taken aback by the idea. The implication from the story was clear enough however, A'Shir's friend probably disappeared for a reason.

"There was a note with it all, in her handwriting," A'Shir shuddered, looking down at her lap and closing her eyes. After a long moment, she cleared her throat and turned up again, "The messages referenced Lady Shiyara Ren'Tauru as being alive and under transport. I don't know where, that wasn't included. Other messages talked about the narrative and one included the footage I shared with you both…"

"For what it's worth, I think your friend was very brave," Tony said, a bit surprised at someone being able to acquire so much. It would have been hard to get it all without being noticed. The reality that A'Shir herself might have been watched as well crossed his mind even as he looked at her.

"She must have trusted you very much to offer you that information at such risk," Truth added empathetically. She gave A'Shir a small smile and the Kul'Raigh returned it with gratitude on her face.

"I never imagined that I'd be grateful to be attacked on the street in Kolos. However, when I saw all of the things in her letter, when I saw what looked like your faces in the footage…I knew I had to tell you.."

"We appreciate it," Tony replied, "If you have a copy of the information it would be helpful…"

A'Shir was already reaching into her handbag. She drew a small data stick from inside and set it on the table in the room, "This is her copy. I've already recycled the terminal I looked at it on."

Tony reached out and took the small stick into his hand, then tossed it to Truth who eyed it for a moment and pulled a small memory analyzer from her belt pouch. The small intel gathering tool had many uses, the primary one of which was bypassing electronic locks but it also had some other useful functionality.

"I'm honestly kind of afraid of that data stick..." A'Shir stated sheepishly, "I'd be glad never to see it again..."

Truth fiddled with the stick for a moment then reported on the contents of it, "It looks like it has usable message meta-data. We should be able to find out where it was routed here in the city..."

Tony nodded, "Do you know anything else about the people your friend was involved with?"

"No," A'Shir replied, "She was very private, very good at the Code of Conduct... She never discussed client details with me. The only breach she ever made was that data stick..."

"What about the time frame, when was she involved?" Tony questioned further. He hoped that with some idea of when the events had been transpiring that the search would be narrowed. A bit of optimism filled him as A'Shir nodded, "She had started with them a week or so before the first attack...the new clients I mean."

"Alright," Tony nodded, "Thanks."

"I don't know how much you'll find on there, but I want to ask you one favor If I could...." stated the Kul'Raigh with a cautious hope in her voice.

"What would be that be?"

"Please find out if Lady Shiyara is alive... and if she is...." A'Shir paused, "Let her come home...It's what her husband would have wanted and its the only way her daughter's memory will live on..."

"We'll try," Tony replied, knowing it was going to be hard to convince anyone to go out looking for Shiyara Ren'Tauru, at least until she was proven to be more directly related to all of what had happened. The fact that she was apparently alive however, was not entirely surprising. Tony had expected as much after Truth's own debrief had hypothesized the same. Who would abduct her however, remained a mystery. It would be hard to hide someone so well known, and so she would never be able to be brought into the public eye. Bragging about the abduction would also have a very real chance of revealing one's identity and crime and as a result, was equally unlikely.

The most interesting thing about it all however was the idea that the Kul'Raigh Companion Guild had such a deep affection toward one of its former members. Lady Shiyara had, as it appeared through A'Shir's words, been a sort of icon to them, someone who was praised and loved. Equally so, her husband and daughter appeared to have the same sort of support.

Admittedly, the sample size was small, Tony only knew one companion to ask, but he had a feeling that she was not alone in her reverence for the royal family. Her friend, the one who was now gone, almost certainly had some sort of deep moral loyalty to them as well given what she had obtained. Tony caught himself wondering what she looked like, who she was. She was probably a companion like A'Shir, but her story was most certainly one of importance, at least to the one who had made the last leg of the journey and delivered the information to someone who might be able to use it.

Tony caught himself eying the less obvious body language A'Shir was giving off. There was nervousness, unhappiness and grief in her posture, her words. It only really manifested when one took a careful look, but the previously visible feelings, now masked, were not gone in their entirety.

"What was her name?" Tony finally asked, catching A'Shir off guard, "Your friend I mean..."

A'Shir's eyes clouded with tears quickly and she gave a tender, grateful smile, blinking rapidly to avoid spilling the moisture from her eyes. Even so, some of it pooled at the edges and rolled down her cheek, "Her name was Ka'Rana,"

Ka'Rana, Tony nodded, he would try his best not to forget. He hoped that he would have a chance to write down the name and, as he glanced to Truth, her gaze told him that she too had noted the name, probably in a far less forgettable way than he would.

"Thanks," He replied with a nod. He would never be ashamed to know the name of someone who apparently offered something that ended up being a boon to he or his people. He wanted to know the names of his allies no matter who they were. Each face, each story meant something.

He hoped that perhaps, A'Shir's friend had survived, that some stroke of fate would have granted her continuation. Part of him however, wondered whether that were possible, if the situation here on Ashor could really be so optimistic. Tony dealt in shades of gray almost everyday. Sometimes it was hard to remember where the standard line was, the normal moral center that most people ascribed to. Remembering sacrifice however, was a surefire way to remind him of where his grounding was.

"What about you?" He asked. A'Shir paused, looking into his eyes carefully. It was as if she was scanning him, assessing how trustworthy he really was. After all, he was a NovaCore operative now, not just a friendly face on the street.

She spoke at last, "I never met the people Ka'Rana worked with. I think I might be safe...I would guess that if they knew what she'd given me, I'd have already been disappeared."

Tony nodded slowly, he didn't quite think that would be the case. Spilling stories had a habit of catching up with people in this sort of situation. Most people who kept things secret by force were entirely uninterested in their hard work coming to naught. Despite that though, the information she had given to them would have to be verified further. Even if it were genuine, the chance that A'Shir had a motive she was not disclosing still existed. It frustrated Tony at times that he saw the potential for a trap where a normal person might have simply been comfortable, but such was life.

"If you need us, you might try dropping another communication like you did before," Truth stated, "Unfortunately, we cannot give you anything to contact us directly."

The Kul'Raigh nodded, taking a breath and drawing her small bag closed in her lap, "Thank you."

She stood and gave a final bit of information as she headed for the door, "The room is paid for several more hours but I doubt you will be staying long."

As she headed to the door, she turned upon reaching it and gave both of the Novians a courteous bow before she turned and tapped the control to open it. Stepping through, she appeared to wait for the door to close before bothering to move.

"Need to analyze this," Truth stated quickly, to which Tony replied with a nod.

"Did you detect anything from her? Signals?" Tony asked.

"No, and the jammer never went off either, I do not think she had anything on her," Truth replied in her normal pragmatic tone.

Tony sighed in relief upon hearing the news, "Good, at least that helps me believe what she said..."

"We can rest here while I analyze this. I do not think we have time to go for pickup or upload," Truth stated frankly, " In the mean time I sent your com a floor plan of this building in case we need it."

Tony nodded and glanced at his forearm. The display there was off but a status light blinked away dutifully, notification of Truth's message.

"Well, lets get studying," He stated, settling in for a good look at the plan while his partner splayed herself out over the couch. With any luck, the information would provide a hot lead.

15 - Breaking and Entering

The wind whipped by, sending Truth's hair into a flurry as she approached, grounded out and flared upward for landing. As she began to rise away from the walkway roof, she gave a mental order for her glider to retract and without delay, the device complied. The wings snapped loudly closed, a series of pops sounding as Truth was left falling forward.

With her feet already in position, Truth hit the ground running, slowing quickly and moving to give Tony some room as he landed in a similar fashion.

With the makeshift runway under them, landing was decidedly easier than it otherwise would have been, though the surprised and confused looks from some of the people below in the walkway, reminded Truth that she and her partner had a very limited window of time in which to make their move.

The intelligence they had been given by A'Shir included enough information to put one of the interplanetary communication brokerages on their radar. It was the likely location through which most of the suspected bad actor's communication passed. Currently, the former Akal'Maru special operator Tamur was the best possible link to what was really going on behind the scenes.

Truth knew that his prior involvement with Shae'Lun and now, appearance here on Ashor was probably not something most would realize. The Federation, even if it knew of him, had little incentive to watch him closely and would likely never have made the connection. Even if they had, something told Truth that the man would never face a problem as a result; he had to be well connected. Regardless, this mission would hopefully reveal potential connections.

Finding a tall building from which to leap and glide onto the pedestrian walkway overlooking the target structure had been more of a challenge than Truth expected. The security in Dau'Kore's most affluent district was all but bristling in many places. She couldn't blame them really. First it was the attack on the King, then whatever had happened against a Nobleman. Death had visited the city in a way it had not for hundreds of years at least. Truth roused herself from her musing and looked to her partner.

Tony was already standing, loading his towline rifle. In moments he and Truth both, standing on the walkway high above the ground below, had prepared to fire.

Truth reached to her belt, grabbing one of the anchor spikes for her weapon and reaching down to her rappelling harness. She pushed the small metallic line feed hanging from her weapon, through a hole in the back of the spike, and when it was finished, pulled a cap from her belt for it.

The cap forced the line out of the way so that the spike to which it was affixed could be shoved into the barrel of the weapon. It would break away once fired. Once cleared the spike would be used as an anchor, the feed mechanism on the weapon would draw the weight bearing cabling through it.

Truth had long ago learned about what the cable was made of to make it light and durable but it usually boiled down to the idea of imitating some unique animals and their methods for constructing tensile fibers.

The wing suit kits had been easy to hide in the raincoats both NovaCore had worn and though they had come with their rifles pre-assembled, the fake sports bags the weapons were hidden in until moments ago, had provided ample concealment. Both of the Novians admitted to feeling a bit naked without their combat rifles, but Truth's trusty sidearm was snugly fastened against her hip regardless.

"Drop confirmed nominal," Tony said calmly over the radio, after which his rifle gave a loud pop.

Truth glanced down after hearing a yelp from someone inside the tube who had been watching, probably since the two landed noisily on the roof. The surprise was certain to be in response to the sound of Tony's towline gun. Truth as well, took aim at the correct place, firing her own rifle. A burst of air sounded, the tool shoving against her shoulder aggressively as it launched its cargo forward. She guessed that anyone inside the walkway was already calling the city police. Who could blame them after what had happened here as of late.

In moments the rifle shuddered, the spike having founds its mark in the outer wall of the target building. The lead line jiggled a bit before Truth tapped the button on her rifle to draw out the anchor and in moments, the heavier cable in the rifle's spool started being drawn away, almost vanishing into the air.

This would probably be the longest part of the transition between buildings, she mused to herself as she watched the now decidedly chaotic state of the tube on which she was standing. Some of the people inside were confused, a few making nervous exits, while some stood, almost in awe about what they saw.

The roof of the walkway was almost entirely clear, a careful examination from below would even give an observer a good look at the tread of Truth's combat boots. A moment or so more however, and she noticed what had to be a security person approaching, prelude to law enforcement but likely powerless to respond. After all, Truth and her partner were standing not inside the tube, but on top of it in the wind. In moments, the perplexed guard was barking into a small radio device on his wrist as he struggled to describe the situation.

Thanks to her augmented hearing, Truth was easily able to understand what he was saying and how he was sure this was some kind of huge problem. When he decided to mention that whoever was on the other end should call the authorities however, Truth felt herself anticipating an eventful entry into the brokerage building.

"Secured, Going in!" Tony radioed before breaking into an aggressive run toward Truth. A meter or so away from her, he turned, leaning to the side and catapulting himself off the walkway. The snap of his glider wings was barely audible from here, but the effect was clear as he began sailing in a lazy arc, toward the target building.

Tony was a fun glider to watch, always having been one of the most adventurous of those in the training for such methods. Even now, he showed his love of the practice, tipping a wing or flaring at just the right moment.

Truth of course, was as perfect as one could be at gliding, accurate to the narrowest of tolerances, but she had always envied her partners ability to improvise and correct. Though he was not always perfect from the start, he ended up close enough through intuition and practice.

"Line secure. Clear," Truth called to her partner via wireless before rearing back. As she prepared to run, she glanced down and made eye contact with the now befuddled security guard inside the tube, who grew more frantic in his outlandish explanation of events. With any luck, the ridiculousness of two people 'Leaping off of the walkway like birds' would not draw enough immediate belief from his unfortunate contact.

Truth gave the man a shrug as she heaved forward, throwing her weight into a dead sprint. In fractions of a second her feet rose, fell and then, her toes pushed off. Racing forward with impossible speed for someone her size and build, the Novian lept forward and to her side as she did.

Gaining just a bit of speed from the fall, and straightening herself out like an arrow, she willed her glider pack open and once more, it responded immediately. The now repaired metallic bars in the frame shot outward, the wing material between them taut as she went into a fast diving turn. She was moving faster than her partner by just enough to arrive almost immediately after he did, but having made sure to avoid crossing their cables by overtaking him. She was thankful that in this instance, her use of the glider was not burdened by the extra weight of an unconscious royal.

Out of the corner of her eye she saw the building still, and as the moments passed, it loomed closer and closer until she was facing it head on. She lurched upward now to bleed off the extra speed she had and reach the correct floor.

With machine precision, Truth angled upward, and in the same instant, she felt her stomach churn as the force of gravity below fought her glider to keep its hold. The fight lasted but a fleeting moment however as she felt her weight moving as it should, with the glider.

Speed dropping quickly, meters ahead, she watched as Tony went near vertical. As he did, he stuck his feet out, cushioning a landing wide legged against the wall and relying on the rappelling harness and cable to keep him against it. His body folded into a right angle now, he glanced over his shoulder and Truth, through her augmented eyes could make out what looked to be his gaze on her position as she raced toward him.

Aiming for the window, she angled straight up, bleeding her speed away quickly. In moments she was near eye level with the pane of glass, and in a moment more she had found her place. Reaching out with one leg now, her foot found the window's lip. She pushed off powerfully, giving herself a final boost upward as she retracted her glider wings.

Wheeling around in the air now, above the window, she rolled until the cable from her harness fed over one shoulder and then, in an inverted crouch, she tugged the cable as hard as she could, pulling herself toward the wall.

The effect was immediate. Her low stance came to rest against the building, her feet finding their marks just above the window as one of her arms held the cable tightly over her shoulder. Upside down now, she stared down at her partner with a broad grin on her face. While he had a penchant for exciting flying sometimes, she definitely loved to show up his landings.

He smiled broadly in response to the unspoken challenge, "I think I need to learn how to land."

Truth nodded, letting some of her cable go as she straightened downward, using her cable as an anchor and feet as a fulcrum. Releasing one hand from the cable, she reached behind her back and slid her hand into the pouch containing a laser window cutter.

With some care, she managed to hand it to her partner who thanked her and hopped along the wall just below the window before gently ascending and planting his boots on the pane itself. With two free hands, Tony affixed the cutter while the suspended Truth looked on, over his shoulder and upside down.

"You telling me you cant put this on with one hand too?" He joked as he fixed the last suction cup.

"You need to feel important too," She joked playfully. Tony smirked over his shoulder at her as he tapped the buttons on the back of the device.

With that, it began to cut, smoking as the laser burned away at the window. Tony slung himself out of the way and Truth watched and waited until the device finished its work. Her partner returned, removing the tool. A large hole in the pane appeared behind the material that had come with it. Tony swung himself into position and climbed through quickly, then, on the inside of the hallway he had entered, tinkered with his rappelling rifle until Truth saw his cable fall limp.

In seconds he had fished the cable through the hole after him, taking with him the spike. Truth followed, swinging acrobatically into the hall after her partner and unfastening her cable anchor in a similar fashion.

With a window so high in the air, there was no external security to speak of. The entry would be unmonitored and as a result, she and her partner would have the initiative in exploiting their opening. Regardless, being detected by anyone could turn problematic. With their timing tonight however, such an occurrence was unlikely.

The evening hours had all but exhausted those who would normally be working in the building or at least, if popular culture was any indicator, they could expect to see very few people on their way around.

As with most buildings in the city that Truth had thus far encountered, there was an available wireless feed, aimed toward visitors, providing some floor layout and other information. Though she had discovered that these public floor layouts had missing areas at times, they seemingly always had the locations of stairs or access ways between levels. It was no surprise then, that she was able to find a map of the building rather quickly by simply asking her computer system to request one. One of the common map formats was available of course, and in fractions of a second, the information was available to her mind as well.

Almost as if she were seeing two worlds at a time, a section of her thoughts perceived the map as clearly as if her own eyes had seen it. She knew however that it was simply in her coprocessor somewhere and nothing about her eyes had changed.

A small hiss sounded as Tony sprayed his face and exposed skin with a mist from one of the bottles he carried and Truth did the same with her own. The compound made her skin feel damp, but it subsided in moments, leaving her with a grimy feeling instead.

Though it was not the most comfortable sensation, the spray would dampen the effect of their exposed skin from thermal sensors that would trigger alarms or activate cameras. Any active cameras which could see in the dark would have to cast an infrared light to see anything and those were something Truth would see long before they were able to detect the intruders.

As a result, this time as always, was one in which the basic security systems in the commercial sector were likely to be of little use in catching dedicated and equipped individuals.

Truth led her partner out of the small corridor and into a larger room, one full of partitions and work areas. She guessed there were at least twenty or thirty work spaces here, each given relative privacy by the panels separating it from its neighbors but still smaller than a real office. The entire room was dark save for the emergency lighting that hung over the doorways on the far walls, but it made for easy movement. Despite that, Truth and her partner both crouched low, moving with quiet purpose. The last thing they needed to do was get any straggler's attention.

Each twisting footstep moved Truth along toward where the map said stairs to the next level up would be, and on that level was the node she had given as a location for a tap into the brokerage mainframe. It would of course, have to have some level of security about it, making Truth wonder exactly what she would have to defeat when she and her partner finally reached their objective.

Step after careful step took Truth down a makeshift hallway between work areas, and, eventually she and her partner reached a doorway. The door was propped open, probably never closed from the look of it, and led into the landing of a stairwell. According to the map and what Truth could see without entering, there would be stairs up and down, on either side of them as soon as they entered. Further, there were several levels tied together by this apparently rather important corridor. It would be likely then, if anyone remained here at these upper levels that they might use the same stairs to get to the nearest express elevator bank.

With great care, Truth threaded her exposed fingertips around the corner of the door frame. Though imperfect, with careful tuning and concentration, the sensors in her fingertips could get a good thermal reading even a few meters away.

The sensor feed told her that the way up was clear enough for now, and a quick repositioning and examination of the way down as well, revealed the same. The sound and temperature of the area she had been able to see, were not indicative of anyone being present and so, cautiously, she poked her head around the corner instead.

No visible reaction followed, although the stairs were apparently fully lit at all hours, making normal passive cameras a possible problem within. Even so, Truth had seen none of them and eventually, moving around the corner herself, found that her partner followed without delay.

The staircase upward was at least three meters wide, with a single metallic tube serving as the railing in sections of stairs. All in all, moving upward even against the wall, was disconcerting from the openness of the location alone.

The upward trek however, concluded rather quickly and without event, leaving Truth and her partner on the floor above where they had entered. Truth double checked with her computers mentally, as to what her inventory of intrusion software was, as she continued leading on.

In moments the report came back, several varieties of all flavors she could imagine needing for the business network. There was even enough to turn the heads of military securities across the galaxy, especially with direct physical access to the networks here in the building.

Moving out of the landing on the new floor, Truth was relieved to find that it was apparently expecting far less traffic at any hour, with no visible windows and fewer lights. It made sense after all, according to the maps she had downloaded of the facility, this was a dedicated server level for the communications routing.

The company billed itself as the local solution to Federation communication but its reach had extended far beyond the borders of the Starlight Compact and ballooned even to international proportion. It was no secret then, why the messages A'Shir had given them revealed their routing through this place.

Thankfully, the lack of windows had created a good situation for examining the rows of faceless humming machines that lay separated from the pair of Novians by thick glass windows. As the pair surveyed the floor, Tony broke the silence, speaking over his radio.

"I think its a clean room, we cant cut in or it'll activate quarantine," He mused. Truth, glancing to where he appeared to be looking, caught a glimpse of the universal clean room symbol that the Hil'Raigh employed across the entirety of the Federation. Thankfully, it was one of the things she and her partner were well versed in reading quickly but she found it interesting in that moment, just how many times she had been on the opposite end of those sorts of signs.

"There's a terminal here, terrible spot though," Tony announced, motioning forward. Truth looked to where he had pointed, noting a single display hanging from the roof nearby. An input shelf hung under the display as well, denoting the obvious use of the terminal.

Quietly, calmly, the pair approached the device, Truth scanning again for infrared spotlights. There was a chance that those sort of things could turn on if the terminal were activated but once she connected she would be unable to do anything about it.

"I am going to have to go full in," She announced looking at the display and input system. It was clear to her as she examined them that such a form of interface would be too slow to get things done in time, as usual. She would need to allow her coprocessors to have a direct connection to the system in order to respond quickly and properly. While trained in the use of Hil'Raigh computers, she was sure that the barrier her flesh presented when interacting with the terminal would prove insurmountable.

"This is a pretty shit location Truth, if the lights turn on they could see us from almost anywhere on the floor."

"We will have to take the risk," Truth replied, turning and sitting, leaning against the thick glass that protected the servers. She ran her finger behind her ear, feeling the small outline of the data access port nestled there. It was almost always covered by her hair but she never forgot about it. She reached to her belt and pulled out the interface cable designed for working with the alien computers and affixed the appropriate end in the socket behind her ear, hearing the plug click softly from the side of her own head.

The other end she held in front of herself for a moment, examining it. Ignoring the machine like feeling she always got when she did this, she reached up to the small access port on the input console and slid the end in.

"Wake me up if something goes wrong?" She smiled at her partner before the world melted away.

There was a searing feeling behind her ear and she yelped as her eyes shot open and she stood suddenly. The reaction was automatic, immediate, and no matter how many times she did it, she never could exert full control of herself until after it was all done. Now on her feet, Truth glanced down at herself, or at least, her body. It was leaning back against a section of thick glass that seemed to fade into nothing around her, in the completely empty abyss into which she always sunk right before entry.

A warm friendly voice chortled to her from every direction at once, her coprocessor adopting Truth's own voice. It was a cheery and eerily artificial tone the computer seemed so fond of, 'Hello Truth, are you ready to enter the system?"

"Yes," Truth replied to the voice.

"I will generate your preferred arming programs," the voice replied.

Suddenly, just ahead, Truth saw a small armory table appear, her handguns and rifles appeared on top, a dazzling array in fact. The selection of weapons, some she did not even own, in real life at least, were strewn over the table like it was an art canvas.

Selecting from the group, Truth chose an array of them, strapping them to herself calmly as she remembered somehow, what each of them represented. Some of them were deterrence programs, some of them were attack programs, a variety she would normally be unable to really understand but in this place, it all seemed quite clear. The perfect abstraction for her training.

"This system is equipped with Aggressive Lock Detection and Heuristic Protocol, please be careful Truth."

Truth nodded and then, once more, the world blinked out. This time however, when things returned, Truth was already standing, a door behind her. Ahead, a facsimile of somewhere in the building she was sitting in. Of course it was not entirely the same, and the building itself upon closer inspection, shared none of the floor plans that she had previously downloaded with her map.

Instead, the map of the world into which she had sunk was based on the layout of the computer system into which she was intruding. After several moments, Tony's voice filled the air, "Looks clean so far Truth."

The thankful announcement made Truth lament the fact that in this state, she could not reply directly. Her mind was only able to receive information from the outside world through her coprocessor and so, Truth asked the machine to acknowledge his announcement on her behalf.

Years before her birth, the first neural interfaces had enabled people with specialized training to infiltrate computer networks like never before, a surge in the power of code breaking. The technology had escalated on both sides until now, it was more of what Truth was used to, with a slightly different set of rules than real life infiltration, but mechanically quite similar.

Processing Truth's mind and its orders, her neural interface would then take a computer action with its suite of software and tools. The result and reply from the other system, if any, would be converted into something that Truth could see, hear or interact with in this virtual world of hers and then she could take further action.

Amazingly, the strongest infiltration weapon still proved to be ingenuity of the mind, strategy and thinking, while tools themselves were only as good as their operator.

The current mission was to find communication records relating to Tamur and possibly Shae'Lun involvement in the recent attacks. Truth hoped that something of that information was left here but was not entirely sure.

Most communications brokerages stored the messages they transferred for a period of weeks at least afterward, ensuring that they were backed up properly. They were of course encrypted with passwords when stored but Tamur's password had been among the bits of information that A'Shir had provided.

"I have located possible matches for you, the locations are in your map Truth," Her own voice informed calmly, "I recommend we attempt to analyze the closest first, security is still unaware of our presence here."

Truth nodded, moving forward in a low crouch away from the exit door, and at the same time, noting its location.

The immaculate halls of the building here, were beyond possibility in the real world. The thin carpet was spotless, there was not a hint of dust in the air and the walls were polished and clean. It was decidedly more maze like in its construction than the reality to which Truth was accustomed.

Rather than navigate all of the corridors however, Truth took advantage of the first available shortcut she saw. A locked door ahead of her blocked what was to be a faster path toward the first collection of messages she was tasked with, but rather than search out a key, she simply reached up to the handle and tugged downward.

After several moments, the door unlocked noisily and swung open. In response, a ripple of sorts rushed over the world around her, the consequence of course, of the forced door. "Undetected, go ahead," Her co-processor announced with a helpful candor.

The first node was not well defended, a collection of holographic disks strewn on an office table. Around her, there were hundreds, perhaps thousands of disks, each stacked neatly in a case. The collection lined the walls but those of interest sat cleanly on the table. Truth walked over to them and twirled the first in her fingers, setting it into a reader device on the table.

Tamur appeared, a hologram of course, having an unintelligible conversation with someone else who was not visible, "The record for the other party is not currently present in the system, audio decryption is in progress."

After a moment longer, Tamur words melted eerily into spoken Hil'Raigh. The sounds were all wrong, an artifact of the reality that they were not really being spoken, but understood digitally. Truth could have listened to them in any language she knew with no problem. Still, the information contained in his message was interesting. He was apparently discussing Vaerlin with whomever it was that this call was placed, specifically, how to keep him in check and watch him. It only took Truth a few moments to listen to the entire thing, it was a short call, but it was evidence at least and she picked the disk out of the machine, putting it into a case on her hip.

Again, a second disk met with the reader, this one with no useful information.

A third disk met its fate in Truth's pouch before she was satisfied with the haul from this particular area. Turning away from the table, she took a few steps, only to see the disks, all in their place on the office table as if they'd never been touched. At the same time, the copies in her pouch told her she had what she needed. The room was in the state she had entered, and therefore, she took it as a sign that she was still undetected by the system which she was now exploring

**

If time were passing normally in this reality, Truth guessed it would have taken a good twenty or thirty minutes to get where she had come to. Now, her pouch was a bit fuller but less so than she had hoped. She had managed to dodge the security cameras in several of the hallways along the way, but her progress had slowed considerably as she had stopped taking the increasingly obvious shortcuts placed in her path. As it seemed to happen, shortcuts littered the inner areas of these systems but the Novian had learned long ago, the danger of using them.

With each action she took, every step or breath, the chance that she was found increased. The more obvious the action, the more likely it was noticed. Though Truth had yet to see any guards, she was sure they were either out there already, or watching and waiting.

Some systems had security that presented itself, obvious and imposing. It usually showed up in the form of guards, weaponized robots or security. This kind was not a wonderful occurrence, but compared to the alternative, much preferred.

The latter, and more dangerous form of security was the kind that quietly went about its business. always out of view no matter where Truth looked. It watched everything that happened, examined every consequence and moved without form through the facsimile worlds Truth occupied while intruding. Only when it had decided it was time for action would the program be represented, and often times, the arrival was well timed and dangerous. With a direct link to the system, a headache was the least of potential worries a would be intruder faced.

Truth had developed a hate for that kind of security, always feeling like something was looking over her shoulder or following behind her only moments after she had been in a particular place. The sense of when she was actively being looked at, when her programs were being monitored and when they weren't, was something she relied on now, after so many scares with earlier missions.

Most civilian networks had the former type of security, loud and easily avoided with Truth's skill set. This network however, increasingly un-nerved Truth as she traveled, wondering just when the security could possibly manifest.

Thus far however, her Coprocessor had been a good companion, helping her whenever possible with tips on routing and finding nearby areas of interest.

Ahead, a large doorway now loomed, with an obvious and clear sign above. In Hil'Raigh it appeared to read something to the effect of "Palace Communication Routing."

The door was already open however, and from within, Truth could hear the sounds of something going on.

Approaching the doorway quietly, she poked her head around the corner, and to her surprise, noticed someone inside, someone definitely not security. The individual had no face, as most avatars in this world did not, but it also lacked armor or protective gear. From the avatar's waist hung a small handgun, but other than that one piece of equipment only the rough, dark and cloudy form of the avatar gave any indication of its presence.

Whoever it was seemed unaware of Truth's arrival, at least for now, and so, with her hand ready on her own weapon, she slipped into the room, behind a bank of filing cabinets, to get a better look.

From this angle it became clear that the avatar was definitely not security. The form calmly and methodically reached into the drawer of one of the cabinets, drew out an array of records and ran a scanning device over each. Periodically, it would stop and toss a record into a small bin at its feet.

Truth gathered after several moments that she was probably witnessing a second intruder, this one destroying certain records, possibly records she needed. However, the individual also appeared to have a vested interest in other things. Truth wondered exactly what the person was gathering, wondering if some of it was related to her own target. The searches had brought her here, and so she knew that Tamur was in records all over this room. Ambushing the target however, was not something she could do as swiftly as she may have in reality.

Unlike the real world, Truth's strength was limited by the software and tools of her own intrusion suite and unfortunately, due to the semi formless nature of the avatar, she had no idea how formidable it might have been. Each moment it was allowed to work however, was one more moment in which something critical could be lost and so, after a moment of decision, Truth drew her weapon and took aim. The fire would probably attract security, but in that case, Truth decided she could try barricading the door somehow until she found something she needed.

"Would you be so kind as to tell Tony he is gong to have to manually disconnect me?" Truth asked calmly, and in a moment, her coprocessor replied, "I will inform him to be ready."

Truth thanked what was more herself than anything as she took aim on the formless avatar and pulled the trigger on her weapon.

The fire let out a loud pop and whine, just like a real railgun would have, but there was no smoke or debris. A jagged hole blew through the shadowy mass ahead but the thing did not fall. Instead, it turned like a caught thief, toward her location before fading into nothing. In the same instant though, there was a cacophony of explosions, throwing Truth against the filing cabinet ahead of her. The cabinet toppled, its drawers spilling noisily and knocking the wind out of her as she crawled onto her hands and knees.

Thick acrid smoke filled the air and in a moment it was clear why the intruder had been so calm and confident. Some kind of aggressive attack software had been laid in anticipation of possible problems and, if need be, the entire archive was to be destroyed instead of letting anyone find any possible data. Now, Truth was inside the rapidly heating room, wondering just how much she'd actually be able to get out of it before she had to leave.

Though it was possible to escape completely unharmed from this sort of situation due to its artificial nature, something about the way the smoke and heat felt told Truth she was better off having Tony pull her cord than trying to escape on her own. Unfortunately, if she had to have her plug pulled she would likely stay unconscious for a few minutes afterward.

"I'm sorry Tony," she said calmly, pushing herself to a comfortable height below the smoke. The cabinet that had spilled open in-front of her was her first target, and rather than examine, Truth simply began grabbing and copying the records into her satchel.

Frantic with the need to save as much data as possible, the Novian worked calmly, both arms grabbing at different records. She felt her satchel bulging and knew she was probably not doing her brain any favors, but kept shoving records into it anyway.

The fire alarms had long since sounded in this artificial world and as a result, security as well, was probably on its way. Truth couldn't decide if she was more interested in avoiding the security or the fire now, but neither of them were close enough to do her harm presently and so she worked.

One set of records caught her eye and without a good way to visualize the information at the moment, amid her surroundings, she called to the air asking her coprocessor for some help.

"What's on this one?" she asked waving it around, then shoving it into the satchel. It was getting far too full, dangerously full now and Truth knew she would not be waking easily from this. Especially since her partner might have to pull her off of the system. Something told her that there was more at work than simple data destruction going on, possibly something outside of her body in the real world.

There was the smell, the heat of fire, getting hot enough that Truth now earnestly considered leaving the room. As her coprocessor announced its findings however, her mind was made up quickly.

"Communication records from the palace. The entire set of these records may be good to have," The system chortled in an almost cheery tone. It was mildly disconcerting to hear such a happy version of her own voice amid the flames and smoke, "Why did you select this one Truth?"

Truth, reaching into the drawer with all of the similar colored record disks she could find, shoveled the drawer worth into her bag and then stood, hefting it. She instantly felt dizzy and disoriented, having trouble navigating almost immediately. She had chosen the record because for some reason or another, in this facsimile world, the coloration of the disk was just right to catch her eye. In her estimation, it was a complete fluke since the coloration was always based on a random hash of the readable data in something like that. Nevertheless it seemed now like fate or something greater had intervened. If Truth had any knowledge of spiritual beings she might have given them credit in that moment, but without any real understanding, she was left to thank nothing in particular.

The weight of the satchel and her sudden dizziness though, were no ones fault but her own. She stumbled forward, coughing on the acrid smoke as she shambled out of the fiery record room into the hall. There were fires outside as well, and in that moment Truth's computers confirmed her growing suspicions.

"The computer system appears to be undergoing a catastrophic failure brought on by an unknown source," the processor informed gravely.

A sudden frantic feeling overcame Truth. She knew that if she did not reach her exit in time, she would have to be forcibly pulled from the system. Then, after that she would be rendered unconscious by a drug cocktail that her systems would automatically administer.

"Please don't drug me," Truth whimpered, leaning against the walls as she moved. There was too much data in the satchel and her mind was already having a hard time coping with such extra information. She needed more space, but there was none left to spare, "I can make it, I promise."

For the first time in years Truth felt a familiar fear, the realization that her computer systems would force her to sleep when she wanted to be awake. She understood why it happened, having dealt with it before but it was no less unpleasant just because she would know about the impact.

It felt like a disconnect with her body, the normally steady stream of input halted forcibly and her mind left to wander some vast quiet expanse she never enjoyed. Then there was the forgetting. She hated forgetting. Sometimes it was days. Sometimes a week. It all just vanished as if it had never happened. It was more disconcerting than any dream state or incapacitation, the reality that she could live and have those moments of her existence taken away.

She remembered the first time she forgot. It was during training years ago with Tony. There had been too much information, too much work going on and her mind was unable to cope. She had broken down, saw things that didn't exist, broken training equipment, and then, forgotten. She had to have the school staff and Tony tell her what she had been studying the last week, she ended up apologizing profusely to people she never remembered harming either. An overload of her senses, from any source despite its extreme rarity was as uncomfortable a thing as Truth had ever experienced. Unfortunately for her, with her mind overburdened from so much extra work, so much special record data taking up space it never was supposed to occupy, she was already feeling the effects. Being unplugged from the computer now, would certainly push her over the edge. The same familiar realization dawned once more, for the first time in years. She was going to sleep no matter what she wanted.

"Don't let me wake up until..." Truth gulped, slumping against the wall, closing her eyes. It did nothing to stop the nausea and the room kept spinning. It was all getting worse by the moment.

"I know Truth, I'll keep you safe and I will try to help make sure you don't forget this time," The computer voice replied calmly, almost soothing.

Truth nodded, "Do it... I can't even see straight..."

With that, spidery veins of nothingness crept into her vision, from the outside toward the inside. The sounds died away, the nausea died away. Everything melted into nothing, and for a moment Truth could still see the satchel in her lap, full of records. She sighed and shook her head, free from the disorientation for just a moment before it all disappeared.

16 - Creative Descent

The message came through the radio clearly enough but when Tony watched his partner slump almost lifelessly into the barrier she rested against, he cursed aloud and moved to her side as quickly as he could. She was limp and rubbery and as he propped her against himself he reached around behind her ear and pulled the connector cable with gentle care. Afterward he reached up and yanked the adapter end from the terminal without ceremony.

"Don't you go forgetting on me," he whispered to her softly, reaching into a small dedicated pocket among his equipment. From within he pulled his recovery pick and slid the cap back. The memory device blinked with a green light and he leaned Truth's body forward just enough to get a good look behind her ear. Pulling her hair aside, he inserted the device and the light blinked once more, this time going red then blinking rapidly.

The machine was, as far as he had been told, designed to assist Truth in the event of a sensory or memory overload. The pair each possessed one, which could be used as many times as needed but had to be reset and cleaned prior to re-use. Each of the devices allowed Truth's coprocessors, which sometimes became overburdened with information, to start dumping their contents without worry of loss.

The risk of a direct neural interface always carried with it the potential for such problems, at least in the general population. The invasiveness of the link on the mind, coupled with the potential problems technology introduced into the natural system, made such interfaces a rarity except among those with damage to their brains.

Truth of course, fit that bill from a young age, and only with the help of the computer machines had she been able to reach more of her potential. Tony sometimes wondered what his partner would have been like without the interface but the idea of the Truth he knew being gone, was something of a worry to him. On some level, part of what made her who she was, was the piece of machinery in her skull.

Truth herself had pointed that out years ago, and since the day she had spoken those words, Tony himself had never questioned the validity of her personality again. He wondered how it might have been to have to come to terms with something that he felt would be so invasive. Regardless of his own feelings, if Truth could handle it, he would not undermine her confidence.

Confidence or not, there were situations Truth could never control. These times, the times when Truth was drugged by her own body, were some of those Tony disliked more than any, because he knew how mentally shaking it was for his partner. She would wake, usually in a panic from what had been happening before. If there was any time Truth's eyes showed fear it was then, when she woke after having been forcibly incapacitated, by the mechanical parts of her body.

At very least, the recovery pick was a valid way to help her retain her memories. The computer would construct a detailed neural map and dump it to the stick, then, while she was unconscious and out of danger later, the same system would repair any damage that had been done to both the technological and biological sides of the interface by the panic. It was rare that damage occurred, but after the first incident years ago, no one wanted to take chances.

Truth would probably be unconscious for quite a while and the drugs that had been administered to her to knock her out were potent. They were released directly in her heart and as a result, propagated to her body in seconds. The challenge as it happened now, would be how to move her effectively. During the time she was unconscious, the most Tony could hope for was a bit of semi-clunky communication with her computer system. It was incapable of doing much more than giving some status updates when Truth's mind was not helping it work. There was an irony there, that the machine Truth's mind relied on so much, in turn, relied on her mind as well.

Finally, the device behind Truth's ear flashed green once more and a reassuring voice line, one in Truth's own voice, came over the radio from her computer, announcing that the recovery map had successfully completed. With any luck, the pick would ensure Truth's memory had not been damaged. Of course, a moment later the machine let Tony know that Truth's sleuthing in the system had produced a reasonable amount of data that was currently being archived and stored.

Tony almost scoffed hearing that. The data was more important than Truth's memory in the eyes of the machine, but really, he had to admit it was true. Truth herself would have wanted to save that information even at the cost of some of the week's memories.

"I hope you know what you are doing," Tony said seriously to his partner's head, hoping the computer heard the message instead of her.

Now, with the device finished doing its work, he reached out to Truth's ear and pulled the pick from the plug nestled there, slipping it into it's place in his belt once more. Now came the task of finding a way out of the building and a place to let Truth rest long enough for her to wake.

Given that her coprocessor had announced an apparently precarious situation in the virtual environment Truth had been exploring, Tony assumed that it was only a matter of time before the manifestations of that situation began to appear in the real world as security guards or police.

The entry location had been several stories up and while he was interested to see if his glider could carry both he and his partner, as Truth had attempted successfully before with princess Kirashira, the possibility of such a plan was immediately discarded by reality.

Kirashira and Truth together formed a reasonably lighter load than he and Truth would, mostly because of the fact that Kirashira was so light. Truth's own weight was enough to turn heads at times but such was the nature of someone whose bones had been plated in metal and whose body was filled with artificial organs and hardening for combat.

From the current level in the building, Tony guessed that he would have trouble reaching any sort of normal exit before some sort of security caught up with him. He began to weigh his options as he leaned down and hefted his partner over one shoulder. Truth slumped over him without response as he wrapped his arm around her ankles and stood once more.

His mind raced over potential avenues of escape. Perhaps he could set a fire or cause another emergency to let whatever escape measures the building had, kick into action on his behalf. He doubted though, that he alone could cause a blaze large enough to trigger the alarms in a way that warranted escape. Most of the tall buildings on NovaCore worlds were equipped with good fire suppression systems that would cause an accidental fire to burn out before doing significant damage. The same he guessed would apply to the Hil'Raigh culture as well, though, for a moment he realized that the fire at the Companion Guild Hall before was confusing for that reason. The immediate problem however, could not be solved by speculating, he needed a plan.

The first thing he decided he would do is try and observe the outside world. Even from this height, looking out of a window might give him an idea of where to go. The current floor however, was not going to be very useful for that course of action. The dark, sterile nature of the level meant that he would have to go down at least one floor to find an external window again.

Exiting through the hole he and Truth had made did cross his mind but the idea was quickly tossed aside. Leaping out of the hole would certainly kill them both, even if Tony tried the wing-suits. Truth had managed it before with Kirashira as a payload but she had the eminent advantage of a limousine driver picking her out of the air. Tony had to make due without any such assistance.

"What would you do in this situation..." Tony asked himself as he entered the stairwell and descended to the level below. His partner of course, did not respond and thankfully, the computer interface inside of her didn't either.

The landing came quickly and Tony moved out of the door. The floor was as he and Truth had left it. Down the hall and around the corner, despite the lowered lighting at this hour, was the telltale sign of light from the outside world filtering through the window they had cut. The opposite direction however, remained unexplored. Raising an eyebrow, Tony turned to the unknown and moved past the array of work spaces in the larger room until he approached the corner around which he had yet to see.

As he moved, he found that instead of more work spaces, a sort of staff room had been organized. He had no idea what standard business layouts were in the Hil'Raigh world but the massive window on the side of the room furthest from him caught his attention more than the layout of couches. The space was easy to move in, some seats and couches surrounding a coffee table. Near the inside wall, counters covered in small appliances framed a large display panel and a selection of utensils and other objects denoted the fact that the unofficial gathering place probably hosted the lunch breaks for whoever worked nearby. It was clean however, making Tony wonder whether anyone used it as regularly as he might have expected.

He approached the window and scanned the outside world with interest, his eyes darting over the featureless walls of the next building over. He sighed and turned, nearly moving away before he impulsively took another glance out the window, looking downward this time.

A spark of hope filled him as he eyed the object more closely. Hope turned to plan almost as soon as he was sure of what he saw. Moving to the couch, Tony set his partner down gently before he tilted her to her side. Hopefully from other places in the room, she would be less visible with the couch back obscuring her body.

Now with eager intent, filled with the goal of his objective, the Novian returned to the window and pulled out his window cutter. He affixed the device to the pane and as he was about to activate it, he sighed and hesitated. There was no way he would be able to crawl through that size of hole while carrying Truth and he had no desire to try and drag her out of it.

Instead, he detached the machine and opted for a far less covert approach. The cutter stowed in seconds and in its place, Tony drew one of his breaching charges from his harness. He uncoiled the rolled up ball and began affixing its semi sticky coating to the window, unrolling it like a thick string. As the cord was placed, he drew the ball onward slowly, meticulously using his other hand to spread and flatten the translucent jelly that contained the explosive itself. Centimeter after centimeter was stuck to the window and Tony turned, repeating the process in a line again. One more corner and then back toward the starting place gave him a good rectangular outline and, upon reaching his starting point, the operative uncoiled the final bit and drew it in a diagonal line toward the middle of the shape he had made.

The center of the ball, now exposed as a blobby mass, was flattened into a disk of material in the middle of the rectangular shape. Next, he drew a small detonator pin and shoved it into the mass in the center. He stepped back to examine his handiwork, preparation for the oncoming destruction of private property. Frowning, he stepped forward again, massaging some of the material at the corners between his fingers until it was to his liking, carefully affixed. At last satisfied, he bounded to where he had laid Truth, a couch meters away.

Noisily hefting one end, he began to rotate the comfortable looking piece of furniture, snagging and messing up the well kept rug below in the process and announcing the impromptu remodel to anyone who might have been nearby.

Thankfully no one appeared in response to the noise and in seconds Tony had his makeshift blast shield. Of course, the charge would not really cause damage inside the room but it was procedure to separate one's self from an explosive detonation even if it was supposed to be controlled. The rectangle loomed ahead in Tony's view and he found the small remote for the device and slipped it into his hand as he hunkered behind the couch. His thumb found the top of the small cylindrical transmitter and after a single beep, he pressed his thumb downward again.

A loud pop burst into the room as the explosive detonated, carrying most of the window outward with it. Fragmented plastic composites blew outward around the edges but a nearly pristine pane of the stuff blew outward. Smokey dust blew around the room for several seconds afterward as the rush of air out of, and then back into the explosion area created a sort of small scale hurricane. Almost immediately, the nicely climate controlled interior of the building began to cycle with outside air and the smoke began to find its way through the opening.

"Hold tight," Tony said to his partner, moving to the now cleanly cut window pane. The hole was large enough that he could for the most part, crouch through it without incident. He approached the edge and looked downward once more to re-acquire his target.

He made the outline quickly, a delivery barge stuck to the side of the neighbor building some several stories down. On its surface, he saw several stacks of boxes and, from the inside of the opposing building, noted what had to be a group of workers transferring the contents of their work platform into the building interior.

He chuckled to himself as he wondered what the work crews would think if they knew what he was planning to do. His mind mulled over the more comical possibilities as he drew his towline rifle parts once more from their case and began assembling them into a functional tool. He watched the crews as they time and again moved out of the access way they were using, grabbed a box or two, and returned to the inside of the building.

There was no real rhythm to it, no real way to obtain the transportation without being seen. Thankfully though, the fact that he had decided to download Captain Roshe's vehicle override software months ago, would pay off once again on this tour. First, he had been able to use the suite of tools to gain control of a limo at the Guild Hall and now, he would be acquiring a maintenance platform too. With any luck, he would be able to steal a whole shuttle before the tour completed.

He began feeding the cable reel and attached the anchor spike to the cable's end while contemplating the idea of trying to perform as many vehicular acquisitions as he could, simply for bragging rights. Unfortunately, his discipline precluded such a thing, but for now at least, he had a valid enough reason to do it.

With the cable launched and anchored above the barge, he could affix one end of the cable reel to another anchor here and use the setup as a zip line. Given the height difference and the distance, he had long ago determined that gliding across the expanse would not be adequate and since he was approaching the flat side of the building directly, there was no good way to slow down a swinging descent either.

The plan played out in his mind. He would begin his journey and barrel into anyone boarding or leaving the barge long enough to confuse the group of them and then he would set to work stealing their transport. There was minimal potential for casualties if he did things quickly and he guessed some bruises would be the only physical reminder that the events had occurred at all. The veracity of the stories the group would tell would never be confirmed, but it would be something that the grandkids would hear about at least.

The optics in Tony's rifle blinked on as he aimed outward. The range to the target and estimated wind direction were displayed in the scope, giving him a clear indicator as to where his shot would land relative to the point of aim. He moved it around until he was comfortable that the drop from the line would not be more than a meter or two and ensured that he would be able to roll out of his impact with the barge deck sans serious injury.

The sound of the rifle firing was rather subdued compared to the percussion of the breaching charge earlier and Tony knew it wouldn't carry across the gap in the buildings. Given the fact that he had yet to see a visible reaction from the crew on the barge, he guessed they had not even heard that much.

A second or so passed before the telltale thunk of the anchor spike finding its place resonated back up the cabling. Tony's rifle blinked the appropriate color, indicating that as far as the spike on the far end was concerned, it was securely in place. There was always a risk that the device broke loose and as Tony pondered that possibility he looked over his shoulder to his companion. He would have to glide to ground if that happened, leaving Truth behind.

In such a case he decided he would notify Truth's coprocessor for all the good it would do. He didn't know if it could revive her more quickly than normal but even if it could, it would not be able to insert the recovery pick containing the neural map. Truth's memories of the immediate time would be gone and she would be disoriented at best, likely lost as to where she was or why. Of course she would quickly figure it out if Tony was able to remain in communication, but it was a possibility he didn't want to entertain further.

With renewed purpose, he stripped the cable reel from his towline rifle and unraveled the remainder. Rather than cut the dozen or so meters more of cabling that remained, he moved back into the room and found the heaviest looking piece of furniture he could. A hefty looking cooler against the wall caught his eye and he tangled the cable around the back and front a couple times, several loops of the tensile material wrapping the rectangular box tightly. Finally exhausting most of the remainder, Tony reloaded the spool so it would feed in the opposite direction and again attached an anchor spike which he loaded into the barrel of his rifle once more.

The thick wall behind the counters served as the opposite anchor for his towline and he carefully found the strongest looking part of it to fire at, burying the metallic spike with a trigger pull. Finally, he had both ends secured, a reasonable towline. Part of the towline kit included a collapsible rider for such cables and as Tony unhooked the empty spool from his rifle, he fumbled for the purpose built piece of rarely used hardware, unfolding the handles as he checked just how taut the cable was.

There was some play in the cord but it wavered less than he thought it might, giving him some marginal confidence at least that it would work for his needs. He slung the rifle over one shoulder finally, knowing he could use it to intimidate the workers even if it were actually unloaded. He had a set of anchor spikes left as well, in a pinch they would make a rather lethal projectile at shorter ranges.

Striding to the window, he took one last survey of the room he was about to leave and reached up above his head, setting the rider onto the cable. A moment later and he took a step forward, then another until finally, he was leaning forward.

As he began to topple out of the building, suspended by the cable, he lifted his feet and, like a pendulum, his body swung forward.

The momentum carried him quickly and as he descended, his speed began increasing. The cable and the rider together sounded off, a grating metal on metal sound that was unique to this sort of situation. Tony had never heard anything quite like it from any other source but this was the first time he had ended up using the towline rifle to form a zip line in between two buildings.

Training had always focused on traversing hard terrain with the zip line setup but never really focused on urban centers. He supposed, as he raced forward, that it was for good reason. The cable shook a bit now as he neared its middle and he wondered just how much force it would take to dislodge the anchors from the artificial construction on either end.

Forward ever more, meter after meter, Tony careened onward, his target rapidly approaching. He lifted his feet in anticipation of the eventual drop and roll landing that he had planned and eyed the barge as he approached. The wind whipped past, the air biting lightly at his skin as he neared his destination but even as he readied himself, he felt a change.

The Novian felt a sudden gust of wind shove him, a burst not too uncommon between such tall buildings but he had not anticipated the strength of this particular situation. Even as the wind subsided, he felt himself come down hard on the cable, and in an instant, the shaking line began to loosen obviously.

He only realized that the anchor spike on the destination end had fallen loose when instead of forward motion, he felt himself losing altitude far more rapidly than he had planned. Instead of the nice targeted landing in the clear space on the barge, he felt himself careening inaccurately. There was no time to deploy his wing suit and avoid a collision with the barge, and so, Tony braced for impact instead.

Whatever was in the boxes the group of workers were transporting made quite a bit of noise as Tony crashed at high speed into a stack of it. The stacked boxes broke before him like toy blocks against an intent child and he crashed through several stacks of hard feeling, maybe jagged, metallic objects.

Even as he broke through the opposite end of the stacks, he noticed the rapidly approaching edge of the barge, and, having careened through the stacks rather than landing on the floor, the waist high railing of the barge was in no way prepared to stop him.

As he rolled, semi helplessly past the threshold, his arms shot out in reflexive desperation and for precious moments he was unsure whether he would even manage to grab hold of anything.

Thankfully, or rather, painfully, he felt his shoulders wrench in violent fashion, drawing a loud curse from him as he felt the jolts of discomfort rise from his fingertips through his upper back. His entry had been far less than discreet. His body hung perilously on the outside of the barge, his legs dangling in useless desperation as the shock threatened to force his fingers to detach from the railing he had managed to grab.

A downward glance told him that a good portion of the cargo he had crashed into was already on its way to the ground below, and he quickly looked back upward, trying to decide what to do. It took a few seconds for him to manage the will to pull himself upward, and as he did, he thanked himself for doing the extra upper body training the past couple weeks.

As his face crested the edge of the barge deck, he looked back over his shoulder to see what he could find out about the crew he was about to displace. One of them was already looking toward the scene in obvious confusion but he failed to notice the Novian hanging from the barge pull himself up. By the time he did, Tony had managed to energize himself enough to slip under the railing and come into a crouch.

Finally, the man noticed him, and his surprise was clear as he began to speak.

Tony cut him off immediately, unslinging his towline rifle and resting it against his hip, pointing it at the man, "Get off the barge!"

The yelling caught the attention of the rest of the group, who, Tony could see inside the building. Apparently this was more than just maintenance, some kind of special delivery service. It made Tony wonder what exactly he had knocked to its destruction some many stories below.

The closest of the deliverymen raised his hands in surrender as Tony's currently disarmed weapon fixated on him. Of course, the man could never have known that it was not actually loaded at the moment and his desire for self preservation precluded the kind of curiosity that Tony himself would have had about the situation.

The others, on noticing an armed intruder holding up one of their own let out an array of surprised yells and generally non-combative expressions. It didn't take long for Tony to herd the helpless crew from near the barge and move to the control console. Industrial equipment was not a hobby but the control consoles on consumer grade Hil'Raigh products were generally descriptive enough that Tony was unsurprised to find a set of well marked buttons there. Even more helpfully, he would not need to use Roshe's software package to bypass any sort of security since the machine was still running.

"Thanks," Tony muttered to himself and keyed the safety gate control. He didn't really feel much gratitude to the delivery crew specifically, but the fact that their vehicle was available gave him some small measure of understanding of what they must have been feeling.

An ever helpful computerized voice announced the fact that the safety gate was now closed, and Tony confirmed it by glancing upward. Indeed the small safety barrier was now in its erect position barring any attempted re-entry of the barge by its crew, unless they were feeling particularly adventurous of course.

None of them appeared to want to take the opportunity however as Tony fired up the engines again. It did not take long for the barge to separate from its docking point and move into the the air between the two buildings. At the speed he was able to get the make shift transport moving, it would not take long for him to reach the brokerage building once more. The sounds of law enforcement sirens filled the air on the front side of the brokerage now however and Tony realized that he had little time remaining to pick up his partner and leave.

After he gathered Truth, Tony decided that he would take the barge to the rear of the brokerage building and land in one of the open areas he had noticed there. Even at that point, he had only nominal ideas as to what he would do about the fact that he would stick out quite obviously while carrying his partner.

Eventually, in the windy corridor, Tony found his barge approaching the hole he had made in the brokerage window. He spun the barge flatly and as he neared the building's side, he tapped the station keeping control, followed by the safety gate toggle.

Even as the gate was retracting, he had moved toward it and stepped into the opening he had made. He moved first to the cooler and the cable there, wrapping up some of the cabling he had used around it. The far end hung limply some several dozen meters below outside but despite that he wanted to make sure he left as little behind as he had to.

Tony fed the cable to the spool in awkward fashion then hit the retraction button. The tool whirred to life and struggled only for a moment as it worked. Tony then moved to his partner's body and hefted her with care. Over one shoulder, he carried her to the barge where he again layed her down amid the remaining cargo on board. It only took a few moments but in that time his rifle had done most of its work already.

He re-entered the building one final time, moving to the anchor in the wall and tapping the release carefully before he hefted the tangled up rifle and cable spool with himself and moved back outward. There would be no firing the rifle for the time being, given how the spool had been retracted. He would have to remove one of the anchors to get the device to feed for a long distance launch but hopefully he would not have to do so in the foreseeable future.

He returned to the barge, moving to the console and toggling the safety gate. A moment later the station keeping was disabled and the barge was, lazily by comparison to his previous zip lining, descending toward the rear of the brokerage building. It would be several minutes before the police reached the floor he and Truth had been on and by the time they did, he hoped to have ditched the vehicle, especially since by now, its crew had likely begun the process of letting someone know what had happened. Tony hoped that the law enforcement vehicles had offloaded their people already, wishing not to get into a firefight with them.

It would definitely be harder for the delivery crew to identify Tony, at least if he found a bench or something to sit on with Truth. As far as they knew, he was alone after all. He smirked down at his partner and returned his attention to the controls.

Unfortunately, the platform lacked in automatic navigation, at least as far as Tony could tell and he couldn't break down his towline gun while he drove. Given the chance, he had hoped for such an opportunity to reduce the risk of being detected when he got to ground but it was entirely likely he would have no such luck.

The descent continued and finally, Tony realized he was paying attention to non-combat details, things like the traffic patterns of flying vehicles above in the airways. That was he guessed, his mental sign that he felt in the clear. Even so, he looked over his shoulder now and again even until he was only dozens of meters from a potential landing point.

The public promenade he had been aiming for was fairly well trafficked out beyond the alley he occupied between the two buildings and so, as he descended, he slowed his forward speed enough to land between the buildings rather than out in the direct public path.

Circling once, then twice, he found a suitably open place to set down the barge and did so with no fanfare. It was certainly not a designated landing zone, but given the simpler navigational control the barge had, it didn't even have the understanding that it had been parked improperly.

As the safety gate once again retracted, Tony noted how happily the barge seemed to settle into station keeping on command, despite the fact that it was nowhere near a landing spot.

Truth felt heavier this time, but that was probably because Tony felt a little more tired now that the adrenaline had died off a bit. Even so, he opted not to carry her over his shoulder, instead carrying her in front of himself and cupping her back and knees with his arms. It would draw hopefully less attention from passerby until he reached some place he could think of the next step for his plan.

As the meters toward the public thoroughfare vanished, he began to look for taxi landing stations. There were some of them on most promenades between buildings and he guessed he would find one or two if he looked hard enough.

None of them however, appeared to be taking in arrivals and no taxis appeared to be stopping at this particular section. The Novian briefly considered commandeering yet another vehicle but as the idea came, it was shoved aside by a more interesting one. A pair of hired mascots in the center of the foot traffic some twenty meters away were happily passing out fliers to those going by. The two Kul'Raigh looked to be companions, ones hired to promote a nearby business. It was apparently not all that uncommon as Tony had seen some companions doing the same in other places too.

"Do you have A'Shir's contact information?" Tony asked over his radio. There was a momentary pause and then finally, a response from Truth's too cheerful sounding computer, "Yes, that information is available. Truth stored this information in a place that prevented it from being vulnerable to the overload."

"Her calling card..." Tony said to himself, then, over the radio he added, "Place a call to her please, route it to me after you do."

Tony heard the sound of a municipal communication line being accessed moments later and seconds after that, a recorded message from A'Shir herself began piping through the channel. It was entirely too proper to be understood easily, but finally, the message halted and a greeting came from the genuine article.

"A'Shir," Tony began, "Hello this is Tony..."

There was a pause, then a reply, "Yes... Tony, what can I do for you?"

"I was wondering if you knew a discreet driver..."

"A discreet driver?" She paused for a long moment and then another reply came, "I understand, where are you?"

"Backside of Dengan Comm Brokerage," Tony began, looking for landmarks. He found a store sign name and read it, "Near the Garment Connection Boutique and the Sensation Aesthetic Center"

He felt silly reading the names so literally but he was not great at reading Hil'Raigh.

There was a small chuckle from the other end but finally an acknowledgment, "I'll send someone I trust, a dark red vehicle. The driver will get out. He wears a kunir hat."

"Right... whats a kunir hat?" Tony asked, searching around now for a bench he could reach before he finished the call. With any luck he could prop Truth to make it look like she was resting against his shoulder.

"It's a sort of ...I wish you had holo-graphics on...I would send you a picture..." A'Shir paused, "The hat will be red too... red hats are not that common, you should recognize it..."

"Alright..." Tony replied, "Thanks..."

"Where would you like him to take you?" came the question.

"Anywhere we can rest..." Tony replied quickly. Locating a bench, he began moving toward it, as yet unnoticed.

"Understood, I have a place then..."

***

The apartment door was nondescript but as A'Shir keyed it, she gestured Tony to follow. He carried Truth through the portal and once he was inside, A'Shir followed. Her shoes were immediately slipped from her feet and placed against the wall next to the door

"Don't worry about your shoes, my feet are just tired," She announced, "Come.."

Tony followed into a side room near the entrance, the one A'Shir had entered. A rather luxurious looking bedroll was already laid out and the Kul'Raigh motioned to it as she spoke, "Is she hurt?"

"No, I don't think so," Tony said, setting Truth down in as comfortable a position as he could manage. She didn't so much as stir. He pulled, the recovery pick from his pocket and knelt down near her, reaching behind her ear and moving back the hair there before he slipped the plug into the jack and covered her ear once more.

A'Shir watched with interest until he stood, "Medicine?"

"Sort of," Tony replied.

She nodded, "Alright, well you are both welcome to rest here..."

"Thanks..."

"I guess you had something to do with the burglary at the brokerage?" she asked. She moved out of the room and slid the sliding door for it partially closed. Tony had never been in a Hil'Raigh residence like this one before. The apartment he and Truth had rented in Kolos was a bit more spacious. This one seemed cheaper, or rather, more discreet. Even getting here had taken a bit of a train ride from An'Jea but A'Shir had been adamant that this was her safest place, a nondescript apartment nestled into a structure at least a hundred or more stories tall. The elevator ride itself had taken a minute or two, and then the stairs the rest of the way. Tony had to admit it was a good place not to be found.

On the inside, it appeared the floor plan was rather basic. A small hallway directly from the door to the back of the place, which opened into a single multipurpose room. Off on one side of the hall was the bedroom he had put Truth to rest in and on the opposite side to that was a washroom and a small laundry alcove.

From here in the hall Tony could see that the multipurpose room contained a kitchen of sorts and what had to be the only place one would entertain guests if they ever came by, a dining room and front room all in one. Off to one side was the sleeping area. It contained a spacious looking bed and next to it, a designer vanity, complete with the accessories Tony might have guessed a companion would keep around. Nearby that was a closed wardrobe.

A'Shir led him back and headed immediately for the kitchen area, motioning to the table, "I guess I was surprised you were still around..."

"Job's not done yet," Tony smirked, feeling grateful, but vulnerable at the same time.

The Kul'Raigh began mixing something into a cup. She then poured some steaming water into the vessel from a dispenser. A small utensil followed and she stirred the aromatic mixture with care before taking a sip. After that, she added what looked to be some kind of condiment to the mix, something Tony couldn't identify. It was probably some sort of Kul'Raigh tea but Tony had never bothered drinking any of the stuff thus far and was likely not to give it a try by this point.

"Glad we got your calling card back in Kolos," Tony finally said, "Very lucky coincidence."

"Fate works that way sometimes," A'Shir gave him a warm smile.

"Sorry to take up your time," Tony replied, "We should be able to leave soon..."

"No need to apologize," she stated in reply, "You and your partner did more than enough for me back in Kolos."

"Quite nice of you to say that"

"Nicer that it was done I think," she said, sipping the cup noisily. The tea smelled strongly, but Tony guessed it missed the mark for Novians to really get the most out of the smell, Truth probably would have had a better experience with it.

"So you keep several residences?" Tony finally asked.

A'Shir nodded, "I have a few, and one at the hall too."

Tony gave his own nod, surprised. He assumed such a thing would be expensive, "Doesn't that get expensive?"

A'Shir nodded once more, "For most people yes,"

"Ah..." Tony said in realization, "Lucrative work huh?"

"My station in The Guild is rather fortuitous in that regard, I admit." A'Shir replied with admirable discretion, "But with that generosity, fate expects also, that I take precautions for my own safety..."

"I don't blame you," Tony replied.

"If one works among the affluent clients long enough, she begins to understand that not all dangers manifest themselves in dark alleys..." A'Shir cautioned seriously, a proverb style caution if Tony had ever heard one.

"But you trust some aliens knowing where this place is?" Tony smirked.

"Not entirely," She replied, adding, "But I hope I can be convinced. Besides you will not be around as long as some of the other concerning characters I've met through work."

The pair sat in silence for a moment and A'Shir set her cup down after several more. It was empty by that time, though the smell of the tea still lingered in the air. Almost as if sensing his train of thought A'Shir looked to him and spoke, "Would you like some tea?"

"No thanks," Tony replied. He had no real love of teas, alien or otherwise. He preferred his drinks to be thicker than that. Even so, the hospitality was welcome, despite the fact that Tony felt on edge anyway. Regardless of how nice A'Shir was, he had to be ready to move and he doubted that he would be able to steal a delivery barge to escape this place as well, if it were compromised.

Once Truth was awake they could decide their exact course of action but for the time being, letting her rest was more important. As he remembered the barge however, Tony's mind was drawn to the memory of his escape from the brokerage tower. The delivery barge had been instrumental, and yet if he were in many of the larger cities in the galaxy, he doubted he would have been able to be so lucky.

"It's kind of interesting to me that there are so many people doing jobs here that robots usually do back home," Tony stated, watching A'Shir's reaction.

She cocked her head to the side a little. Giving a sort of half nod she began her explanation. "That's probably because of Naturalism, a concept many foreigners pick up on when they visit."

"Naturalism. I think I've heard it before," He replied, "Something about people should not have robot arms and stuff right?"

A'Shir giggled lightly. Tony of course, had heard Truth relate to him, the small bit of such a concept that she had experienced with Kirashira back on the ship. The limited explanation he had received was centered on people with artificial implants but A'Shir was sure to provide a more general explanation.

"Well sort of," She replied, "The Natural aesthetic is of paramount importance, so a fake looking arm is generally not something you want in the Federation. But most of the time, regenerative techniques can salvage a limb so losing one would be extremely rare..."

"Natural, but it doesn't include genetically engineering I take it?"

"No, engineering is considered of importance because it has its foundations in the natural world. On the other hand, trying to create something that passes itself off as nature is a... touchy... subject." She explained, "That's why most of the robots you see, if you ever see them, are for assembly lines or heavy lifting. That doesn't even include some of the rebel statements one might make by bending the standard either."

"Seems inefficient," Tony replied, "Back home the taxi driver who took us here or picked me up would probably have just been a robot car."

A'Shir smiled, "It is inefficient. By design."

Tony was nominally surprised by the answer, it did not make much sense to him.

"In a society like ours, where the real logistics are automated and hidden from view, having a living body do work is something of a prize. For us, the worker and the receiver of the effort are gaining something intangibly beneficial, the expenditure of living energy. A robot of any kind cannot offer that."

Tony eyed the Kul'Raigh critically. That point of view was assuredly alien but rather than reply in words which might sound accusatory, he finally shrugged. This was an alien society after all, "I guess I never thought of it that way."

A'Shir smiled broadly, "That's partly the Kul'Raigh influence on society over the generations. There was an old saying, 'What can a Kul'Raigh do that a robot can't?'"

"Guess you took it as a challenge," Tony replied.

The Kul'Raigh nodded and stood a small smile on her face. Moving to place her cup in the wash tray on the counter, she replied, "The Companion Guild was one of the first organizations to be borne of that effort. Eventually, everyone just sort of realized that they liked the idea of people still living and breathing together. Frankly I find it comforting."

"I have a feeling there is quite a bit to learn," Tony replied diplomatically, "Unfortunately, I don't think I have time to absorb all the local customs."

The companion shrugged and pulled a small bag of something from a shelf near the counter she stood next to, drawing out a piece of whatever it was and sticking it in her mouth happily. She appeared to chew a bit as she took the bag with her back to the table. Gesturing, she offered the bag. Tony looked inside and found one of the few things he remembered eating back in his acclamation training for the stationing in Kolos.

"Thanks," He said, taking one of the thin wafer like crackers from inside.

"Unfortunately I only have books here, I turned off the entertainment center feeds months ago, otherwise I'd offer them," A'Shir announced. She moved to the couch in the center of the room as she continued speaking, "I have some book keeping to take care of but you are welcome to rest as long as you like."

"Alright," Tony replied, he took another wafer and chewed it thoughtfully as he watched his host sit down and pull a slate from a pocket in her robe. She began tapping away at it with focus.

Finally, Tony stretched in the seat he occupied, then, pulled his towline rifle and the filled up spool from before, and set them on the table. Now came the unenviable task of disassembling the tool after it had been used for zip lining. While he had broken down the barrel of it already, the meat of the rifle was still in the state it had been earlier. With a sigh, he got to work, glancing up now and again to keep an eye on his host.

17 - Anti-Social

There were of course, potentially worse ways to spend a day but the idea of playing babysitter sat near the top of Tony's personal list of bad options. Getting an extraction shuttle had been relatively easy, thanks to A'Shir's help in transport, but Truth was still being medically evaluated by doctor's orders. Standard procedure with Truth seemed at times, to be made up as it went, but thankfully at least, the rest might do her some good.

She had woken up after the incident with very little loss of memory but rules were rules and because of her history with that sort of mental overload, they were more strict. A clean bill of health and a physical evaluation from the acting physician, was enough to overcome the standard rules for recovery time from wounds. Conversely, Truth had a hard time limit off duty whenever she was dosed. It would be a few days at least, in which she was officially off roster. The theory was it gave her time to recover, to think and regain her full mental faculty because the interfaces were not always perfect. In reality, Tony knew what everyone else, including Truth knew; it was more about observing her behavior than anything.

Still, the time off would let Truth be removed from the unofficial ambassador duty she had assumed since Kirashira had boarded the ship. As Tony glanced down at the data slate in his hand once more however, he felt the unease of being the primary point of interaction with the Princess creep into his mind. She was not dangerous, not really, but the idea of what she might be, made him dread any sort of personal contact.

Tony had to admit that as far as people from the Federation went, he had limited experience. Despite that, the way they always seemed to think about or talk about his people and their nation bugged him anyway. He wondered how the Admiralty had ever expected an ambassador to be useful on Ashor at all. Nothing he had read or heard from the endeavor had ever yielded the kind of basic political understanding that even the Terrans had managed.

Still, he had a job to do, a favor for Truth at least, and an order of sorts from Thorsh. The Admiral could not be bothered with the day to day of the Princess' whims and since the analysts were busy pouring over the information Truth had gathered, that left he and his partner without an official mission for at least some time. Time enough for him to take a while reaching the guest quarters.

Every NovaCore ship had its own set, some were improvised and some dedicated. This vessel featured the latter, a relatively large cabin space designed for up to two occupants. Tony had previously occupied the room with Truth but ever since their guest had been discharged from the infirmary, she had been Truth's room mate. Even though it had only been a day or two, Truth already had some interesting tidbits to share.

As a result, reaching the door to the guest quarters was something of a tense moment. Kirashira was inside by request, until an escort came to pick her up. Would she react badly to a change in who she had waiting on her flippant whims?

Tony keyed the door call and waited, clearing his throat. He wore now, his light regulation dress, a tank top and dark combat pants. His familiar red belt bisected the ensemble and his holsters were unattached to it. Was the Princess expecting dress uniform? He smirked to himself, imagining odd greeting scenarios until finally, the door slid aside.

Princess Kirashira appeared in the portal and for a moment Tony forgot about the fact that he was observing a foreign royal. She wore a pair of combat pants, Truth's size by the look of it, and a form hugging shirt, both of which probably came from the requisition office. By all standards she almost looked passably familiar to the ship. When her voice sounded though, the illusion broke apart, articulate Hil'Raigh filling the air, "Hello Major."

"Princess," Tony replied with a nod of acknowledgment. A salute was out of the question, being that she was a foreign official and not technically a head of state either, at least not yet, "I'm your escort for the day."

"You?" She looked surprised, scrutinizing Tony with obvious care, "What about your partner?"

"Truth is indisposed," Tony replied diplomatically, "So you got me instead."

"Truth mentioned the observation deck before," Kirashira stated, "I'd like to visit it."

Tony nodded, "She said you were interested. We can head there before we go to the tailor."

Kirashira gave a nod and exited the guest quarters, the door sliding closed behind her. Tony turned on his heel and began leading at his normal pace. In moments it was clear that Kirashira was not used to having her pace dictated as she fell behind. A flustered look filled her features and she hopped forward to keep up until Tony slowed down enough for her to keep up. While not entirely intentional, the idea that he was dealing with a coddled royal made him wonder what he could get away with. The idea that he wanted to keep Kirashira off guard settled in his mind but for diplomacy's sake he pushed the urges to the rear.

At very least a walk to the observation deck would be enough to have some time to talk to Kirashira directly. She had, by Truth's report, been something of a mixed interaction. At times she would appear and act as if she were comfortable and relaxed. Then, at other times, something would change and she would become standoffish. There were likely a combination of factors to blame for that behavior, Tony guessed, but no concrete answers. Truth was good at reading people's honesty and discomfort but she was far from a perfect socialite. As a result Tony guessed there was probably some sort of thing that she was overlooking, something that, thanks to her constant computerized companion, she was missing. Tony, guessed that, in Truth's position he would have made a similar judgment about the Princess. After all, she had just lost her parents and the confirmation of her father's death had already been delivered. Her mother was as yet unaccounted for but the popular assumption was that she had also been killed. The chance that she wasn't, was something Tony himself had only recently considered thanks to A'Shir.

Kirashira was an enigma to be sure. Truth had not revealed all that much about their conversations and at this point Tony guessed it was more a matter of not having tried to dig very deeply. She was going to be emotional, probably as long as she was on the ship, at least due to what she had been through. It didn't help that she was in a foreign environment surrounded by things she did not understand. Even still, Tony was bothered by the idea that Truth was somehow a problem for her. He contemplated for a moment, on whether his desire to figure it out was important enough to hold on to.

Kirashira was stuck here for now, and to work with her, to work on her behalf, he felt he had no choice but to understand it. Even if he couldn't change her mind, he had to understand what the limitations would be on her cooperation in the future.

"So what else is there to do on this spaceship," Kirashira asked at last.

"Depends," Tony replied, then explained further,"You might not find many things you are used to on a ship like this since most of the space on board is tailored to naval personnel."

"You don't have many leisure activities on board then?" She asked.

"There are some good physical training rooms on board, The social hall..." Tony shrugged, "There are some game rooms. I honestly don't know what a member of your royal family does in their spare time, so it's hard to recommend anything."

"I like dancing, my mother taught me a number of them," She replied, "Much of my time was spent studying how to do my father's job. Learning. I like to learn."

"There are some low impact exercise rooms on board, you might be able to dance there. No private venues though," Tony replied, adding, "Unless you feel like dancing in your room."

"Truth and I went to one of the training areas, there were some crew there," Kirashira stated, "I didn't mind given the circumstance."

"What kind of things do you have to study to be in charge of a country anyway?" Tony asked, raising a brow.

Kirashira sighed, a sound Tony guessed was a resignation to relax if a little. She was silent for a while, but not in a defiant way. Her body language took a contemplative tone, one that made Tony more curious. At last she spoke, "I have to learn some of everything, at least enough to work with the people who are directly in charge of it. Economic management, diplomacy, finance, technology, even some military strategy."

Tony chuckled, military strategy coming out of the Starlight Compact was not something he had ever imagined possible, "I thought your nation was pacifist."

"We have been for quite a long time, it's a sort of Ren'Tauru tradition," She began, "They say it started after the civil war during the exodus."

"I don't know much about that, I only hear the name every so often when it comes to the Federation."

"It's a pretty important part of our history but most people who live in the Federation still don't know many details," Kirashira replied, an educational tone in her voice now.

"I find it a bit hard to believe," Tony replied, "Especially since, as I recall, the story involves a giant transport ship?"

Kirashira nodded and Tony continued, worried he would strike another chord. Regardless, he pressed forward, voicing his skepticism, "I just don't see how you could misplace such a big thing after you spent so much energy making it."

To his relief, Kirashira simply shrugged, "I don't have a good answer for that, it seems a bit fantastic if you take it at face value."

Finally, the pair reached the double doors to the observation deck Tony had been wanting to reach. Of course, it was an observation deck in its function and name but the reality was that it, like almost every other part of the ship was not tied to the outer hull of the ship at all. The window here in this room was little more than extremely high resolution display, that, given the visual sensors and other instruments on the outside of the ship, displayed a crystal clear picture of whatever celestial object that an observer might wish to look at.

Under normal operating conditions the screen was set to display images of the planet around which the vessel was orbiting, making for a currently striking view of Ashor below. Rather than a real image though, the picture was color enhanced and often magnified to showcase detail and give the viewer a sense of connection to the displayed image.

At times, observation decks like this were used as screening rooms for classic entertainment or crew training sessions. Now however, during the middle of a duty shift, the place was unoccupied save Tony and his guest.

Passing through the doors, which slid closed behind, Tony led the way into the room with Kirashira in tow. The interior of the room was dominated by a selection of comfortable looking couches along the outer walls save the side against the display. Several more chairs covered in the same leather like material were arranged throughout the room to have a view of the screen as well.

Breaking up the furniture placements were sets of artificial plants with broad flat leaves, lifelike enough that they added to the ambiance of the room without requiring any upkeep save being dusted clean every few days.

The swirling, clouded atmosphere of Ashor made a striking contrast to its broad ocean and the largest of its continents far below. Like a majority of the normally habitable worlds in the galaxy, large oceans dominated most of the globe and were broken up in their expansive reach by the masses of land across the surface.

Tony knew little of Ashor save that the weather was rather mild and that the wind currents on the surface made for temperate weather during most of the year. There was little in the way of axial tilt and as a result the equatorial belt of the planet was fixed in a tighter band than the NovaCore's capitol world. It's rotational speed was marginally slower than his own home and the size of the planet made for a gravity in line with most other major metropolitan planetary centers.

From here in orbit, it was hard to imagine that the lives and actions of so many on the surface were irrevocably tied to the fate of the single individual who was here by his side. She was being given the chance or maybe forced, to observe her home in a way she probably had done few times before.

"It's a nice planet," Tony said at last. Kirashira had already taken a seat observing the slowly rotating planet on the screen, a sort of reverence displayed in her body language as she stared intently. Either she had no idea the image was processed or she did not care, Tony guessed.

At long last, the Monarch spoke, sounding far more exhausted than previous, a tone of resignation in her voice as she asked her question, "How much longer until I can go home?"

That was a question Tony had no idea how to answer. It was for her own benefit that she was here at all, safe from the ravages of the world that had already consumed at least her father, perhaps her mother too.

"I don't have an answer to that," He replied with a diplomatic hint, trying to sound as much the ambassador as he knew how, "We'd naturally prefer to keep you here for your own safety, at least until we can be sure you will be safe again."

"I'll never be safe again," She replied, her voice foreboding. It betrayed a deep sense of pessimism that Tony guessed, was far from momentary, but rather, representative of the situation as she saw it playing out, "Not after what happened, I don't know how I can be safe anymore..."

"We can help you make changes," Tony offered, "Security practices, intelligence, I'm sure there are options."

"And when you and Truth go home?" She turned, looking to him with a critical need for assurance, assurance he could not provide. The idea that he and Truth were where Kirashira's mind went first however, was interesting. Tony would have assumed she understood the context of his meaning, knowing that he was only referring to his own government in broad terms, rather than he and Truth directly.

Even so, he took it as a sign that perhaps some headway would be made in the future. If she felt like the two NovaCore would provide help personally, perhaps there would be a chance that she would be more than just marginally cooperative later.

"We will try and see what we can do to help you solve this, not just for today or tomorrow, but to make sure it goes right as long as it can, that has always been the goal," Tony reiterated with confidence. He hoped that the way he said it sounded as assuring as he hoped in her native tongue.

There was a long silence with Kirashira returning her attention to Ashor. She seemed so lost in the sight of the planet that Tony wondered exactly what sort of spiritual foundation she relied on. He had heard that there were a variety of beliefs related to celestial objects in the Federation and maybe she was one of those who observed some form of those sorts of faiths. Still, there was more than spiritual reverence in her eyes, something that he understood when the yearning in them became clear.

She was not looking in awe or reverence but in memorial. He imagined that her eyes were searching, probing the sky to look for her home, to look down from the heavens upon the life she used to have, one she could no longer live-; a life stolen.

"I never realized how much I could miss a single planet," She said at length.

Tony stared at the screen for a while, glancing between it and the Princess.

"Truth says you both went to the training bay," He began, hoping that starting even some sort of conversation would get the royal talking.

She looked to him and nodded, remaining silent for a long while, "I have never been very physically inclined but it was a nice change of pace for me."

"I'm surprised. You handled yourself pretty well on the surface before, despite being tired, " Tony replied curiously.

"That's mostly biology," Kirashira replied with an honest disappointment, "I got given the genetics for it."

"Genetics," Tony smirked, "We know all about that."

Kirashira was silent for a moment, "Isn't it more than that though?"

"Training?" Tony guessed.

"No, I mean, Truth." She replied, "She's not... Like everyone else."

The discomfort in Kirashira's voice was obvious and Tony raised a brow, "Well she is a little awkward at times, I'll give you that."

"No, I mean, her body," The Princess insisted, almost like she was defending some as yet un-presented argument. Now intrigued, the Major wondered just what his guest was hinting at. Of course Truth was different, so was everyone Tony had interacted with, at least on some level. It was true of most anyone save the few people Tony labeled into insular collectives, ones he rarely saw or spoke to anymore.

"I'm afraid I don't follow," Tony replied with a shrug.

"She's modified with machines."

Tony smirked, "Well yeah, so am I. Tons of people are...I mean, you're genetically engineered too right?"

The royal looked frustrated, glancing to the ground for a moment, "No, not like Truth, she's different."

"What do you mean then?" Tony asked, his curiosity practically oozing now.

"Her eyes, the lines under her skin, the way she talks..." Kirashira rattled off a few of the important reasons that Truth was different. Listening, Tony realized that some of those things were true, Truth's eyes had a distinct look to them, and if one looked carefully they would certainly catch evidence of some of her hardening and protective enhancements through her skin as well. What he found himself bugged by the most however, was an implication that Truth was somehow off putting. For some reason, that alone stuck in Tony's mind from the short list.

"You mean you don't get along," Tony clarified. The Princess shook her head negatively.

"No, she's very polite. I just...I don't know if I should have someone who is changed in such a way be my guide here," she replied, "I think I could be more comfortable otherwise."

"Truth didn't volunteer for that job, Princess," Tony said, feeling defensive. The idea that Truth was being seen as less in Kirashira's eyes was frustrating to him. He had always looked out for Truth, it had always been that way, and in return, she did the same. Now, Tony felt that he was a wolf whose pack mate had been attacked by someone from the outside, he had to defend her. Kirashira did not reply and so Tony continued, "Truth was asked to guide you around because some people felt that your similar features would help you get along."

"I appreciate that," Kirashira replied, not backing down. She was calm however, despite the feeling bleeding into her voice she maintained herself in a dignified way, "But it would probably be best if she did not have to undertake that duty anymore."

"I don't understand why that's a problem," Tony replied in frustration.

"Because Truth is... its not something you'd understand, your people do that all the time. We don't. We don't put enhanced parts into people, we just try to make sure they start off with the best ones possible."

"It sounds to me like you are picking a problem out where there isn't one," Tony asserted, "No one decided to give Truth artificial parts for the hell of it."

"Oh really?" She shook her head, looking annoyed now, "It's just like you people, to come and take what you don't understand because you think it will provide you some kind of military benefit down the line. Consequences be damned."

"We might not need those advantages if your Federation was not breathing down our necks all the time. Talk about enhanced soldiers, I don't think I've heard of any of your natural people going into combat before some convenient gene hacks."

"We optimize what we have, we don't replace it."

"Sounds pretty hypocritical coming from a Len'Raigh like yourself," Tony replied, throwing in the Hil'Raigh slang for a genetically engineered art baby. It was one of the few words he had bothered picking up that had no direct parallel in his own language, probably because of the slightly insulting connotation it carried. While genetic engineering was common before birth in the Federation, not everyone had the ability to tweak and tailor every aspect of the desired child along the way, nor to the extent that royalty could. As a result, the term had come to into its own as a pejorative against the people who had been given such a silver spoon from the moment of their conception, "Truth has had to work to live from the moment of her birth, she has had to survive. You've probably never even got a cold."

"Work to live? Seems like she was designed to kill, not live," Kirashira jabbed, "There's a reason most civilized people don't go as far as yours!"

"You have no idea how much she suffered before she got those replacement organs, She was dying in more ways than you could count with that amazing royal education of yours!" Tony stood his ground, he had no interest in dealing with such a brat, "She had to have them, she didn't ask for them!"

"She never would have had those problems if your people were not playing divine with Kul'Raigh genes! No child gets born with those kind of severe problems when those who understand them are in charge!" Kirashira replied, further adding to the frustration Tony felt building.

"Right, you just erase the child, I forgot," Tony retorted with deep sarcasm filling his voice.

"That's not true!" Kirashira snapped.

"I guess having everything not work out for once just sets you off on everyone who has succeeded despite the obstacles," Tony jabbed, "But when you get the silver spoon your entire life it must really hurt to be shoved back into reality."

The Princess smoldered but he continued, "If Truth would have had all the perfect doctors, all the expensive amazing geneticists, peer review of her genome before it was ever sequenced, all the shit you got for free... She never would have had to have ANY of those things done! No surgeries! No pain! No crying that she was alive at all! You had it all and you get touchy and selfish the moment it's not working out. Welcome to the real world Princess!"

The royal began shaking her head angrily and got up to leave, her lip quivering. She winced a little as she fought back the obvious onset of tears. Was she that thin skinned? was she so weak as to break under such minuscule criticism? Tony almost continued but instead he just stewed angrily, remembering the hospital visits to Truth's bedside, the times she cried because the pain wouldn't stop, the times she couldn't take anymore medicine without overdosing. He was reminded of the stumbles, the failings, the way Truth had struggled to re-learn her world after each different surgery, after each replacement. The way her life changed each time. He remembered the innocent girl who liked coloring books, stuck in a hospital bed every day. He was angry. Kirashira had no right, none at all, to accuse her of anything.

He felt himself overloaded for the first time in years. The kind of smoldering frustration that he had not felt since his days as a cadet in the academy boiling now in his heart. He had put it past him, the behavior of other cadets, the insults he sometimes got, the ones Truth received from the jealousy of others.

None of that was like this though. Truth had not risked her life for those cadets back then, she was in training like they were. But for the one who Truth had been wounded saving, one who Truth had risked the life she had clung to so long, to have such an attitude was nigh unforgivable.

Glancing over his shoulder Tony realized Kirashira was gone now, probably wandering helplessly around the ship. She would eventually be picked up by security or he would be paged... He didn't care.

18 – Reflection

How long had it been? Tony looked over to the still slowly rotating globe of Ashor. He wondered just how long it would take before he got paged by someone on the command staff for causing an international incident. He felt a bit sheepish now, but he was still mad. Sheepish that he had let himself get so frustrated but angry because Truth was the focus of it all.

At the end of the day he had to admit to himself that despite all of the work that had gone into helping he and his partner stay level headed under all conditions, disrespect of his closest ally got to him in a way nothing else ever could.

It had been so many years now since Truth had been introduced to him, it felt like a lifetime ago. Even so, he could remember the first day vividly, those moments when Admiral Thorsh had ushered him into Truth's hospital room. Tony, being one of the successful clones was being brought to try and cheer up one of the malfunctioning ones. He did not know it at the time but that was the goal really.

Truth had been sitting upright in her bed, diligently selecting from among a set of coloring sticks. It was ancient technology, something odd and out of place. The first words Tony had asked were of course, why she was using those old things to color when a slate could do any color she wanted. She said she liked the feeling of the paper.

Tony sighed, recalling those events. Knowing what he knew now, the things Truth said back in those days carried so much more weight. She liked the paper because she had already been losing her sense of touch. The roughness of the paper compared to a screen made it more appealing to her degenerating mind.

Over the years, he had never been given any full explanation, and he guessed that Truth probably hid some of the complications from him as she had learned of them. What he did know however, was that when parts of her had been replaced, it was due to a failing, a new problem brought on by her condition.

Tony had learned from Thorsh years later that Truth was considered by some in the program to be a lost cause. The idea of bringing another of the clone batch to cheer her up, was seen as a waste of time and energy that was better spent educating him instead.

Thorsh however, had apparently seen it differently. Tony had never been told about the specifics of the man's involvement in the cloning program. He only knew that it was what had saved Truth's life and given Tony someone more important than any friendship could hope to replicate. What he did know however, was that the Admiral was just the same as he was now, he was a taker of calculated risk for what he deemed a moral imperative. He had decided that if Truth was to deteriorate, that she deserved a friend in her short life, one to bolster what she did get to do.

At first, Tony had not enjoyed the visits, he did not like coloring with Truth, he did not like sitting in the hospital next to her bed. Truth was an alien anyway, he'd said sometimes. Of course, she had grown on him, a helpful nudge from Thorsh had pushed things along but looking back, Tony expected he would have eventually befriended Truth regardless.

The first years of their friendship were not what Tony would have imagined as a child of that age and yet, they had turned out to be something unique. He had gone to the primary school in the hospital with Truth, a place where those undergoing radical treatment or terminal illness care were allowed to spend their time with those they could relate to. Tony of course was the odd one out there.

He knew at times, looking at his peers that he was one of the few who would ever have all the opportunity life usually held, one of the few gifted with the genes to make it all work. How many others were from cloning programs he did not know, and frankly, he was glad not to know. He always looked back to the programs with mixed feelings.

On the one hand, he owed his existence to them, he was a product of their success. The costs however, could be quantified easily for him. He had watched what Truth had been through, and despite his ego, his desire to be right, Kirashira was not entirely wrong in her earlier assertions. She had contended that if true experts had overseen Truth's sequencing that the outcome of the process would have been different. In that case, perhaps they would never have met.

Tony had speculated with his partner at times that perhaps she had been meant for deep cover, more than just serving in the force. They both understood why it would be attempted and yet, for some reason, both seemed to agree without words, that there was moral ambiguity there.

Cloning super soldiers was something that had, hundreds of years ago been a dream for his people. Part of the civil wars that had wracked the Novian home world before the split into two nation states, had involved the first attempts at genetic manipulation, gene hacking as it was called.

Still, technology of that type had only been used in a minor fashion, augmenting and adjusting. Making Novians more capable of living in space without severe health problems or giving them better strength and speed were its common uses. Most of that was a natural thing these days, part of standard gene therapy for most people.

He and Truth however had been something new, something unprecedented. The entirety of the program, all of its details had never been disclosed, but the implications were clear enough in Truth's existence. The ability to manipulate genetics as well as the Hil'Raigh, presented a striking ethical dilemma.

Tony had met the geneticist and researcher responsible for most of Truth's implant technologies and the neural interface she had received, one Dr. Malory. The woman was a headstrong, scientifically minded person who valued the end result almost too much. Tony never got a good read on her personality and it was probably because it had been years since he had ever met her in person. Now, with all of his training he was sure he could read her better, but there was little reason for him to contact her now. She was the project director back in the day and that was as much as Tony was allowed to know. Even Admiral Thorsh, the most honest and friendly man Tony had known, was oddly tight lipped about the entire project series.

Tony had been a successful experiment and the moral obligation posed by Truth was less severe now that she was more or less able to live her life free of disability. In fact, she was better off from a tactical standpoint than anything she would have been before.

That reality always made Tony think however. He wondered at times whether the condition Truth had found herself in had stemmed entirely from genetics and whether some of it was not allowed to happen for testing things like the neural interface.

No, he shook his head. He knew some few scientists, he'd even met some people involved in the cloning project. None of them had seemed that callous, not even Dr. Malory.

The possibility though, was insidious enough that Tony stood, pacing a bit to clear his mind. He didn't want to go there or ask those questions. For him, he reminded himself, it was enough that Truth was alive and well. She was safe and she was able to live her life as she chose. Thankfully that meant she was pretty close by most of the time.

That was what the whole argument with Kirashira had boiled down to in the end. Tony hated the idea of his partner and ally, his dearest friend, being insulted at all. She had succeeded despite the challenges her artificial parts had presented, not because of them. Admittedly she benefited from them time and again these days but that was in Tony's opinion, a long overdue reward for what she had overcome earlier in life. If anyone deserved success to come of strife, it was Truth.

As he thought, there was a knock at the portal leading into the observation deck. A knuckle rapping on the open doorway. Tony turned and immediately shot to his feet, saluting, "Admiral!"

The man smirked and entered without fanfare. He wore his command officer cap still, meaning he had probably come from a duty position on the command deck. Tony's stomach prepared for the reprimand he would receive. Thorsh was a father figure of sorts but he did have his moments of strictness, especially when one misbehaved.

"Major," He finally said, moving to sit in the vacancy left by Kirashira. She had been gone at least a half hour now and Tony guessed Thorsh or someone on the staff had found her wandering unhappily.

"If it's about the Princess sir," Tony began, eying his commander, "I will be able to explain my reasoning, though I realize now it was probably better handled with more tact sir."

"Sit down Major," Thorsh replied casually, "Let's talk first..."

"Yes sir," Tony said a bit of tension leaving him as he sat, a little more stiffly now than he had before.

"So what made you sit in here while our guest was wandering alone? Must have been mentally stimulating," Thorsh asked.

"I thought she had clearances sir, I wouldn't have let her walk out if..."

"She didn't walk anywhere restricted Major," Thorsh replied, "What were you occupied with?"

Tony sighed, feeling at least a little more comfortable, "I was just thinking about when I met Truth... All we've been through since then. The stupid way you tricked me as a kid..."

The officer smiled broadly, a good wholesome smile. He nodded in understanding, "As I recall, I tricked you into becoming friends, right?"

Tony smirked and shook his head, "More or less sir."

"What did I say again? I bet you don't understand how to be her friend because she is sick. I will find you a different friend if you can't handle this," The man recited gleefully. Tony laughed at the words, he could never remember them exactly but that sounded like what they must have been.

"How'd it work?" Thorsh followed up and looked over to Tony who cleared his throat, realizing now that it was not just reflective memory hour, but some sort of lesson of example.

"Too well sometimes," Tony replied honestly, remembering what had sparked the argument in the first place. The Admiral gave a knowing smile and Tony cocked his head in understanding, "How'd you know?"

Thorsh shrugged, "That kind of thing always set you off when you were younger too, I just guessed. Once you told me you were thinking about Truth I knew I was right."

Tony nodded, "I just… It's not fair. Kirashira got given a leg up on everything and everybody and she is criticizing Truth just for being alive…"

"I can understand how that might make you unhappy," Thorsh admitted, motioning with his head to the planet in the screen, "Especially after what you two have been through so far on this…"

"Yeah, it makes me mad," Tony replied.

"Well that puts us in a predicament then Major," He continued, "Because our objective; helping Princess Ren'Tauru? Making sure we keep the lid on this before it explodes in our faces? That all hasn't changed."

"I understand sir," Tony replied in embarrassment.

"Having a pissing match with someone so important… damnit Major I can't have that…" Thorsh chastised. His rebuke was cutting not because of tone, but because of who was delivering it, "We both know who should have stepped away. No question about that. You have a bigger duty to attend to than defending your partner every time some snot nose comes by and insults her."

"I know sir," Tony replied with a nod, trying to relay with his tone of voice, the very same.

"And you know what makes me more annoyed than anything about what happened?" Thorsh asked.

"I wouldn't presume to know in this case," Tony said, looking up to the officer with intent.

"That I probably would have done the same thing in your position," Thorsh replied with a hint of irony in his voice. He sighed deeply and leaned back in the couch he occupied, muttering a curse to himself and shaking his head.

"I doubt it sir, you are the most collected person I've ever met," Tony replied, he meant every word. Thorsh was a sort of bulwark. Tony attributed much of his own growth in the area of patience to the man's influence.

"Not always," The Admiral replied, "I wasn't always what you think I was…"

"That's hard to imagine sir," Tony replied.

"When I was your age, I was as prickly as a spined Caclian Fruit. I'm amazed I got a command at all," The man related exhaustedly. Tony could not help but picture the plump round red fruit from his homeworld and its myriad of wispy spikes. They got into ones skin and irritated it for weeks if not treated with the right kind of ointment. The fruit tasted only okay, no amazing reason to even eat them save the challenge in getting one peeled with one's bare hands.

"I can't say I've had the pleasure of eating one of those in a while," Tony joked.

"You just might have to get one out of food storage for this little outburst," Thorsh replied with partial seriousness. Tony nodded though and as Thorsh caught his eyes, he cleared his throat.

"I've half a mind to simply make you another challenge you can't refuse on the Kirashira situation..."

"You know they say lightning doesn't strike twice in the same place sir," Tony smirked.

"I don't know what you said to her, but she managed to sequester herself in the guest quarters again without incident. I'm calling you lucky on that front but I hope you understand how stupid I feel that it happened like it did... I have to make sure this works..."

"I take responsibility for what I said sir..." Tony replied.

Thorsh shook his head, "I only got a small call with her before she had enough. It took every bit of social wrangling I've learned over the years to get her to a point where she will probably talk to you again."

"You talked to her?" Tony's heart sank.

"Of course I did," Thorsh replied seriously, "Because when the people under my command make a mistake, it bites me."

Tony wanted to apologize but nothing came, he had no way to sound genuine enough. He simply nodded instead. Putting the man before him in a position of disadvantage was something he felt absurdly guilty for. Not only had he disappointed one of his role models, but one of the top leaders of his nation. It was rare that a person got a personal reprimand from a member of the Admiralty but here he was, receiving one.

"I'll do my best to mend the fence sir," Tony said at last. He still wanted to set Kirashira straight in a way but that could wait. Maybe if they developed some sort of real understanding then perhaps she could be convinced and if they couldn't, well, that was not Tony's immediate problem. The mission was the real goal and Kirashira, despite her mannerisms, was key to its success.

"Do we have anything from the data Truth got?" Tony finally asked, curious to know whether there had been much information of use in what Truth had overloaded herself to obtain.

The Admiral groaned slowly, a drawn out groan. It was not an enthusiastic gesture in the slightest and Tony wondered at why the question seemed to sap away his commander's enthusiasm. At length, the officer replied, giving a sigh before he did so, "It's sticky. A bit of everything the holo-verse could throw out and then some..."

Tony grimaced. The worlds created in most action holos were far from realistic in the general case, the spy thrillers mostly got things wrong. As a result, real life mirroring them was something of a bad sign in this sort of business.

"No idea who that other actor Truth found was, but the information she did get points to the tip of a very large iceberg that seems to encompass nobility and power brokers from across the Federation," Thorsh replied.

"You don't mean..."

"I do," Thorsh replied gravely, "It's very likely to be them, the Knights."

Tony sighed deeply. Most of the time the enigmatic organization was rumor and conspiracy. NovaCore intelligence had long suspected that something resembling it had existed but no one had ever managed to piece together a useful narrative.

As rumor had it, the network was decentralized and separated into echelons. Each tier knew nothing about anything beyond the people in charge and subordinate to it. It helped keep things secure when no one person knew anything about the entire organization.

Furthermore, the conventional wisdom said that the Knights were independent of any Federation member state, acting in their own interests for some kind of moral crusade type of reason.

Tony had never believed much of it but the Knights always came up as the joke perpetrator of any action no one could pin to any other agency in the Federation. It was a sort of running gag to say the Knights had orchestrated a plan or carried out a plot.

"You're sure?" Tony smirked, unable to contain himself at the idea of the crack pot theories probably having some weight to them now. It would blow the lid off of much of the surveillance that came out of the Federation if it were true. The real question was how anything had leaked out. The secrecy till now had been good enough that nothing had broken through.

"So what changed that we suddenly know it's them?" Tony pressed.

"Well... It looks like they are working with the would-be regent, Vaerlin. They are also likely employing the Shae'Lun people you've been dealing with."

"All that from the communication's brokerage?" Tony asked skeptically. It seemed like a large leap to find out such a thing from what would have normally been useful mostly for finding new leads instead.

"Well, it appears that Vaerlin does not trust his new associates as much as they might think. The information we got given before by the Kul'Raigh coupled with some of this new stuff sheds a lot of light on the situation."

"I'd love to be enlightened," Tony replied.

"It's not a crystal clear picture, but it makes enough sense when you see what kind of information he was gathering," Thorsh explained, "Apparently Vaerlin is a bit paranoid about the Shae'Lun liaison he's been working with."

"That was stored in the databank there, huh? How haven't they figured out that he is trying to watch them back?" Tony was skeptical that any organization that powerful would be spied upon by an ally of their underling.

"It was not all stored, not fully, it was in the process of being deleted when Truth came across it all," Thorsh replied, "All the comm monitoring we have been able to do thus far has indicated that there was actually some server damage at the brokerage as a result of whatever program caused trouble for Truth in there."

Tony sighed, "Yeah I remember her mentioning that. So you think that she saw a hostile program or something?"

"Possibly a contractor for Vaerlin, I don't know for sure but that turned into a dead lead, they covered their tracks better than anyone the analysts on board had ever seen," Thorsh stated grimly. The idea that whatever opposition the mission faced might be fractured in some way was a relief, if but a small one.

"So we have some partials that are basically information dumps on Vaerlin's allies?" Tony clarified.

"More or less. It isn't perfect but using the information A'Shir provided you before, we've been able to correlate more than we thought, or so I am told. Until the official comes across my desk it's all in the air."

"The Kul'Raigh mentioned Kirashira's mother, any info on that?" Tony finally asked, recalling the conversation with A'Shir.

Thorsh however, sighed and shook his head, "No leads"

Tony nodded. Kirashira's mother might still be alive, but wherever she was, it was still some place well hidden.

"Of course, don't tell Kirashira anything about that," Thorsh finally said, "That's the last thing she needs, false hope."

"Of course sir."

"I'll let you know if we learn anything new about the mother but I have to admit I could see someone taking her alive for leverage if they had to."

"I figured that would be the only reason," Tony said, unsurprised that both he and the Admiral thought the same.

"Regardless," Thorsh said, stretching a bit and, on his feet, pacing, "I want you to see what you can do with Kirashira but give her a bit of time to calm down before you try to patch things up, an hour or two should do the trick..."

"You can tell how much time that takes now?" Tony smiled, stopping short of anything insubordinate and nodded, "Will do sir."

Thorsh gave a curt nod and finished, "Good, then in that case, I'm turning in until morning watch, don't do anything that gets me woken up, hmm?"

"You have my word sir," Tony replied.

The officer left through the portal, turning to the left as he departed, looking astute and smart despite his apparent fatigue. Tony hated being in briefings all day and guessed that Admiral Thorsh had dealt with that sort of environment for most of his.

Still, the information he had relayed toward the end of his visit was something of a revelation, something Tony instantly wanted to capitalize on. If the enemy that they were engaged with had problems with the unity of their objectives between people or supporters, it would be something to exploit at some point during the mission.

He had to admit though, that the Admiral asserting the existence of the enigmatic Hil'Raigh Knights was a bit disconcerting. While Tony knew what most people in the intelligence world knew of the rumor surrounding them, real representations of their activities were so hard to come by as to make them all but a ghost. If they really were involved, things would likely be more delicate the closer to resolution the situation became.

Vaerlin, the duke of the Compact was apparently their chosen useful idiot in the endeavor but what was it all for? Tony had to wonder what motivated them. Surely it was not the King, he was not unpopular enough. His policies were not so controversial as to destroy potential economic concerns on a scale that justified such risks against him. As a result, the question as to why they had been involved at all weighed heavily on Tony's mind.

They were the stuff of rumor, enigma, a shadow that had existed for hundreds of years behind the scenes of the Federation. If they had the pull to accomplish regime change within the Federation itself then the reality of their influence was probably not something that could be disputed. Tony was sure as he decided to head to the mess hall himself, that the news of their existence would change the way his people collected intelligence and analyzed it. Thankfully however, that meant he would never have to worry about becoming a desk officer and listening to briefings from analysts all day every day.

With a smile at the irony, Tony set out, thankful to his adversaries in some small way, of being devious enough that they kept him from being sucked into the world of paperwork war fighting.

19 - Betrayer Revealed

The argument had hurt in ways she had never imagined it would. It was not just the words, but what they meant. Why wouldn't he just let it go, let things change like she had wanted? Was it always to be this way from now on? With others deciding what she could and could not do? Would it be like when she was a child under care with maids and servants dictating what was best? Even retreat to this room felt like defeat, sequestered in her cell of the prison in which she was kept, a foreign ship far from her home. The tears had not come, not for long at least, she had forced them away, demanded of them that they stay themselves for her benefit.

What benefit that effort had gained her was as yet unclear however; she was no less miserable. The only difference now was that she was unable to release the feelings she held inside with the aid of her tears. Part of her had kept asking to be left alone, to cry to wail or to moan as it wished. Her ego, her conscious mind however, ruled now, an iron fist, one full of fiery frustration intent on saving face. It was not ideal but what was in this world?

She frowned again, she had been frowning for at least an hour now and she felt it in her face, the discomfort of continued anger. Even so, the call from the Admiral had done so little to assuage her frustrations that it couldn't be helped. He had made overtures; he was friendly, but for what reason? It was obvious to Kirashira that his call was for his own benefit as it always would be, with everyone no matter who.

Anyone who spoke to her wanted something, that was how it was before, that was how it always would be. They wanted her power, her influence, her blessing, all because she had a name to put behind it.

She did not want to give a name to anyone, her influence was not for sale and her authority or power was for her alone. She was tired of feeling chased only to find that it was for her purchase that people seemed to value her. Her parents had shielded her from the bulk of it in the past but they were gone. They couldn't help, they would never be able to turn away the fake praise or the power brokering that would surround her for the rest of her life.

She was not ready for that reality. She hated it, the responsibility. She needed more time and the Divines knew it, everyone knew it, not the least of which was her father, her mother. Why couldn't they have held on? Why did they have to be taken away?

The questions brought a wave of grief, her heart aching, threatening the fire of her conscious conviction. She stifled the questions, a tyrant in her own mind, willing them to silence as she stood up from the desk. The entire room was cramped and she almost cursed it for that reason. She wanted a real room, not a container tucked away in the bowels of a NovaCore prison among the stars. The bunks were set into the walls, mounted billets that lifted up on hinges to offer more storage space.

What in hell used all of the space on this ship anyway? Hil'Raigh ships, at least the ones she had toured in her life, had far more available space. Even the small ones were more aesthetically pleasing, and she guessed that she would find most ships from across the galaxy to be a step up from the vaunted NovaCore Navy.

Two people? For this room? She scoffed aloud, eying the upper bunk with a fierce, accusatory gaze. It was empty now of course because the malfunctioning robot who normally inhabited it, was probably undergoing some kind of upgrade process, more power to demolish things on Ashor perhaps. Kirashira paused, the reasonable part of her mind objected, apologizing to no one in particular for thinking such a thing. Was Truth really that bad?

It didn't matter, not now. Kirashira silenced the dissenting thought, her ego winning out again. She had argued almost as much before. She still wanted to win, she was not going to back down, not even if she had left that field of battle behind.

Still, this room was lonely and though she was loathe to admit it to anyone, She wanted company more than she wanted to be angry and alone, even if it was a Novian. Part of her hoped for and missed the company of a personal bodyguard, someone to talk to. Or was it the fact that the bodyguard would never contradict her openly?

She huffed and moved to the billet that was hers, the one formerly occupied by Major Karo. It was stiff, the pad in the bed was so much less comfortable than what she had grown up with and she almost rolled out of the thing in disgust. Her apathy however, won out in that moment and she stayed, staring up at the blank display mounted above her face.

She felt torn, despite her frustrations, the better part of her heart pleaded for some level of empathy, some more royal decorum than she was allowing herself at present. Her thoughts broiled haphazardly for moments more however, a sea of retorts, witty and biting, the right things to say to win an argument. She played out scenarios, wondering what would have let her hold her ground better, it was not as if the NovaCore officer was some pillar of wit.

If that was the case however, why had she decided to leave? Weakness and frustration were the only real answer she could come up with, despite her best efforts to save face in her own mind. But was her frustration really so unreasonable?

There was no denying what he had said. Kirashira was engineered to be perfect in every possible way her parents could offer. That meant a myriad of modifications had been undertaken to make her smarter, more physically capable, more attractive and that even her mood, the hormonal balancing act of the Kul'Raigh body, was highly curated.

She had never faced the reality before, but seeing the NovaCore, being spoken to so plainly about her own origins had made her wonder, it had planted a seed. If she was engineered, was she really all that unique or special? Was she as valuable to her parents as they had claimed or could they have just modified the genetics and tried again if she had not worked properly? Would they have gone through all of the trouble like Truth's people had supposedly done to salvage her? Would they have just thrown her out and started over?

The very question, even unanswered, made tears well in her eyes, unbidden. She felt sick. She remembered what she had learned about the process of genetic engineering and pre-selection. It made her scared to know that she only existed at the behest of someone else. There was no chance in her existence. She felt unwanted not because she was alone but because she was the only thing that had been chosen.

The unique combination of everything, the very fabric of her life, her personality, her mind and heart, it was only there because her parents had chosen it, not because it was what she was destined for. She rolled to her side and whimpered helplessly, remembering her mother's face and wondering. Would she have smiled the same way if Kirashira had imperfections? Would she have held her closely or soothed her tears? Was it the fact that her mother and father had preselected that specific version of their daughter, that had made them appear so loving?

The cool air of the foreign warship billet made for no comfort at all. There were no answers here. She was wrapped into a cubby hole in space, far from home, far from a shoulder to cry on, far from the very people she desperately needed to still love her. Now, she would never be able to ask.

A surge of tears ran down her cheeks as the question she now so desperately needed an answer to would never receive one. One moment was all she wanted, one chance. She had felt a spark of it before, with her father and yet, now she was so unsure. How had life and its experiences not given her that knowledge in surety? She almost cursed the stars themselves and the ancestors there for being so enigmatic and contrary but she held her peace, suffering alone.

If there was ever a time she had questioned every modicum of value she had it was now. She questioned whether she was a worthy daughter, a worthy child. She questioned whether she was a ruler, a leader. She questioned whether she was worthy of the effort that had gone into saving her life already.

She sobbed, an object without price being rescued at risk? It was too much, too much to ask even the NovaCore to risk such a thing and she felt guilty. She felt guilty railing against Truth knowing what she had done already. She felt sad knowing that the two who might understand at least a bit of what she felt were now, because of her own actions, on the other team.

She curled tightly, pulling the blanket of her bed out from under her shuddering body and laying it over herself before she curled up, the pillow on which she rested dampening more and more.

***

Her father's face, her mother lifeless, they lay amid the strewn rubble, fiery and hellish, of the Guild Hall. There was no safety here, no solace, the world of her dreams had betrayed her. She shuddered in horror, her bloodied hands having done nothing to save them. Her glamor, her fanciful robes, everything affluent about her royalty was laid bare now and there was only the smell of flesh, smoldering. She screamed to them, they didn't wake, nor did they stir. Another call, they faded, they were slipping away, further and further. She had to chase them, make them come back. Her mind raced and she screamed out one last time.

She bolted desperately, sliding out of her massive bed, the confines of her room feeling hollow and lifeless, there was no warmth here now. Her legs hit ground, there were no sandals but she had no time for room sandals, she had to stop the party, stop it all before it happened, it was the only way.

Shooting to her feet, Kirashira felt the hard tile of her palatial bedroom thundering below her footfalls until she crashed headlong into a wall. Pain lanced through her body as she recoiled, a shot of agony up her spine as her tail-bone hit hard ground. She was frantic, now perturbed. Who had rearranged her room like this? Who would do such a thing?

She looked around the room helplessly, trying to find out where the door was relative to her bed. If someone had moved her bed while she slept, then there was no telling where she was inside the once familiar space.

Her bookshelves were gone however, her closet gone. Her bathroom was gone, her recliners, everything. Shan'Li wasn't even there reading and it was dark, darker than it should have been. The cold air of this strange featureless environment bit at her skin and she shuddered for a moment, her agony momentarily forgotten.

Only when she heard stirring from behind, from above, did her mind finally remember. This was the real world. The palace was the dream. The place she had come from was not the place she had really been. She had fallen asleep on the bed in the NovaCore ship's guest quarters, the room she shared with the NovaCore robot.

If she was here, now, it meant she had failed. She had never stopped the party. She had not warned her parents. They were gone for good and she was alone.

The throbbing in her hands, her rump, it did nothing to slow the onset of the agony she felt. The faces in her dream were so familiar, down to the details. Her mother's birthmark was the same, her father's nose, the fragrance he always wore, it was all right, it was all correct. The memory she had was so hard to manage at times and yet, when it was left to its own devices, it betrayed her in vicious fashion. As if it had been sent to destroy her soul, it had recalled what it had needed to drive a spear of pain so deeply, that she already felt the tears streaming down her face again. Not this, not again. Her mind pleaded. She wanted to be free, not once more in this hell called life.

"I couldn't stop it from happening", Kirashira wailed, "I wanted to but I couldn't stop it."

Images of her father's lifeless body flooded back. She had shaken him, called his name. He had laid, forever silenced. Could she have saved him? His lifeless eyes were accusatory in her mind and she whimpered aloud even more.

"Why didn't I know what to do? I should have been able to do something!"

The agony of this defeat was more than her mind could bear. Had she just chosen more interest in medicine, maybe if her hobbies had been different, she could have done something to save her father, she might have been able to stop her mother from being blown to pieces or thrown from the Guild Hall to her death. If only she hadn't chosen the Guild Hall for her party, nothing would have happened like it did. She was guilty, she was the one who had failed and no one else.

Every accusation, every doom she could imagine was waiting for her now. Every pair of eyes seeking justice would surely see through any guise she could muster. Between her sobs, she drew in air, raggedly. Her lungs tortured her, burning, her eyes throbbing, her head pounding too. It was all too much. She willed in that moment that it would all just stop, that she could just cease to be, vanishing into the eternal night of nothingness. That was the only way it would stop.

She shivered in the cold, waiting to simply die, wondering how long it would be until her grief claimed her soul. Her heart churned, burning and tormented, the smell of flesh, of blood, fresh in her mind.

She almost didn't notice the touch against her shoulder, but it was so unexpected, so ethereal that it jarred her. She jumped despite herself, shuddering in her prison of grief until someone from the outside, someone outside the prison, spoke the one word she realized could punch a hole in its walls.

The way Kirashira's name fell from the mouth of her rescuer, was to her, the sound of ancestral angels, a soothing gentleness not fit for the mortal world. It carried with it all the concern and care that Kirashira imagined any sort of verbal communication could muster and it hung like a standard in the air, bidding her to escape, to fight and leave the prison of her mind.

She clung to the word like a lifeline, remembering that she could not be alone, not when someone else was there, not if they could call to her soul like they had. She mustered all the strength she could and finally managed to turn, to glance at the one who had spoken.

A set of artificial eyes stared back, their unique lines fixed and focused, the face they were part of twisted in concern and wonder. It was the Novian, Truth. She knelt by Kirashira now in the quiet cold of the guest quarters and for once, Kirashira had no idea what to think of her.

"You were dreaming," Truth finally stated, rubbing Kirashira's shoulder. The contact felt good, it was gentle and assuring.

There was a long pause, a silence in which Kirashira was reminded of how she had picked out the sound of the air flow system before, something she was not keen to hear all the time. This truly was an alien ship.

"I guess I was," Kirashira finally managed, caught utterly off guard by the disarming way her room mate had thus far handled the situation,"Sorry."

She moved to stand, feeling sheepish, but her legs were weak, they buckled and she fell forward. Truth caught her with ease and set her down again, her concern unabated, "I am worried that your dream was so painful Kirashira."

Was Truth a mind reader now too? How did she know just how bad it was? Kirashira recalled the words she had spoken after waking, her lamentations, and wondered if she had said more in her sleep. She felt vulnerable, completely off guard now. She was at Truth's mercy. What would the NovaCore do with that power?

"How can I help you?" Truth said at last. Help? Truth wanted to help her? Kirashira's mind was caught in its bias. How could Truth, the one she had complained about, wanted to be freed of, want to help her. Surely she had been told of Kirashira's distrust, her disdain for the artificial Novian. Even so, there was no hint of guile there, only an honest look of intent. Kirashira was at a loss for words,"I don't know."

She had no choice but to reply with naked honesty as well, giving in kind what Truth had apparently done already. It was only after a few moments that Kirashira realized her utter confusion had halted her tears, and though she was shivering, it was because the air was too cold, not because she had lost control of her body.

"I don't know how to feel good again Truth," Kirashira finally admitted. The words made her eyes tear up again as quickly as they had stopped. The reality expressed by her voice was inescapable.

The Novian nodded, looking over Kirashira with concern, "I do not yet know either. I cannot fully understand your loss. But I want to try."

The words made Kirashira smile despite herself. She nodded and took a breath, controlling the emotional roller coaster.

"What happened was not your fault," Truth finally stated,"You did not choose to have your family or anyone else harmed."

Kirashira breathed shakily, controlling what she could. She tried to put the images out of her mind again, "I didn't have to have the party there."

"Please stop blaming yourself Kirashira," Truth replied in earnest, "You will only do harm if you do. No one wants that to happen."

"You barely know me. It might be the right thing that I feel sad."

"No. I know that it is not the right thing despite barely knowing you," Truth replied, "We all know that. Everyone on this ship, knows that."

The expression made Kirashira's heart churn, but this time with a burst of warmth, a feeling of being cared for that, for long days, she had never felt. Truth continued, "I cannot imagine how difficult this situation has been for you, but I am sorry if my behavior has made it worse. Tony told me you were uncomfortable."

Kirashira felt guilty hearing it. It seemed so silly now, the argument, her feelings before. What had made her so apathetic to that idea? Why had Truth been so frustrating? She owed the Novian an answer, some fairness. It was the least she could do and so, she opened her mouth, wondering whether she would regret the words.

"I apologize Truth," She began, "I just... Have never met someone like you before, with all of your enhancements. It made me nervous, especially knowing what your job is."

Truth nodded intently, listening with no hint of judgment in her gaze.

"And I sort of selfishly felt like your people were trying to steal mine and use them against us because you are so Kul'Raigh looking."

The Novian appeared to consider the revelation for a moment, then spoke, looking concerned as she finished, "I understand how some of those things could be upsetting. Unfortunately I cannot change them."

"No, you're right," Kirashira admitted, "You can't. You shouldn't have to either."

"But I cannot expect your opinion to change in an instant," Truth replied, "It would be unfair of me or anyone else to expect it. Are you sure you would not prefer a different liaison?"

Kirashira shook her head, feeling now, immensely grateful, "I don't think I'll need a different one."

"If you change your mind I will not be offended," Truth offered, then she went silent, just sitting and waiting.

The Princess mulled over the turn of events, shocked in a way but not ungrateful for them. She was amazed, dumbfounded really and it came out as she spoke, "Why do you care how I feel Truth?"

Her room mate replied without any hesitation, looking to her directly. She took on a matter of fact tone as she spoke, "I have been alone too."

There was a long silence and Kirashira felt in her mind, that she no longer could justify to herself, holding Truth in any regard lower than anyone else. The person before her was at very least, as nice if not nicer than she was and more than likely, well rounded and careful in ways Kirashira had never had to even learn existed, due to her royal station.

"Thanks." Kirashira replied, not sure what more she could say. Her mind would certainly have to process for a while, what had just occurred. Even though the haunting memories of the past days, the dreams, had yet to fully subside, she knew she had a chance at least, of finding support to deal with them. There would be struggles and it would surely challenge her in ways she had yet to realize, but for once, for the first time since the attack, she felt like there was a road forward.

Even as she contemplated the idea. Truth appeared lost in thought for a moment and then, she stood, speaking, "The Admiral has some news for you. It seems urgent."

Kirashira tensed and looked up to the Novian next to her. The gravity of her tone made short work of any potential lethargy that the Princess harbored however, and she began to stand. The shakiness of minutes ago was gone now and though her body felt exhausted, she stood without trouble. A blessing or curse, Kirashira wasn't sure but she had fallen asleep in one of the outfits given her by her hosts. As a result, she gave herself a simple look over and shrugged. If there was urgent news and no chance for prying camera crews or other nosy eyes, she supposed it would not be too terrible for her to avoid complete preparation before stepping out of her room. At the palace, she would never have conceived of such a thing but without Shan'Li to assist her and make the process more painless, she felt little choice in the matter.

The hallway came quickly and Truth led the way. The maze of corridors on the ship was making steadily more sense, at least the route from the guest quarters to the nearest internal tram terminal. Truth's pace however, conveyed a sort of urgency that Kirashira had only briefly been privy to see back on Ashor. Given that she now at least knew her guide's name and was not completely drained, she noted that it was with some intent that Truth's footfalls made their marks on the deck plating. The brisk pace continued up until the tram station.

Entering the open space in familiar fashion, Truth led the way into an already waiting carriage and Kirashira followed. The trip began moments later and Kirashira was left wondering what exactly the news was that had Truth so hasty. It had to be bad, big and bad. It was probably news from the Federation.

Finally, the door chimed and Truth led the way outward once more. Her brisk pace continued as she moved past a pair of heavily armed guards. A thick looking door was propped partially open and the pair slipped through the gap. Kirashira had never been to this part of the ship before, only having visited a meeting room or two near her lodging. The overall relaxed pace of life on the vessel she had come to expect was far from reflected here however. There was a bustle akin to Truth's own in this area, something that had Kirashira even more nervous. Was it always this way?

Twists, turns and finally a door. Truth keyed the handle by its side and stepped in. Kirashira followed, the darkened room playing host to an array of faces the monarch had never seen. There was a large table here, a series of chairs, a holo-projector. Across the table the familiar Admiral Thorsh stood as Kirashira entered. The rest of the assembled individuals followed suit, giving respectful bows. Kirashira, dumbfounded for a moment, returned the bows in kind before taking the seat Truth was offering.

"Welcome, Princess Ren'Tauru of the Starlight Compact," The Admiral said colloquially in her native tongue. She thanked him and he sat, as did the rest. "As this meeting pertains to your nation's political situation, I will be conducting my business with you directly in your native tongue, if that is acceptable?"

Kirashira nodded, curious, "Yes of course."

She glanced around, noting an ear piece with each of the attendant officers, probably for translation. She wondered who would be translating but as she glanced to Truth, she decided it was obvious.

"I wanted to bring you in for a meeting with the senior staff because we have some troubling news.." Thorsh began, "As of zero eight hours, approximately two hours ago, The Federation Council has opted to open a war council against the NovaCore. Effective immediately, diplomatic ties are suspended pending outcome of the council vote."

The words hung in the air like a deathly cloud. There was a deafening silence in which Kirashira managed to finally pick out the air recycler again. Even after several more moments, the silence continued until finally, she replied.

"Obviously, there must be a great confusion as to the reason behind what happened to my family..."

Thorsh nodded, "We believe some element within the Federation is presenting doctored evidence which paints the blame for the attacks on your people and government squarely on the NovaCore. More specifically, Major Karo and Truth, who you well know."

Kirashira nodded, "Definitely not true,"

"I am authorized to return you to your people in preparation for the war council and strategic planning... however... I do have a request to make before that.."

The Princess nodded slowly and waited, at length the officer spoke once more, "I was wondering if rather than simply dropping you on Ashor, we could trouble you to suspend the council, at least until the government of the Starlight Compact is crystallized."

The request was clear. He wanted her help, her political capitol. She almost cringed but remembered that this was a different situation. He wanted her help not just for himself but to avoid a conflict. If there was one thing the Princess had garnered from the man over the course of being trapped on board his ship, it was that he was not a war seeker by any means.

"I may be able to do that. If I am available but not present at the council, it has to suspend until I can arrive to vote..."

Thorsh nodded, "Incidentally, it appears that regency proceedings for your nation have been moving forward quickly. More quickly than anticipated. The potential regent might attempt to attend and vote for you."

"I don't understand. The requisite period has only just passed. To seek regency so quickly is..."

"Happening right now, Duke Arash Vaerlin." Thorsh replied gravely.

Kirashira's head swam. The idea that someone would so quickly seek her father's throne was unfathomable. There was a protocol to this sort of thing, especially regency and it was established long ago. Violations of that protocol in Sho'Alar years prior should have had no baring on her own nations handling of such a situation. Even so, the idea that it was happening was disturbing. Instantly, the Princess was annoyed, not only by the proceedings but that she had not known. Just how long had the NovaCore not said a word. She curled her lip and nodded, almost having to bite her tongue to remain silent.

"I see," She replied icily, "Then it appears we do not have much time to reach Shar'Jya."

The Admiral squirmed but Kirashira pressed, "If you would like me to intercede on your nation's behalf, Admiral, then we have to depart for Shar'Jya immediately."

By hyperspace it would take days and if Vaerlin was planning on attending in her place he might be on the way soon. They had to leave now to beat any vote that could be cast. Of course, she had heard that NovaCore Naval vessels were inexplicably faster than the superior Hil'Raigh ships in some interstellar cases. That rumor however, was not enough to assuage her concerns now.

The Admiral nodded and spoke aloud, now in his native tongue across the table to a man seated near its middle. He saluted smartly, called to a couple more and they exited the room.

"We will make preparations to leave as soon as possible," Thorsh explained to her, "What else can we do in the mean time?"

Kirashira racked her brain, she had no idea how to stop a war council other than preventing it from voting. Her father had never taught her how to willfully disrupt Federation proceedings, that would probably have come after her birthday when she was able to wield some measure of official power. Now, he would never have that chance.

"I should probably call someone, in the case that we cannot reach the capitol in time." She explained at last, wondering just who she could call. Only one name stood out to her.

The Admiral eyed her carefully then nodded at last, "Alright, we can make the comm system available soon as well, but we will need some preparation time to keep the ship obscured."

Kirashira nodded and looked around the room. All the eyes in it were on her. For all intents and purposes, it appeared that they were not only interested in, but reliant on her today. She hoped that she was up to the challenge.

Her heart called, softly, a gentle request to whatever afterlife her father had been sent, to let him look down on the situation and guide her in some way. If she had at least one ancestor to make a difference, she wanted it to be her father and no one else. There was no reaction, her heart did not swell and she felt no different after the thought, but hoped perhaps he was already listening.

PART THREE

RECLAIMING THE THRONE

20 - Business as Usual

The meetings until today had all been going well. After a brief introduction to this morning's guest, the attendant had finally come by, dropping off another tray of refreshments before exiting the room. The conversation lulled of course until she was gone, not something to be discussed in front of a mere servant.

"I feel that you understand the complexities of our situation on the border Duke Vaerlin," said Vaerlin's guest, finally resuming the discussion. He stood now and moved to the refreshment tray, picking up one of the snacks and popping it into his mouth. Negotiating like this was not all that common for Vaerlin, who relied more on his aides to take care of things. With matters such as the impending regency vote however, he wanted to make sure he tied things off himself.

"I can certainly empathize with the problems the reforms would have on the economy in your region," Vaerlin replied with a diplomatic smile, "It's a shame not all of the other regions in the Compact can fully grasp that complexity."

Dealing with other nobles was a chore at times, but was always interesting, each had their own lusts or desires in government. Each had a unique problem, and there was always a unique solution for each one. Lord Laelum had been dealing with an economic decline, one he was apparently certain was the fault of Kul'Raigh trade unions changing their rules under the previous king of the Starlight Compact. For a well loved king, Ren'Tauru had certainly stretched the boundaries of what was allowed under the laws that governed all of the Federation members.

The structure of society in the Federation had long been in place thanks to the ancient Concord of Abner, an agreement made hundreds of years before anyone alive currently had been born. The exact specifics of the agreement had varied by the account one chose to use for recalling it, with some historical societies citing widely unsupported provisions that they purported as part of the agreement. The general consensus however, was that the Kul'Raigh were more guest, than equal in a truly Hil'Raigh society. They had been given the gift of continuance by the inclusion in Abner's exodus fleet and as a result, owed to their hosts, the Hil'Raigh, a level of deference in the future society.

Further modifications had occurred to the agreement after the Great Rebellion in the Exodus fleet, one widely shown to be started by Kul'Raigh extremists. The subsequent changes had codified a number of things and among those were a lack of equal societal status in government. The Kul'Raigh were to be their own society in a sense, symbiotic with the Hil'Raigh government but not without immunity to its laws. Genetic re-engineering and other things that Vaerlin himself found to be impossible provisions by modern standards, had also been put into the official transcript. Now, the agreement and the rest were history, already part of the Federation's charter.

Vaerlin had never fully understood all of the intricacies of the Concord and regarded it more as ancient dogma than good policy. Some in the Federation, however, held the agreement in almost religious regard. Any deviation from its perceived provisions became a sort of heresy among their circles. It was the latter school of thought that heavily dominated the neighboring Sho'Alar state and much of the upper echelons of Hil'Raigh society as a whole. Because of that strict adherence to tradition, it was unsurprising then, that Laelum, who hailed from the very same neighbor, was almost always at odds with Kul'Raigh organizations.

Despite lacking in a complete understanding of the Concord, Vaerlin had long ago learned that he and the other nobility, but also Hil'Raigh in general, were who he was to really represent in his line of work. He did not outright hate the Kul'Raigh but when it came to making choices for the future of the Hil'Raigh society, his decision was foregone.

The birth of King Ren'Tauru's daughter, half Kul'Raigh, had shaken the standard, putting the true line of descent into the hands of someone born in the throes of indoctrination from a Kul'Raigh mother. At least, that was how Vaerlin had to think to truly interact with his contemporaries. He had his own moments, moments where those feelings rang entirely true to him as well, but at times he caught himself wondering about their validity.

"I can assure you Lord Laelum, your holding has my ear. As Regent I would be capable of ensuring that beneficial trade routes are not cut by the Transportation Guild either." Vaerlin continued, pressing to a topic he knew would have value to his guest. The Interstellar Transportation Guild was one of several organizations that had a sizable Kul'Raigh membership. If King Ren'Tauru's reform programs had come to be, they certainly would have consolidated as much trade through the Compact's central region as possible.

"I am glad to hear that, though I am more concerned about the over reach of the Companion Guild than anything else at present," Laelum responded critically.

Vaerlin nodded. The Kul'Raigh Companion Guild had far outgrown its original purpose. No longer did it simply represent a unified group of standards for etiquette and decorum for Companions. The growth had not only taken the form of new memberships and Consorts. It was not only instructors, artisans and their limited support structure but a network that had begun branching into an increasing variety of sectors.

The Guild now had influence in many major metropolitan centers across the Federation. They enjoyed offices even on Shar'Jya, the Federation Capitol world. The only place they had yet to make inroads of course, was Sho'Alar, where they were outlawed. The Guild had grown to more prominence than even Vaerlin had imagined in prior years and had been bolstered for years now by Shiyara Ya'Lae's popularity. After King Ren'Tauru had married her, most people understood it to mean an extension of the Guild's unofficial political influence. This was of course despite explicit denials by the Guild's leadership and the King himself.

"As I hear, the Companions are ripe to simply absorb the Transportation Guild, I might limit them at the same time I talk to the Transportation Guild," Vaerlin quipped sarcastically. It was a cynical bit of dark humor circulated among the nobility, the all consuming Companion Guild continually expanding its influence. The nobleman sighed and glanced to Vaerlin, tired rather than amused at the joke.

"My question for you Vaerlin, is this," The man finally posited, "If elected regent, how would you curb the influence of that organization in not just mine, but other regions?"

The duke was given pause by the question. He had researched some potential solutions to the problem before the meeting and he was sure to surprise his guest.

"I'd make a concession..." Vaerlin began, eying his guest. When no immediate outburst came, Vaerlin continued, "The Guild has power because some of the laws we have allow for them to exist. The Guild does a service, fills a need. If the Federation instead, offers that service, there is no need for a Guild."

Vaerlin's guest smiled and nodded, a hint of realization in his eyes as Vaerlin continued, "The Guild has teeth only because the complacency of our leaders until now, has made them necessary. An effective regency would of course, follow in the vein of Ren'Tauru reform but... perhaps in a different shape than he had originally planned..."

Laelum smirked, "It's almost poetic how good that would sound in a speech isn't it Duke Vaerlin?"

The two shared a chuckle and the nobleman stood, nodding happily, "In that case Vaerlin, you can count on my vote for regency. I look forward to your historic reforms."

Vaerlin nodded and stood in response, bowing to his guest, escorting him toward the door. The finality of the meeting had gone quickly, something he was glad for, especially since his wrist band had been nagging him for minutes now about an urgent message. He opened the door and offered his guest a parting word, "I'll make sure you are included in the panel discussing that topic when it occurs. Until then I look forward to your voice on Shar'Jya."

"Be well Vaerlin," Laelum turned, moving to his waiting entourage of assistants in the foyer outside of Vaerlin's office. The Duke had been enjoying his estate more as of late and with each passing day it looked as if it would soon become to be the estate of the regent. Laelum after all, was representative of many more voices. Vaerlin's associates had been tight lipped about most of the behind the scenes brokering they had managed but the sometimes unexpected support had come through from a wide variety of sources. In truth, it made the Duke nervous, to know that those he was involved with could manage it without him knowing how.

The recent problem at the comm brokerage he had been using had been a warning to him to keep his head low and he was sure that those responsible were among his associates. The report he had received, although brief, from his data contractor, was simple. Whomever had been responsible for the intrusion had been well prepared, better than anyone the contractor had ever dealt with despite their years of experience.

If the nobleman was wrong and the break in had been the work of someone else, the NovaCore for example, he had far less to worry about. The NovaCore could in no way present useful and credible threats to his regency in the Federation council, they had already been too heavily implicated in the attacks that had taken place here in the Compact. Their reputation was near non-existent even before the blame had been falling, but now, with public opinion being so properly shaped, their influence was near moot.

Even more so, knowing about who he was working with would probably set their intelligence agents ablaze with conspiracy theory. They would be so interested in who he was aligned with that any direct threat from the NovaCore to him was minimal. They would surely be more interested in his associates even if they had managed to get their hands on anything usable.

No, the real threat here was his own allies, the people he had been working with. With the power at their disposal it was entirely possible that he, Vaerlin, could outlive his usefulness before he'd had enough time to build a significant defense, a reality that weighed on his mind more and more as time went on.

Still, the motivations for their helping him, for ousting the Ren'Tauru family, remained something of a mystery. It seemed unlikely that all of them were concerned about the Kul'Raigh reforms. Even despite agreeing to check the Companion Guild, Vaerlin himself felt it was more a symbolic gesture than any needed policy decision.

What had triggered it all? Scientific advancement was finally entering a new cycle of growth. The Federation was peaceful save encounters with pirates and other largely inconsequential actors. Even way finding and exploration, an area of the Federation economy which had been docile for years, was making a comeback. Recent discoveries had been dominating headlines for weeks, at least before the attacks on the Ren'Tauru family. With so much to gain by the continued peaceful climate, Vaerlin wondered if some among his associates simply were not restless power brokers.

Perhaps he was over analyzing, perhaps it was just a confluence of factors well timed. Indeed, with some of his meetings thus far, it had seemed that way. Each person who came into his office had been after something unique. Some wanted their holding to be given a better seat at economic talks, and some simply disliked Kul'Raigh, like Laelum. Some simply wanted power for themselves, and in exchange, they would support near anyone who offered it.

Of greatest importance however, was that most nobles in the Compact had been coming around to the idea of regency. With the length of time that the Compact had gone officially ungoverned by a state head, even the staunchest of royalists were starting to warm to the idea despite the short timetable.

Still, the vanished Kirashira Ren'Tauru made Vaerlin nervous. She could technically become a thorn in his side. Her continued absence however, had gone from a novelty foreign involvement conspiracy, to a question of self preservation. He had started to consider at least, the idea that his own associates had managed to find and deal with her, all without him knowing. That was probably the most chilling prospect he could face and of course, he did not want to believe it could be, it made the situation far too complex.

The way Tamur was so tight lipped about their efforts to locate her coupled with the complete lack of communication from them on the issue, had driven Vaerlin's paranoia. For being such an important part of the plan, he had thought that Kirashira would remain a significant topic until she was resolved. Based on what he'd seen from his allies, he appeared to be incorrect. With a moment more of contemplation following, Vaerlin returned to his office and sat down at the desk he had abandoned the moment his guest had arrived.

Sighing, he reached to the mug he had been neglecting there, a sip of the now tepid liquid inside confirming his suspicions. He set the mug aside in disgust, his face curling. He hated cold tea. He groaned and took a look at the slate on the desk.

The report before him had been compiled with the best of intentions, but the new aide, the one who had replaced the young man killed in the prior attack, was far less capable. He did not organize things like Vaerlin wanted, at least, it felt like he lacked the nuance of the former assistant.

A tinge of guilt crossed Vaerlin's mind but he reached out to the tea once more, sipping it deliberately now as a form of mental penance. The bitterness of the liquid took his mind off of the cost in lives, of his otherwise clean ascension to leadership of the Compact. At least he was not a Kul'Raigh, he mused to himself. It would have been worse otherwise.

Could it have been that an overwhelming number of his associates detested the idea of a Kul'Raigh ruler so much as to wish the destruction of the Ren'Tauru family before it happened? He sipped the tea again as he pondered the question. Cursing himself for his continued consumption of the substance, he slid it comfortably out of reach now on the desk before he returned to his chair. A bit of time to ask some questions was all he wanted.

Of course, he doubted it would come, and he had consigned himself to the fact that probing Tamur when he was busy dealing with something else was probably the best way to dig at that kind of information. Tamur couldn't admit his mistakes without potential problems and so it was a sort of cat and mouse with the mercenary, getting him to say something without playing the hand so overtly that he became angry or uncooperative.

Thus far, that strategy had netted only a few gems of information. They were certainly useful gems though, and shed at least a bit of light on his associates. They painted the picture of an organization with largely the same end goal but showed that some parts of it seemed to take its information obfuscation less seriously than others. For all its tight lipped-ness, it seemed that Vaerlin's desire to know that which should not be known, was at least in line with the kind of activity some of the other higher-ups were accustomed to using. He guessed most of them were doing it for the same reasons he was, self preservation. Most of the things Vaerlin had pieced together pointed to old names, probably connected to Sho'Alar. It was unsurprising too, given how much friction some of their leadership had with neighboring King Ren'Tauru up until his demise.

Vaerlin's wristband vibrated once more, prompting a groan. He finally tapped the control on the device and spoke, "Yes?"

The reply came curtly, a familiar, gruff voice, "There's a problem, you should come by."

***

Vaerlin stretched as he exited the courier vehicle, one of course, approved by his associates. Even as the door of it closed, its engines began winding up until it started to lift off for its own departure. The less than reputable brokers in Dau'Kore had certainly created a profitable market for discreet transportation operators. Here, under dozens of meters of solid ground above, Vaerlin had finally arrived at Tamur's base of operations.

At least, that's what he thought it was. He had never been given any official description of the area and the fact that it was nestled between two large factory consortiums in the underground manufacturing sector of Dau'Kore, was enough to tell him that it was a temporary fixture. From the look of it, it was an older generational industrial office, one that perhaps had served to house workers or some other function that required a landing pad lacking complete automation. Truth be told however, Vaerlin had no exact idea as to the location, just that its neighbors were automated factories. The transportation corridors under the city distinctly lacked any sort of signage, intended only to be driven by automatic vehicle traffic.

Tamur was already on the platform ahead, looking unhappy as usual. His arms were crossed over his chest and he did not so much as take a single step to Vaerlin, making the noble come to him instead. Once Vaerlin was comfortably in talking range, Tamur finally opened up, "Come on, I'll show you."

Vaerlin shrugged, considering some kind of witty jab at the merc's lack of decorum. Instead however, he simply kept the thought to himself. With Tamur it almost never had the intended effect anyway. If there was one thing Vaerlin detested about his liaison, it was that the man seemed to have all of the social grace of a rock when it came to dealing with the nobility.

It was therefore, something of a blessing that Tamur and his thugs had largely receded to their lair here underground rather than being all over the city. It seemed to the nobleman, that the prior, regular contact was more of a phase of the pre-created plan than it was any sort of actual interest in Vaerlin's well being. After the framing attack, Tamur had kept out of the public eye, giving Vaerlin the chance to publicly re-evaluate his choice of security contractors. It was an opportunity he had gladly taken.

The landing pad led way to a set of rust red industrial double doors, little more than thick metal plates on sliding tracks. Though ragged in appearance, they rolled open without issue as Tamur led the way through them. The walls here were a drab reinforced concrete and the roof carried visible power conduits harnessed to it by anchor points which were drilled directly into the structure. The floor was not much different save the fact that it was clean of debris and featured a somewhat more polished finish than the walls themselves. The decorator here was not winning any awards.

Tamur led the way through a maze of corridors until finally, he brought Vaerlin to a broad, open, room. Whatever it had been, it was now a command center of sorts, with bundles of cabling running along the bottom of most of the wall. Holographic displays and workstations dominated the space with a large holo-tank occupying one corner of the room. It was situated next to what appeared to be a set of windows looking into a room beyond.

Tamur motioned for Vaerlin to step inside the somewhat cluttered environment, one that looked to be hastily established, and moved to one of his people. For the moment, the Duke was free to explore the room and he wandered toward the windows he had noted earlier. As he had suspected, they overlooked a large room below, a former factory floor that had been converted into a mix of barracks and storage area, with cots and crates making up a majority of the space there.

A large table, some benches and what looked to be some hastily installed portable lavatory facilities rounded out the bulk of the room. The number of people in the command center and in the room below made Vaerlin wonder just what he had walked into. There were more faces than he could have imagined being needed for the plan, milling about and he instantly decided that his business had to be a fraction of whatever the people here were engaged in.

His scrutiny of the facility was interrupted with a rough call from across the room, "Vaerlin."

Tamur's voice carried but it was apparent from his demeanor that his mood was probably more foul than normal. From a distance, Vaerlin finally decided that the man looked tired. Approaching the station Tamur had been standing next to, he finally offered acknowledgment, waiting to see whatever wonderful problem the mercenary planned to present to him. Part of him wondered if it was a cynical announcement of betrayal. That never came however as the display flitted to life and revealed instead, a familiar face.

"You know this Kul'Raigh?" Tamur asked quickly.

Vaerlin nodded, she was a face he remembered, "Yes I think I've seen her before, She was a servant of Shiyara Ren'Tauru until Kirashira was born..."

"Good," Tamur replied, standing straight rather than leaning over the desk as he had been.

"I'm sorry I don't quite follow," Vaerlin replied.

"She appears to have had contact with Kirashira recently," Tamur explained, "My people are moving out to obtain her."

"Contact with Kirashira?" Vaerlin was perturbed. His regency flashed before his eyes, "What do you mean?"

"It appears we were right," Tamur said, "Kirashira was extracted by the NovaCore after the attack. She'd been dark since then but recently sent this person a message."

"What about?" Vaerlin's head swam, he was angry, afraid, all at once. He was mad that it had even come to this, Kirashira should have been eliminated properly from the outset. He almost leveled the accusation at Tamur but somehow knew that would get him nowhere. Tamur was not directly responsible for that, his people were, even if they were incompetent. He had probably already done something about the failing. While Vaerlin hated to admit it, Tamur was a proactive leader at least.

"Shar'Jya," replied Tamur.

Vaerlin felt anger flare in his heart, he clenched his fists and closed his eyes, seething for a moment, "How is she getting there? Did she secure transport?"

"Probably the NovaCore," Tamur shrugged, "They are not going to shove her on a transport at this point."

"And what are you planning to do about it?" Vaerlin pressed immediately.

Tamur's reply came after a moment, "An idea has been put forward but it's not something our associates can take care of on their own."

"What is it?!" Vaerlin continued, sounding a bit too desperate.

"It's a several step process," Tamur replied, "First we need access to Kirashira."

"What a wonderful idea!" Vaerlin snarled and turned stepping away from the console.

"All you have to do is remind the Elite Guard that Kirashira was taken captive and coerced into making positive statements on behalf of the NovaCore. As long as she is in their custody she cant be trusted." Tamur replied carefully.

The absurdity! Vaerlin almost screamed, it was all so close. He hated the idea instantly but, as he processed the words instead of simply reacting, he felt himself calm quite a bit, "Go on..."

"Kirashira's whereabouts will not be publicly disclosed until she shows up in council," Tamur replied, "No real limit once she's in our control."

"And how do we get her to take a detour?" Vaerlin frowned.

"I prefer injuring people myself, but she also trusts her servant," Tamur replied motioning with his shoulder to the Kul'Raigh on the screen, "You mentioned that servant used to serve her mother correct?"

"Yes, but I think you knew that."

"Then we put the mother up as collateral for the servant to help things go smoothly," Tamur replied, "She won't be able to let her former mistress come to harm if she can avoid it."

"So confident?" Vaerlin almost groaned aloud. The plan could not hinge on a servant Kul'Raigh.

"We have methods Vaerlin," Tamur replied darkly, "Your job is going to be to make sure you have the guard rescue Kirashira like the good little tool they are. If we can get her to Shar'Jya, my associates can ensure she is surrounded by a number of sympathetic individuals."

"And what then? We coerce a statement?"

"Your creative mind can think of something Vaerlin," Tamur mused, a hint of his familiar sarcasm returning, "It's your regency after all."

"Your people could have done this the first time," Vaerlin quipped icily.

Tamur cocked a brow, his sarcasm had returned apparently, "You could always keep her around as a puppet. Just in case your regency failed..."

The jab was not something Vaerlin wanted to entertain, he eyed the merc with obvious contempt.

"Just make sure your people do their part this time," Vaerlin said at length.

"I'll let you hold the gun this time Vaerlin," Tamur smirked, "If you can stomach it..."

Vaerlin hated Tamur. He hated the way that his own annoyance or frustration seemed to make the man happy. It was infuriating. Tamur had gone from disgruntled and curt, to rude and obnoxious in so few minutes. The Duke wished he had never had to deal with the man but knew that he had no choice, at least for now.

21 - Under Way

The NovaCore ship felt all the more cramped now. Perhaps it was because of the news. The war council itself had been unsurprising but the fact that one of the nobles had already managed to push regency proceedings into action was disturbing. She felt betrayed and couldn't help but wonder how involved this aspiring regent was with the death of her family. She wanted to question him, to have him chained and brought before her. Her surroundings reminded her she had painfully little power, especially to do something like that.

She was the sole member of her government, even more, her family, on board this ship and there was only so much she could ask of her rescuers. With a hasty trip to Shar'Jya on the horizon and having had so little time to try and unwind fully, she felt at odds with herself. She was now being taken back to the world of politics, the one she had been isolated from for days now. It would not be a pretty return, it would be rough, painful even.

First there would be the condolences, then the questions, and then, the worst. Her stomach churned as she thought of actually arriving on Shar'Jya. She did not even have the proper clothing for a royal arrival. Even if her birthday robe had not been damaged, the stylists on board this ship were utterly unprepared for the task. At best, she would look the part of a noble who had fallen on hard financial times. Without even her own clothing to use however, she was forced to rely on promises, hopes.

Arrival in the Shar'Jya system by a royal was supposed to be something of an event, and the royal in question always had to look the part. That was just how things were done. It was already odd that she would arrive on a NovaCore ship, let alone without the regalia she really needed. Her best hope was to have them repair and clean the robes she had been wearing for her birthday. With any luck the assurances of the Admiral would come through and they could at least manage to make the clothing she had worn with her arrival look clean, crisp and regal. It would never match the majesty of a royal arrival outfit, and Kirashira lacked almost all of the accessories she would otherwise have had. Given the circumstances however, she was sure there was room for understanding in not making a perfect showing this time. She hoped at least.

Even if she was hampered, she had to do her best, if only for the fact that she had to look strong from the moment of her return. She was the true heir to the throne, but if the nobility had already been considering a regent, so soon, it meant she would still have to deal with the contest. She had to show the strength required to prevent people from backing a regent.

That was what she hated most, she decided, the fact that even though she was the legitimate ruler, she would have to prove it. It was frustrating as anything she could think of about the whole situation.

Part of her was still angry that she had not been informed, feeling like the NovaCore must have known about the regency proceedings before they ever mentioned it. She had wondered why they didn't say anything until it had reached such a point.

Realistically though, what should they have done? They couldn't have stopped the proceedings and with such a thing going on, the reality that they were in fact, protecting her life like they claimed, seemed all the more believable.

Would the people that took her family return to finish the job? She shuddered. She hated admitting to the fact that here, on the NovaCore ship, she really did feel safe. The prospect of being out there again, in a place where people would be her enemy but she would not know where they were, was chilling to say the least.

Even if she never suffered the same fate as her parents, the world of Federation politics would never be the same. The guard duties would be bigger, bodyguard details would be bolstered, she'd have to wear body armor all the time too. It would be like the old days, the days the Hil'Raigh had thought to have left behind and for what? One person to become a regent?

The sound of someone's throat clearing behind her made her turn. It was Major Karo.

"The tailor's said they took your measurements already?"

Kirashira nodded, "Yes, I visited them after the meeting."

Karo made a motion that showed he approved, "They are pretty good on this ship. I think you'll be surprised."

Kirashira shook her head, "I hope so. Appearances are of great importance when you make an arrival."

The observation deck had become a sort of refuge from the isolation of sitting in the guest room while Truth attended to her own minor duties on board. She and Major Karo had no doubt been planning their next missions.

"When are we leaving?" Kirashira finally asked. The ship as far as she knew, had made no effort to move toward the star in the system, the only place they could hope to catch a hyperspace corridor to Shar'Jya. A subspace trip would take over a month but it did not seem the NovaCore had any sense of urgency about their departure.

"We will be in a few minutes actually..." the NovaCore officer checked a small device on his wrist and entered the observation deck proper.

A few minutes, Kirashira sighed. Who knew how long it would take once they decided to get underway. A few minutes plus however long that took.

"I thought NovaCore Ship's were fast..." Kirashira jabbed lightly, "I didn't expect getting on our way would take so long."

"Well you gotta charge the jump core up first right?" The Novian smiled lightly.

Kirashira knew enough to know one did not charge their drive until they reached the hyperspace departure point, something that was tens of millions of kilometers from her planet.

"I guess I have to take your word for it," She replied.

The man smirked, raising a brow, "I assure you we will be under way faster than you realize, On our way to Shar'Jya even, it's just not a place you arrive at without some planning ahead is all."

"I have to admit I have no idea how your people use the corridors," She finally admitted.

"You'd be surprised," he replied, adding, "Though to be honest we don't use the corridors much differently from yours."

Kirashira sighed, feeling like she was being given the run around. Whatever technique it was her hosts used, it was probably something they weren't allowed to share directly. With any luck that meant it was something as fast as the common wisdom seemed to dictate. Having no real knowledge about what the Federation actually knew, she was at a disadvantage in that regard. Of course, her father had probably known a thing or two...

Major Karo moved ahead eying the image of Ashor on the wall. When Kirashira had learned it was a screen and not a window she had been a bit disappointed. By any Hil'Raigh standard, a screen was inadequate, one needed a true connection to the celestial world, one that only came by viewing its true reflected light directly. Apparently the NovaCore did not agree.

There was still an oddness about the Major, something Kirashira did not fully understand. Even after she had smoothed things over at least a bit with Truth, the man seemed a bit hard to read. He was friendly, but still so guarded that Kirashira felt nervous in his company at times. Ironically, the one she'd had the most trouble with initially, Truth, was more of a friend now.

Was it proper to call her that? She had been extremely nice, especially since Kirashira's unfortunate dream. Still, she was a little odd and the Princess had to admit it would take getting used to. She would have to overcome her immediate instinctual feelings to fully appreciate the Novian host. Now though Kirashira was not sure that would happen. It would take time and time was something she now felt she lacked, at least if the ship got underway this century.

As she mused however, a deep droning filled the air. It was broken up by a shrill klaxon that oscillated from high to low pitch. The noise was prolific, startling and immediately unsettling. The royal almost slid from the seat she had occupied as it pierced her ears. Whatever it was, it was certain to be of some importance. Even before she could ask however. The loud drone stopped and the klaxon was interrupted by an even toned computer voice. It spoke in words she did not understand repeating the same message several times in Novian before cutting off. As it did, the warning siren changed into a rapid cacophony at a tempo that made her heart race. Loud speakers in the hallway proclaimed some other Novian words and then the siren cut off. For a moment, Kirashira was unsure what to do, glued now to the chair in fear. Even as she felt her confidence returning however, the ship shuddered violently, or at least, it felt violent. She looked to the Major who simply gave her a knowing smile, amid the shaking of the deck beneath him. He was apparently un-phased by the ruckus transition of the ship.

Kirashira had heard in her study of history that the oldest hyperdrives suffered from oscillation problems, something that apparently required them to be fit with massive dampening devices in order to avoid damaging the ship they were mounted in. Perhaps that was what was going on. With no real window, she was unsure. The image of Ashor, probably recorded footage at this point, was still playing on the screen as if nothing was wrong.

The shaking of the vessel continued for a moment and then a noticeable surge made her stomach churn. She felt like it was going to leap out of her body and yet, the plants, the Major, none of them moved. Had she imagined it?

She tried to stand, no longer feeling all that safe in the observation deck but felt nauseated immediately and collapsed back into the seat, gripping the armrests more tightly than she thought possible.

It was a good half minute or so before she worked up the fortitude to speak, swallowing and directing her attention to the NovaCore officer before her, "I take it that we are underway?"

He nodded and smiled, turning to the observation screen. His fingers poked at the small control panel off to the side of the device and in moments the image of Ashor melted away. The edges of the screen burnt out first, a reddish hue consuming the image from the edges and moving inward until the familiar planet was gone.

In its wake was the image of something nebulous and cloudy. It reminded Kirashira of images from gas giant atmospheric probes. For several moments the cloudiness rolled by the screen and then, the clouds broke. In the screen now was a space, something almost undefinable, something she had trouble understanding.

Stretching away from the point of view above and below were walls of the same nebulous phenomenon. There were arcs of what she guessed to be lightning dancing between the distant clouds. Some of the blasts of energy burned ineffectually into empty space and in their wake, pinkish red cloud congealed before melting away into nothingness once more. The scene was grotesquely enticing, a strangeness so un-nerving to her eyes that she couldn't turn away despite the uneasiness she felt looking to it.

"What is this?" She asked.

"It's what under way looks like," Karo responded, clasping his hands behind his back. His characteristic hint of sarcasm permeated the comment.

In the distance, Kirashira could make out what had to be shafts of nebulous gas like material. They stretched from the top of the expanse to the bottom, connecting the floor and ceiling of the place like giant columns. They twirled and twisted however, not stationary. They writhed, blasting more of the energetic arcs she had noticed before into the space around them.

"Are we dead?" She asked finally, feeling eerily like the place she was seeing matched the descriptions of some hells described in a few ancient texts.

"I sure hope not," the officer replied with a snicker, "Or the perfect safety record of the jump drives is going right down the tubes..."

"I guess this explains..." Kirashira thought for a moment, "Well... It doesn't explain anything really..."

Karo laughed again, "I'm not qualified to explain what you are looking at so it's probably for the best."

He continued however, "But in simple terms... this is how you get around really, really fast."

"You mean, this is how you get into..." She paused, "Is this what hyperspace looks like from inside your ships?"

The man shook his head, "Nope. Looks like a giant vortex from the inside of a corridor just like it does on your ships."

The Princess stood now and moved closer to the screen. It was like something out of a dream or a story. What she was seeing felt surreal, yet hollow. There was nothing inherently assuring about it all and she could not help but wonder whether the sense of her hair standing on end was because of the unfamiliarity or something else entirely.

"It's got sound," The man smirked.

"In space…." Kirashira replied incredulously. Her people had radios on some ships that traveled hyperspace just to make interesting tourist songs out of the signals.

"I don't really know if you call this place that," He replied, keying the screen control.

The room's speakers crackled online with a subtle hum. A soft low lazy sound, not unlike the planet songs Kirashira herself had heard in planetariums or science tutoring. It was different however in ways she soon began to identify. For one thing, the arcing bursts far and wide seemed to reverberate through the hum. Regular melodies almost felt like they rippled from the disturbances but as quickly as they came, they faded away. Even so, there was a consistent tone. It was subtle but once she heard it once she couldn't block it even if she tried to focus on something else, "I don't know how to describe it."

"Yeah, you probably hear it better than most Novians. Truth says Kul'Raigh ears would be better at hearing it than ours," He explained, "Something about the shape and the membrane for sound transmission…"

"You can't hear it then?"

"I can…sort-of. I have really nice ears for a Novian. Most people on the ship probably couldn't though." He smirked and tapped his earlobe. She wondered if he had implants there too. He had mentioned something about more than genetic enhancement before. Almost as if anticipating her next question, he spoke.

"Most stuff out here makes some kind of weird noise actually," He said looking momentarily serious, "Lot's of weird stuff to see too if you poke around for a while."

"How much have you poked around here?" She asked, now curious.

"I'm not an explorer, so not much. But I hear it's pretty challenging work to map this stuff, takes fortitude," He replied, turning away from the screen after cutting the speakers. Even though the sound was gone, Kirashira felt like she could almost hear it reverberating even still, the low rhythmic humming still fresh in her mind.

"I'm hungry, let's eat. Truth said she'll meet us in the galley," He announced.

Kirashira nodded, following him toward the door. A glance over her shoulder was the last look she decided she wanted to have of the oddity outside, at least for the time being. The path to the mess hall was one she had learned enough of but it was always nice to have a guide anyway.

"How long do you think we have?" She asked, "You said we would be there quickly…"

"I can't say specifically, I'm no expert in it. But it should be at least enough time for people to work on your clothes," The officer replied with a shrug.

"I hope so," she stated, "It's important that I put on a good image for the arrival, Even if its on your ship and without all of the normal revelry."

"Never knew taking a trip to the seat of government was such an occasion in the Federation."

"Each member state contributes to make sure the other leaders are honored appropriately when they arrive, it helps keep the peace," Kirashira explained.

"Hmm," He gave her a glance but said nothing further for a moment, simply leading the way forward.

"I'm nervous," She said eventually, "I've never done this without my parents."

"You'll probably be fine," the Novian replied, "But if it makes you feel any better, everyone on this ship is probably more nervous than you are about going to Shar'Jya."

Kirashira quipped a small sound of surprise at the assertion. What did they have to be nervous about. Apparently hearing her unspoken question however, her guide explained, "Going to Shar'Jya and, as discussed, making ourselves visible and obvious to your people there is not something any ship from the NovaCore would ever do if it had a choice..."

She had not thought of it from that angle. For her the arrival was what mattered but the very real anxiety that some of those on the ship probably felt about the trip was not something she had contemplated until now,

"Can't be helped really," He shrugged once more, "That's what the mission needs. Besides, how many other NovaCore ships get to say they waltzed into the Shar'Jya system?"

He seemed to take pleasure in the idea of reaching the seat of the Federation and she understood that much. It was something of a point of pride really, being in your adversary's capitol system. As long as the NovaCore did not cause any trouble it would be a peaceful reception she had decided. No one in the Elite Guard would attack a verified envoy ship.

"Do you have to make a speech?"

She sighed and nodded, responding to the Novian's question, "I have to say a bit, some customary greetings really. Not a prepared speech by any means. Still, I should probably take the time to think of some things to say."

"People are going to want to hear from you, especially about us," He coached.

Kirashira smirked, he wanted her to say something positive about the NovaCore? That was pushing it. She could say they were acceptable hosts, gracious even, and that their help was important to her being there on Shar'Jya. Open praise however, would have to wait until she had dealt with the regency problem. She couldn't take the risk of looking too friendly with the Federation's rival so soon after leaving their care. If she did people would become suspicious. With her luck, they would make claims of undue influence regardless of just how independent she really was, something that hung over her head like a cloud now.

"I'll try to put in a good word without embellishing," She replied taking a diplomatic tone, adding, "I wish I could say more but it might not be the best time..."

"I'd suspect foreign influence too," the Major said in candid response, "No need to be shy about that. Your stay hasn't been perfect after all."

"No it hasn't" Kirashira replied, remembering her spat of argument with the man who was currently with her, her trouble with Truth, her emotional roller coaster. It was very far from an ideal length of time. To say it was bad however, she felt was not doing justice to the good that had happened. She had, despite herself, managed to make some small steps of progress regardless and that was something to be celebrated. Though not perfect, her hosts had shown courtesy, genuine concern and in the case of Admiral Thorsh and Truth especially, a level of compassion. Compassion, a concept she had thought NovaCore incapable of and yet now she was thinking of them providing it. Truth's face came up in her mind and she sighed. The bastardized version of a Kul'Raigh in so many ways and yet, she was something that Kirashira had to admit was uniquely special. The level of empathy that she had shown so recently was not far gone from the Royal's mind.

It was a difficult situation, to feel obligated to one she at most, wanted neutrality with. Thankfully, the Major interrupted the reflection with his own musings, "I have to admit, you are not entirely who I thought you were."

He continued, "And after thinking about it, I feel like you have good leadership potential for your people after all. You're not as... frustrating... as I might have implied earlier.."

"Thank you," Kirashira replied, a bit surprised at his sudden change of attitude. It was a sort of non apology, but it was more than nothing. A few moments more and she asked. "What prompted that?"

"Something about ego," The officer sighed.

Confused, Kirashira regarded him with a raised brow for a moment, pursing her lips until, at last, she decided it was best to let him alone in his musing. For now, the smell of the galley's offerings ahead was enough to ensure that the conversation would change regardless, and with it, Kirashira would gain a moment more of respite before the coming storm.

22 - Bitter Welcome

The stage had been set, at least as well as Tony imagined it could have. The bridge was looking as clean as he could ever remember, though he had to admit he never really visited for any length of time. Today was an exception however and it was clear as the technicians did their final checks on the holo-tank in the middle of the space, that something was different about it all.

The apparatus was normally used for giving the ship's acting commander a better view of the world around the ship from deep inside. Rather than visual sensors, the various suites of detection devices on a NovaCore ship relayed a three dimensional map that was projected holographically. The tank also doubled as a high definition communication device for conducting communications within a fleet.

The techs, as Tony had been told, were making the adjustments that were needed to allow the machine to produce a hologram that could be sent and read by Hil'Raigh vessels instead of those from the NovaCore Navy. It was all apparently part of the plan when arriving.

The whole business had most of the crew on edge despite how calm and collected they all acted, it was something that Tony had learned to spot. Between he and Truth, they had yet to see someone on board that did not seem at least a bit distracted by the idea of taking their ship right to the heart of the Federation. Further still, the plan did not stop there, going so far as announcing their presence for all to see.

It was how things were done apparently, something both Thorsh and the ships commanding officer had confirmed. Even so, a Shar'Jya arrival was something that Tony felt he was not alone in wishing he could opt out of.

Kirashira had been a more reasonable guest since they had departed from Ashor and he had to guess it was because her mental energy was at least partly focused on the coming hours. He couldn't blame her really. Though she had generally been more positive toward Truth as well, it was still unclear to Tony whether she had moved past her apparent misgivings about his partner.

Either way, with an arrival coming, and definite Shar'Jya Elite Guard presence in the near future, he guessed she might be off of the ship sooner than anyone had planned. Thorsh had insisted she accept a NovaCore entourage, namely Tony and his partner as personal guards, until the whole political situation was resolved. It was a selfish move but it looked good on the outside at least. The safer she was the more likely things would go positively, for the NovaCore anyway.

Even so, she had waffled, not giving him a full answer yet. As a result Tony had assumed she intended the opposite, getting home. It was part of why he had, despite mending the fence a bit with the royal, kept his distance. She was for all intents and purposes, still a potential adversary. It all depended on what she did once she was not on the NovaCore ship.

It was easy to be someone's friend when you were stuck at their home, but once you went back to your own, you were free to deal with them as you chose. While he doubted she would directly antagonize the NovaCore, he was still skeptical that she would provide much in the way of political relief for his nation. Averting the war council was all he could realistically hope to see happen, and that was because it was in her own nation's interest as well. It was a sentiment he and Truth did not exactly share.

His partner believed apparently, in the good nature of the Princess despite her previous attitude. It made sense in a way, they had spent more time together and perhaps as a result, Truth knew something she could not really explain. Either that or Truth was blinded by the hope of redemption in the eyes of this individual, someone she was not obligated to in any way yet seemed to be drawn to.

The connection there was ambiguous and it seemed to Tony that he had for the first time in quite a while, encountered a facet of his partner that made little sense to him. He had grown to know her so well that a surprise like that was now a rarity and yet, it had happened. One thing was certain, Truth would always keep him guessing.

Guessing however was not in the cards for their guest. She stood only meters away, mumbling to herself as she examined a data slate. She wore the finery she had been rescued in, cleaned and repaired as well as possible on board a Navy vessel.

The clothing had not been damaged much, or so it was said. It had been stained and dirtied but beyond that there was little preventing it from being usable again. Given that it was quite literally the only royal garb on-board, the cleaning and repair had become a priority the moment of departure from Ashor.

Of course, in the real royal world, that clothing probably would have been destroyed and remade but there was no option for such a thing during Alternate Planar Travel, nor on a NovaCore ship in general.

A diversity of talent from the crew had come together to give Kirashira as much of a royal presence as one could muster from the ranks of a Naval crew. While it was not at the level of the herds of stylists and consultants most nobility and affluent Hil'Raigh seemed to keep in the wings, it was enough to put Kirashira into eye catching territory once again. She looked rather regal, for an alien at least.

Her white robes hung from her frame with little slack, tailored to fit from her torso to her hips. Only below the hips, where the garment split apart to expose some of her legs was there any real give to it. The sleeves were long and puffy as well, completing the overdone look that was signature of Hil'Raigh high society. Tony had not bothered looking in detail at the garment before, but seeing it now, finally understood why she had been able to run, her legs freed enough to move. Apparently it was not just that survival was a powerful motivator.

Beyond the garment and its bushy red trim however, Kirashira had been given a layer of cosmetic work that was at least passably similar to what she'd had back home. Her hair was pulled not into the fancy, impossible to replicate style it had been on the night of rescue, but instead pulled back more like Truth's own. The odd lengths of some bits of her hair however, attested to the fact that it had to have been custom cut to work with the extravagant royal styles she was used to. There was no hope of anyone on board this ship finding out how to make those happen.

Still, despite her lesser equipped support staff for the day, she seemed to be doing well enough, if a bit nervous. She kept fidgeting, mouthing words then looking down at the slate and shaking her head before trying again.

It was a speech or something, some kind of statement at least, something Tony had no interest in reading through prior to now because it had started off with such vague political platitudes as were apparently required in this situation. Thanks for this, thanks for that, hello and thanks for welcoming me, thanks for this. I'm so and so. It all seemed too fake and rehearsed, less tradition and more wrote memorization.

Kirashira had of course, insisted that despite how it appeared, the tradition was actually quite important even if it turned rather repetitive for people who went to and from the capitol world often. Royals she had said, did not arrive more than a few times a year, with nobles, who had far less to do in the way of arriving, visiting in their stead at times. It was an interesting cultural lesson, but it was one that Tony had surely filed in his short term memory.

It would only be mere minutes now until the NovaCore ship entered Shar'Jya space. The Elite Guard, a Federation military force responsible for all the security in the capital, would have ships all over the place and despite the extremely effective drive masking technologies employed by most NovaCore ships, none of it would matter when they began transmitting.

Admiral Thorsh paced around near the command walk among the various operational stations meters away, analyzing the work of the crew, probably to avoid thinking about the arguably suicidal proposition he had convinced the ship and its crew to entertain in coming to Shar'Jya at all.

Kirashira, near the holo-tank, finally set the slate she had been reading from down and began to pace awkwardly. She glanced over to Tony and his partner only for a moment before looking as if she was lost once again. It was probably nervousness that drove her. If only she knew the half of it.

A loud warning klaxon sounded, a long droning signal that indicated preparations for leaving alternate planar space. The otherwise subdued bridge turned to a flurry of vocal activity as stations called out statuses to each other. All of the major systems and departments would report ready before any attempt to return to normal space was made. If anyone failed to check in, it would mean immediate general quarters and the whole thing would be put on hold pending a review.

Tony had never actually been on a ship where that had happened, and as far as he knew it was something that had only ever happened one time in the past, decades ago on a single ship. As with any story coming out of alternate planar space travel, there were so many versions, so many imagined boogie men conjured up by the fevered minds of the space faring crews that, the Major had never been confident he'd heard the real story. Even so, a failure to report meant a marine detachment without question.

One by one however, the main departments were sounding off through their liaisons on the bridge. First was gunnery, engineering, navigation, docking control and operations, All of the major sections.

The ships speaker system popped to life and a computerized voice announced the return to normal space was pending. Tony thought the name they had chosen for it, surfacing, was apt, given how the ship seemed to move when it was making the return trip. Even so, this was no normal return, they were going to arrive in one of the most heavily patrolled, heavily defended places in the known galaxy, an enemy stronghold if there ever was one. Caution could not be overstated, and so, while standard procedure dictated a warning alarm before surfacing, general battle alert sounded instead. In any other circumstance that meant Tony, Truth and Kirashira would be kicked off of the bridge, but since the only adequate communicator was located there, Kirashira had to stay and as a result, her assigned liaisons did too.

"Last chance to change your mind admiral," The captain called to Admiral Thorsh. It was a good natured reminder of the danger everyone now faced. Thorsh simply nodded giving a flick of his wrist, pointing squarely at the captain in reply, "Go."

With that command, a final alarm sounded and the ships computer came over the loudspeaker once more announcing the surfacing process. Tony looked to his charge, Kirashira, as she got the clue quickly and leaned forward, holding onto the railing running around the holo-tank in front of her. The large circular table and its holograms sputtered, the light dying in the thing as the ship shook, almost as if it were digging through solid ground to return back to the space it belonged to. Within moments the shaking stopped, the ship lurching as the environmental systems normalized the feeling.

The bridge itself quieted for a moment and then, in an instant, the massive wall screens that ran the length of the room began flaring to life. Large enhanced imagery of the system, a full panorama, covered the walls of the bridge. Moments after that, blips began to appear, outlined meticulously. It was always something to see, watching just how quickly NovaCore sensors managed to isolate and pinpoint alien ships against the stars. Dot after dot appeared and it was clear, rather quickly that by sheer volume, this was more than just a stronghold. It was more of a hive.

No NovaCore ship had ever actually traveled to this system, at least in any official capacity or one that Tony had heard of. Now, he felt like he had an idea why. The status indicators on the tops and bottom of the displays counted into the hundreds now, already flashing a desperate red as if to indicate the computer core's unspoken protest at being dragged to such a place.

Finally however, an iconic, if oft unheard alarm sounded. Learning all of the different warning signals on a ship was something of an art, but this one was clear enough, the perimeter alert warning. It had probably turned on automatically because of the high alert condition, once one of the closer Hil'Raigh ships was detected and categorized.

Those were the more dangerous ones as far as the NovaCore were concerned, smaller, stealthier military vessels. Thankfully it probably had not detected the NovaCore in kind, but that was anyone's guess now.

"Plot flight path to avoid perimeter violation..." The executive officer chortled. Thorsh was like a stone ahead, watching the screens. Tony wondered what he was thinking now but it was a little late to decide. Coming all this way already had more or less committed the ship and its crew to the mission until it was done.

Tony glanced over to Kirashira who looked even more nervous. It was as if the apprehension of being a Novian here at Shar'Jya had infected her too. Of course, Tony knew better, her arrival was now a reality, and that was what had made her nervous.

At length, she composed herself and let go of the railing she had been white knuckling, stretching her delicate fingers without a word as she looked onward, a bit of curiosity mixed in with her attempts at being regal.

No Hil'Raigh had ever seen what she just had and if she were anyone else, she probably would have been prevented from being on the bridge to see it. Thorsh however, had stuck his neck out for her before, securing a promise of her cooperation and offering a bit of vulnerability to ensure she understood the gravity of his request.

"Transmission Array deployed," came an unseen voice from the crowd of crew ahead, sitting among the consoles below the command walk.

With that, the recorder for the tank swung down. A double jointed appendage with an array of cameras and scanners on the end. It flipped down from its holding area above the holo-tank and rotated around it on a track until it was on the opposite side of Kirashira. Tony watched as she eyed the device, gulped and then stood firmly.

"Transmission go for Hil'Raigh patrol ship," another crew announced. There was a pause, an awkward one until finally, Kirashira caught the Admiral motioning to her. She nodded and one of the senior staff relayed the order to begin the transmission in response to her gesture.

"Hil'Raigh Ship," She paused, gulping, then taking a breath, she seemed to gain a shred of confidence, "This is Kirashira Ren'Tauru of the Starlight Compact, Daughter of Gou'Ran of the Ren'Tauru Dynasty."

There was a long pause and yet, no reply. Kirashira spoke again, the same words. Again, no reply. Confused looks crossed from officer to commander among the bridge crew but a single voice rose out of the silence, "Sir! Hil'Raigh Patrol ship is coming at us full burn, weapons hot!"

"Targeting?" The quick, urgent query from the ship's captain sounded, "Do they have us?"

"Unknown sir..."

"Shut down that damn transmitter!" another voice, the ships executive officer sounded, following with, "Clear the tank!"

The holographic imager folded away immediately and Tony stepped forward to Kirashira. He tugged her arm to move her aside as she stepped back, confused, "What's going on?"

"Your patrol ship isn't responding and it is coming in aggressively," Tony replied.

"What!?" Kirashira seemed more than just surprised, she was offended, annoyed even, "What kind of accusation is that?"

Tony almost rolled his eyes. She couldn't even understand the conversation now taking place around the holographic map in the holo-tank.

The image had shifted from nothing to the NovaCore destroyer at the tank's center. Spheres representing various perimeters and distances from the ship glowed faintly as a detailed three dimensional model of the incoming Hil'Raigh patrol ship closed. It was of course, small in size as the distances were large. Even so, the speed of approach, the vector, it was something Tony knew spelled trouble. As he thought it, a curse erupted from the Captain as he examined the situation.

"Deflectors Full. Engage full burn evasive pattern Teros Negal. Charge Points!" He barked. The bridge replied immediately.

The order resounded several times. Once was enough of course, for Tony to know he and his partner were going to be leaving the bridge with their charge rather soon but there was always the chance that she was able to talk to someone. Thankfully, one of the bridge officers had already been thinking the same, approaching the trio and motioning for them to follow.

"Come on Princess," Tony requested grimly, "We might be able to stop this from becoming a fight..."

"Fight!?" She was aghast. She immediately scurried forward to the comm station and, when offered a transmitter, began barking into it urgently.

"Pulse Plasma in the vac!" A shout came from the command walk.

Tony glanced to the holo-tank, a series of small dots, bright red dots, hurtled from the Hil'Raigh ship toward his own. Fascination and a sense of dread gripped him as he watched the dots eek their way ever closer until the first passed by. The second vanished, probably intercepted. The third however passed through the bright red sphere closest to the holographic representation of the ship. A fraction of a second later and there was a violent shudder. Metal echoed in protest from some unknown place on-board.

Sirens, warning alarms, whatever one wanted to call them, they were not something anyone wanted to hear. The Hil'Raigh salvo had hit home in at least one place. It was only as Tony contemplated his vessel returning fire, that the reality of a firefight set in. Even so, the holo-tank was already sharing terrible news. More Hil'Raigh ships were on their way and long range fire had already been dropped by several of them.

NovaCore ships were tough, well designed and resilient in the face of dangerous odds. Taking on several enemies at once was not impossible for them, but they had already given themselves away with the transmitters earlier. It would be next to impossible to evade any effective fire with that disadvantage in play.

"Return fire sir?"

"Negative, Kul'Sanir is on scopes."

Kul'Sanir, the Elite Guard Flagship. It could punch this ship in half easily with the kind of power it packed. It was one of the big hitters among navies in the galaxy, a ship whose sole purpose was to protect a single planet in the vastness of it all. Even so, it was not one anyone had ever decided to pick a fight with and Tony couldn't blame the captain for not trying his luck.

"They are going to move to board," Tony muttered to himself, watching as the patrol ship veered wide in the holo-tank, delaying its approach for apparently more backup.

"We've gotta go," Tony announced, moving to Kirashira and tugging her quickly away from the communication console. She protested only a moment before someone among the bridge crew announced several boarding craft on sensors, probably from the incoming flagship.

The befuddled Royal squirmed little as she was escorted from the bridge into the hallway. The command deck itself was bustling with activity in any case. Standard procedure for this situation dictated that Tony and his partner prepare to repel boarding parties but with Kirashira to look after, he guessed that was not an option.

A cryptic order, general order twelve was repeated over the comm several times. Tony shook his head. Whatever was going on was not a fight. Truth gave him a grave look as the announcement looped a second time.

"There goes the jump drive..." Tony said with a sigh. General order twelve was a simple idea, sabotage the ships main drives so an enemy force could not use them to reverse engineer the method of FTL travel used by the NovaCore. To a lesser degree, advanced weapons or other secret technologies would also be destroyed. That meant that within minutes the ship's computer core was going to be a molten hunk of silicon and metal fragments as well.

"We need to get to a safe zone," Truth stated calmly. Tony nodded in response. Since Truth and Tony were not part of the ship's crew, and they had the required training to avoid detection and evade capture, they were obligated to avoid detainment or capture by the enemy to ensure all of the last requirements of general order twelve were carried out. A safe zone was a small secret compartment on the ship not logged in the floor plans or schematics that provided access to some discreet access-ways and maintenance shafts leading almost anywhere on board. Furthermore, it hosted an armory of its own and sets of survival gear and other tools.

Sets of markings embedded in standard signage told those who were trained where they would need to go in order to access such an area and usually the command staff was expected to carry out the bulk of general order twelve followup. Tony knew he and his partner were better suited to being sneaky than being captured.

They began on their way quickly, Kirashira en tow. The ship shook again as they walked, indicating that there was still most certainly incoming fire.

"You think they'd get the picture since we aren't shooting back." Tony said with an unhappy sneer.

"Apparently not," Truth replied.

"Where are we going?" Kirashira asked. For a moment Tony had forgotten about their guest not having any reason to be brought to a safe zone. He looked over his shoulder at her and opened his mouth. Even as he did so, his words caught in his throat.

Down the hall behind them, the hull plating bulged awkwardly. Then finally, the shake of incoming fire rattled it. Even as the shockwave reverberated through the walls, Tony was already diving to shove the Princess to the ground. Truth followed as hellish fire burst through the deformed bulkhead a dozen or so meters down the hall. A lance of white hot energy erupting through the metal like a nail through soft wood.

The beam of energy flooded awkwardly into the corridor, cascading over the far walls with fiery determination as the concussion of the torpedo impact rattled the deck plating. The air smelt of ozone, burning heat and Tony felt his lungs struggle for the next breath.

The heat subsided. It had taken mere fractions of a second for the display to burn into life but it was now replaced by a rush as the air desperately attempted to fill the void. The plasma torpedo had consumed the very air Tony's lungs so desperately yearned to take in, fueling its own destructive energies with devious intent.

Tony struggled upward, pulling Kirashira quickly. He knew what was coming next, even before the hallway blared to life with warnings. The running air continued despite filling in the gap. It kept flowing despite adequately subduing the fire. No, there would be no more fire here, not without air.

The cold of space, the touch of the void poked at Tony's senses as he felt the hallway's atmosphere pick up violent speed, venting angrily into the unknown without regard for he or his companions in the hallway. The sound of sirens, warning beacons, they all faded as the air carrying the clarion calls was removed from the hallway, expelled into the lifeless nothing outside. Truth had managed to grab onto something while Tony found himself leaving the floor against his will.

He struggled for a moment as he felt the Princess leave his grip, no, she had been shoved close enough to the emergency bulkhead that she was wedged inside, it had yet to close. He however, had no such luck. The ground was betraying him, the air inviting him along for the ride into space. It was a ride he did not want to take but what could he do. No skill ever prepared him for this, nothing had ever taught him how to swim without a space suit in the black.

He felt himself picking up speed as he raced toward the hole in the hull that threatened to drag him into the vacuum. Oddly, as he approached the jagged mess, he realized he was likely to be impaled on some debris or the jagged edges of the penetration before he ever actually hit space itself.

His fingers slipped along the bulkheads, finding no purchase for agonizing moments until at last. He felt them find a hold, one of the support structures along the wall. He gripped tightly, struggling for breath amid the violent torrent as he looked around. Dirt, dust, it all felt like violent hail now as it pelted his skin, his face. Flecks of metal bounced off of his uniform here or there and the generally horrific circumstance was made only marginally better by the fact that he saw Truth shoving Kirashira through the emergency bulkhead meters away. The door had not closed and until it did, the compartment would keep venting. He contemplated calling out, asking her to close the thing, but he realized he probably couldn't have been heard over the sound of the decompression anyway. It was only going to take seconds for the automatic lockout to begin regardless.

For once in a long time, Tony realized he had no idea what to do.

23 - Swimming in Space

Truth had felt the shudder of the ship as the bulkhead behind began to deform but even then it had exploded outward so quickly that she could not have done anything more than dive for the nearby doorway.

The open hatch seemed an inviting target. Truth lept forward towards it and her partner lobbed himself into Kirashira, shoving the Princess forward. She collapsed to the ground of course as Truth began scurrying forward. The intense heat of a plasma explosion licking at her from behind, she wrested Kirashira's wrist with a sort of calculated violence, tugging her along. There was no question in Truth's mind about what was going to unfold.

At first, the deafening pop resounded down the corridor, a shock of what little dust or dirt littered the place directed through the open hatches on either side of the compartment like an unseen punch, a gust of wind. Even as quickly as it had happened though, the voraciousness of the vacuum of space made its hunger known, eagerly sucking through the newly minted hole like a thirsty traveler with a straw standing in his way of a cool beverage.

Truth shoved Kirashira through the hatch, glancing over her shoulder only a moment more as the initial gust of air, now in reverse, punched at her from the front. Kirashira was immediately pinned inside the hatchway, a precarious position to say the least. Tony however, had no such luck and was sucked violently backward.

As she braced herself, Truth made out his form, clinging helplessly to one of the frames in the hall. His face was a mask of wind whipped helplessness, his eyes nearly closed in the wake of the violent outtake of air. In seconds his life would be forfeit and he would be lost to the void forever. It was a fate that awaited the entire section of the ship as well, one that the automatic emergency bulkheads were designed to prevent, even if it meant sacrificing a few brave souls along the way.

He looked stable enough, but with only seconds to act, Truth summoned her strength to shove Kirashira around to the safe side of the bulkhead. There was only a mere moment of time to save her partner and she had to act. She crawled through the doorway between the sections, looking back to analyze his situation. There was nothing to throw him, no cables, no rope, nothing that would guide him toward her, even if he could manage holding on.

It did not take long for the environmental warning sirens to kick in, something that meant the ship was now going through the process of deciding just how quickly and with what bulkheads it was going to stop the breach. Once it made those choices, it took precious seconds of time to override, time Truth did not feel she would have. There was no time to guess, a loud thud sounded down the hall, then another.

The flow of air slowed but until the hole she now looked through shut, the leak would continue. She recalled as quickly as her neural interface allowed, the schematics of the ship, the locations of the emergency bulkheads nearby even as the time ticked away. She looked to her partner, he was struggling still to hold. Another thud, but the air did not slow much at all that time. The ship was getting close, the reactionary measure impossible to stop.

Then, in a burst of inspiration, Truth bolted to her feet, running the meters to the next access-way in desperate fashion. She made the journey in an instant, with speed she had no idea her body possessed. At the top of her lungs, she yelled into the noisy air, hoping that someone would hear, knowing at least that Tony would but worried at the same time for her charge only meters away, "Exhale and hold your breath!"

With those words she mashed the flashing emergency control on the bulkhead. In a fraction of a second the bulkhead slid closed, so violently in fact that it shook the wall against which she leaned. In seconds more however, the icy chill of nothing began to claw at her skin. She looked over her shoulder as the system shut off the artificial gravity in the compartment and a desperately grasping royal squirmed through the air meters away.

"Go now" Truth radioed pushing off of the wall toward Kirashira, who looked more like a choking fish than a Princess, her face turning bright red. There was no reply from her partner and Kirashira's desperate eyes locked to Truth as they waited. Unlike the two NovaCore, Kirashira's body had most certainly not been enhanced to provide a more effective survival time in such a situation and it showed.

Had Truth scarified the Princess to save her partner? Had she doomed the NovaCore to war for nothing but selfishness? Had she made the right choice? Her mind desperately wanted vindication now, proof that she had done the right thing, but in that moment, despair crept into her thoughts.

The fractions of time passed as eternities, Truth's mind racing through every possible scenario as quickly as she could muster. She had to wonder, she had no choice. As she floated there however, her senses tingled and she glanced to the side. Her ragged, red faced partner looking about to choke, though not as bad as Kirashira did. He floated through the hatch with a surprising amount of speed, probably what had used the last of his air. He was careening out of control toward the far wall but he looked to have moved into the safety of Truth's intact compartment. Despite being uncertain, as to whether he had fully cleared the hatch, Truth reached out and gripped the handle next to the door before mashing the emergency close. The bulkhead sealed and the breach in the hull disappeared from view. A finger stroke more and the room changed.

It was an odd sensation as sound bled back into the room, it was a violent hissing, but also, the sound of sirens, they returned, sounds had returned. Truth could feel herself coughing, looking down to Kirashira who gasped the incoming air like life itself. Tony had found a hand hold on the far wall and coughed helplessly as well, finding air to give his body peace once more.

The artificial gravity was still offline in the compartment but given how Kirashira had shifted and the fact that Truth herself felt the ship dragging her by her outstretched arm, she guessed the main engines were also off.

"Damnit," coughed Tony from across the room. Truth turning her attention to Kirashira. She looked dazed, sick and overall unhappy but more or less alive, more than she would have been if the torpedo had punctured the hull in front of the trio instead of dozens of meters behind. She was however, in an obvious position of helplessness, squirming uncomfortably.

Truth examined the control panel carefully and keyed another button. A light tugging sensation took hold of her, dragging her weight downward. It was enough to let Kirashira settle to the floor and Truth felt her own feet contact moments later.

Tony finished his bout of coughing and called over, "Remind me to wear the mag boots on board these ships..."

Truth felt a bit guilty. Having artificial gravity tended to make the oldest rules of the space navy more of a cultural history than something commonly enforced. Modern weaponry tended to kill most anyone in compartments it impacted so current crews didn't bother wearing the magnetic boots as often. Those that did were usually career Navy, people who actually dealt with regular gravity outages. While Truth and her partner had been trained at length in vacuum operations, that usually came with careful preparation and most importantly, space suits for the occasion.

"On the bright side we can all say we have gone vac swimming," Truth replied with an exasperated half laugh. Tony shrugged, slowly walking over, probably to ensure he did not flip himself from the ground like Kirashira had done when attempting to stand. She comically flailed about but seemed to get the hang of it in time to land on her knees and try again.

"If I ever get in a bragging contest with a Marine I'll bring that up," Tony replied sarcastically, with a cough.

Of course, the number of signals and warnings on the ship did not abate long enough for much of a real conversation. Within seconds the boarding alarm had sounded as well.

"Guess we should have expected that too," Tony quipped, "Let's get to the safe zone before our friends show up to greet us..."

Truth nodded calling to Kirashira who looked a bit shaken but far more coherent than Truth would have expected given what had just happened, "Princess... are you able to walk?"

The royal stood, lacking confidence. She moved in an awkward and deliberate way within the minimal gravity she was afforded here. Her shaky voice gave a reply "Yes... I can walk.."

"I never expected to have a torpedo detonate so close to me," Truth added at length.

Her partner was already busy trying to override the lock on the door that sealed them from the as yet unaffected areas of the ship. It would take seconds at least, for the environmental control to decide it trusted the crew enough to open the door. The blinking lights on the panel told Truth the same story. At last however, the bulkhead cracked, then the door receded into the roof above. The emergency sealant from the thick metal door left a slimy residue all over the door frame's internal surfaces. Otherwise one would never have known that behind them the sleeping lion of space was sealed away, waiting for its next chance at a snack.

Tony was already checking wall signage as he moved. The threshold of the door was an infinitely awkward boundary as Truth followed, the differences in the gravity of both compartments disorienting. While almost nothing remained in the space they were exiting, this portion of the hallway with full environmental control, had carried on like nothing was amiss.

Kirashira followed after the two NovaCore, Truth was not surprised to see her have to stop herself from retching as she passed into normal gravity and stumbled, holding her mouth. All of the queasiness from a first time zero-g experience might have been the introduction to the nausea, but the differential in the door frame must have tweaked just the right places in her head to become a problem. Thankfully for Kirashira, her slow heavy breathing while kneeling on the floor was apparently enough to calm her stomach and despite looking worse for wear, she stood again.

"They shot us," Kirashira finally stated, a hint of surprise in her voice, "I can't believe they shot at us..."

Tony, in the lead, examining signs and following some of the more cryptic symbols embedded in them, only looked over his shoulders and Truth could swear she saw him roll his eyes. To him, it would have been obvious but Kirashira's befuddlement did make some logical sense regardless.

The Elite had the sworn duty to protect and defend the rulers of all of the Federation member states when they entered the Shar'Jya system. It was more than a charge but a point of honor, a tradition that had gone on for centuries now. To violate that long standing practice constituted a serious breach of etiquette and trust. As Kirashira had put it in the moments leading up to their arrival on the bridge before, it was a mark against the Federation itself.

"I'm sure they had a good made up reason for pulling the trigger," Tony quipped as he eyed a sign hanging from the roof above. They were getting close to one of the safe areas on the ship now.

"No reason is good enough," Kirashira countered.

"Good or not they are playing for keeps it looks like," Tony replied.

"They have boarded this vessel and likely intend to capture it," Truth explained to Kirashira as the trio traced turn after turn down the corridors. There were few crew in this area, most of them having taken their shelter in the command deck nearby or back at the various duty posts they held during combat, none of those postings included hallways amidships.

"No, No they can't," Kirashira replied.

"Well General Order 12 is already in effect, I think our Captain would disagree with you on that," Tony replied, frustration had crept into his voice.

"No you don't understand," Kirashira stopped following, pausing for a moment. The trio came to a halt and Tony regarded her, apparently what she had hoped for as when he did, she continued speaking, "I won't let them. As far as the law is concerned, this ship is an embassy because I am on it..."

"Well we can't exactly tell them that now can we..." Tony said.

"I can..." Kirashira replied.

Tony eyed her for a moment, "I'm not going to Hil'Raigh jail... Truth and I need to get to our little private armory near here, part of our job in this situation..."

"Then leave me here," Kirashira said with intent, she looked completely conscious of what she was asking.

"And put you in their hands?" Tony quipped, motioning toward nothing in particular and pointing. His arm had gone in the wrong direction if he was intending to point to where the patrol ship had fired from but it was a minor detail. His concern however, was something Truth had not expected as he continued to speak, "I didn't come all this way to let you get put into the hands of people who can't be trusted to guard you Kirashira."

"They are the best guards in the Federation..." She replied.

"And they already shot at you once!" Tony replied, stopping again, "I can't let that happen."

Inside, Truth knew he was wrong. He had to relent, there was no choice. The ship and its crew needed Kirashira's influence on their side and if Truth and her partner took Kirashira on another wild rescue, there would be hell to pay not for them, but for those already being captured.

"Tony," Truth said aloud.

He shook his head, "Not like this... Not after all this..."

"Then follow me..." Kirashira said suddenly, moving closer to Tony than Truth had ever seen her dare, "Escape, then follow me… keep me safe... I know you can…."

The Novian paused, his pride obviously in a battle with his strategic sense. Whatever he chose, Truth planned to go along with it regardless but she had a feeling she already knew what that choice would be. The moment however, the exchange, was something of a new experience for Truth.

In all her life she had never observed a moment in which she felt truer reconciliation had occurred between two who were at odds. Kirashira's expression was one of obvious nervousness. Tony's words had most certainly reminded her of the danger she could face among her own and yet she was asking for that chance. The simpleness of the appeal was one that had unexpectedly shut down any resistance that Truth could have imagined from her partner. She felt a stir of… something, in her heart but was not sure exactly how to understand it really. The moment faded quickly as it came but there was a marked change, a new determination gripped her partner's face and a steel eyed resolve took hold. He looked as he should have, the partner Truth wanted, the one she hoped for every time a challenge arose. He looked like the kind of partner she wanted to be in return and as she looked to him, she felt her own resolve grow in kind. They would succeed, that is what they always did.

"Alright," he finally said, "But only if you let us give you something first…."

"Okay..." Kirashira replied, "What do I need?"

"Do you remember the object the Ambassador for our people used on Ashor, the night of the attack on your family?" Truth questioned.

The royal nodded, a pang of regret coming across her face, "I put it on the window for him..."

"A device like that will help us locate you on the surface…." Truth explained.

Kirashira nodded immediately, managing a small smile, "Good."

"We have some really nice ones in the safe area..." Tony added, leading the way forward.

The trio moved with more urgency than ever, Truth listening with intent, hoping not to hear the footfalls of Hil'Raigh marines but ready to run if she did, they could not afford to be caught out.

Thankfully, the proximity to the safe area was something she had misjudged by a compartment and as Tony brought himself to a pause before an innocuous looking piece of plating on the wall, she knew they had arrived.

She knelt at one end, Tony on the opposite side as they pried their fingertips under the edges. Kirashira looked on as the two found what they were looking for. In moments the plate came free. Behind it was a hole, one leading into the space between decks here, underneath a storage room and above what was probably a maintenance cabinet on the deck below. Space inside would be less than ideal for three, but thankfully, only two had to enter.

Tony slipped inside, Kirashira eying the hole skeptically until the Major shimmied up to the opening again, handing a pair of small rod like devices outward. One was a long range transmitter and one was a universal locater beacon. The larger one would help the Novians locate the Princess on the ground and the smaller would help them find her indoors once they arrived.

"Use the big one to mark your general location..." Truth instructed, "The smaller one is for us to find you in a building..."

"Okay," She replied, "Do I need a window?"

"No," Truth replied, "These are newer than the Ambassador's beacon... Open air for the big one works a bit better though if you can..."

"Okay," She said once more, looking suddenly more nervous.

She set the two down on the deck and for a moment, looked between Tony in the shaft on his belly, and Truth, then she leaned forward. A sudden unexpected embrace locked Truth for a moment as the Princess gave her a squeeze, "Thank you."

Truth nodded, returning the hug lightly before Kirashira pulled back, rubbing her eye clean, "Where do you think I should go to get found quickly..."

Tony vanished back into the tunnel he had poked out of, leaving Truth to give the instruction. By all accounts, it would be easy if the Princess could reach one of the larger corridors. Truth formulated the instructions in her mind and relayed them quickly. A turn here, a turn there, looking for a particular sign, then another turn. Kirashira showed no signs of misunderstanding and stood quickly, jogging at a light pace. She looked back to examine Truth once more before she turned away again and took a corner out of view.

"You coming?" Tony called from inside the safe area proper. It could not have been very large given how his voice sounded coming out of it. Truth reached for the deck plate the two had removed, a pair of handles on the inside, ones that would be easily hidden from view. She slipped her feet into the hole, putting them in first as she took both handles in her grip and slid backward. She squirmed along until the plate connected and, with a rough tug, she heard the latches pop back into place.

A half a meter more and she felt her feet sliding against level ground rather than the inclined tunnel. She slipped out of the tube she'd occupied and moved to a crouch, turning to face the small room.

The cramped interior of the safe room made clear that it was purpose built, placed into an area where it's presence would be hard to notice, at least until those who used it to prepare themselves were long gone. As far as Truth could remember this was one of the only times Hil'Raigh forces had actually boarded a NovaCore ship since the armistice years ago. The safe areas had been someone's brain child, some designer or engineer somewhere with an idea of how to cram some kind of extra redundancy into NovaCore ships. If she and Tony evaded capture today, it would very likely become a sort of staple for all future design in practice rather than just principle.

The most unfortunate part about the safe area was the unavoidable fact that the armory selection inside was rather slim. Most of the gear inside was aimed toward sabotaging critical systems on board the ship to prevent them from falling into enemy hands. Each section would take care of its own under normal circumstances, but when a section failed to accomplish that goal, it fell to the specially trained instead. Thus far however, no extra order for the destruction of systems had yet been given. Truth had a feeling that it was coming regardless though. The Hil'Raigh Military higher ups seemed to have a healthy and thriving interest in exactly how it was the NovaCore ships traveled between star systems. They had themselves, in all of their Hil'Raigh wisdom, apparently never stumbled upon the secrets of Alternate Planar Travel as the NovaCore had so long ago.

The result of that lack of ingenuity, was of course, an endless game of cat and mouse. The Hil'Raigh wanted NovaCore jump drives and it was sure to be one of the first unofficial objectives the boarding Hil'Raigh would have; secure the main drive. In contrast, the NovaCore did everything in their power to prevent the technology from even surviving, let alone being studied, under circumstances like these. While the invaders probably had a good idea of where it was located, they likely were not prepared for the fact that actual access to the drive's compartment was controlled by time locks. The command deck and the drive compartment were both heavily shielded internal structures but the drive compartment itself was built such that even weapons which would conceivably puncture the command deck's thick armor would have trouble denting the drive compartment. The added mass according to designers, was helpful in making the thing work but that was about the extent of Truth's knowledge of the devices.

Their operation was as closely guarded a secret as anything Truth had ever known and the number of people who actually understood the interstellar drives in their entirety was numbered in the thousands back on the NovaCore homeworld. Those few, sequestered into the highest security facilities on the surface, were those on which the NovaCore's reach into the stars rested. Standard procedure therefore, demanded that the sabotage timer on the drive was already in effect and would activate automatically unless canceled. Unless the engineering chief or one of the ship's commanding officers disabled the countdown, the drive would find itself mangled into an unidentifiable state. The rumor had it that accidents in production of the devices had actually given the NovaCore engineers the idea on how to make them sabotage themselves for that purpose, but it was as with most things surrounding the systems, a mystery. Truth guessed that some of the massive armor shell around the drive was probably to protect the crew from such potential failures and that it simply doubled as a convenient protection for the drive itself.

Tony nearby, poured over a digital map of the ship. It indicated the sections which had reported completion of their hostile boarding preparations. An indicator also announced the status of the main computer in its work to purge secured information. Anything not already relayed to High Command was being forwarded via a tunneling signal before it was purged locally. Unfortunately once that process concluded, the jump drive programming software and the communications software that allowed access to the NovaCore signal network would be deleted as well. The powerful main computer would be relegated to the simple job of managing the life support computers and sublight engines, something a group of home computers could probably accomplish.

A snicker escaped her partner as he keyed through the information, "Thorsh ordered a high resolution imaging scan of the surface."

Truth felt herself smile a little, "Making the most of the chance."

"I suppose a ship this close to the planet makes a better scanner than a long range probe poking around the outskirts of the system," Tony replied.

Truth nodded as her partner began keying information into the console he was kneeling at. She moved to the gear lockers along the wall and pressed her fingertip against the keypad on one of them before sliding the door open. The cavity was packed with conceivably useful gear, among which Truth found a familiar sight.

Hanging in the black leather gunbelt at the top of the locker was one of Truth's favorite weapons. She reached to the belt and pulled it from the locker, wrapping it around her waist as she knelt. The heavy, almost unwieldy firearm stored in the side holster dragged against the floor here in the safe area, "They have SD-19's in here."

"Bad news for our friends," Tony quipped.

Siteran Dynamics back home was one of the producers of military weapons for the NovaCore and both Truth and her partner had an affinity for their makes. They specialized in railgun style firearms and the SD-19 was no exception to their tradition of excellence. The long railed weapon was considered to be a sidearm, though the 19 series featured an extending brace for firing with more stability. The non existent stock and the sidearm profile of the weapon meant that unlike rifle style arms, the SD-19's capacitor bank and magazine were one in the same, a single long cylinder that slotted into a place in the rear of the weapon. The unconventional magazine design was part of the draw for most people that liked it. Truth herself loved them because of the fact that when she properly braced them, she could use two at a time.

"Have they located Kirashira?" Truth reminded her partner as she latched the clasp on the belt around her waist, tugging it to make sure it was secure. She reached down to her hip, strapping the front end of the large holster around her leg carefully.

"No idea..." Tony replied. "Might as well check in with the command deck and ask..."

Tony's voice sounded aloud and via radio as he whispered. His voice carried over the communications implant in Truth's ear as well as the air around her, "Command Deck this is Karo, checking in at safe zone Faralae."

Truth glanced up at the plaque from which Tony had read the name. Each zone was named so that the small number of those on board who knew where they were, could identify the location quickly. There was silence in the comm line, probably because that set of words meant that whoever was sitting at the comm station on the bridge had received the communication and was patching the call to one of the senior officers there. At length a familiar voice sounded. Admiral Thorsh's calm tone had not changed despite being boarded but Truth wondered if he was doing his best to make sure of that, "Hello Major, good to hear your voice. Confirm Faralae."

"We split up with Kirashira sir," Tony explained, "She said she wanted to stop them from ransacking the ship... in so many words."

"Affirm Major," Thorsh replied, "I will have someone see if they can pull her up on the internal monitors."

Thorsh paused for a moment then began speaking again, "I have a feeling they ignored Kirashira's message because of our friends that started all of this. She's going to be in trouble soon I'd say. They will try and get her under their control before she can establish herself."

"Felt the same sir, we gave her some beacons."

"Then I guess I don't need to tell you; We have the fate of everyone on board and a lot of people back home riding on you making good," Thorsh stated, adding, "We will take care of the ship up here, I have an indignant Hil'Raigh captain wanting to gloat at us on the line. If Kirashira pulls some strings and I'm sure she will, I might be able to knock the smirk off of his face..."

"Fatal Order sir?"

"Keep Kirashira alive." Thorsh replied, "That is your Fatal Order."

"Understood," Tony replied. Truth stated the same and could almost see Thorsh nodding in her mind. Fatal Order was not a phrase Truth had expected to hear on the current mission but it made sense. In the event that everyone on the ship was captured, interned or killed, or that the ship was scuttled or otherwise destroyed, the assigned Fatal Order was the one task any survivor was to do their utmost to accomplish at any cost. In general, 'Survive, escape and harass the enemy' was the standard Fatal Order, rarely overwritten by any commanding officer. When it was however, it underscored the gravity of concern surrounding a particular objective. Truth remembered hearing stories when she was younger about the people who were of the elite, those who operated under the assumption that every mission was a fatal order. She never imagined she would be one of them.

The order however, felt at least a bit more imposing than it otherwise could have. Kirashira was on her way toward those who should have been ready to protect and defend her. As far as the Shar'Jya Elite were concerned, Truth guessed they would do just that, as their duty demanded. It was once she was out of their direct care, once her own nation's political structure got a hold of her that Truth knew things would change. When that would be however, and how it would happen was anyone's guess at present.

It would be hard to quickly erase Kirashira after she was ferried to the surface. They needed more time to set up a narrative or a story. The Shar'Jya Marines would inevitably see or notice something if she was in their care while any plan was enacted against her. Instead, those looking to remove her from power would have to find a way to get her out of the public eye. It would take connections and a massive amount of political capital to move on such a deal. Kirashira was too dangerous to touch now after so much furor surrounding her parents and so, the pool of potential partners in crime was going to shrink more than it would for any other sort of operation.

"How long do you think it will take to reach a pod?" Tony asked finally, glancing to his partner. She keyed a second locker and began handing him the gear, a gunbelt, a long service trench-coat, some magazines and an armor vest.

Truth thought it over for a moment and shrugged, "Not long, we should get going while there is still likely to be debris floating around in space nearby."

Tony sighed, taking the belt and slipping it around his waist. He nodded however and took the rest of the equipment as it was offered. That would not be long. The burning question remained however, where to land. Anywhere near the metropolis below and a landing pod would be hard to hide.

"Pull up a map of the capitol city," Tony requested, almost as if he had read Truth's mind, "Let's see if we can't find a nature preserve or something to crash into."

"If we could land in a lake that would be best..." Truth stated, pulling up a map in her brain. Of course, topographical maps of Shar'Jya did exist and were publicly available but no high resolution military scans really happened to exist in the databases on board. If they did they would have been in the process of deletion anyway, save the utterly incomplete one ordered by Thorsh. Only the non secure data was going to remain on the computers and so, as Truth trawled through the different options, she settled on some tourism brochures for the capitol sector of Shar'Jya.

If Dau'Kore was a city, then the Federation's primary legislative center was nothing short of a metropolis. Hundreds of millions of people were packed into the urban environment and its surrounding suburbs, things the tourism materials seemed happy to mention. What it did mean at least was that if one reached the city, it would be relatively easy to blend in due to the sheer volume of people present.

"We will also want some surface leads in the city," Truth said as she examined the maps.

"Do we have any informants on the surface?" Tony piped over the radio.

"Not presently," Thorsh replied, "The last ones had to move out because the Imperial Alliance did a rotation. All the Novian face's had to change and we had not put a new one into place in their program yet..."

Truth listened carefully as her mind located a good place, or at least, a reasonable one. Landing there would probably attract attention. A second option presented itself, more direct, likely to cause suspicion in the middle of the city itself and yet, dangerously acceptable. Truth knew little about the exact layout of the city but the tourist materials, maps and public transportation maps painted a picture of a city much like Dau'Kore in construction, if dwarfing it in scale. Unlike the Compact's capitol however, Shar'Jya City was quite literally the coast line of the land mass on which it rested. At some points the construction extended a kilometer or more out to sea on artificial wharfs and building. A wall of tide breakers and weather stop construction appeared on all of the maps just before the point that the continental shelf appeared to dip drastically into the depths. The sea was allowed inland to a series of artificial lakes by canals which appeared to be a point of purposeful design rather than a natural occurrence.

"We could land the pod..." Truth scooted over to the terminal her partner had been using earlier and keyed some strokes on the control pad. A moment later the image she had been viewing in her mind showed up on the screen and she pointed, "Right here."

Tony eyed the screen, raising a brow and saying nothing. His visible skepticism however, prompted Truth to explain, "It is the most central of landing locations."

Tony laughed, "Yeah but it's a lake in the middle of the city..."

Truth shrugged, "And the bottom of the lake is as noted in the tourism brochure, a natural lake bed, made of traditional salt lake silt and sand, hosting natural wildlife native to the coast line."

Her partner looked confused for a moment, eying her critically. She gave a knowing smile and he finally seemed to understand.

"Jumping out of an escape pod before it buries itself a couple meters underwater in the mud..." Tony replied, "Of course that's your plan."

Truth smiled broadly, it was an exciting form of egress. Normally an insertion pod fired a retro rocket to slow itself down before it hit the ground. The slowing was barely enough to make sure the occupants survived. The pods were always mangled beyond repair in any case and so Truth guessed turning the rocket off would let the vessel impact at a far higher speed. If the conical heat shield was never detached, it would allow the pod to slip into the water before hitting the much more rigid lake bed below. Any explosion of energy would be gobbled up by the mass of the lake on top. It was doubly useful in that it would keep the authorities digging for at very least, hours if not days to figure out what had happened. Overall, the distraction it would cause would become useful at letting them escape their own individual landing spots and meet up.

"So we go in late at night so we are hard to see but the red hot pod goes flaming into the lake. We land with the halo kits..." Tony concluded, "I've heard of crazier plans...Jumping out a window in a wing-suit with two people comes to mind..."

"That one worked," Truth said with an educational tone, "And this one is likely to be safer..."

"Safe being a relative term," Tony replied, "Just don't open your chute too late and hit something in the traffic lane..."

"Get hit by something in the traffic lane," She corrected, "Far more likely than us hitting something, and more lethal."

"That gives us what... a couple minutes from breaking atmosphere to choose a location and leap out of the pod before we are too low and crash anyway..."

"Not quite," Truth stated, "We'd have to come in steep to get a good camera shot of the city from above, that gives us about twenty seconds or so to select a landing site and egress. Essentially once the hatch is relatively safe to open... we are going to jump out."

Tony shook his head and smiled a bit, "I hate your plans. What if the hatch sends the thing off course?"

"I'll program the guidance computer to induce a spin just as we are about to jump out. At that speed it should stabilize the pod long enough for it to go where we want but you are welcome to stay here," Truth said with a gentle jab of her partner's midsection, "If you do however, you do not get to complain when I complete the mission alone in that case...or when I mention it every single day for the rest of your life."

"That's true, You'd never let me live it down," Tony replied, "Besides, we are together on this no matter what."

Part of her wondered if the math was wrong and they would have less than twenty seconds. A wind gust here, a missed angle there and there was certainly a recipe for disaster. As her partner nodded however, Truth smiled to herself. He had trusted her, like he always did.

24 - Rescuers

The ship had never felt so foreign, even after her first moments aboard. She had only just begun to be able to navigate the limited area around the guest quarters but that was nothing like here. Of course, the hallway looked the same as it did in other places but the reality of the location nagged. Each time she turned a new corner, dutifully attempting to follow the given directions, she felt increasingly uneasy.

Kirashira had never felt so alone on board the NovaCore vessel as she did now. She kept hoping that Truth or Major Karo would show up and offer a pointer or decide she was best left in their capable hands. Despite that, they didn't come, it was after all, wishful thinking. There was nothing to do now but carry on.

The two devices they had given her, both of the metal tubes, had been a bit of a marvel at first but she wondered now whether examining them as she had walked was why she now felt so lost. She stowed them finally, in the pockets in her robe. The discreet, cavernous pouches allowed them inside easily and they would be entirely invisible from the outside.

Part of her wondered just how much searching or examination would happen after she was recovered by her people. Were they going to examine every centimeter? Even so, the difficulty in hiding the gift's from her friends quickly slid to the forefront of her mind. It was ironic that when confronted with Hil'Raigh boarding the NovaCore ship she was on, that she felt instead like one of those being invaded rather than one being rescued.

The directions had finally run out as Kirashira made one last turn and she could see why she had been led there. It was one of the main hallways. Was it anywhere near the disaster they had dealt with earlier? Even as she recalled the scene, the difficulty breathing, the lack of artificial gravity, she felt sick.

She was certainly going to have a talk with whoever was in charge about that, or have their commission at worst. In their apparent zeal to deal the NovaCore ship a blow, they had indiscriminately torn at least one hole in it, probably more. Who knew how many had died as a result and for what? To rescue Kirashira?

She scoffed. Their rescue efforts had nearly killed her, something she planned to emphasize angrily when she got the chance. It was one thing to interdict a ship and stop it. It was an entirely different one to blow holes in it in order to rescue someone on board.

Kirashira began pacing, the several meter wide main hallway giving her a good view in either direction. Eventually she was greeted by a sea of words. For a moment she was stunned, looking to the source. Who was it rambling at her? It took her a moment to realize that in fact, she was being called to in Hil'Raigh, her own tongue. She had become so used to hearing NovaCore crew passing information back and forth that anything not obviously directed at her had started bouncing off days ago. Instead she was hearing her own language.

The words were a bit stunning regardless. She was not used to being ordered to do anything, by anybody, save maybe her father. No one else had the authority except really, her mother. The latter however had never used that sort of method to get Kirashira to do anything in all the years she'd been alive, preferring instead to manipulate the outcome in other ways. As a result, Kirashira's mind immediately decided to stand firm, to ignore and look annoyed. She did it only for a few seconds and once she realized there were in fact, weapons being pointed at her from several meters down the hall, a mix of fear and outrage swept over her. Surely, whoever was in charge of this operation would hear of these kinds of behaviors.

She finally decided to listen, at least partly. Moving to sit calmly on the floor, rather than lay on the ground. She lowered herself down, legs out to the side and leaning on one hand with what she assumed was an annoyed smirk on her face toward the ringleader of the eager Hil'Raigh rescue team. How many of them were scurrying around the ship right now looking for her? She was not even bothered by the idea of sitting on the metal deck plate if it meant putting a strong face toward even her own rescuers.

The action appeared to have some effect however and eventually, after some obvious radio chatter, Hil'Raigh Marines, clad in the garb of the Shar'Jya Elite, moved around the corner to come to her aid. Some moved past, securing side corridors, calling all clears as they formed a perimeter. Eventually, the Ring leader broke the protective line of bodies loosely placed around the Princess. He, like all of them, wore a dark blue environmental suit.

Body armor plates covered his torso, shoulders, thighs and shins, strapped around him with careful precision. Like his peers, he was clad in a full helmet and probably a personal air supply. He was, of course, ready for anything as was the motto of the Elite. Ready for anything at least except Kirashira.

She looked up at him disdainfully as he approached and when she refused his offered hand as assistance in standing, he shifted uneasily for a moment. His position here meant that like all those serving the Federation's capitol, he was culturally savvy enough to recognize the sleight from his superior. Finally having made a bit of a point, Kirashira stood, on her own, and brushed off her robe, making sure to give him yet another non verbal cue, "I hope you don't plan on pointing your weapons at me again in the future."

The words were filled with just enough of a bite to underscore their seriousness. The marine immediately reached for his helmet and twisted. A momentary hiss followed and he removed it completely, holding it under his arm as he let his rifle hang from his shoulder. He looked to be not more than a few years older than Kirashira herself, but that was about all she could gather from his face alone. Unlike some long term combat veterans, he had no visible scars. It meant that he was too fresh for them or he had simply undergone gene regeneration therapy to get rid of them if he'd had them at all. Given that it was a Shar'Jya posting, Kirashira guessed the latter.

She examined the rank insignia at last, on the neck of the man's suit and it identified him as an Adjunct Commander, one of the middling officers of the Shar'Jya Infantry Corps. He would have a superior nearby, one which was probably on board currently. His ship's captain might also have come, depending on how confident he was that his people would find Kirashira quickly. At last, after securing his helmet, he replied smartly, "My apologies your highness, we wanted to be sure it was really you."

"And you are now satisfied?" She replied.

"More or less," He stated diplomatically, "Standard genetic verification would be appreciated..."

Kirashira sighed and nodded. The Adjunct Commander produced a small phial which she spit into. A moment later he had drawn a device from his belt and inserted the tube of her spit. It only took a few moments, but they were long moments. At last however, the device beeped and showed a light.

"Your Highness," He stated with a nod,"Please, come with us to the secured landing zone."

"You may lead, Adjunct Commander," Kirashira stated, motioning to him with her hand.

A nod and a smart turn of the heel brought the commander to about face. He began moving again, his rifle ready as he led onward. The group of his people herding Kirashira forward in a sort of protective ring of bodies as they moved.

It was official, she was royalty again, not just a guest. She almost immediately missed some of the freedom's her position here on the NovaCore ship had afforded her, the ability to be ignored when she wanted, not by request but simply by being unavailable. Returning to her people meant a return to responsibility, to life, to danger.

The last thought made her a bit sick to her stomach. She immediately caught herself looking at each of those around her, watching for sudden movements. What if one of them was involved with what had happened to her parents? Suddenly, the transmitters in her pockets became all the more important to her. They were more now, than fancy electronics, but lifelines. She decided that she needed them with her at all times no matter who she was with or how safe she felt.

The discomfort continued, a feeling that faded a bit but never completely as she was led down corridors. It took time, how long she had no idea but it felt like an eternity. The world around her gained eventual familiarity however as she began to pick out details of what she knew. Based on her memory, she was nearing the docking bay for the ship, a likely landing location once the vessel had been secured. It did not take long for the infirmary where she had stayed before to come into view. She wondered if the doctor there, the one whose name she had never learned, was okay. Had she been harmed in the boarding?

"How many have your people captured?" Kirashira asked, spurred by curiosity.

"Several Dozen," The Adjunct replied, "We are in the process of securing the ship from stem to stern."

"I want your people to stop," she stated bluntly, remembering the assertion she had made to the NovaCore now. For a moment, her fears subsided and her mind fixated on the new goal.

"You'll have to speak to my superior your Highness, but we are almost there," He replied grimly.

If he was upset by the suggestion he did not show it and only after she was shepherded into the docking bay did Kirashira feel the perimeter of escorts loosen. In fact, it dissolved almost completely. One or two remained, the rest staying at the docking bay door with their comrades while the officer led Kirashira into the space.

She had been here before but it was larger now than she remembered, at least three stories tall. NovaCore ships hung silently from the roof in many places. A few had been damaged or obviously shoved aside by the boarding craft. Among the cleaner pads one shuttle stood in contrast. It was probably that of the commander of the operation. He became clear enough as he turned to face the oncoming royal smartly.

The Adjunct Commander called loudly to him and he quickly dismissed his aides. In a moment more Kirashira's guide stopped, gesturing forward to allow her the rest of the way on her own. Behind the officer, the dull red glow of the NovaCore docking bay's environmental field tinted a view of the starry space.

"Your Highness," the man began.

"Captain," Kirashira replied, "Would you care to tell me why you attempted to murder me with your attack?"

The man looked surprised, genuinely. At length he replied, "I... I had no idea you were targeted your Highness..."

"One of your weapons punctured the ship while I was with my NovaCore escorts..." She continued. She paused for a moment, knowing that if her people were capturing the ship they would try to account for everyone listed on the manifests. She looked as sullen as possible, hoping that clever wording and body language would deceive the officer into thinking that number had decreased by at least two, "They sealed a bulkhead to prevent me from being sucked into space... Something that should not have been needed..."

"I assure you your Highness we had no intention of targeting you or your... escorts.." he replied, "There will be a thorough investigation of which torpedo attack caused the damage I assure you. We will begin at once upon securing the vessel."

"You will stop securing this vessel Captain," Kirashira retorted quickly, mustering any bit of authority her frame could offer, "I order you to cease your boarding action immediately!"

"Your Highness..."

"Now!" she yelled, "Stop this now!"

She saw heads turn out of the corner of her eye and pressed the advantage heatedly, "I declare this ship an Embassy of the Starlight Compact and House Ren'Tauru! Any hostile action against a member of this ship's crew or the ship itself will be seen as an act of aggression against me personally! You will immediately release all detained NovaCore crew and personnel! You will cease all attempts at recovery actions on this ship! You will tow this vessel to a military berth and notify the NovaCore so they can send a repair vessel at once! If you are incapable of understanding that imperative then I will demand your immediate replacement and take your commission before your chain of command! Is that clear?"

The general din of activity that had permeated the bay was gone. A rapt attention focused on the two. Kirashira eyed the man and for an all to brief moment, she felt his defiance waxing. His eyes were strong, he was proud. He was the victor over the NovaCore. Who was this short brat to tell him what to do?

The visible struggle ended almost as quickly as it started however and he nodded at last, looking a bit dejected but obeying nonetheless. Kirashira, of course, had no direct line to anyone in the Shar'Jya chain of military command but she knew that an upset royal would be capable of demolishing one of the Elite's career in military service in perpetuity, if they complained enough.

While there was no official requirement for someone to obey orders from a royal like that, to ignore them outright was seen as a serious breach of etiquette. The only orders that were to be actively refused were those which presented a clear danger to the Federation, a commander's crew or other member states. It was one of the important lessons that Kirashira had learned from her father years ago; taking charge of the guard. The diplomatic angle was of course, a powerful deterrent in and of itself. Kirashira knew her privileges there.

Anyone she wanted to be, could be appointed as an envoy on her behalf. It was entirely her discretion to allow someone to serve in such an ambassadorial capacity for her personal affairs at any time she needed. It was something that most royals did regularly too. There was always a loss of the unseen currency of political capital that seemed to grease the wheels of every chamber of the Federation's cooperative legislation when one over used the privilege, but it was a way of life regardless.

The Princess had decided however, that her father had some of that influence left over and he would want her to leverage it for something useful, seeing as he was no longer around to take advantage of any of it.

At last, the officer made a call on his wrist band. The mood in the bay changed quickly back to business but it was a different kind. The dozens of NovaCore personnel sitting with their hands and ankles bound in groups around the bay were left wondering exactly what had happened but Kirashira felt at very least, like she had repaid some of the hospitality given her before.

"We'd like to ensure all of our teams are recalled and contact is made with the command staff of this ship before releasing any of their crew we've detained," The officer began explaining. Based on what he'd said over the radio, he was likely the captain of one of the patrol ships. At length he added, "For everyone's safety of course..."

Kirashira nodded, making a concession to let the officer win some small victory. She needed to let him have something in return for what she had asked and as long as the requests were innocuous, she would agree, "That's fine."

"I will notify Shar'Jya command of the request for berthing the NovaCore vessel at an appropriate orbital facility. Though I was earlier informed that they unfortunately sabotaged their main drive system upon our boarding. As a result they will require towing. It may take some time," He added.

The NovaCore really were paranoid, Kirashira had to admit. They had already broken their ship? It brought to her recollection one of the strategic briefings she had attended years ago here on Shar'Jya. The Hil'Raigh military had been interested in the NovaCore's interstellar reach, how they seemed impervious to the new hyperspace gate restricting technologies that had been deployed only a year before.

They wanted a NovaCore ship's drive core for that purpose then. Now, it was in their hands, only, apparently sabotaged already. At risk of sounding like a foreign sympathizer with the implication, Kirashira replied, "I had no idea the NovaCore were so desperately protective of their secrets captain."

Being genuinely surprised at the lengths that her hosts would go to hide things made it easy to be genuine in her reply. The officer shrugged, "Eventually perhaps we will find out what makes the ships tick... However, given the circumstance Princess, I must ask if you would grant me the leave to return to my vessel and better coordinate the efforts you've requested. Adjunct Commander Joshim will be able to assist you, given you've already met him."

The Princess nodded and turned to glance toward the Adjunct Commander. He appeared to be paying at least marginal attention. She hoped she had been able to do enough.

***

The landing bay had become a hornets nest soon after the captain had returned to the bridge of his own ship. Kirashira was ushered onto a shuttle and left under assurances, assurances only, that her requests were being honored. She had for no small measure of time since, doubted the veracity of the claims but it had been time to go regardless.

Was it enough? She hoped so. She hoped that her efforts on their behalf had in some small way, saved lives but more than that, she wanted to prove she was trustworthy. Her reputation with the NovaCore she had just left, rested on the backs of the capable Shar'Jya Elite. It was always possible, however unlikely, that she was promptly ignored soon after she was no longer in a position to obstruct anyone's work on the ship.

She had put that concern to rest as much as her racing mind would allow for now however. Instead she was left pacing in the room she had been waiting. Under any normal circumstance, she would have been escorted in pomp and circumstance to the capitol world, vessels becoming the honor guard of her own. Instead, out the view port nearby, she could see a set of tugs laboriously getting the damaged NovaCore ship to speed.

She had learned since her departure from it, just how much the outside had been pock marked by debris. Before she was given the quarters she now occupied, she had overheard some people talking about how some of the torpedoes fired at the thing had been prematurely detonated by the NovaCore defenses, hence some of the more radical markings on the outer hull. The gravity of the breach that had nearly taken her life and that of Truth and Major Karo however, was a bit more humbling than modern art. Even without any kind of instruction in the matter,

Kirashira was immediately aware of exactly where it had happened as her own ship followed alongside the NovaCore one.

A deep pit and a bulge in what looked to be the thick metal plating on the outside of the ship gave way to a more surgical hole near the middle of the damage. It was of course, impossible to make out any exact detail at this distance but Kirashira knew simply by looking at it, that it was the hole which had attempted to suffocate the three of them.

The pit she had felt in her stomach earlier, returned when she wondered just why this weapon did so much damage and all of the others did not. To assume that someone on board the ship had relayed her location however, was something even her current paranoia could not accept. Even so, somehow, she felt like the fear was justified, the fear that even there on the NovaCore vessel, the people who had taken her father and mother away had tried to do the same to her in the easiest way possible, a big misunderstanding.

The loneliness of the space here was something she had to admit to, something she was fighting against in her mind. The ship she had boarded had much the same level of empty space for her to pace in outside, in fact her guest quarters were far larger than the NovaCore had offered. Even so, for all the space, it felt empty. She hated the thoughts she now felt compelled to, wondering just how much normalcy she would ever claw back from all of this. Her life before had been busy, but largely without major concerns such as these. Living every day from this point forward looking over her shoulder was not something she could tolerate. It made her feel exhausted, exploited even.

She turned away from the NovaCore ship, with the same motion trying to mentally move on from her time there. She could not wallow in the safety of the metallic beasts people called starships, not when she had a kingdom to run, not when she had her parents to do justice for. For better or worse, she was here now, on her way to the place she'd asked to go. She reached into her pockets and gave an exploratory feel for the transmitters that Truth and the Major had given her before. They were still there, safe.

Would they actually come if she needed them? She wondered a bit about that since she had left them. They'd already risked quite a bit so she guessed they would try, but what if someone found the transmitters or they didn't work right? What if someone took them away? She shuddered. It made her realize that she needed something more than friends to ever feel confident again. She would need someone like her bodyguard before, Shan'Li.

The name gave her pause. Shan'Li was after all her only true friend before all of this had happened, a bodyguard and confidant that she had always trusted. Of all the people she had left, perhaps Shan'Li was one of the few she could count on, but even so, she needed something more concrete than that. Shan'Li had not been there at the time of the attack, she had been somewhere but not where she was needed. All of this might have been avoided if that were different.

Kirashira did not want to blame her closest friend, her confidant, but what choice did she have? Her mind would not let go. The creeping feeling of distrust had been mounting ever since the brief call she'd been able to make to the bodyguard before. Why did Shan'Li not help her?

Her mind twisted and churned for a moment before she finally came to an inescapable conclusion about all of it. She cared about Shan'Li as much as before certainly, but nothing, not even Shan'Li, no vestige of her former life was enough to offer the security she simply had to have. She needed something new, something self created, self mastered, something of her own making. It was time to move on from the good intentions of her parents in selecting guards, maids or servants, that was her own job now and it had to be for as long as she could envision.

Part of her wished she could simply hire Tony, or Truth for the job. Ridiculous hopes. They were foreign military personnel, not exactly up for hire, and even if they finished their careers, it would be years from now. Kirashira needed trustworthy people sooner rather than later. Where did one find such people?

Shan'Li had been a servant of her mother from birth and when Kirashira was old enough to need a guard, the Kul'Raigh, almost an older sister, had been quickly assigned to her. There was something there, something valuable in that time. Shan'Li knew nothing else and with most royal bodyguards it was the same. The Princess, soon to be queen, could not wait for a fresh face to be born and raised into the life of her guard. It would take at least a decade and a half, a time table that did nothing for the here and now.

For the time being, she would rely on the discretion and hospitality of the Shar'Jya guard, she had little choice in the matter at least until she could build a far more meaningful personal security force once more. After that, perhaps she could try to move past some of the difficulties her mind was mulling over. For the immediate future she had to focus after all, on getting her nation back from the would-be regent Vaerlin.

She had requested a full documenting of political activity by the man and the proposals being made by and to the Compact since her disappearance when she'd arrived on board. It was something she was yet to receive. It left her wondering about how headstrong and wildly brash the man's efforts might have been. She knew he did not waste much time but just how quickly had this all been proposed? Hours after the attack? Days? Kirashira sighed. No amount of nobility would ever truly be able to give her the peace of mind she needed to govern, not with snakes like Vaerlin itching for control of the state the moment a chance appeared. It made him look incredibly guilty.

Unfortunately, any meaningful change to the system of royals and the nobility was likely to meet with near rock solid resistance from those who stood to lose their political influence if things changed. The political landscape of the Federation was their home, the land that provided their bounty. They were never going to support any changes which restricted their access to it. Of all the burdens Kirashira felt she had been saddled with, perhaps the system of government she'd inherited was the one she was most apprehensive about. For now, only time would tell her what she should worry about most.

The gentle chime of the door sounded, breaking Kirashira free of the window through which she was gazing out into the world and she called to the visitor after clearing her throat. She tried to project as much confident authority in her voice as she felt comfortable with. It came out worse than she'd hoped, but passable enough. The door unlocked at her response and her visitor stepped in. Kirashira eyed the entrant carefully, recognizing him as the Adjunct Commander who she had dealt with before. He saluted her smartly and she gave a shallow bow in return, padding barefoot toward where he stood in the entry of the room. That was one thing Kirashira had to admit she was glad to have again, carpeted guest quarters.

The man carried a data pad in his hands and offered it with an explanation, "A relevant compilation of internal political matters as submitted by your government, your Highness."

Kirashira raised a brow, stepped forward and accepted the slate, looking up to the commander. He stood a good quarter meter taller than her at least. After the quick glance, she returned to the pad. A number of entries about regency proceedings filled the slots. The rest were about the most important of functions she had missed. She sighed as she skimmed the titles and then thanked the commander. At last, she set the slate on one of the small tables in the room, "Is that all Commander?"

"That is all your Highness," He replied, saluting smartly. When he did not move, the royal eyed him critically.

She pressed him further, "If you have more to say Adjunct Commander, please tell me what it is."

"I'd like to offer my condolences," He said finally, "On the passing of your parents."

Kirashira nodded and let out her breath slowly as the man continued, "I speak for many when I say, We shed our tears with you, your highness, know you are not alone."

"Thank you Adjunct Commander," Kirashira said, glancing to him and maintaining her composure, it was challenging.

"If I may ask," The Adjunct Commander stated quizzically.

Kirashira looked to him and gave him an unenthusiastic shrug, he accepted the invitation immediately, "Did the NovaCore really treat you well?"

"They saved my life," She replied without hesitation, locking eyes with the man, "And they treated me well. I'm grateful to them."

The words seemed to impact him like a foreign language. He appeared visibly, to process the information for a long moment, then, at last, he nodded and snapped to a smart salute, "Then we are also grateful to them, Princess Ren'Tauru."

With that Kirashira gave him a nod and dismissed him. She turned back to the slate as she heard the door open and began looking through the things presented to her. She moved to the couch and curled comfortably.

"Thank you for the data pad Commander," Kirashira called to the leaving man.

"You are welcome Princess, and, I'm sorry it has to be this way, for everyone's safety," came the reply.

Startled by the proximity of the reply Kirashira looked up to where it had come from only to notice the commander standing at the couch she was sitting on, "What do you think you are doing!?"

She paused, what she had said was not what her mouth had said. She tried again, jumbled. Finally she tried to scream, that too failed her, everything was failing now especially her eyesight. Only now, as she began to slump in her chair, Kirashira realized that the man was holding a medical injector in his gloved hand. It had been on his belt earlier. How long had he been carrying it?

25 - Skyfire

The crawl ways were not as open as Tony remembered them in training, they seemed to be reduced in size on modern ships. Truth led the way, crawling along ahead of him, both of them having gathered kits from the safe area lockers and equipped themselves in as complete a fashion as they could.

Their ship was being towed, and while the official word was that the vessel had been designated as a 'protected zone' it had not stopped the Hil'Raigh from keeping themselves a few squads of marines here or there. They still controlled the docking bay and of course, were not going to be happy at the idea of two of the NovaCore crew poking around as if they were looking for a way down to the planet below. Despite the supposed political protection they'd been granted, Tony knew for certain that Thorsh and the other command staff had still not opened the command deck doors, keeping the entire thing sealed tight. This was of course, despite assurances by the wonderful Hil'Raigh hosts.

Tony rolled his eyes. He wondered what Kirashira had said to the Hil'Raigh forces, but guessed that they were perhaps, being a bit liberal in interpreting her requests. It already seemed like she was a memory. He and Truth had been crawling through the access-ways for what seemed like a half hour or more. They had been at it since before the tugs had arrived and even now that they were attached and hauling.

When they had left the safe area, they had been on the clock to beat the towing. As long as the ship was in the debris field from its own damage, pulling it out was going to be slow and steady. A careful process would ensue but because the heaviest of the damage had come from one side, it was not going to take long to pull the ship free once the tugs got underway. While the debris was not a problem for the NovaCore ship, Tony guessed that the armor fragments blasted free of it's hull would have been problems for any of the non military ships sent to bring them to berth. There would be orbital cleanup crews hunting metal bits for at least a week, maybe more. Unfortunately, the immediate concern was leaving the ship before it was impossible.

Truth wriggled around a turn ahead, padding at a fairly ridiculous pace through the tunnels. At last however, Truth announced over direct radio that they had arrived. She stopped, layed on her stomach ahead and moved forward, sliding up to an access way panel ahead.

The pair went silent, Tony like a rock statue, waiting for his partner's signal. Truth used meticulous care as she threaded her fingertips into the latches on the panel in front of her. One by one, she pried the latches free with a quiet click. The first, a second, a third and at last the fourth came free.

Next, Truth let go and reached for the handles welded to the rear of the panel. She lifted the lightweight panel and set it aside without a sound. She then wormed her way forward more, crawling to the lip of the opening. Carefully, she hung her head through the hole, her hair dangling around her like a mop. She pulled back briskly and nodded to Tony before scooting around the side of the hole. At last she dropped her feet through and followed with the rest of her body, a low thud sounding in the room below as she landed. Tony followed, in moments finding his way around the opening and then dropping down. His feet hit the ground more softly than Truth's own.

The room was dark. Emergency lighting, the kind active at all times, was the only thing online here. Despite the marginal lighting, the corridor was well lit enough to see. The length of the space was a good thirty or so meters, small dots of track lighting on the floor edges to one side. On one side was a solid metal wall, thick armored plating that served to bolster the launch racks. The other side of the corridor was one of similar imposing thickness. Instead of unbroken solid metal however, elongated hexagonal portals, tall enough for Truth to squeeze through standing, lined the wall at regular intervals. Each of them featured a single set of indicator lights, all of which were glowing a faint green. Behind each was a launch pod and the green indicators meant that they were all ready to be used.

The tub of a room underscored how dangerous it really was to have a launch bay for such small craft accessible from the inside of the ship. It presented such a striking structural weakness to meld the inner hull and well protected outer section, that the designers had opted to cover all sides in thicker plating. The result was a cramped, nearly soundproof and uncomfortable interior.

Truth moved to one of the doors and keyed it with haste. The door responded without question or fanfare, though some sort of alarm bell was certain to be ringing on the bridge about the pod being accessed. The portal popped as the atmospheric seal was disengaged, and then, the lighting in the pod kicked on. The interior was well lit, washed out and lacking in comfort. The dull gray of the paneling inside underscored not the effort for comfort, but the aim to make each pod effectual. Truth slipped inside, contorting herself like a sort of gymnast to get over the flight seat in the doorway and move to her own.

At last, she slid into her seat, reaching up to the control panel in front of her. In total, she had about thirty centimeters of headroom between herself and the panel she worked with. Tony followed her in, moving to the seat she had passed over, folding out the cushion and settling in. He reached to either side of himself and took the six point harness, joining it in over his chest like Truth had done.

"All Clear?" Truth inquired, her finger hovering over an ominous looking red button.

"All my limbs are inside..." Tony said, thinking aloud. He began checking to make sure he did in fact have all of his limbs and clothing inside the pod. Once he confirmed it, he finalized, "Clear."

"Sealing," Truth responded, tapping the button. The hatch shut with violent speed as a loud, uncomfortably deafening siren sounded in the cabin. A computerized voice indicated that the pod was in fact, pressurized and ready for launch.

"Programming for lazy launch," Truth announced, a few more keystrokes following. Tony sighed and leaned back in his seat as Truth worked. A lazy launch at least, would be far less violent than the norm. Of course, pretending to be a piece of debris meant that the pair would be floating aimlessly in space, tumbling in weightlessness while the tugs and their mothership moved on, carrying the NovaCore vessel as their prize.

"Ready when you are Captain," Tony said at last. Truth nodded and reached up for a final sequence. At last her button presses took away the artificial gravity. Tony felt his body lose its weight and glanced over to Truth, whose hair was now following her head around like lost ribbon in a stagnant wind. How she managed with it, he didn't know but she was not slowed down in the slightest. A moment more and he felt a gentle churning as the pod was spun, the only visible indicator of the motion being the artificial attitude display ahead of him.

"Launch in three," Truth announced. Tony counted off the seconds in his mind as Truth held onto her harness. With a sudden jolt, the pod shuddered and Tony felt shoved into his seat for a moment. The pop was enough to shake the entire cabin, but not violent enough to cause much in the way of discomfort, unless one startled easily at least.

The normal anticipation, an intense, aggressive acceleration that followed the main escape motor firing never came. Instead, Tony was left with instrument panels to see what was going on. That was for most, the hardest part of it all, relying completely on instruments. The pods had only minuscule windows for structural purposes, making the entire affair of entering one, an eerie and unpleasant experience for those not versed in it.

Indeed, there were some crew who had to be assigned to duty stations near the larger pods or escape shuttles because they were mentally unfit for the claustrophobia induced by the two seat variety. As a matter of course, the two seat models were the most durable of them all. It was always a trade.

Tony drew in a long breath, closing his eyes for a moment, acclimating to an environment where gravity was no longer felt. Truth was doing the same, something Tony could hear. The exercise helped most people acclimate more readily. After a moment he opened his eyes glancing to an ominous red handle on the hatch he had come through to enter, "I hope the override latches work."

"Indeed," Truth replied. As she did there was a click from somewhere in the cabin. The air recycler kicked in a moment later, a low hum filling the space now.

"Do we have any comms?"

"Not until we are clear of the tugs," Truth replied, "We will drift clear of the debris field in... seven hours."

"Just keep the tumbling to a minimum would you?" Tony replied sighing, "What do you think is going to happen when the dust settles?"

"I.. suppose we will go home." She replied, choosing her words with care.

Tony smirked and shook his head,"Always a realist."

Truth smiled despite herself, looking momentarily sheepish, "Sorry."

Eventually however she spoke again, "I have not been afraid in years Tony. But, I think I am now."

Tony nodded and eyed his partner directly, wondering why she felt as she did. To him the mission was grim, but not something to fear.

"Why's that?"

"I do not want to lose a friend..." She said turning to face the control panel ahead of her, looking sullen.

Tony huffed and shook his head, leaning against his headrest. Either Truth was insane, or she was still so childlike in her own way, that she was impossible to refute. Some part of the terminally ill little girl that had been stuck in those hospital rooms was always going to be alive in her. No amount of implants or computer coprocessors would be able to erase it.

When he was sad or annoyed, it was easy to deal with, but when something had touched Truth like the current situation, it was hard for him to feel anything but care. He felt his own youth well up, the care for Truth he felt, the kind he had hidden behind immature bravado years before.

"We won't lose her, I promise," He said at last, committed in his heart to the very same. Truth gave him a thankful smile and leaned back in her chair, closing her eyes. Tony was left for the moment. He reached to his wrist and set his watch to wake him soon. He then looked to the instrument panel above, ensuring that it was not showing any alerts as he leaned back against his own cushion.

***

The cabin was churning as Tony opened his eyes. It took a moment for his brain to realize that it was not the cabin, but the entire ship that was lazily rotating even now. Truth was carefully clicking away at a keypad in front of herself, "Anything good?"

"I have been trying to use the public records system to find out if there are any organizations on the surface that I could cross reference with some of the data we recovered in the communications brokerage," Truth explained.

"Any luck?"

"Some," She replied. Tony's display flickered and changed visuals as she sent his screen the same image. A short list of names appeared on the screen, only one of which was a private individual, the other four were corporations.

"All affiliated?"

"Yes but only some of them have industrial space," Truth replied.

"Because it's easier to hide things, and people, in them.." Tony said grimly.

"Exactly."

"Well lets cross reference some of the properties, see if we can tie any..." Tony trailed off as he watched his partner. She had broken away from the topic at hand, a blinking light on the control panel catching her attention.

"Problem?"

"I set this pod to accept the emergency transponder beacon signal from Kirashira," Truth replied.

"Wait... already?"

"Apparently,"

"Where?"

"Moving," Truth stated grimly," I cannot get a good fix because of the speed... It will not cross reference either because we do not have a satellite constellation deployed."

"Are we clear to burn?" Tony asked.

Truth nodded, reaching up to key the pad again, "We might have to cancel our water landing..."

"The trash didn't waste much time did it?"

"Understandable, if she got to the public it would have been problematic for them," Truth replied, "I am going to set us in."

"Wait, we need to know where she's being taken," Tony replied.

"The beacon may be discovered before then..."

"If we find out where... We can use the pod as a projectile." Tony stated calmly.

"That runs the risk of harming Kirashira," Truth objected.

"There!" Tony frantically pointed at the map screen Truth had put on the displays. The transponder signal appeared to have stopped moving.

"Getting the floor plan..." Truth replied with a frantic excitement in her voice.

Tony tensed unhappily as he waited. Truth clicking away with a furious intensity on the computer console she was manipulating. This was the kind of situation he hated most, waiting to take action when he knew time was against them both. They had to land the pod as close to the target location as they could, and from the map he had seen, the original landing location or any safe water body landing was going to be impossible.

"The complex is two square kilometers, owned by a Hydroponics and Agricultural processing company," Truth announced.

"On the list?"

"Yes on the list..."

At very least the prior research had been accurate enough to catch something related.

"Several stories above and below ground, regular transportation traffic, mostly automated."

"Any good hardened places?"

"Surplus freezers and store rooms in the lower levels. Most of them will be empty because the shipping season just finished."

"Alright, give me a map," Tony requested, the adrenaline in his veins elevating his voice. The map came up even as he felt the pod shifting.

"I am setting us in for burn. If I can I am going to land on a grain loader, it should be a good diversion..." Truth explained.

"By land on you mean..."

"Projectile, yes," Truth replied.

"Buy some stock in their competitors first..." Tony replied, heavy sarcasm permeating his voice as he began examining the map of the complex. The two dimensional screen did far less to explain the geometry of the place than a three dimensional hologram. Thankfully at least, the screen could display a facsimile of the spatial model with enough clarity that he could get an idea of what Truth was talking about.

The freezers became obvious in moments, buried in the basement where they would be least affected by external temperature changes. There were only a few of them that looked secure enough to control traffic in a regulated way and Tony immediately began comparing them against the locations of landing pads. The most secure freezer, closest to a landing pad was the right guess, he was sure of it.

Even as he started looking, he knew that the fine point beacon they had given to Kirashira would be less effective underground. It would have reduced range and potency or worse.

At last, Tony found on the map, what would have been his own first choice for a secure location at the facility. It was two floors below the surface with only two accessible entry ways. From the look of the blueprints, it appeared that it would be easy to cover both entrances and set up cross fire or defensive zones at regular intervals on the way to the freezers. With Truth's further assertion that the place would be near empty, the spot on the map solidified itself as the best candidate, "Think I found us a likely location."

Truth nodded and continued with her own work, likely punching in a landing vector. The assumption was confirmed as she spoke aloud once more, "Descent path confirmed, we will have some time for a couple corrective burns at high altitude. I set the landing location as one of the larger grain loading docks."

"Fire it up," Tony replied, glancing to his partner.

She nodded and reached up to the control panel again, "Roll Action."

Tony felt his stomach doing gymnastics while the rest of his body tried to catch up, a jolt one direction, then on a different axis. The process occurred several more times and then a set of shudders from thrusters on all sides brought the craft to a lazy motionlessness in space. The gentle rotation had finally stopped, the feeling on his organs subsiding.

"Entry Burn in Five, Four, Three, Two, One," Truth tapped a button on the controls and quickly recoiled to her harness straps. She clenched her eyes as the pod was rocked by the primer explosive firing. The sudden burst of energy blew through the craft, throwing both passengers into the bottoms of their seats with a violent thunder. In immediate followup, the main engine fired and Tony felt his body struggling against the aggressive acceleration. Without a pilot suit, even his enhanced body struggled against the rush of blood out of his upper extremities and he felt himself go lightheaded. The instrument panel was a blur, impossible to see with such power being expended from the pod's engine system.

"Thrust to maximum," Truth managed even as the acceleration on Tony's frame reached an overwhelming level. He felt like he was going to be squished through the cover on his seat like some kind of extruded cheese. The world began to fade as the numbers on the speed indicator for the pod relative to the planet below rolled rapidly upward. It was not that every pod was supposed to re-enter the atmosphere at such unsafe speeds, more that Truth had programmed the thing to such a thin margin that they'd be lucky to have any heat shield left by the time they came through the atmosphere.

Suddenly the engine cut, Tony thrown for a second into his shoulder straps. There was a moments respite and he huffed, the sound of the air recycler the only sound between he and his partner's breath. Even as he considered talking however, making a joke of some kind to lighten the mood, He looked over at his partner and she still had her eyes closed, breathing at a regular rhythm.

The expression on her face told him just how little margin she must have given them both and he was at once, nervous. Rather than say anything to that effect however, he simply settled into his seat. He wondered if it would be all that painful to have a pod like this burn up on re-entry. He did not get much time to contemplate it however as a new set of tremors rocked the cabin. The ship rolled suddenly, an automated precision roll just in time to point the engine compartment toward the planet. A series of thuds sounded as the heat shield closed around the engine nozzle.

A simple alarm underscored the fact that the front end of the pod was soon to be a blazing fireball hotter than a plasma torpedo as it burned through Shar'Jya's atmosphere. It would be flying at a pace that would make most test pilots blush with inadequacy, one well beyond documented norms or safety margins. The deafening, throaty sound of the engine firing before, paled in comparison to the crescendo of fire licking around the vessel. A simple glance to one of the tiny cabin windows on the side showed Tony all he needed to see, the fire licked past the window tentatively at first, then more vigorously until the whipping lines broke into a blazing white heat so intense he had to look away. He tried to shout something, but the shuddering cabin and its raucous sound drowned out even the sound in his head, driving the words from his mind as quickly as they'd come. He only managed a nervous laugh instead.

The fiery descent, something that normally could take minutes, was passing at a pace that Tony could only guess at. The shaking continued, on and on as his seat bottom threatened to carry him through the roof or turn him into a pancake. He was not sure which.

He stole a glance at the speed indicator above, even as the numbers blurred. As quickly as the numbers had been rolling up before, they rolled down almost as fast now, but the speed was ramping quickly, something he felt in his body as the force of acceleration. A helpful, if ominous two dimensional depiction of the craft in a dedicated panel above, showed the heat shield section, flashing a brilliant red.

A series of indicators revealed the remaining ablative thickness of each of the six protective panels that had enshrouded the craft's engine. Tony watched the decimal points tick away as the craft melted through the sky of the alien world below. The shaking began to slow as the thicker atmosphere damped the movement of the pod, bringing a noticeable pressure on his internals.

The computer happily announced that atmospheric penetration had been successful. Control surfaces were deployed a moment later and Tony looked out the window once more. The dark night sky of Shar'Jya stretched away into the horizon. In glide now, with control surfaces, the ride was quite smooth despite the speed. The heat shield was likely still bright as a plasma torch in the sky but was no longer melting, at least according to the instrument panel.

Truth's eyes snapped open a moment after the automated message and she was already working once again. It was a moment or two more before the landing camera feed blinked to life on the multifunction screen in front of Tony, telemetry data overlayed on the video image. The ominous looking counter in the top right corner of the scene could only be one thing and it counted down into the double digits now.

Tony watched as the craft made minute course corrections, one after the other, the landing point dot flitting on the screen with each. The infrared camera did a good job despite the night however, of providing a good view of the facility to which they were headed. The blueprints did not do justice to the place at first, but at length Tony managed to pick out the pad he had decided would be the likely landing location for Kirashira's abductors.

His instinct proved at least partly correct, a transport shuttle appeared to be resting on the pad there.

"I see a ship, probably theirs," Tony called to Truth, reaching up to focus his camera view on the shuttle location. He quickly ordered the computer to give him the coordinates and it chortled happily. He held up his wrist computer and the device beeped after downloading the information.

"Landing data up."

Truth nodded and began programming the ejection sequence into the computer as she spoke, "Check HALO."

Tony punched a button on his side of the panel, the computer began running a check on the parachute pack built into his seat, at last it showed green, "Green. Check HALO."

"Green!" Truth yelled back, taking a deep breath. She looked over to him and nodded, an unspoken promise exchanged between the two, "Ready Egress."

"Go."

Truth reached to a lever between the two seats and tugged. A loud buzzer sounded and Tony reached for his own to jump start the ejection, tugging it.

He could swear he never managed to pull the thing the full way but by the time he understood where he was, he was no longer in the cabin of the drop pod. A shower of safety batting flew past him as he was rolled and thrashed around by his seat. He cursed to himself as, once the seat was righted, he heard an insistent computerized voice in his ear, over and over asking him to cut the seat or automatic landing procedures would be initiated instead.

He had done HALO drops before, and even ejected for practice, but he only realized he had a cut on his arm as he looked down to the side of his ejector seat to verify he was clear of the pod. The tumbling world had largely begun to settle as he grabbed the release handle. Even so, the constant spinning he'd endured as a would be piece of space debris still weighed on his senses. The bare bones frame of an ejector seat fell away from his body a moment later, causing him to swear again as it fell from beneath him, pulled out from under his body by the small drogue chute on-board.

He was now left tumbling forward in free fall. Landing telemetry appeared mercifully from his ocular implant and he used his limbs to direct his body onto the vector recommended by the information he saw. Even as he angled in, he heard Truth announce her clearance from her own ejector seat over the radio. He responded with the same, feeling an intense relief to be in control of himself once more, but especially knowing that his partner had survived.

So preoccupied with landing, Tony had barely noticed the now ravaged drop pod tumbling away at breakneck speed below. It was still smoking, glowing with intense heat as it plummeted toward the ground exactly where it had been asked to land. Under normal circumstances the pod would open its heat shield and fire the engine to slow and land safely. Because Truth had overridden the safe landing in favor of ejection, this pod was instead, doomed to serve as a destructive and violent distraction for anyone in the complex.

Tony felt a bit of gratitude as he watched the abandoned vessel fall to the ground below, The on board computer struggled and, with the help of the aerodynamic shape, got it under control at last. He was struck in that moment by the inanimate object that had conveyed them here and despite the fact that it was a mass produced piece of machinery present on every NovaCore ship, he whispered a sort of gratitude to it.

There was just enough time to watch it career nearly on point, into the broad landing pad that the automated grain barges used for picking up new shipments. The initial impact was catastrophic and a violent explosion appeared, a visible shockwave expanding through the air around the chaos as the pod became a hefty battering ram.

The harvester nearest the landing pad was tossed into the air, listing lazily as it's partially filled grain hold caused it to easily imbalance. Tony watched with rapt fascination, even as the sound finally reached him, the destruction playing out like a concert below. One harvester careened into another, which crumpled helplessly amid the gouts of hellfire unleashed by the impacting drop pod. Tony guessed in his head, just how much monetary damage they had caused and smirked to himself, unable to fully contain his childlike glee at seeing such heavy machinery tossed around like toys during a tantrum.

His attention returned however to his descent and in seconds more, he reached to the cord on his harness and pulled it with all his strength. He was immediately slowed, strung, feeling like the hand of heaven had reached down and plucked him from his downward path. Of course, he had continued falling the entire time, but the sudden change in speed from the parachute sliding out of its pack on his backside, made him feel all the more grateful.

His speed was high still and so he reached above himself to tug the controls, flaring quickly to bleed it away. Coming in at night with a parachute was not something he had done often, usually using a wing suit or something fancier for night operations. His enhanced vision however, gave him a good idea of where he could land and how clear it was. As long as he and Truth could land without being immediately seen, it would give them an advantage.

As Tony drifted ever closer to the facility he heard the sounds of the fire alarms from below, echoing into the air. From up high it had been so small looking but as he neared the ground, he realized just how expansive the place really was. Fuel explosions were uncommon in modern automated transporters like the ones landed here, and so, the cause of the danger wrought by the landing pod's impact would probably give any astute individual a good idea that something was amiss. Tony was however, counting on apathy as he found an open space behind a building next to the landing pad he had been trying to get to. He flared again, turning tight and directing himself inward. He lifted his legs up as if to sit and descended with practiced finesse until he felt his feet touch ground.

With mechanical efficiency, he reached across his chest and unbuckled his harness even as he rolled the impact off. He was out of his roll and crouching even before his chute hit the ground, the lazy, now empty harness carried forward several more meters before the chute itself came to rest on the dirt.

"On the ground," He radioed, drawing the weapon Truth had given him earlier from its elongated holster and gripped it carefully in his hands as he moved from the open ground to the wall of the building nearby. He was pleasantly surprised as Truth touched down in the same space, meters from where he had. Her landing was cut short as, when she was meter or so from the ground, she released her harness and tumbled forward, rolling into a ball, getting to her feet and heading to him at the wall.

"Plated bones are cheaters bones," Tony said to her with a smile as she reached the wall and drew her weapon.

"And you will never break them," She replied. With that she was probing the corner and, once satisfied, slipped around it with her weapon high and ready. Tony followed, back-stepping around to keep his eyes to the rear as she led onward. If it were anyone else leading the way, Tony would have been unable to keep much of his attention on the rear quarter but with Truth, he trusted completely. Especially now when it really counted, he knew that with Truth leading, there was nothing to fear. Only as they stopped moving did he steal a glance back over his shoulder.

The landing pad ahead was raised on a bed of support structure, at least three quarters of a meter tall underneath. Fueling equipment and electrical generator connections dotted the underside of the structure but Truth led them both under, on their way to the door Tony had earlier designated as an entry point.

"Two," Truth announced over the radio.

Tony focused forward, quickly identifying two armed guards as they looked on toward the fire in the distance. A quick perimeter scan showed no more obvious signs of enemy activity, at least, not that were watching the two men by the staircase ahead.

"I'm right," Tony announced.

"Left," Truth replied, "Same uniforms as the Guild Hall,"

Tony took a knee, aiming his weapon just above the neck protector of his target before pulling the trigger.

The ever quiet firearm gave a single sharp crack as the projectile was expelled and buried itself in the target. Truth's own trigger pull sounded almost in the same instant. Both of the Hil'Raigh before them fell forward, lifeless.

Tony approached his kill, immediately taking his ankles and pulling him backward into the shadowy confines of the landing pad's underbelly.

"They have gloves and visors on, security is probably based on key cards or something rather than biometric," Tony said, disarming the hostile. He reached down and examined the carbine the man was carrying. A high fire rate, low signature weapon. Definitely military grade and designed for discreet operations. Tony took the downed Hil'Raigh's weapon and looked it over. He did not want to risk it exploding in his hand due to lack of authentication. While most of them would simply refuse to fire, there was no telling with black market finds. Almost as soon as he had looked over the grip however, he noticed the usual identification interface upon it.

"Found an ident-patch," Truth said as she stripped her target's glove off. A small bump on the back of it showed where the identification came from.

"Black market guns with the identification removed but they kept the user tags," Tony said, tossing the useless weapon aside.

Tony and his partner moved out from the safety of their location and headed to the staircase the men had been hovering around. Dug into the ground at its bottom was a single door. It was a thick metallic portal with no visible handle. A simple keypad on the side of the door frame underscored the industrial nature of the building it allowed access to. With a concrete stairwell descending several meters into the ground ahead, Tony was sure now of the path he had charted to reach the underground.

Tony moved first, sliding into the stairwell enough to poke his head above the lip of it and cover his partner as she scurried in a low crouch, across the meters of open space and descended the stairs with rapid precision.

Taking the stolen glove in her hand, she put the back of the it against the keypad and it blinked in acceptance, not realizing it was instead allowing access to intruders. Upon hearing the door crack, Tony turned fully from the world above, taking the stairs two at a time until he reached the threshold and entered the corridor behind. Individually, he and Truth were a force to be reckoned with. Together however, he knew there was nothing that could stand in their way.

26 - Trapped

Kirashira teetered exhaustedly and slumped to the side, collapsing against the wall again. Her head was pounding as if someone had installed an automatic hammer in her skull. She took a deep breath and regained her footing, shuddering in the cold of the room as she moved toward the door. The fuzzy outline of the portal wavered in her eyes and as she stumbled forward, she felt sick. Her stomach threatened her as she finally closed one eye, her breathing ragged and uneven.

She reached out to the door handle, missing, then trying again, felt the cold metal in her hand. She tugged hard and it didn't budge. She whimpered and shook the handle angrily. Still the door resisted. The anger turned to desperation as she thrashed the handle with all the strength she could muster. She bashed the door with her hand helplessly, pounding against it and shouting. Why she shouted, she didn't know, but she did.

Her palm was raw now, from being smashed against the door, it throbbed almost as much as her head. She felt a wave of nausea and slumped forward against the door, hanging from the handle. At last she collapsed to her knees in front of it and crumpled forward in agony. She was still bleeding from somewhere on her head, whatever had hit her earlier had not been kind. As she tried to cry, she felt herself give a dry heave instead, bile rising in her stomach.

She remembered waking up before, waking up and seeing Shan'Li, her servant. Those were the only two in the room. She had asked her servant what was going on and the Kul'Raigh had simply asked her to calm down, as if that were possible. Even as she tried to remember, she knew that she had some sort of concussion. She tried to speak aloud, and thankfully, her words came out.

The words she spoke were of no comfort, the affectionate name her mother had given to her father years ago. It was what she and her mother had called the man when they wanted to show their trust and care for him. It was the most intimate address a daughter could have for their parent. It was the Kul'Raigh tradition to shorten the name and put the intimate suffix on the end of it for those closest to one's self. Despite the age old invocations, the spiritual feelings about how such a caring utterance brought comfort, rang hollow now.

She repeated the words and sobbed quietly in the unknown place, wondering at what moment her true end would come. Shan'Li had asked her to just let them have what they wanted and promised that they'd let her go. Kirashira felt the rage she'd felt earlier at the betrayal boil up in her heart. She could still remember what it felt like springing from the bed and screeching at her servant with the shattered heart of a broken friend. The scuffle had been brief, a princess was not near as strong or as well trained as her bodyguard was.

Kirashira was pulled from her momentary memory, her anguish paused as utter fear crept into her body. The sound of the door handle clicking was enough to send her scurrying from the door to the far side of the sterile room. Was it a storage room? Whatever it was it had no place to hide.

The latch sounded and the door slid open unceremoniously. One body, two bodies. Kirashira closed her left eye again, fighting against the double vision as she leaned against a support column and eyed the entrants. Both were familiar, only one issuing the sense of dread in her heart.

The nobleman from the two entrants immediately looked disgusted and gave a curt barb to his cohort, "By the Stars, You are an animal Tamur!"

The other man shrugged, "She was very uncooperative Vaerlin."

The nobleman scurried forward, his fanciful garb rustling around him as he approached. Kirashira almost sprung from her place to move but was stuck there, fear overtaking her as she clung, white knuckled to the few places her fingers had found purchase on the support before her.

Rather than lash out to strike her, the man pulled his sash off and offered it to Kirashira, shooting an angry glance at the man he'd called Tamur.

Kirashira timidly accepted the sash before reaching out and putting it immediately against the place on her head she remembered finding blood earlier. Her hair was matted with the stuff there and she felt sickened as the texture contacted her fingers. She whimpered timidly as the reality of it all came rushing back, her lip quivering and her eyes filling with tears as she eyed the Duke.

"Princess..." The man said. He reached out but Kirashira recoiled like a sprung snake.

"You traitor," She said icily.

"Princess please, this is not the time..." He replied.

The anger she had felt before was nothing compared to now. If she'd have been given a weapon, the man before her would have been fighting for his life already.

"I need your cooperation Princess, for everyone's benefit. I want to resolve this so we can all go home..."

"You robbed me of mine!" She screamed with bitter contempt, her fathers bloodied face in her mind as she stared down the man, "You are never going home Vaerlin!"

Tamur, the man who'd struck her earlier, causing the head wound in the first place, gave a laugh as he heard the outburst. He moved to the one piece of furniture in the room, a chair Kirashira had tried to throw at the door earlier. It had done nothing, she had collapsed doing so and the chair was undamaged. He flipped the chair to a usable position, turning it backward and sat in it, straddling the chair back to rest his arms on it.

"Kirashira, Do not think I am a monster," Vaerlin said. His words rang hollow, "I'm not like them, I assure you."

"Then why did you kill my parents!"

"I didn't Kirashira!" He retorted, with such force that it sounded genuine, "By the Stars I would never have killed your father!"

"Then why is he dead?" Kirashira sobbed.

"They were going to do it anyway!" Vaerlin replied with what appeared to be his version of righteous indignation, "I never asked them to!"

"Why should I believe you?" She spat back, lowering herself to the floor and turning away as she nursed her wound. Yelling made her head hurt even more. The sobbing and crying did nothing to help her either. Kirashira glanced to Tamur who gave no visible indication as to the truthfulness of Vaerlin's words.

"My parents didn't do anything Vaerlin," Kirashira said at last, "Why would you help them?"

"Nothing?" Vaerlin began to pace, scoffing aloud, "I assure you, your father was doing far more than nothing to me!"

Kirashira eyed the man and felt dumbfounded. She knew about the council seat, but would the nobleman really have done this, cooperated over that single seat? It was unreal, an impossible reality.

He continued, now ranting. "Your father promised to destroy everything I had worked for! My life's work, all my accomplishments!"

"My father was rotating you through the council, almost every noble gets rotated at least once..."

"Rotated!" Vaerlin laughed, "Rotated you call it! What a euphemism! Your father wanted to ruin me and everyone like me. He wanted the throne to have all of the power. Return power to the crown, that was his motto and it endangered the fabric of the Federation."

The man turned and pointed accusingly, "No Kirashira, your father did more than nothing, he created a climate that made him an enemy to too many!"

Tamur snickered from across the room and interjected, his unwelcome voice sounding easily in the small room, "Don't be so naive Vaerlin, he only made one wrong enemy, not a bunch of them. If you are going to pretend to be honest with the Princess, at least be consistent..."

The merc stood and took a few steps toward the pair, "You are such an innocent little collateral damage Princess, you really just have no idea do you?"

"Vaerlin here wanted to be in charge, he asked us for help in making it happen," He said with a smirk.

"That's not true! Your man solicited me! Outside the council Chambers!" Vaerlin replied.

"You are the one who asked for Shiyara as a prize Vaerlin, Not me." Tamur replied.

"What are you trying to do!" Vaerlin snarled curling his fists angrily, turning to face the other man.

"Just being honest, since we are all being honest now," Tamur replied, shrugging. He was a good thirty centimeters taller than Vaerlin was and his broad muscular frame betrayed his obvious advantage over the smaller nobleman.

"You are free to leave!" Vaerlin angrily gestured toward the door.

Tamur smirked and walked back to his chair instead, sitting again.

Kirashira however, was in disbelief as the argument between the two had mentioned her mother.

"My mother is alive?" She asked with sudden clarity, not caring who answered.

Vaerlin sighed and turned. Tamur just shrugged in response.

"Tell me!" Kirashira insisted, "What have you done to her?"

"She's fine!" Vaerlin retorted in a sharp, defensive tone.

"For now," Tamur added from his part of the room. Kirashira already hated the man.

"I did not think you'd cooperate..." Vaerlin began, "So we decided to spare your mother..."

"Cooperate?" Kirashira replied, disgusted, "With your regency bid you mean..."

"The Compact needs a course correction Kirashira," he continued, "It's not just for me..."

"You are going to try and force me to do what you want because you have my mother..."

"I'd appreciate your cooperation," Vaerlin replied with a diplomatic and corrective tone, "Your mother just helps facilitate that."

"Let me see her," Kirashira replied.

"She's not here," Vaerlin stated, he began pacing once more. He would wear a hole in the metal floor by the time this ended.

"Then I have nothing more to say to you..." Kirashira replied.

Vaerlin sighed loudly and worked his fingers, clenching and uncurling his hands. Tamur however, piped up at last, "I told you she wasn't going to cooperate, should have just shot her and dealt with the aftermath of it at that point."

"No!" Vaerlin replied, "I don't need you killing more of the royal family! The servant was bad enough today!"

Kirashira shuddered, she didn't remember what had happened, she had not seen it. She had heard a shot but that was all.

"She tried to plant a transmitter on the shuttle Vaerlin, don't be willfully ignorant," Tamur replied dismissively.

"You didn't have to leave her there," Vaerlin responded in disgust.

Tamur shrugged again, "I'm not sure what you want me to do about your moral problems with all this Vaerlin. It's always been a dirty business."

"Maybe it wouldn't be so dirty if people like you, let people like me take care of things," Vaerlin retorted.

"You wanted a throne, you got one. We've been over this. You can either get the princess to agree and put this to rest for now, until you inevitably have her killed, or you can put her down right now and we can move on."

"Kirashira, I promise you, I have no intention of harming you, or your mother, you need to do what is best for yourself and your people. Your mother needs you too and I promise you will be able to see her as soon as we can make a deal..." the Duke assured brazenly. Kirashira almost spat at him, but the idea of her mother, probably locked up somewhere worse than this, enduring what? Only the stars knew.

The young monarch's mind raced as she wished her mother to safety. She knew it meant nothing though, none of her wishes came true anymore, not a single one of them. Was she really willing to let her mother be lost forever over this? It was a set of words on a page in history. Did it really matter whose name those words were?

She looked at Vaerlin, then Tamur. The latter's accusations however, poisoned her well of goodwill. She could not help but believe that somehow, the cynical man was right. When things had settled, why not get rid of Kirashira and her mother both? Who was to say that Vaerlin would ever let her have her mother back anyway.

Perhaps he would keep her out of reach, taunting Kirashira as long as she lived to keep her under his thumb. Even so, the options were clear. She would bargain for her mother's life and her own or she would be killed. She would likely be killed anyway at some point but there was always a chance she lived if she waited for it to come later.

She felt angry, helpless and most of all, alone. This was the kind of time she wanted her parents at her side, something she would never have again. Her throbbing head, her broken body, her pain, both physical and spiritual, it was all hers to bear and hers alone.

Even as she sat, waiting, dazed and unable to decide on anything. She knew she was being presented with an offer to capitulate and potentially live, or be killed now anyway. She looked up at Vaerlin even as Tamur reached to his ear and looked concerned. He quickly stood, shoving the chair out from under himself and moved to the door with haste. The door slammed closed behind him and Kirashira heard it lock noisily.

"So you're going to kill me anyway?" She asked at last, looking up to the man before her, "After all the talk about how you didn't want to do any of this violence?"

"Kirashira..." He sighed, "They won't let you live, I've tried reasoning with them and..."

"What about you Vaerlin?' Kirashira interrupted his justification, "When are they coming for you too?"

The man looked stunned and Kirashira pressed him, "You must know they won't tolerate having you around very long either..."

"I know too much... They won't risk it. I know too much about the organization, about Tamur. They can't do anything to me without that information finding its way out of the dark." He retorted, his voice betrayed his obvious uncertainty.

"You don't sound like you believe that, Neither did the man with you..." Kirashira jabbed icily, exposing the advantage in Vaerlin's weakened mental exterior, "My blood won't even be dry before you are killed Vaerlin... I promise you that..."

"They need me to oil the machine that is the Federation Political System, without it things will grind to a halt, there will be investigations, people will be found..." He replied, "I am too valuable..."

"You can't hold them off forever Vaerlin..."

"I won't have to! I just need to hold a sword over one or two heads!" He snarled.

Just as he finished speaking, Tamur burst into the room again, "Make the choice Vaerlin, we don't have any more time..."

Before he could stammer a reply, Kirashira called to the brute, "You shouldn't have made a deal with Vaerlin..."

The man raised a brow and eyed the Princess carefully, even as he drew his sidearm and slid a power cell into it.

"Why's that Princess?" He replied, the cell clicking into place.

"Because, he's been spying on you."

The man smirked and casually sauntered away from the door, his sidearm looking rather small in his hand. It was of course , no less dangerous. Shan'Li carried one like it at all times before and when Kirashira had gone to her gun practice, it had shown its dangerous colors.

"Is that so?"

"He told me he knows all about you and your organization.."

Vaerlin stammered a reply, approaching Tamur like a sniveling weasel but the man roughly shoved him aside and stepped forward. His imposing figure came to rest only a half meter away from Kirashira's sitting frame. She looked up at him, still holding Vaerlin's sash on her wound, "He's already planning on betraying you... he's just waiting for his chance to expose you and turn you in."

"Outrageous!" Vaerlin snarled, "Can't you see she's just trying to turn us against each other!"

"And when have you actually acted like you are on our side of this Vaerlin," Tamur turned to him.

As he did, Kirashira noticed a small ring on the Tamur's finger, one hidden from view until now. It was a small, nondescript band. It wrapped around the base of his pinky-finger. Kirashira knew that kind of ring, she knew why it was on his finger. Her mother hand long ago taught her that when a Kul'Raigh was adopted by a Hil'Raigh family, they gave their adoptive parent a small band as a token of gratitude. It was there because they shared no blood. As a result the ring was given to signify the unification. She wondered who had given it to the man and why, what were they like, what was their name.

For a moment, she felt a tinge of compassion for the brutish man as she realized that he of all people, was not someone she expected to have such a soft side. She felt guilty for a moment, wondering if that adopted child would ever know what their adoptive father did in secret. Shan'Li had given her mother and father such rings years ago. Seeing what was before her, Kirashira saw a chance to drive a permanent wedge between her captors, recalling the large man's name from earlier and blurted out, "He said he'd kill your daughter Tamur."

The man turned with immediate fury toward the noble and grabbed him by the neck of his robe, shoving him roughly against the support frame. He braced Vaerlin there with one arm as his free hand toyed with the handgun, "Is that so?"

"I don't even know what you're talking about let me go!"

"He's lying," Kirashira pressed, seeing the uncontrolled fury on Tamur's face. If she was going to be killed, she'd see to it that Vaerlin never left the room either. His own double dealings would be his end today.

Tamur holstered his weapon with violent speed and smashed the puny noble against the column, "I never liked you much anyway Vaerlin but if you think you can play games with our people, you are even stupider than I thought."

With that he let Vaerlin slump against the column and wound back his arm. Vaerlin's feet had barely hit the ground before a vicious right hook impacted him and sent him reeling. He stumbled dazedly and landed on his hands and knees. He looked utterly shocked, his face revealing a mix of astonishment and disbelief.

He rubbed his lip and when his hand came away bloodied, he turned in utter horror to the taller, steaming man near him. It was not horror at the man's frame, no, Kirashira knew the look. It was the look of a social better in such astonishment that someone who he deemed beneath him, would dare challenge him so openly.

Kirashira scrambled away from the two and Tamur remained unmoving for a moment until Vaerlin stood. He had the look of someone who'd been wronged impossibly now. He was now going to do anything he could to ruin Tamur. Seeing his face, his expression shift so suddenly, made Kirashira realize that although Tamur may have been bluffing earlier about Vaerlin's intent to kill her after things settled, he was probably correct after all. The sheer contempt in his eyes betrayed the fact that it was not violence he abhorred, but getting his hands dirty.

Even as Tamur fumed at the nobleman, the skinnier man reached down the front of his robe, attempting to hide his motion from Tamur. The latter, seeing the Duke squirm, immediately charged him. His shoulder impacted Vaerlin's body roughly and the thing he'd been reaching for clattered to the floor nearby. A small concealable handgun lay on the ground near them both.

Kirashira looked to the two as they scuffled. Tamur threw a few insults, Vaerlin retorted angrily and the larger man pummeled the duke a few times. After taking a few blows, Vaerlin delivered a rough jab to the pressure point in Tamur's armpit.

Tamur howled as the sudden pain incapacitated his arm and Vaerlin scrambled free. He bolted across the distance to his handgun and scooped it up even as Tamur charged him again. The nobleman fired a wild shot, a white hot blast arcing into the roof, melting some metal into vapor as Tamur again impacted him, this time shoving him into the door. The door shook violently as Vaerlin ricocheted from its surface and collapsed on the ground. Tamur followed with a kick to Vaerlin's ribs, an aggressive brutal gesture which caused the now enfeebled nobleman to crash roughly on the ground, his weapon skittering away from him again, this time sliding toward Kirashira instead.

With that, Tamur drew his own weapon and fired into Vaerlin's leg. The noble howled in agony as his robe was punctured with white heat. He scrambled away with one leg now unmoving for only a moment more before he collapsed due to pain. Tamur took aim again and fired into his back as he lay on the ground, returning silence to the room.

Kirashira gulped, the sudden brutal end to the duke shocking her in a way she had never been disturbed before. His unmoving body, his still open, fearful eyes. She shuddered and turned away in disgust as the smell of burnt flesh mixed with melted metal in the room, the smell of life burned away by white hot plasma.

She regretted speaking at all despite the fact that she was convinced Vaerlin would have done just as she had said. Now, only solemn footsteps sounded. She scurried toward the pistol ahead of her on the ground and gripped it helplessly as she turned to face Tamur. He already had his weapon pointed at her. She shakily pointed Vaerlin's own at him. Could she kill? She angrily willed her fingers to crush the trigger but nothing happened.

"Ironic that it ended this way isn't it?" The man said.

Even as he moved closer, he eyed Kirashira with an awkward tenderness, "I wish you didn't look like her but I'd be lying if I said you didn't..."

Another step forward.

Kirashira squeezed the trigger again and nothing happened, Tamur simply smirked. "I sabotaged his power cell yesterday, In fact I'm amazed it worked at all... You might say I had a feeling..."

Kirashira whimpered helplessly and closed her eyes, dropping the gun and curling into a scared, desperate ball. She buried her head behind folded arms and sobbed into her knees.

A loud sheering sound filled her ears and she realized, she had never been shot before. This must have been what it felt like to have nerve overload. Heat, vicious biting heat and impossible noise, overwhelming the senses. She was already in so much pain that she couldn't even tell where she was hit. Was it the top of her head? Her torso? Was she going to be killed by dozens of minor shots?

Even as she thought about what she'd say to her father when she finally saw him again, she felt a gratitude for all the people who had tried so much to help her. She remembered their faces. She remembered the NovaCore, Truth especially. The silly, innocent smile that the Novian would do when Kirashira seemed to manage some happiness despite herself, on board the ship she had formerly called a prison. If only she could have been there now. Safe. Protected. Valued.

That memory was pleasant. Truth spoke nicely, she was friendly. Major Karo was rude at first, but he was not bad, he was genuine enough when Kirashira had come to spend a bit more time with him. They were nice people. Thorsh had risked his entire crew just to bring her all the way here. Even despite being captured. Shan'Li had tried to help too, Kirashira realized. Perhaps there was something of value to her end anyway, perhaps she had been something better than a lazy royal who sat in the safety of a palace all her life.

She was prepared to say her peace, the final thing she should do as a dying mortal. She heard a thud and opened her eyes. She was laying on her side now her ears ringing viciously and her vision blurred. She became acutely aware of the fact that she could not feel her arm at all but this was definitely not the afterlife. Was it some kind of hell? Maybe the people who had told her hell was real were right and she was there instead. After all, she was in pain still, and hell was painful.

An angry guttural yell sounded nearby and Kirashira turned enough to see the most odd of sights. A familiar frame was climbing off of a the meat hunk Tamur.

The Novian recoiled from the man's frame as he lashed out violently in response, getting to his feet.

Kirashira finally realized who it was despite her vision.

The ambusher pressed his advantage and moved against Tamur with surgical precision. Major Karo roughly attempting to bury his knife in Tamur's chest. His blow was deflected however and the Major's advantageous weapon was wrenched from his hand within moments. Undeterred, the Novian twisted, contorting just enough to give himself leverage once more. He pulled free of the grapple and broke away from the Hil'Raigh's grasp.

Kirashira felt as if she was watching some sort of ancient bloodsport now, the two circling each other with death in their eyes as they lashed out, testing each others defenses lightly. Neither of them committed in full as a punch flew from Tamur and Karo retaliated with a rough kick. His leg sailed through the air like the tip of a whip and he damped the blow as Tamur pulled back instead of pressing in.

Kirashira knew nothing of styles but could distinctly tell that Karo favored using his legs for offensive work and his arms defensively. Tamur on the other hand, seemed to mix both more readily. Despite that, neither seemed to be able to land many effectual blows, testing misses and glancing hits turned into deflections.

Tamur grinned and asked his opponent what he'd studied. Rather than replying the Novian came in with a new stance. Tamur baited an attack and as Karo made a kick, the Hil'Raigh looked like he was going to bolt. Instead, he pressed in, exploiting the opening but the apparent feint by Karo turned forceful just before impact, slamming against Tamur's torso roughly.

Tamur staggered to the side, his attempted attack abandoned to recover footing against his adversary. Karo probed again, trying for another attack but this time Tamur reacted with his own cunning. As Karo's leg came in, Tamur caught and grabbed. He held the officer's calf and ankle tightly. He then gave an aggressive tug on the limb he'd grasped. The motion sent Karo into a tumble but as he fell, he whipped himself violently. He spun into a graceful escape as the sudden twisting motion freed him from Tamur's grasp. Even as he landed, not fully footed, Tamur moved in and landed an aggressive punch that the Novian couldn't deflect. Though blocked, the blow squared on Karo's forearm. If what Kirashira had felt earlier from Tamur's lighter hit was any indication, the blow had to be painful.

The abrupt block paused the action only for a moment as Tamur followed up with another strike from the other side. This time Karo's deflection paid off and the Hulk's own momentum carried him into the Major's waiting knee. The blow had effect and Tamur stumbled forward after the attack while his opponent backed off nimbly.

There was a sound now, a loud cracking sound and Kirashira looked toward where it seemed to sound. Only now did she realize what the intense heat and noise had come from earlier. The metal door to the room was mangled, punched inward and barely hanging from one of its hinges. It still smoked, caked in soot and grime. From what, she had no idea but her hunch immediately turned to some sort of explosive charge.

Outside the room, she could barely make out the figure of Truth, framed by the door portal itself as whatever adversary she was dealing with exchanged fire with her. White hot beams of energy lanced into the walls as she ducked into cover and then retaliated with her own firearm.

At once, Kirashira knew that if the Major had used most of his ammo, something she assumed because he'd charged with a knife, then Truth was certain to be running low. A pit formed in Kirashira's stomach as a yell returned her attention to the fight playing out here inside the room.

Tamur stumbled away from a roughly deflected blow as Karo's leg caused a noisy thud on the ground. He recoiled quickly but Tamur took advantage of the over committed strike, landing a strong blow against the Novian's side, and as he stumbled, his back.

The Major went to the ground, rolling out to the side and slipping back to his feet quickly enough to ward off further advance. He followed with a snapping kick that seemed powerful enough to have removed Tamur's head if he had continued forward.

Kirashira wondered just how long this would last as Truth emptied a few more shots at her unseen adversaries outside. Despite it all, despite wanting to, Kirashira was powerless to help. She dared not go near the brawl here in the room she was trapped inside of for fear of being outright killed by a stray attack from either combatant. With her head already so clouded she wondered if she would even remember watching any of it.

Tamur pressed and Karo fell back, then the roles reversed. Watching, the Princess knew there would be an abrupt end soon, once the first true mistake was made. In her heart she felt that her friends would win the day, but even so, the beating of it felt more like a warning as time went on.

She watched another exchange and just in time, witnessed Major Karo stumble. As he did, Tamur's strike connected with his arm in a brutal way. The Novian winced and yelled as he was downed, brought to the floor and pinned quickly by the larger, weightier person. Kirashira's fear was only deepened as she noted the Hil'Raigh aggressively throttling his enemy.

He glanced up at her for a moment, his gaze promising to seal her fate next. The Major's hands scrambled around the floor for a moment and then with sudden urgency, one of them lanced up to Tamur. The Knife glinted in Karo's hand, abandoned before but returned to its master fatefully as it plunged upward into Tamur's muscle bound frame. The shock was enough to let the Major wriggle free and he jabbed again, with vicious intent. Even from here, the disgusting thunk of the knife was audible. Kirashira felt her stomach churn, even worse than it had when she had seen Vaerlin gunned down. She could not help but envision the bloody altercation.

The attack freed Karo at last and Tamur's aggressive strength was already fading. He stumbled and stood as Karo coughed hoarsely and circled. The altercation had brought the two close by now and Kirashira could see their faces clearly.

The intent which Tamur had shown before when looking at Kirashira was one of confidence, one of calculation, but in looking at Karo, Kirashira saw something even more humbling. His will was clear, his bloody knife dripped even now and his eyes told the story of something larger than a single man. There was something primal in them, something that made Kirashira afraid, not for herself, but for anyone caught in their gaze. She saw something in his eyes that explained instantly, what he was capable of. She was both curious and disturbed at the same time.

Re-armed, faced with impending death and standing between his charge and one who sought to harm them, the sudden explosion of viciousness from Karo made Kirashira shudder. He raced forward with an angry yell. Tamur deflected one blow but took another. There was a pause. Karo circled again then with another aggressive dance, racing forward once more. As Tamur attempted to deflect him, Karo twisted by on the side, bringing his leg roughly into the back of Tamur's knees. Even as the hulk stumbled forward, his knees roughly impacting the floor, Karo twisted again.

He gritted his teeth and from behind, over Tamur's shoulder, thrust his knife into the front side of Tamur's neck.

The scene froze and Tamur squirmed only briefly until Karo, shuddering, let go of the knife and let him fall forward into his own blood. The Novian glanced to Kirashira quickly and then scurried toward Tamur's firearm in the far corner of the room, coughing roughly as he did so. A violent jet of plasma spurted out the end of it as he scooped it up and fired it into Tamur's body for certainty.

He then slumped against the wall and dropped the gun, huffing in pain.

Truth appeared in the door after several more moments, Kirashira paralyzed, unable to even look at Tamur or Vaerlin. She could not bring herself to look at the Major either because of the single glance he'd given her earlier. It made her afraid of him. She had no idea what he was capable of and now...

There was a touch at her shoulder and she recoiled suddenly with a whimper. Truth kneeling nearby,"We're here to save you Kirashira..."

Tears welled in her eyes as she looked up to the Novian. Her fear melted. She was unable to speak but she looked over to Karo as he sighed, nursing himself against the wall.

Truth had already let her go and moved across the room, kneeling by her partner and softly speaking to him in their own tongue. When Truth's voice cracked and she hugged him tightly, Kirashira realized that there was no animal there. No, he was no animal, he was her rescuer and the rescue had come at a permanent price.

Working up the courage to move at last, Kirashira carefully made her way to the two. Truth had rolled up Karo's pant leg, revealing a severe burn on one of his calves. He had cuts and bruises on his arm and a large contusion on his face. His neck was red and he huffed softly, not speaking. As Kirashira neared though, he must have sensed her.

His eyes opened and he looked over to her. His physical tiredness appeared to do little to dampen his gaze. He looked not like an angry cornered animal now, but a concerned friend, more than that even. His gaze reminded Kirashira of the way that her parents had looked to her with complete care and concern. His eyes had betrayed what lurked inside in the officer. He was obtuse and upsetting at times, but there was a loyalty in them that was clear and proud.

Kirashira felt humbled that she of all people, would warrant any of that kind of care but the moments of eye contact were lost as Truth worked on him. She made a small quip in Novian, giving him a smile and laughing, he smiled and laughed too, less enthusiastically, but clearly.

Noting that his good arm was the one she was next to, Kirashira slid against the wall next to him took his hand in hers, feeling every emotion imaginable. It all came through at once, but as she felt gratitude, her heart swelled and she hugged onto the officer's arm like a child clinging to its parent, her soft, tender thank yous, embellished with the most holy of honorifics, echoed in the silence of the room amid her tears of thankful joy at being given yet again, the chance for life.

27 - Transcendant Bond

The world had been a whirlwind since the landing. Now, it all seemed to be settling into something. What exactly, Truth had no idea but a clarity distinctly lacking in the past few days was finally returning. Still, despite that, she was unsure of what to do with all of the personal attention she was getting. The swarms of dutiful attendants had coalesced around Kirashira almost the moment she was out of bed, and, since that time, had continued with her a tightening of security that would have made one of the Admiralty blush.

Truth couldn't blame the precaution on anything other than experience. With what had happened recently, even the most ardent of pacifists in the Federation were being forced to admit that this was a special circumstance. Even so, the level of protection being provided now, made Truth wonder why it was not that way before. Tragedy had made it a more salient point perhaps.

Truth had never been in a resort before, only briefly living in Kolos and having been unable to do much more than settle into the place before things turned wild. As a result, the constant assessment of her needs by complete strangers was something of a novelty, at least at first.

Now, she was unsure of what to think, her ever skeptical nature informing her judgment on just about anyone who came asking about her needing a drink or anything else. At least Tony did not have to have conversations with them on the grounds of doctor's orders. Instead, he sat idly in the chair next to Truth's tapping his fingers with the beat of the music that played over the loud speaker. He was sipping at some too fruity beverage he'd been given earlier in the day.

An approaching gaggle of attendants signaled the arrival of the one who'd put them into the facility in the first place. It was only after several moments that she squirmed free of the near incessant protective ring that was following her all over. Who was providing all of the security was not clear, but there were distinctly more Kul'Raigh in the group than Truth assumed a normal entourage would include.

The monarch who'd just extricated herself smiled and approached the two NovaCore, bidding her support staff to stay at bay while she met them. She moved to them calmly and smiled a bit as she approached. Most of her bruises had been healed now, a point made obvious by her light robe and the fact that it exposed her shoulders, arms and the sides of her torso. The halter top was a far cry from the naval duty uniform she'd been given while living with the NovaCore on their ship.

What she lacked in the familiar wardrobe, she made up for with a more energetic warmth than she'd had almost the entire time Truth had known her thus far. She was obviously feeling more relaxed and judging by her expression, not the least bit bothered with all the attention her people were showering on her now.

Kirashira had of course, been far from idle since her rescue, issuing an immediate veto on the war council proceedings as one of the three required votes to make the council go forward. After that she had re-opened the diplomatic mission with the NovaCore. It had been closed when reports had initially implicated the NovaCore in the attacks. Now it was already reaching out to Truth's own government to request a new ambassador. Truth had even heard something about a memorial for the prior one but nothing further had reached her.

Yes, Kirashira had been busy thus far but what she planned to do next was anyone's guess. Truth assumed it would not be mourning. The princess had mentioned before, that she had to finalize her ascension to the throne. The vacancy left by her fathers death needed to be filled, especially now that the head of the interim government, Vaerlin, was dead. Kirashira was a far cry now from the battered and displaced royal she'd been only days before. Now she was in charge again, people listened to her opinion and did what she asked, even if they did not agree.

Rescuing her had come with a price, there were a number of lives lost, but most of them were those of hostile forces. The official circumstances had yet to be released to the public, but the reality of Vaerlin's betrayal had already received a public explanation of sorts. What most in the Federation probably did not realize however, was just how much distrust Vaerlin had of his co-conspirators.

The people he'd worked with had been planning, at least in Vaerlin's own opinion, to double cross him. As such he'd amassed a sizable amount of information on them in return.

It was a wealth of self protection in its own way, a bargaining chip that Vaerlin's unique connections and talents had amassed. It had all been for naught, at least in Vaerlin's case, but it painted the dark and compelling picture of a deep rot in the Federation as a whole. The information had hit the net hours ago, starting in foreign nations first and it was only now propagating back to the Federation. There was no hiding Vaerlin's last act of defiance against those who'd killed him in the end.

Truth wondered whether Kirashira had seen anything of it yet. The last they'd talked directly was minutes before several armed response team members pointed weapons in their faces back at the agricultural processing plant. Since then Truth had yet to communicate with the monarch, only hearing of her deeds and requests through the all too eager staff here.

The assistance though was at very least, well informed and professional. The Royal's influence had been felt however, long before they'd had face to face contact once more. First it was in ensuring that Truth and her partner were released from the custody of law enforcement and instead, brought to the highly secure medical resort they now rested in.

Truth herself needed little here and in all fairness, neither did her partner. A quick nanite injection and some bed rest is all their own doctor would have provided. Even so, the relaxation had been authorized, or perhaps, forced, by Admiral Thorsh and as a result, the two operatives now made their time sitting amid a curated mixture of gardens, pools and spas.

"Truth!" Kirashira said at last, and quickly approached as Truth stood. If it weren't for their similar sizes, Truth wondered just how the intense hug would have felt. There was a tight squeeze and Kirashira made sure that Truth knew it was more than just a show.

"And Tony!" She pulled free and moved to Tony next, who, despite his neck brace had made a hasty exit from his chair to receive the gesture.

Her partner smiled, rather than smirking when she referred to him by name but said nothing in reply. At last they settled in once again, Kirashira finding a kneeling stool and taking the only un-used piece of furniture at the small gathering place.

As Truth began offering her own seat, Kirashira gave a good natured scowl and laughed, waving her back into place.

"It is good to see you Kirashira," Truth began. "And seeing you smile so much is wonderful."

"Thank you," she replied, "It's because of you two."

Tony shrugged in reply, all in a days work. Truth smirked at him and a genuine laugh escaped their visitor.

"I hope you've been able to hear from Admiral Thorsh," She continued, "I tried to make sure he was put in touch with you both."

"I have spoken to him, thank you," Truth replied.

Kirashira piped up again, "I wanted to ask you both, if you'd come to my coronation ceremony as guests."

"I'd be honored to attend Kirashira, and I am sure Tony would as well," Truth said, glancing to her partner who simply nodded.

"Good, I already cleared it with Admiral Thorsh, who is also coming, and the Captain... and your ship's doctor."

"Do you need help planning the security?" Truth asked carefully.

Kirashira shook her head, "No, but thank you. This time my people should get it right. Though... I do have a request..."

"What is it?"

"I'd like you to be my escorts," She replied.

"Escorts?" Truth inquired, earnest curiosity filling her mind as she wondered what exactly she was being asked to do.

"You arrive with me at the shrine, and well... you walk... with me. That's it really." She replied.

"That does not sound too difficult," Truth replied.

"And you have to wear a special robe too..." Kirashira added, "And some other things, but its really not that bad..."

She began smiling warmly and the obvious gravity of the request began to sink in. Rather than be turned away however, Truth felt a sense of pride knowing she was being asked for something so personal and traditional. Of course, it would require approval from the Admiral.

"I already asked Admiral Thorsh, he granted permission..." Kirashira pre-empted. She had certainly grown to know the two NovaCore a bit.

"Then we will help." Truth replied.

"Good!" Kirashira chortled happily, "There are a few dress rehearsals before the main event, but you have a few days to get that brace off and have the robes made. You will have to be measured today... My personal tailor will make sure you have robes made in NovaCore colors for the occasion and will consult with your government, on appropriate placement of any insignia or required regalia you may have..."

"We appreciate your enthusiasm Kirashira," Truth replied, stunned. She had very little she could respond with. It was not every day that such a candid and in any other circumstance, ridiculous, request would have come across her ears but today was an exception. She had to remind herself that she was dealing with a head of state now, and not a political refugee.

"It will be hard to get back into running things... I just hope I do a good job, there are so many things I missed while I was away..." Kirashira said with a half smile. She looked tired as she said the words.

"I assume you have already been informed of Vaerlin's information dump?" Truth asked. The knowledge would soon be public everywhere anyway but it was very likely Kirashira had been given a preliminary notice on it.

Kirashira nodded and her face grew sullen as she spoke, "I've heard some of it, bits and pieces. I don't know if I will ever be able to make myself read it word for word..."

Truth nodded. As far as she had seen the information contained therein was a mixture of topics. Some of the information consisted of dirt agathered on people who Vaerlin should not have been able to identify but did. Other topics included things like Vaerlin's own personal notes on the entire affair and his dealings with the people he'd met. Vaerlin's personal notes were perhaps the most compelling part of it all but at the same time, that was likely to make reading them hard for someone in Kirashira's position. It was akin to understanding the mind of a person who'd been instrumental in the death of family, something most would never desire to learn about. For Truth, it was a narrative, and though it was familiar due to her involvement in the mission, she had no such misgivings.

Perhaps the most important part of the dump of information was that it had confirmed the existence of some organization, unnamed of course in the notes, but clearly representative of what the NovaCore had always dubbed the Hil'Raigh Knights. The group was a sort of half joke in intelligence. It had always been a shadowy group to which so many seemingly unconnected dealings were attributed, that it had become a gag to assign blame to them for every little thing one could not properly assess. Despite that, the dump by Vaerlin solidified, at least in Truth's own mind, the existence of such an organization. The schizophrenic nature of the group's dealings observed thus far probably had a basis in reality too.

Vaerlin's notes detailed rather copiously, his research into his co-conspirators and their organization. With the help of unnamed parties, he'd amassed a wealth of information that painted a sort of incomplete web of influence and corruption in the Federation as a whole and its individual member states. Some people in that web had been named, others were still a mystery but a distinct division of style seemed to exist among them. While one side appeared more ideologically driven, the other appeared more interested in the religion of greed and influence.

Unfortunately, details beyond the names of a few, likely lower level members of the organization, had been sparse. Even with Vaerlin's talent for double crossing and hoarding information, he'd been unable to amass much beyond a few contacts. The picture therefore was an incomplete canvas on which a few names, driven by greed appeared to mesh with, at some level, a broader, more powerful organization whose influence spanned the entirety of the Hil'Raigh Federation.

"I know Vaerlin had many notes, did he perhaps note your mother's status?" Truth asked at last.

Kirashira nodded and bit her lip for a moment. She looked at Tony, then Truth, "I'm told that my mother's last known location was incorrect. The rescue team did not find her there."

Her announcement was a humbling one. Duke Vaerlin's information drop had included that information but it was already wrong. Who knew if it was ever correct at all.

"I am sorry to hear that Kirashira," Truth replied trying to look as concerned as she could.

"I'm sure whatever happened to her will be clear soon," Kirashira stated, appearing to change mental gears, "But I wanted to let you know that I appreciated your admiral's willingness to help locate her."

"It would be a pleasure to help return her to you, Kirashira," Truth affirmed.

"Whatever happens, I wanted you to know that she'd be grateful. So would my father," Kirashira began, her eyes glistening, "She was so important to him..."

"I am sad I never knew your father Kirashira," Truth replied, her voice gentle and empathetic, "He sounds like a good person."

"He really tried at least," The princess replied, "Sometimes he didn't know what to say or do, like anyone I guess, but he tried..."

"That is one of the most important parts of life I think," Truth stated, adopting a partially philosophical tone.

"I won't be mourning him yet," Kirashira stated with blunt intent, "I just... I can't do it right now. It feels so fresh with all of these politics again...I don't think I can have a funeral ceremony until I know whether I have to mourn my mother too..."

"I understand. I hope that can come at a time that you feel more prepared," Truth nodded and so did Tony, who gave a concerned look and slid to the bottom of his recliner, sitting closer to Kirashira there on her stool. She gave a thankful smile and regarded the two NovaCore with care.

"I'll have a separation ceremony at least. Father deserves that much. But I don't think I can do his funeral rites yet. I just..." She trailed off sadly, her lip quivering.

"I have heard that your culture practices two distinct ceremonies. Perhaps you could tell me about the difference?" Truth asked. She'd heard of both but wanted to give Kirashira a chance to feel that she was important. It also helped that it would provide a chance for her to be distracted from her obvious grief.

Kirashira nodded and sniffled a little, smiling with a grateful look as she began to explain, "At a separation ceremony, the attendees say a personal goodbye and let their own spirit release it's hold on the deceased. They plot their stars and recite the words from their star plot."

Truth nodded, she'd heard of such a thing but not exactly why it was done. She guessed Tony was in the same position as he was visibly listening.

Kirashira took a breath and paused for a moment then spoke again, her voice cracking despite her best effort, "During the funeral..."

She paused and wiped her eyes, but at last, continued, "A funeral is how we free the soul of the dead completely. It absolves their spirit of its obligations to us in the mortal world but in the Kul'Raigh Tradition..."

Kirashira sniffled, wiping her eyes, "In Kul'Raigh Tradition it's the last time we can plead to the divines to let us see our loved one again in the after life. I cannot have a funeral without letting my mother plead. I can't. I won't. It would be so wrong..."

"So you cannot have a funeral until you know whether she's alive and if she is, you want to have her here..." Truth summarized.

The princess whimpered and nodded helplessly. The gravity of the situation for her came down in a new way. Truth felt immediately sad, empty inside knowing that somehow, the thing that was supposed to ease the difficulty in losing a loved one had such a painful hold over her friend. After all, the beliefs that any culture had when it pertained to death were invariably aimed toward easing the loss in some way, in making it feel less permanent and damaging. Yet here, Kirashira was paralyzed by them because of her desire to see her mother gain the benefit she'd been taught existed.

"Kirashira, I have no way to fully understand how much pain that is causing you," Truth began. She'd never felt such compassion in her life and it was clear to her as her own eyes began forming tears, "But I do know that all spiritual interpretations in your culture say that your divines are good, just and fair. They will not rob your mother."

The princess whimpered in a mixture of what had to be relief and emotional release. Perhaps outside assurance was what she wanted, perhaps the idea that a NovaCore offered their own interpretation had helped. Truth had no idea, at least until the monarch slid off of her stool and offered a tight, needy hug. She kept crying but there was a difference to the tears. No longer was it simply anguish, but release. It was something she'd shared just a part of before on the ship after Kirashira's dream, but now somehow, that initial vulnerability, the initial trust, had borne fruit.

Truth returned the gesture as best she could, having never felt entirely comfortable with such contact, but as she glanced to her partner over Kirashira's shoulder and noted that he was picking moisture out of his own eyes, she knew that he understood just how empathetic the words had sounded.

At last, Kirashira released Truth. As she turned to move to her seat, she instead gave Tony a tight squeeze as well. It was shorter lived but the intent was clear. She truly did seem to value them both. The fact that she'd asked them to be a part of her coronation at all, now carried such a weight as to make it feel like the most important assignment Truth had yet been given in her life. A mixture of humility and pride filled Truth's heart and she knew that no matter how life might drag them all apart from each other, there would always be a bond.

28 - Triumphant Queen

Tony cleared his throat again, feeling a familiar dryness that had been dogging him since the fight with the Hil'Raigh Mercenary days ago. Despite the recovery therapy and the work of the medical nano robots he'd been administered, it had persisted more than he'd liked. Of course, it was a small price to pay for being able to breath or speak normally despite the injury.

At the very least he had been brought to the realization that Hil'Raigh medicine was a significantly advanced field, even from what he was used to. While the NovaCore had been using nano-technology for decades now, the Federation had elevated it to an art form. For once, it had seemed like there was something that felt advanced enough in their civilization to warrant the old age they claimed it had.

He reached out and took the small bottle he'd been given to drink, taking a swig of the stuff and feeling the cool cascade of liquid coating his parched throat. Perhaps it was not just the injuries but the fact that the room was dry enough to give the most remote deserts a contest. Truth nearby, appeared to have no such problem as she glanced around the room idly, letting Kirashira's attendants finalize the trim on her personalized robe. No matter what Tony felt about traditional Hil'Raigh garb, he had to admit that the tailors had done some of the most interesting and compelling work he'd ever seen.

While Kirashira's royal colors he'd learned, were primarily red and white, the tailors had worked to create robes of black, with red trim and silver accents. Other than replacing silver for the normal gold, the colors were the same as a standard dress uniform would have had. Despite the familiar looking palette, the attention to making the Hil'Raigh style of clothing uniquely NovaCore had been something of a surprise.

It was a learning experience in how these kinds of clothes worked however, something that Tony did not find unwelcome, at least when he'd heard the robe's designer explain his method and effort. The robe's outer layer was a hefty garment designed with limited ballistic and thermal protections in mind while the inner layer was a light, breathable fabric designed for comfort. The outer piece had been designed with a broad cut over the chest, placing the seam over the left breast and down the left side of the torso, much like the more familiar uniform's Tony was used to for formal functions.

Instead of a rank insignia on the shoulder however, a carefully placed mark occupied a place on the high neck of the robe, which extended from the base of the neck to the underside of the jaw line. The aggressive styling apparently reflected in part, the design that Kirashira had chosen for her own clothing.

Truth was finally released after tilting her head back and letting the attendant carefully clasp the neck of her robe. As soon as the trio began to move toward the door she was already squirming around a bit, looking mildly uncomfortable.

"Don't look too much like you are being choked," Tony joked.

Truth looked to him and reached up to the neck, covertly un-clasping it immediately after the attendants left, "I find it quite uncomfortable in the neck area. Otherwise it is fine."

"I'm not used to clothing that is designed to be so accentuating," Tony replied, glancing over his partner and then down at himself. Though the robe was not tight in the way of movement, it was tight in the areas of the body that did not move much, more so than most clothing Tony was used to. Apparently that was a staple of this kind of fashion, "It looks nice on you though."

Truth smirked and brushed herself a little, examining her figure then shrugging. It was an oddity really, to see his partner dressed like this. She already looked so much like a native of the Federation. Now she was wearing clothing fit for her genes. The fact that she was less than enthused about some of the cuts on the robe was ironic, at least a bit.

The waiting room was not all that large, a table and some couches. There were no windows here and the door on the side through which the attendants had exited was, while expensive looking, rather bland overall. It was a stark contrast to the outside of the building.

The dress rehearsals had allowed both NovaCore to get a good look at the venue prior and though Tony was not one for architecture, he had to admit that it was an impressive place.

These sort of ceremonies apparently took place at the same shrine on Shar'Jya for every royal house no matter who it was. If selected as a regent, Arash Vaerlin would have had his own ceremony here instead. Of course, the scope was different depending on who was doing what. As it seemed however, there was quite a bit of work that would go into the ceremony and the celebrations that followed regardless of whom it was for. Tony still remembered the large group of companions that had been practicing their coordinated dance routine at one of the stages in the shrine the previous day.

He and Truth had the simplest of jobs in the entire thing, at least in terms of steps to remember. They just had to walk, and make sure they stopped and let Kirashira lead at several points along the journey. It was a direct path from here in the preparation building to the ceremony hall in which the official transfer of power would take place. The low thumping in the air was already starting up again as fireworks were dropped from patrolling fighters and police ships above the shrine.

Guessing at the cost of the entire affair had been something Tony had abandoned after that had begun during the first dress rehearsal. They'd used real fireworks then to ensure they fell only in the designated airspace and never near the path of travel for anyone on the ground. Of course, the queen to be had been replaced by a look alike volunteer from the Kul'Raigh Companion Guild during the dress rehearsals. Since the dress rehearsal had featured stand in clothing as well, it had made Tony wonder exactly what Kirashira would look like today.

He had not seen her since they'd left the medical resort. His musing was interrupted as the door slid open and a grave looking Hil'Raigh official stepped in. The man stood about as tall as Tony did, wearing a robe much less finely detailed than his own but obviously expensive. He regarded both Truth and Tony but scowled immediately as he noticed Truth's collar. He cleared his throat loudly and gestured to it before he began to speak, "Are you ready?"

"Ready," Tony replied.

Truth adjusted her collar back to the intended aesthetic with a sigh and then nodded as well. The gesture appeared to placate the man's unhappiness and he turned smartly, "Follow me. And please remember, during the ceremony, you should not speak to the queen."

Tony snickered, he had to admit he had been a bit of a problem at times during the dress rehearsal, mostly because he had felt challenged by Kirashira's stand in. He could not remember exactly what precipitated the simple contest he'd had with her but he had felt he won. He'd gotten her to start talking back. It had not gone un-noticed. To assure his guide now, Tony spoke, "Of course, Lips are sealed."

The man turned, looking over his shoulder as he guided the two out of the waiting room. He rolled his eyes and turned back forward almost as soon as he had. Tony could not remember seeing him before but it seemed par for the course that some Hil'Raigh he'd never met had some preconditioned idea about him. The man seemed composed and in control, a perfect challenge.

"Will you be at the after party?" Tony finally asked as they turned the corner. The guide gave a single laugh despite himself and sighed, just in time to stand both Tony and Truth in front of a set of double doors. He gestured for them to take their places, then glanced down the long hallway. At the far end was another set of doors that led to the outside world. A series of low thuds sounded above, followed by crackling, "Please wait here, and of course, refrain from adjusting your clothing further."

He glanced at Truth who nodded studiously before he looked over both NovaCore's clothes. Appearing satisfied, he stepped back and gave them both a respectful bow, one after the other. After bowing he turned and began down the hall, disappearing into a side door. In the utter silence, doing something to go against the grain was almost irresistible for Tony as he stood dutifully, but his self control won out. Only when he glanced to Truth did he have to block a laugh as she scowled and rubbed her neck woefully.

"Guess I'm the real winner, the brace made it easy to wear this," Tony quipped quietly.

Truth glanced over, "They should have just given you one of these. It would have been more effective."

Tony snickered to himself as the double doors cracked open nearby. Like everything in this building, they were made of wood. Their polished surfaces glinted only barely in the light of the well disguised lanterns hanging from the center of the hallway's roof.

From within the room behind came a Kul'Raigh wearing the robes of a temple attendant, someone who probably lived and worked at the shrine they now occupied. She carried with her, two familiar black fabric bundles. She passed between the two NovaCore wordlessly and, once past them, set her cargo down. With careful diligence, she knelt, picked up the top of the two objects and handed it to Truth. She knelt, turned and grabbed the second bundle, handing it to Tony before finally stepping back toward the doors, "Please inspect your arms to ensure they are functioning properly."

With that she retreated into the double doors and slid them closed. Tony peeled back the cloth case quickly, revealing a pristine Hil'Raigh Plasma rifle. The artistic darkened black metal finish a mix of silver and metallic red trim on the its chassis underscored the most expensive looking firearm Tony had ever been given to hold. It was a familiar platform, one of the long range military variants. When he pulled it from the case completely and gripped the handle, the small display under the base of the rear scope aperture blinked to life. His own name, spelled out in Hil'Raigh was displayed for a moment before the display switched to an ammunition count in the dozens.

"Very nice hardware," He mused to Truth, who nodded seriously.

A durable looking black leather strap hung from the weapon, braced at both ends by silvery metal clips. It was clear that the weapon had been fired only a few times ever, probably in ensuring proper operation when manufactured. The reality that he and Truth had been given weapons with powercells in them already, carried immediate gravity and when the doors slid open again, the reason for that was clear.

Tony looked up to see a beaming and proud visage, one that made him smile immediately. Kirashira stepped through the door with a grace that Tony had never seen in another person, a gentle confidence that underscored her station. Her brilliant white robe was accented with a complex layering of sashes and hanging portions, all trimmed in red. Rather than the puffy red velvet like material of the robe she'd been wearing on the day of her rescue, the wispy fur like appearance of trim, along with the carefully crafted highlight and color gradient underscored it's value. The white fabric appeared even to change color itself.

While the weapon in his hand had been impressive, the live artwork before him made him pause. Kirashira's face had been made to look so pristine she almost looked fake. There was meticulous detail in everything from her lashes to the corners of her mouth. Her hair cascaded down the sides of her head past her shoulders and behind her head hovered a large, slowly rotating disk, or rather, what passed for a crown in Hil'Raigh society.

Tony cleared his throat and quickly slung his rifle over his shoulder, reminded of what the thing was for; protecting the person before him.

She looked to both NovaCore happily but did not speak or burst into a hug, only smiling at them both before looking forward smartly and being composed.

Tony and Truth both, assumed positions on either side of her as per the practice sessions. At last, she took a step, signaling the trio to move forward in unison. With careful precision, Tony took his footfalls one at a time down the hall in solemn reverence. One after the other, looking forward and not so much as stealing a glance at Kirashira or Truth, his movement continued. Step after step took them toward the exit to the building and as they approached the portal to the outside, the two guards flanking both sides of it quickly reached into the middle of the doors, unlocking them and sliding them open as they stepped out of the way. The concussive sounds of the aerial celebration outside became immediately louder as the wooden panels slid open.

Through the doorway, Tony caught a glimpse of the familiar path ahead. Outside, meters beyond the set of stairs leading away from the building was the bridge over which he, Kirashira and Truth would pass. The pond underneath was filled with lilies and other aquatic plants while it was fed fresh water from waterfalls on either side.

On both sides of the pond were the two paths around which non royalty were forced to traverse the pond's central position and in the center of the bridge was a tall gate frame with no door, through which Kirashira would have to pass first. Several more such constructions dotted the way up the stairs at the far end of the pond until finally, the trio would arrive at the coronation hall.

The carefully placed lighting, combined with the darkening sky of the almost completely set sun, created an artistic aesthetic here, using the traditional wooden buildings as part of the exhibit while, above, frantic bursts of light began to intensify. Kirashira stepped down the stairs.

In perfect coordination, a series of pops above sounded in the same moment that her feet hit the solid ground in front of the stairs and a new phase of the ceremony had begun. Tony stole a quick glance at his charge, unable to see much detail while forcing his head to stay forward. Her smile had not faded, though it was more subdued, her eyes revealing her concentration on the ritual at hand. Even as she began moving toward the bridge, Tony's ear piece relayed a softly spoken message, "Kirashira is descending the first stair, security zone one."

A meter or two more let Tony take in the familiar sight of the well lit ascent, several gates and flat sections ahead with lights focused on them. Kirashira kept her steady pace and the trio moved forward until their feet touched the wood of the bridge. Another security announcement filled the radio channel as she did so. Feeling his foot hit the surface, Tony immediately paused. Only when Kirashira was several steps ahead, did he and Truth un-shoulder their weapons.

With his right hand cupping the butt of the rifle and his left arm level across his chest, hand gripping the barrel, Tony stepped forward smartly, knowing Truth had performed the same action. They advanced at Kirashira's pace, taking care to remain as exactly far away from her as they could, never moving closer or falling behind.

When she finally stopped before the gate in the middle of the low bridge, the two NovaCore stopped as well. Kirashira stepped forward and bowed before the gate, pausing for the small ritual prayer she was to offer there. Tony could not see her simple hand gestures as she at last, clapped them together loudly and gave one final bow before stepping forward through the gate. As she did, bursts of white light shot upward from either side of the complex, giant beams of glory reaching into the sky from the spotlights mounted there. Once again, the impressive coordination of the ceremony was paying off and Tony felt a tremor of awe in himself as both the sound and light reflected in the same instant, her passage.

Finally, she began walking forward once more, a slow methodical pace until she reached the end of the bridge and paused. Once she'd paused, both Tony and his partner moved forward quickly, flanking her once more on either side. They re-shouldered their weapons, kicked their heals together and waited. Kirashira began walking forward again and the two moved with her once more.

"Escorts, prepare for ascent to zone three," The careful order came.

Now ahead of them was yet another gate but flanking it on either side were some of the temple attendants with baskets of flower petals. Tony and Truth drew out their distance carefully, now following by a good half meter as Kirashira briefly paused in front of the gate and stepped through. At the same time another set of light beams lanced skyward, more fireworks went off and the temple's attendants began moving ahead of Kirashira on the sides of the path, though never stepping on it themselves. They laid a carpet of flower petals carefully, each handful tossed out in such a practiced way that Tony wondered how long it had taken them to make such a simple action look so choreographed.

A set of stairs followed, and then another gate, at which two more attendants were waiting. As Kirashira passed through, yet another set of lights brightened the sky along with two heady thuds that shook Tony's chest to the core. Now, above, the ships had abandoned their lazy patterns of flight, forming up in slow cruises, their hulls lit by bright lights. They flew in careful formations, dipping the wing in reverence to the place on the ground where Kirashira had just passed.

The slow passage of ships above was timed with a chaotic increase in firework blasts and explosions. The festive atmosphere reaching a head as Kirashira approached the last gate in front of her self and the shrine ahead. Her feet had long since stopped treading on the detailed carpet laid out for her, instead finding only the carpet of petals that was being draped along in front of her with meticulous care. She paused now at the last gate and visibly took a breath. The pause lasted long moments until finally the monarch stepped through.

In the same moment, the formations overhead broke, one by one. As each craft broke away, it flared its engines aggressively, a maelstrom of loud bursts in the sky, shaking through the metropolis surrounding the shrine. In the same moment, the darkened horizon blared to intense joyous life as the awe inspiring skyline of Shar'Jya, the heart of the Hil'Raigh's precious capitol, joined in. A cacophony of joyous cheers sounded as the lucky few allowed here to the shrine, previously silent, were at last allowed to share in the celebration. Kirashira shuddered visibly ahead at the raucous cacophony, her forward motion paused as she could not help but look around herself. Here at the highest point in the temple ground, she could see over the temple walls and it was no doubt impossible to fully take in.

The city itself was so large that when the first dress rehearsal had taken place and Tony had got a good look at it from up there, he himself had gotten out of step with the rest of the entourage. Now, with Kirashira paused, he wondered if she would simply stop and cry there, instead however, she moved forward.

"Security check zone four is clear," Came a Hil'Raigh voice over the ear piece. Only after the announcement was made did Kirashira begin moving forward once more until at last, she reached the shrine stairs. Tony and Truth stopped there and un-shouldered their weapons as the radio announced the next step, "Prepare weapons."

Carrying his rifle at the ready, Tony quickly fingered the safety, making sure it was still engaged as he ascended in careful unison with Truth. Only when they'd reached the top did Kirashira step forward. Tony put his back to the wall here and Truth did the same on the opposite side of the door. Kirashira reached to the middle of the doors and, gripping the handles for both, slid them both open with purpose.

Tony watched her carefully now out of the side of his vision, turning just enough to get a full view of her as she gave a small prayer and then reached behind her head, her fingers disappearing into her hair. Her long nails tugged some of the hair out of place but two waiting attendants quickly ascended the stair and reached up to the crown hanging in mid-air behind her. The two Hil'Raigh men carefully pulled the metallic disk from its suspended place and moved to the side as Kirashira turned, facing back the way she'd come.

The attendants disappeared into the shrine behind her and at last, Tony saw the Federation's prime minister step forward, moving to the small set of shrine stairs. He ascended, his own guards stopping short at the bottom of the stairs. He pulled a thick set of bound metal plates from under his arm and then, with some difficulty, hefted the book and opened it.

He cleared his throat and spoke to Kirashira, his voice echoing through the air on speakers, "Kirashira of House Ren'Tauru, Daughter of Gou'Ran, Daughter of Shiyara. Child of the Stars, May your grace, poise and leadership be a beacon to your people and to our great federation."

Kirashira locked eyes with the man confidently.

"Let all of our stars witness your throne Kirashira and let the histories of our people revere your reign. May you reign in peace, prosperity and with the blessing of the dearest of our honored Ancestors. May you find in the halls of your sovereignty, love, respect and dignity worthy of a Queen."

Kirashira nodded and carefully reached out, placing her hand on the open page of the book. She closed her eyes as she rested her hand, whispering something softly, unheard aloud. Quickly afterward she withdrew her hand and the prime minister stepped back, closing his codex and descending the stairs with careful back steps.

Once he had moved, a large, even more ornate looking disk appeared from within the shrine behind Kirashira, carried by the same attendants who'd whisked away her prior crown.

The new crown and its intense filigree glinted in the varying light, its shiny silver finish sparkling as the four deep red gems mounted at the edges refracted and cascaded light all over. As the crown was let loose by the attendants, it quickly found its place, hanging weightlessly behind Kirashira's head. Each attendant then produced a pair of smaller gems mounted in metallic frames. From the bottom of each hung long red ribbons.

The attendants carefully released them into the air behind the crown and each was carried by unseen forces to a proper position, the ribbons gently fluttering in the wind. One of the men whispered something to Kirashira and the two helpers quickly scurried back into the shrine, the doors closing behind them.

Kirashira stepped forward with a broad smile on her face, to the edge of the stairs. She took in the assembled, looking once more, over the horizon, the ships in the sky, the barges on which joyous observers were riding in the air far away. At last, she took a breath and, at the top of her lungs, yelled out the words that not even the stand in had been allowed to say aloud, "Kalei'Shei Akari'Hijran!"

The phrase had no literal translation to his own tongue, something that never was said much in Hil'Raigh society either. It was apparently a phrase that had old religious meanings, praising the two deities common to the two cultures that made up the Federation. Once she had spoken the words however, she was no longer required to maintain any sort of rehearsed composure and instead of standing there, She began waving frantically to everything she could see. Even as she began her excited thanks to the assembled crowd a loudly yelled order was shouted from the crowd. Groups of Shar'Jya security forces in assigned sections below took aim to the specified clear spaces in the sky.

Tony lifted his weapon and aimed at the same area.

"Awaiting your order, escorts."

Tony heard the words in his ears and in that moment, he stole another glance to Kirashira and his partner. The ever burning question in his heart, the desire to know that what he had done had been for something greater than himself was answered in completeness. Here today, Kirashira's joy, the excitement and optimism that permeated every aspect of the festivities had answered that question with such force that he had to actively prevent his eyes from moistening.

Kirashira was going to be one of the best leaders that had lived for her people, he decided, if for no other reason than she was strong enough to stand before her people and the Federation even after she'd suffered so much. It filled his heart with pride to know that today, he and Truth had done more to secure peace for their own people and those nameless millions watching that night, than so many years of fighting had. Today's gift was not only to Kirashira and the Federation and her people but to his own nation. It was to be both an end and a new beginning, a chance for the same infectious optimism to reach across the stars themselves and find place in so many who had always wondered whether a day like this could ever be. The scene before him reaffirmed within, feelings of duty and honor, a sense of gravitas and hope that overshadowed even the day of his graduation into the service. Today, he, his partner, Kirashira and so many more had done the impossible.

Filled with an intensity of an overwhelming pride, Tony took aim into the sky and yelled aloud his order, thankful that Truth had let him make the call as he squeezed the trigger himself, "Gun salute! Honor to your Queen!"

The thunder of five hundred rifles lighting the sky from the temple and barges hanging there in the air, lanced into the night. Despite the dusk, their honor overwhelmed the darkness and signaled the dawn of a bright, new day.

Epilogue

By the time Anshi had reached her suite on Shar'Jya, the official coverage had ended at last. The networks had all transitioned to political analysts and pundits going over the proceedings. The coronation ceremony for the newest Queen of the Starlight Compact had been a resounding media success; The first half Kul'Raigh queen ever to touch the throne of any Federation power. She was not a full Kul'Raigh no, but she was the daughter of one of the greatest.

"Turn off the holo please," Anshi said into the air, and in a moment, the holographic projector cut out, leaving the room in silence.

The Kul'Raigh at last slipped the extravagant shawl she'd been wearing to keep her shoulders warm from its perch, setting it on the foot of her bed. The whisps of artificial fur were dyed with prismatic colors so radiant that they twinkled even in the softer light of her bedroom. She fell back back on the bed for a moment, and once she felt her large crown against the back of her head, she reached into the hairpiece there and turned off the levitator. When she sat up again, the disk was laying on the bed inert, along with all of the associated dangles and accessories that formed a small cloud of expensive metal in it's wake when it was on. Eventually she stood, reaching behind herself and clicked open the hidden clasps and buckles of her form fitting dress. At last, she was free of the day's exertions.

The Kul'Raigh Companion Guild's High Matron had enjoyed the festivities up to, during and after the coronation, perhaps a little too much. Her head throbbed from lack of sleep and the consumption of far too many rounds of spirited beverages. A chime sounded from the other room, announcing the completion of her tea, the kind prescribed by the Guild to preempt hangovers. It never seemed to fail, at least for Kul'Raigh. She finally set her extravagant shoes aside and padded over the cool artificial stone floor to the kitchen. She found the finished tea making thermos mounted in the socket on the counter and pulled it free, clicking the latch and pouring the steeped, hot drink, into a nondescript mug.

Thankfully despite her partial inebriation, she had not succumbed to foolish temptations or made any social missteps. If she had it would have been some level of news. Some network somewhere who disliked the Guild, probably an Akal'Maru station, would have tried to taint the whole proceeding if Anshi had made a mistake. It was likely that the new queen would not even know that the

Guild's High Matron and several attendants, had been present at the coronation, overlooking the last leg of the journey, not until some politicking Hil'Raigh Noble made a fuss about it at least. After all, those seats in the witness' gallery could have been given to some noble house from an unimportant backwater.

Anshi scoffed, as if any Hil'Raigh noble was somehow her superior. She would let them think so at least, because that was the order of the world in which she and the Guild lived. Letting them think what they would was their business, it did not matter in the end. When the strings needed proper pulling, Anshi was sure that she of all people would be more than able to find the threads she needed to tug on. Perhaps that was why she had been so drawn to the dossier of the late Duke Arash Vaerlin. When his information dump had hit the networks in foreign nations, it was something of a jumble. He had either obfuscated it on purpose, or he had been terrible at taking notes in a way that made sense to the world at large.

Regardless, the Guild's own analysts had sifted through much of the information and the hard copy they'd provided to their High Matron, along with the juicier corroborations only possible from the Guild's generous network of information gatherers, always felt like it was burning a hole in her pocket when the slate was not in hand. Of all of the information contained there, one thing was of particular interest to her. She knew of course, the same thing weighed on the mind of every Kul'Raigh this side of the frontier. Anyone with a passing loyalty to the Companion Guild and even most of the unaffiliated were still waiting for the news, the word; what had happened to Lady Shiyara? Until that little bit of information was known, it would be impossible for Anshi, or anyone else, to rest.

Anshi sighed, remembering the decades prior, the times when Lady Shiyara had been a companion, one of the most talented and loved. The lady had been Anshi's protege, a direct subordinate in the guild. They'd become good personal friends, talking of the world, the peoples in it, their work and even possible futures, late into the depths of those nights. Anshi had personally trained Shiyara in every discipline she could manage, and when she could not do so on her own, she had hired the best instructors and teachers. Shiyara was an idol of Anshi's personal creation; a perfect icon of all that was truly Kul'Raigh. She'd been made to be an avatar of everything that the Guild represented and that training, combined with her personality had produced a marvel. The reality of it all was something Anshi knew, it was something Shiyara knew. It was something Gou'Ran, the late king, had known. It was no secret to those who really understood the Companion Guild at the time either.

Of course, that was all hushed backroom talk now, no one would say such a scandalous thing in public since the marriage. Anshi had seen Shiyara's relationship with King Gou'Ran blossom, she had lamented it as a theft of Kul'Raigh treasure from their people.

Despite that, she had been the first in line to provide the most expensive wedding gifts she could manage when the time came. When Shiyara had announced the conception of their daughter, Princess Kirashira, once again, Anshi had been there with gifts and well wishes, not only hers, but of a people.

Now, once again, Anshi would step forward. It would not be easy, it had been difficult having one so important taken just out of reach by the order of the world. For all she was, despite her subordinate position, Shiyara was and would remain a dear friend who Anshi could no longer contact any time she wanted for fear of damaging her husband's, now her daughter's, political powers. She was a confidant that the High Matron could not confide in lest the Compact's royal government come to know the Guild's inner workings. Shiyara was now a treasure which could no longer be treasured by the one who had crafted it.

Anshi sighed and took the slate from her pocket, powering it up. At the first instance of Shiyara's name in the section she had been studying, she shook her head and chucked the slate onto the couch in haphazard fashion. She quickly returned to her bed chamber.

The High Matron had people whose job it was to connect the dots. They were experts, paid well for their work, She need not burden herself with it. She knew this and never forgot it, yet she could never shake the feeling that she was not doing enough if she was not personally involved in finding Shiyara. Anshi wanted to do something, anything, to resolve and bring the hellishness to an end. As she sat on the foot of her opulent bed, sipping her tea, wiggling her toes in the warm air to stretch them, she felt alone for the first time in a long while. The room was large, the bed had been designed for more than one occupant. The room itself a sort of miniature palace that only someone like Anshi could rest in. Only the Guild's High Matron could sit in such a place and feel lonely rather than be left in awe.

"Place a call to the front desk, I'd like to review my appointments for tomorrow," She said at last. Whether or not anyone ever saw Shiyara again, Anshi could do nothing about it for the moment. Once that changed however, she would be at the head of the dragon that she and generations of companions before, had cultivated just for such purposes. The Guild never forgot its own, no matter how much their choices hurt, and Anshi was to be the face of that Guild as long as fate would allow.

Author's Note

Dear Reader,

Thank you for taking the time to read my book. I am flattered that in the busy modern era, you would choose to provide my work with the attention that you have. If you are reading this, it means you reached the end of a narrative that was a long time coming, and one that challenged me in so many ways. My life was at points along the journey, a tumultuous chaos that felt as if it would never end. I suppose I would be lying if I said that anyone on this earth is ever "out of the woods" completely but thanks to enthusiasm and excitement from those close to me, I persevered and finished this work.

It is my hope that you will consider yourself of value to me, not the least reason of which is that you read my work.

I hope that in the efforts you undertake, that you understand that it is possible someday, somehow to overcome some of the challenges we face, as the characters in this book attempted to do. This is despite the fact that we may not have clean or easy resolutions to our challenges in the moment we feel we need them most.

My book is not intended to be an allegory of any kind, but if you can come away with at least something of a more hopeful outlook, or even if you just enjoyed the ride for the story's sake, I would like to think that is a job well done by the writing.

To all those of you aspiring creators who struggle, or perhaps to those whose struggles take the forefront and prevent the release of the creativity they want to share; Know that you do not have to be alone. In the words of a band I love, Incubus, and a song of theirs that has been increasingly valuable to me in my times of challenge, "Don't let the world bring you down, not everyone here is that fucked up and cold. Remember why you came and while you're alive, experience the warmth before you grow old."

I hope that this work, and hopefully future works I create to share stories, can find your eyes again. I would love for you to be able to take a journey with my characters and worlds once more. You can even visit my website (shameless self promotion incoming) at www.starofashor.com if you are so inclined. I promise I put effort into the things I post there. Until next time, take care and stay safe out there.

-T

About the Author

T. has been a creative individual and lover of telling stories for many years. The story of Star of Ashor was originally conceived in their mind many years ago during middle school. Through several iterations, efforts and even a previously completed manuscript, T. has worked tirelessly to refine and create a world that they feel incorporates a good measure of creativity, passion and excitement for fictional writing. Star of Ashor is an entirely self published work, and all of the efforts to bring it to the readers were undertaken by the author alone, with some select help from those who were kind enough to read and give feedback on some advance copies of the manuscript.

Star of Ashor is T's first published work and is the culmination of many efforts, but should not be seen as an end point. Star of Ashor is and always will be a starting point for a larger story and serve as a reminder of what can be accomplished by an individual in our modern era. It will hopefully serve to inspire not only T, but other aspiring creators in future writing projects in a variety of genre's and settings.

The author T, chose to go by a shortened name for the writing of the book in order to allow for some personal freedom in their identity. While it is not supposed to be some well kept secret, there is a level of trepidation that every author faces when writing, one that can challenge them. Due to personal struggles and conflicts in T's life, it was chosen that rather than spelling out what T. represents, a shortened version of the name would be used instead. This was an effort to give T. the freedom to feel removed from personal challenges and instead allow them to focus on an unbiased and clear, story focused presentation, for readers of the work.

T. hopes that everyone regardless of who they are, can find something to enjoy in the work they produce, and the characters, people, places and especially, world building choices that have gone into the Star of Ashor world are of particular importance to the author. Each of the choices made, in some way, represents a form of the Author's expression, and while the story being told is and never will be an allegory, T. has long hoped that by telling stories with interesting and compelling characters, those who read such works will be able to be provided with food for their thoughts, even outside of fiction.

Coming Soon

Did you know that Star of Ashor is only the first of a series of books that the author wants to write?

That's right, Star of Ashor will (hopefully) become a series!

If you read through the whole book, and enjoyed it, you'll be pleased to find that you can get a sneak peak at the (as yet untitled) upcoming second book in the series right here!

1 - Cornered Wolf

Truth ran her fingers over the fire control group, a mental checklist in her mind while she carefully eyed the controls of her rifle. The sound of the shuttle's engines whined as her stomach lurched. Nearby, her partner stood at last, nodding to her. She regarded him for a moment before slinging her rifle on her shoulder and moving to the already open rear ramp of the vehicle.

The outside air whipped past the opening as the bitter chill of the night sky began to fill the cabin. Ahead, a marginally lit building top rested. The gunner called out over the radio after a moment and the instant later, the mounted weapon he held blared to life. A cascade of pops sounding as a set of five breaching spikes burrowed into the wall ahead. Truth and her partner backed away, ducking into the cabin and hunkering down even as the gunner ducked and curled around. Yelling aloud, the man set the spikes aflame with a button press.

In that same instant, the wall was lanced with blindingly hot bursts of energy. A perfectly rectangular section of the wall was sheered clear of its support. An explosion followed an instant later and the well built structure blasted into the building like a piece of tissue paper.

The moment had come, and Truth stood, waiting for a clear line. With the gunner shirking out of the way. She readied herself. Her mind cleared and saw the motion she would take. A moment more was all it took.

By the time her conscious mind caught up with the reality of her running at breakneck pace toward the edge of the loading ramp, her coprocessors had already compensated for every footfall. Every aspect of her mind was now tuned into one purpose, crossing the gap.

As she felt her feet leave solid ground, her thighs and calves pulsing with vigor, her arms thrown forward, she identified two momentarily stunned targets in the breached room ahead. Truth felt her feet hit the floor of the room, one littered with dust, debris and fragments of rapidly cooling metal. Feeling her grip fail her, she tumbled forward into a roll. The move put her at the feet of one of the two she'd seen.

Uncoiling like a wound spring, she called on her mind and body to give her the perfect motion against the target. In the fraction of a second she had managed to look upon the target she had identified it. He wore body armor regarded as a standard heavy security contractor. A full helmet, gloves, shin guards, vest and chemical protection gear. Already rising, she was at last given the point of impact she should seek.

The stunned target, having barely started trying to get to his feet was brought low immediately, Truth's leg sweeping him roughly to the ground. The man impacted the floor with a loud thud and Truth's leg continued past him as she spun to a low crouch. Her body moved with complete fluidity, practiced unnatural precision. Every ounce of her momentum, every part of the energy she'd given herself in the run helped propel it, and a moment later the same leg was raised high.

Like a dropped hammer, Truth let out a guttural yell, bringing the heel of her combat boot roughly onto the combatant's chest. The blow would guarantee his incapacitation before his comrade inevitably came to his senses. A loud thud sounded, along with a hapless groan when Truth's foot connected. She put her weight to that leg immediately, throwing her torso aside with violent force, an acrobatic spin that brought her airborne again, out of reach of the drunken grapple attempted by the man's comrade.

Landing, she loosened her stance , ready for attack or defense all at once. The man moved toward her and her eyes flitted over every detail of his motion. The points of his body, his joints, his projected path and momentum were all there in Truth's mind. Every flaw and every natural motion predicted with machine accuracy. She gritted her teeth and surged forward. As the man moved to block, she dropped into a slide, his arm passing overhead. She drew back her arm as her body moved along and at the right moment, snapped her hand forward in a thrust.

The violent push upward was accompanied by a disturbingly clear crack, the sound of ruined joint and sinew. Truth's flat palm broke toward the assailant's elbow with such force that the plating and armor on his forearm, prevented it from moving upward as quickly as it needed to. In real time, her sensory systems analyzed what must have been the intended joint separation. While not lethal, it would put anyone who suffered from such a move in such agonizing pain as to incapacitate them for a significant period, or make them pass out completely.

It appeared this target was of the latter variety, as his body took a couple shambling steps then collapsed forward as if he'd died.

At last Truth stood, moving to the windless groaning merc she had first attacked. Reaching down, she forcibly unclasped his helmet chin strap and tugged it off of him. She glanced over him. Her mind fixed on eliminating him in that moment, the efficiency of the situation almost demanding it. There was a cold calculation to the way the coprocessors determined threats. It was always disturbing to her at times outside of battle, but in the heat of combat, when her life was in it's hands so completely, Her mind tended to surrender. She reared back her hand, flattening it for a lethal throat strike.

Her hand moved again, with practiced precision, glancing the man's neck at a critical pressure point, leaving him to groan and go limp. The indicators were clear, he would live, but he would have balance problems for a while.

Truth stood straight again, glancing down, then back to the hovering shuttle.

"Clear entry," She stated at last, watching as the shuttle lazily positioned the ramp such that her partner was able to hop into the newly created entry hole, rather than vaulting through it like she had done.

Tony glanced over both of the incapacitated mercs, "Alive?"

"Yes," Truth replied, though she had to admit the second one almost never made it. It wasn't that she was averse to harming or even killing people who would try to do the same to her given the chance. A second glance at the merc reminded her that above all, the mission was one of recovery and prisoners would be useful for information at very least. Even so, there was a tinge of wonder in her mind, as to whether she really had complete control of herself when things were so intense. She would have never planned the motions like that, yet her mind figured out in instants how to incapacitate or kill almost anyone she met in battle regardless of her conscious input. It was an unconscious part of her coprocessor, part she sometimes had misgivings about.

"More intel," Tony replied with a nod. In that moment, Truth felt at once, calmed. The way her partner didn't ever question what she did or why cleared those doubts. A moment more and he was on the radio, indicating to the assisting Hil'Raigh forces where they could pick up two hostiles.

With that, the two made ready to enter the building proper. While the room they'd entered had been planned, the estimates on hostile forces demanded that at least several more of the mercenaries, members of the Hil'Raigh knights, were on the premises. The number of them were of course, employed by various security companies. With the help of Federation investigators, Kirashira Ren'Tauru's newly formed circle of advisor's was already taking aim on the organization behind the scenes. By piecing together the late Duke Arash Vaerlin's dumped information on the Knights, the investigations had uncovered a bevy of connections underpinning some of the larger institutions in the Federation. While no official connections to member state governments had been uncovered as yet, Truth was skeptical. If anything, the prior mission had taught her that the Federation, while impressive in many ways, had its own share of rot beneath the surface.

Thankfully however, Truth and her partner were not required to understand or even attempt to clean any of that up. They were currently serving as training and combat adviser assets for the newly minted Starlight Compact Special Response Service. It was a branch of combatants created at Kirashira's order, with input and advice from the NovaCore and the understanding of Hil'Raigh Military personnel. The stated goal was to prevent any sort of the kind of tragedy that had occurred with Kirashira's parents, but also to provide the largely pacifistic nation with a tool of scalpel like precision. In this case, the dry run for the organization was to attempt a rescue of Kirashira's mother at the building in question.

Lady Shiyara Ren'Tauru, the wife of the late king, mother of the Queen, was, contrary to Truth's initial feelings on the way things would develop, still remembered well. Part of that was likely the Kul'Raigh Companion Guild's doing. Though headquartered in the Starlight Compact, The Guild had made manifest, in every one of its holdings, the reality of her continued absence. It was interesting for Truth to see such an organization venerate and revere one of its former members to the point of near sainthood. Buildings large and small, from the Companion Guild Hall back on Ashor, to the Guild's Shar'Jya holding, were decorated, draped in massive banners, surrounded by the glowing banners of light that served as billboards in Hil'Raigh metropolises. How much of the piecing together of Lady Shiyara's location had come from their help, Truth was unsure, but the reality of their support meant that no one in public life could fail to remember or acknowledge her disappearance. With luck, the saga of her long absence would finally be resolved. Queen Kirashira would finally be able to hold the ceremonies to put her father's spirit at rest, and hopefully, Truth's friend would find some measure of solace that had been robbed of her by the series of events leading to this very day.

Without a word, truth looked to her partner who nodded and pushed the keypad allowing access out of the room into the hall. Truth's mind was drawn once again to the immediacies of the mission at hand, and she followed him through the door as it slid aside. Tony flanked to one side, and Truth took the other. Once the hallway was confirmed empty, Tony began leading the way, with Truth covering the rear arc as she followed. As they moved, a loud pop and burst sounded somewhere else.

With sky-scraping constructions so large, it was often the case that the designers would make efforts to compartmentalize areas in each of their creations. A building such as this would house dozens of large firms, a mix of offices, residential and commercial space. The current compartment as it stood, was one rented to a shipping company, one tied to the Knight's by investigation. According to plan, there were a trio of teams entering the compartment from different locations. Truth and Tony had entered on the top floor, a second team was slated to enter through a maintenance shaft between compartments near the middle of the structure. The final team, made mostly of Hil'Raigh law enforcement, was to enter via the main door with breaching charges. The loud pop sounding therefore, had to indicate that the law enforcers had received their go signal.

Airspace around the building had been cleared under the pretense of a priority shipment bound for a nearby tower, a semi regular occurrence in this part of Shar'Jya's cityscape. With it, a communications and power blackout to the compartment had been imposed moments before Truth and Tony had arrived to breach. With such a sudden entry, the enforcers were likely to have success in overwhelming and then flooding into the compartment without much meaningful resistance.

The objective to which Tony was leading, was an office room, that, according to the floor plan, would overlook the main inventory warehouse. Intelligence had indicated that within that warehouse, was a modified cargo container in which several cryogenics pods were housed. Inside one of them, was supposed to be the prize.

Truth backed along after her companion carefully as the sounds of commotion rang through the walls now. The law enforcement entry had of course, not gone un-noticed and some variety of fighting had broken out, the sounds of Hil'Raigh plasma rifle's echoing now, amid muffled yells.

The sounds cascaded through the air, and dimly lit hallways were an obstacle only for the unprepared. Truth's eyes had already seamlessly added extra vision mode's to the feed, ensuring her perception was crisp as she could want. Even so, she had to admit the false color addition made by the alternative inputs tended to blow some colors out of proportion even for her practiced mind.

Tony keyed a door from behind Truth as she followed along. She was so used to pair movement now that doing so required very little in the way of verification on his motion. Where he went, she knew to follow, even when looking the opposite direction. Of course, it helped to have extra sensory inputs that he lacked, but even when the roles were reversed, he still did a better job than anyone Truth had ever met.

A word of clearance told Truth they had entered their target room and she broke from her following to take position near one of the windows overlooking the warehouse. The office they had entered was well kept, clean and very business like.

The whole operation was of course, legitimate enough that smuggling a few extra cargo containers here or there would hardly be noticed in such a massive economy as that which powered Shar'Jya's Metropolis. Truth pushed past the carbon copy desks and chairs moving to the window. Finally, reaching a good position, she looked out over the floor, scanning with care.

Her mind ignored most of the detail, looking first, for people amid the inventory. Finding none, she resolved then, to see if she could see much else. In moments, the law enforcers who had breached would begin spreading out over the room to look for the container they had been assigned. The sounds of combat had died down and now, silence waited. Truth had half expected some civilian employee to be around even during these off hours, but so far none had been found. The radio chatter now coming in from the link to the Hil'Raigh had made no mention of it either.

At last however, Truth noted the infrared floodlights of their allies bathing over the warehouse floor. Eventually, visible figures followed, though, fewer than Truth had expected to see for such an important mission. They started fanning out over the floor. With power still cut, they were left to their assisted vision devices. Now it was time to wait.

"Let's hope she's down there somewhere," Tony said at last, finally speaking. His vision was also augmented, though less heavily than Truth's own. It was likely he was having more trouble with some of the details at that distance in darkness.

"I agree," Truth replied, watching the Hil'Raigh move around the room in their search pattern. The officers below moved with a trained precision, the kind that Truth had come to expect from any sort of incident team. Even so, something about the way they moved reminded her of something she had seen specifically. In the Hil'Raigh Federation, many of those in work such as this had received military specialized training from a security agency. With holdings and nations so vast, the number of such companies was rather staggering, at least by NovaCore standards.

With the NovaCore, everyone was obligated to perform national service in some variety, and therefore, almost everyone got some level of training in some minor military doctrines and soldiering. While it was argued by foreigners as "inefficient" it also meant that the NovaCore had no real private security firms. High level security back home, was almost entirely a government function, with organizations reimbursing the national economy for any drain that their security needs imposed. Regardless, the coherence of training displayed below made Truth wonder just how many of the officers had gone to the same training school.

"Looks like we found it, intact and running on internal power still," Truth heard over the radio channel. Shiyara was there, and likely alive inside whatever container had just been located. Truth perked up and looked for where the confirmation had come from below. After moments of scanning, she saw a group of the Hil'Raigh congregating around the container they'd identified.

"Prep for extract, lets clean up," The radio stated at last, but only the command channel was audible, "Get a handle on the power would you?"

Truth glanced over to her partner who had slumped a bit with what had to be relief. He was mid sigh, rubbing his eyes. A smile returned to her as he opened them and saw her looking, one which she returned.

In that moment, the power was restored to the compartment, the lights in the office flicking back to life. Truth's vision adjusted in an instant, and the false color, blown out reds and greens, vanished in an instant. The office was decidedly more drab inside without them however. Truth took a glance down at the assembled, armored law enforcers below, watching as they brought what looked to be a mag-lev cargo dolly around to pick up the container. On the far end of the warehouse, a large garage door began rolling upward.

"Moving fast," Tony snickered, "Already pulling out the container."

"Yes," Truth replied, though, she realized as she did so, that she was entranced by something she had finally noticed, a nagging from her coprocessor. Her eyes fixated on a specific point in the distance, almost by compulsion, and only after willfully disregarding the feeling for a moment, then looking there herself, did Truth realize why.

"Tony what's that insignia?" She asked motioning to one of the Hil'Raigh's shoulder pads. The black body armor suit was relatively standard fare, and like most security or police firms, bore an insignia on it.

"I've never seen that one... It's not local law enforcement though..." Tony furrowed his brow.

Even as he did however, Truth's mind was filled with alarm bells, warnings. Without hesitation, she charged her partner, diving atop him and bowling him to the ground. An instant later, the air behind her exploded into a fiery maelstrom, the window of the office turned into a rain of glass shrapnel. The heat of fire licked at Truth's body through even the armor she wore and the concussive shock sent her mind reeling, her coprocessor already screaming in its own way, giving real time status updates for her body parts.

Dumbfounded, dazed, Truth landed atop her partner, who crashed through one of the simple mass market desks that filled the office. Behind and ahead, anything and everything that was not bolted down took on a mind of its own, an airborne trek from the mind of an insane fairy tale. Mugs, data tablets, chairs, the few hard copy documents along with more than one family photo and at least one child's award, were sent flying. The chaos of fire, mixed with the cacophony of sheered metal and torn carpet. The smell of chemicals, the kind Truth knew from demolition training, was already filling the air, mixed with the smoke. Reminded of so few days earlier when a torpedo had hull breached only a dozen or so meters away, Truth decided that this noise and chaos, was definitely more violent.

Thick acrid smoke began to bellow from ruined computer terminals and the smell of burned electronics, cheap fire retardant carpet smoldering, and the unmistakable hint of a breaching charge, now dominated Truth's nose. Her hands and feet all worked, or, according to her coprocessor they did, and her eyes, they seemed functional. Her hearing had been disabled at least for a few milliseconds, the artificial sense and its machinery overloaded by the blast but returning gradually. Unfortunately, thanks to the concussion, there was already lasting damage reported to the sensitive instrumentation inside.

Even so, with the world a dull thudding racket and head throbbing, the near lifeless look on her partner's face sent her mind into panic. He was not dead, his heart was still functioning properly, and as Truth lifted herself from his body coughing, she noted that his brain probably hadn't ceased either, since he was still breathing. At last, his eyes cracked open. He groaned and winced as Truth pulled herself from his body, letting him get off of the apparently rather sturdy surface he had overturned and landed on top of.

He groaned, rolling, rather than standing, to move.

A cursory check of his body revealed no obvious wounds, though he would probably have hearing damage as well. Thankfully, his radio implant appeared to be functioning as he groaned when Truth sent him a wordless message, "Can you feel your body?"

The groan was enough, and when he moved his legs, then hands, getting on all fours, Truth turned from him and immediately assessed the damage behind her. The hole behind her had definitely been made by a breaching charge, a breaching charge cannon in fact. Yes, that was it. Truth recalled in that moment, the image that had sent her into the panic. From the corner of her eye, barely visible really, she'd noticed one of the Hil'Raigh taking aim with a breaching gun, one not unlike the kind that would have been used to enter the shipping company's compartment in the first place.

With no telling whether the man believed he'd killed them both, there was always a chance he took a second shot. Even as Truth got ready to drag her companion from his place, she heard another blast, this time across the warehouse. Her heart sank as she realized that the newly assembled Special Response Service team, the one who'd entered from the other side of the compartment, also slated to overlook the warehouse by now, was likely the victim of the second blast.

"Gotta move!" She yelled aloud. Tony barely responded, attesting to his trouble hearing, but even more worrying for Truth was the fact that the natural audio from her own ears came through with such a muffled distortion that it sounded as if she had poured glue into her ears. It was true that her hearing was powerful, resilient even, but to be sensitive, the systems that worked within it were not impervious to sudden pressure waves. The nanites in her blood would try to repair the damage but until there were no guarantees of field repair even being possible. Certainly her partner would have no such luck and would likely need some corrective medical care regardless.

Tony's lethargic response was instantly aggravating, not because he was not willing, but because Truth's mind was already moving at a million meters per second once more. The combat high returned. No, this time it was not a combat high, it was something more, something Truth hated. This kind of feeling was the kind she dreaded if for no other reason than it meant danger lurked nearby. Adding to the worry though, was just how hard it was to think rationally when her coprocessor switched into a preservation at any cost mindset.

In an instant, her options were flooding by like a raging river. Leave Tony behind? Call for help? Move to Cover? Fight?

The torrent of thoughts ripped past. Truth forcibly discarded anything at all, relating to her partner's demise, refusing them outright. It didn't stop the simulating, the hypothesizing, but it meant she could at very least, ignore any of the results of those lines of thinking. The instant of thought, was cut short as heavy footfalls in the hallway outside sounded, heralding the confirmation of the kill by the newly revealed enemy. Even despite herself, one thing was already completely clear to Truth, neither of the two she heard would leave the room.

With frantic speed, she brought her weapon toward the door, the railgun's heft perfectly understood. In the same instant that the final ghost image was made reality by the hint of muzzle and body armor pushing through the doorway she now faced, Truth's muzzle found a shot. Though not ideal, it was enough to buy time, and so, she pulled the trigger.

A flash and a shower of sparks, along with an audible pop sounded almost in the same instant as the rifle in Truth's arm blazed to hellish life. The projectile it sent ripping through the air with violent, sudden and force. Truth felt the air around her moved by the pressure but ignored it almost entirely as her senses fixated on the one thing she demanded of herself in that moment: survival.

Before the sabot casing on the slug had even broken free, it had struck the target in the thigh. The case buried partially in the thigh armor of the target before being stripped away from the intended payload and in a fraction of an instant more, Truth already noted how the target was stumbling, rather than walking. Complete muscle failure, a failure of the leg, was bound to occur when a shot like that shattered the leg bone. While Hil'Raigh body armor was able to stop most standard issue NovaCore rifles, the variety to which Truth and her partner were accustomed faced far fewer problems, especially at such close ranges. What they paid in weight was made up for by sheer performance and this was no exception.

Truth watched the lead man stumble into the room, his balance vanishing as quickly as his chance for survival. The sudden attack seemed to slow his comrade down however, and, not expecting those who'd just been licked by an explosion to be capable of fighting back, both of them were doomed from the start. Their attempted ambush had never counted on the NovaCore doing what they'd done to make Truth.

Though his reflexes were quick, Truth's trigger finger was quicker, and the second target received an unhealthy center of mass shot that sent him reeling back visibly. The shot took him even as he had attempted to trigger his own burst on Truth. His speed, his haste and his surprise however, had made the shot lance by harmlessly into the wall, boring a white hot hole. His shattered body recoiled visibly as the deceptively small hole in his chest plate signaled his end, the tink of punctured composites and metal barely audible to Truth's damaged ears.

The race in Truth's mind had not abated. Targeting plans, options, movement plans of her own all still raced along. The bevy of information almost felt hallucinogenic as it rushed through her now aching head. Even so, she kept to the basics first.

Heart was racing, but only minor stress.

Limbs were all functional and not in shock.

Eyes still worked properly.

Lungs were smoky but fine.

Muscles were responding to control inputs.

Skeleton, undamaged.

Skin bruised, minor burns possible but no shrapnel punctures.

Hearing was damaged but usable and her radio systems were fine.

At last, a moment to think to react without instinct alone, presented itself and Truth tugged Tony again. This time, he responded more coherently. He moved to a crouch and took a place near Truth, behind the overturned desk he'd been shoved into. He looked utterly dazed, uncomfortable and even angry, but still, he looked alive and he was not trailing a river of blood behind him. By the time he finished moving he had his back to the desk and was groaning uncomfortably, rubbing one side of his head.

Rather than speaking, he opened his mouth and then simply shook his head. He glanced over at Truth, then checked his rifle in his lap before bringing it to a more ready position.

He was definitely in Truth's hands now, something his look was clear on. His eyes told her enough, there was a willingness, though it was certainly dampened by his state currently. Truth moved to the window frame nearby, poking a quick glance down into the warehouse as Tony trained his rifle on the door.

Down below, the group of of what were supposed to be law enforcement had largely abandoned their task of simply putting Shiyara's container onto the mag-lev dolly they'd found, and were instead, taking covering positions. It was only as Truth heard a yell and pulled back behind the wall, followed a moment later by a white hot beam surging past and into the roof, that she realized they were fully aware. They knew they'd failed to kill at least someone now, and they were not taking chances. The radio channel with them had long been dead, and with the yells they were likely sharing near impossible to decipher, Truth was left to wonder as to what she would do. The hostiles would likely not stick around, it was insanity to try it. Word of the betrayal would eventually spread and backup would arrive. No, what they were doing had to be more immediate. It was not killing the NovaCore they were attempting.

A realization his Truth's mind. They were likely there to extract their precious cargo, perhaps on behalf of the Knights themselves.

Truth's mind was greeted by a rage, an annoyance, a sort of fury that at this stage, so close to finishing this important mission, she could be denied it. If she tried to fight, to draw more attention to herself and her partner, she would bring them into danger. Was pressing the chance, trying to attack in such a state, worth it at all? No, she decided. Becoming a plasma burnt corpse was not going to fix anything. Letting her partner die was not either. The mission was important, but so was living to see it through. Today, life was what she had to choose, despite the urge building in her mind to poke around the corner again and take a quick shot, hoping someone didn't respond in time.

A bore of plasma tore through the nearby floor, vaporizing half of what looked to be a digitally photographed family portrait and its frame. There was no time for playing hide and seek here, No gadgetry, no tactic, nothing really, but withdrawing to a safer place. At very least, the rear half of the room was likely to be less vulnerable to random blind shots.

Truth peeled away from the wall and scurried away from it, tapping her partner on the shoulder and bidding him to follow. Once the pair found a desk near the far side of the room, Truth turned it over for the minor concealment it could provide. The contents of its surface were already strewn about the room, so as it thudded against the carpet, there was little else in the way of noise.

With Tony now coherent enough to help watch the door, Truth tried to pull part of her attention away from the frantic overload of survival ideas. Unfortunately however, her next course of action, contacting help, was thwarted when no appropriate communications mechanism responded over her radios. After trying several, she finally resigned herself to the fact that the hostiles were likely employing some sort of jamming field here.

Across the warehouse, the muffled sounds of vehicle engines coursed through the door Truth had seen opening earlier. She guessed, from the sound, that a vehicle of some considerable boldness had landed outside, probably in a bid to pick up its allies and their cargo. Was it worth risking a look?

Truth fought her instincts for a long moment, and at last, moved along the inner wall of the room, away from the breach and window she had looked through before. Pushing prone, she carefully crept forward enough to nestle the muzzle of her rifle amid some of the debris hanging over the edge of the of the destruction. The action however, was not to fire on anyone, but to give her electronic optics a chance to get a view of the world below. With a quick request to her coprocessor, the admittedly more rudimentary input from the rifle scope was added to her mind. The sudden clash of visible information, from two completely separate points of view made her feel light headed for a moment, and after a moment of the uncomfortable feeling, her coprocessors put together a more coherent mix of vision, one that stopped making her feel so nauseated.

Already, in her new window to the outside world, Truth could see what looked like the underbelly of a Hil'Raigh commercial lifter. They were industrial vehicles used to transport single high priority cargo containers. While it was pressurized and reasonably durable, few firms operated the particular model Truth saw in any sort of surface to orbit capacity. Even so, the container, the reason for the mission, was clearly being taken out onto the landing pad to be snatched up by the cargo crane on the thing's underside.

Truth counted a number of hostiles, even a few still covering back where she had come from, but certainly not with the visual acuity to notice the very minor protrusion of her rifle over the precipice. Even so, she dared not fire upon them since the durability of the wall and floor of the office was demonstrably not strong enough to protect her body from reprisal. Instead, she observed, trying to figure out exactly what information she could gain from her observations. She scanned for faces, nameplates, insignias, and her coprocessor announced it was collecting a bevy of other information, like analyzing the way some of them walked. Unfortunately however, all of that information was likely to be incomplete or non existent. All of the faces were fully covered, the armor worn by the hostiles of a variety designed to resist environmental hazards. The insignias on a few of their shoulder plates however, were visible. They did not appear in any of the databases Truth's brain could access while offline, but there was still a chance that bringing that information home would yield leads.

The hostiles covering the office she and Tony occupied pulled back gradually to meet with their comrades, who were now giving hand signals to the pilot of the shuttle and securing the magnetic clamps from their crane ship. A few moments more and the clamps had been attached. The container lurched from the ground, dragged upward a meter or so into the embrace of the mothership. With their prize secured, the group broke into a quick race to reach the door to the inside of the craft. The frustration in Truth's mind mounted as she watched her adversaries vanish into the safety of their metallic shell. All the work that had gone into the mission was now moot. Not only had the mission failed, but would likely prove a serious setback for the fledgling program that Kirashira had authorized. At once though, Truth's mind realized that whatever had happened here today, had not happened without cooperation. Someone, somewhere, on the outside, someone with access to Kirashira's more closely guarded planning, had to have helped their allies.

It was only when Truth saw one of the hostiles pull his helmet off, apparently bantering with his comrades, that she decided to do something. The smirk on his face toward the carnage within the building was enough to steel her resolve. The enemy may have won the day, but the war Truth had declared was far from over and their whole group would know it. After taking a moment to let her system's analyze and store as much of the facial structure and detail as she felt she could afford, Truth used her mind to key the optics in. There was no time for a good shot, a planned shot, but at very least, a shot across the bow so to speak, would remind the enemy that they would never so easily vanquish NovaCore fighters.

The man's arm presented itself, as the best part still visible on his body and Truth loosed a shot toward it. The jolt of her improperly braced gun sent the rifle itself off kilter almost immediately, but in the time it had taken to fling the rifle away, the shot had struck home. While by no means lethal, the glancing blow to the man's arm plate had resulted in sending him spinning out of view. Rather than try to return fire from such exposed positions, the man's comrades wisely ducked behind their vehicle and, in moments more, the ship's engines flared loudly. The craft began to ascend slowly out of view, but was already turning and changing course before it vanished completely. Regardless of how damaging Truth's fire had been, it had certainly startled the hostiles enough to take their situation seriously again.

Even despite their apparent departure however, Truth wasted no effort in keeping herself concealed. She crawled backward a half meter or so before crouching and moving back to her groggy partner. Tony stared intently down his rifle scope, pointing toward the door with single minded focus. Sitting next to him behind their make shift cover, Truth decided it would be best to wait until friendly backup came to check on what went wrong, rather than stick her neck out again. With a sigh, she braced her rifle on the desk and sat, waiting for potential threats. With any luck, the next people who showed up wouldn't be trying to kill her.

www.ingramcontent.com/pod-product-compliance
Lightning Source LLC
Chambersburg PA
CBHW032131190626
46814CB00005BA/1653